The Books of Outremer:

THE DEVIL IN THE DUST
TOWER OF THE KING'S DAUGHTER
A DARK WAY TO GLORY
FEAST OF THE KING'S SHADOW
HAND OF THE KING'S EVIL
THE END OF ALL ROADS

Visit the series website at
www.outremer.co.uk

A DARK WAY TO GLORY

The Third Book of Outremer

CHAZ BRENCHLEY

ACE BOOKS, NEW YORK

This is a work of fiction. Names, characters, places, and incidents either are the product of the author's imagination or are used fictitiously, and any resemblance to actual persons, living or dead, business establishments, events, or locales is entirely coincidental.

A DARK WAY TO GLORY

An Ace Book / published by arrangement with the author

PRINTING HISTORY

Originally published as part of *The Feast of the King's Shadow*, Orbit / 2000
Ace mass-market edition / August 2003

For information address: Orbit,
a division of Little, Brown and Company (UK),
Brettenham House, Lancaster Place, London WC2E 7EN.

ISBN: 0-441-01086-5

ACE®
Ace Books are published by The Berkley Publishing Group,
a division of Penguin Group (USA) Inc.,
375 Hudson Street, New York, New York 10014.
ACE and the "A" design
are trademarks belonging to Penguin Group (USA) Inc.

PRINTED IN THE UNITED STATES OF AMERICA

10 9 8 7 6 5 4 3 2 1

Big hearts are big houses,
with a spare room for friends.
This one's for Richard and Jane.

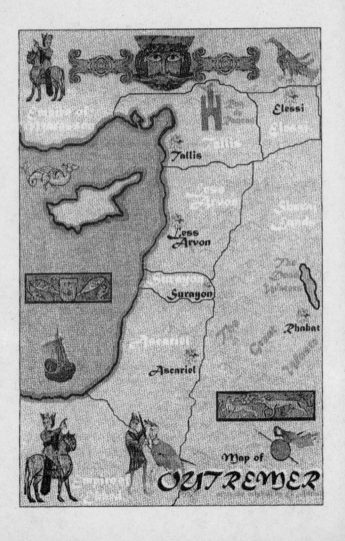

Map of
OUTREMER

Qul 'a 'uuzu bi Rabbin Naas,
Malikin Naas,
'Ilaahin Naas,
Minsharril waswaasil khan Naas,
'Allazii yuwas wisu fii suduurin Naasi,
Minal Jinnati wan Naas.

AL-QUR'AAN, 114, NAAS, 1–6

HE HAD COME out of the west in the early morning, running now as he had run all night, hard on their trail. Four horses and one afoot, it had been simple—he'd said—in these soft lands, even in the dark. He had done what he could to hide or mask that trail, though, against anyone else's following.

His name was Jemel, he'd said, the women knew him. He had sworn to guide them safely to Rhabat. Then the Patric horsemen had come and taken them the other way, back to the castle. He'd followed then—and did not say why—and had followed again this night when they'd burst the gate and come riding out, a party of four and one. He'd tried to keep up with that one at least, the one on foot, the runner; but that one had outrun the horses, and Jemel could not. So he had followed, at his best pace.

And had found them in a gully, resting and watering their horses. Dismounted, they had faced him as a group, and yet they were not; not even four and one, the runner divided from the riders, though certainly that was true.

There had been tensions everywhere. That had made it easier.

The old man, the crippled man had asked him what he wanted. He'd said that he was oath-bound to the women, to take them to Rhabat. The bearded man had laughed shortly, though he'd said nothing.

"But if we know the way, they do not need your guidance now."

"You need my help, perhaps. I said, I have disguised your trail for you, which you could not. You would have been caught by now, without me."

"If we don't want you," from the bearded man, "why do you want to come?"

His eyes had moved of themselves, inexorably sideways to the one young man of their party, the one who kept his distance from the horses; the one who kept his silence, his head lowered, his eyes hooded and hidden.

Too late to hide them from Jemel. He had seen, he knew.

"Your road lies with mine," was all he'd said, as mild as he could make it. And then, when that had seemed not to be enough, "We can be useful to each other. You need another sword, and one who is of the desert; I would be stupid to travel alone, here where your soldiers boil like bees at my back, or there where a man alone can die of a single bee sting . . ."

"Enough of this." The bearded man again, brutally abrupt. "Tell the truth, boy. You want to come because of him, don't you?" A jerk of his head, towards the silent one. "Because of what he is."

"He is not yours."

"Indeed not. I don't want him, never did. We're stuck with him now, though—so yes, I think we'll take him to Rhabat. Why not? It should be interesting, if nothing more. You'll excuse me if I decline to follow you, though. I suspect I know the way there at least as well as you, and likely better."

"I think Jemel should come," one of the women had

said instantly: not the one he'd saved from the 'ifrit, the other, the one who spoke his tongue and had shown some signs of decency, half-veiling her face when he'd appeared, though she'd let that veil slip mind and fingers soon. The other had simply gazed at him bare-faced, judgemental.

"Oh heavens, girl, so do I think he should come. Why not?" Again, as though it had been all a bitter joke. "He'll make the perfect addition to our party. We've already got the escaped prisoner, condemned to death for heresy and tortured till he can barely move, till he must use another's strength to ride with; we've got the runaway baroness who rides to Rhabat because a djinni told her to, and her companion who goes to spite her father."

"The djinni sent me too," the girl objected. "And I'd go in any case, to be with Julianne."

"Of course: the girl who goes for loyalty, obedience and love, and so to spite her father. That father himself, who goes to prevent a war, if he is able; and who takes in his baggage, running at his stirrup-rein, the very weapon which can win that war. Who is a boy from the one side, possessed by a spirit from the other; whatever he does, he will betray himself. All we need now is another boy, and one who wants that war more than he wants any other thing in life, am I right?"

No, he had not been right, he was too late for that. A month before, yes, certainly; but not by then. By then what Jemel had wanted most was vengeance. But he'd said nothing of that, and so the bearded man had nodded, sure of his own cynical judgement.

"Join us, Jemel," he'd said, "and welcome. We are a party of fools; there's always room for a little more foolishness."

1

Sand Dancers

AT THIS DISTANCE she thought they looked like dancers, blurred figures who swirled and stamped and left strange trails in the sand. Black silhouettes, hazed by the heat so that they would flicker and jerk, vanish almost for moments too brief to count.

At this distance, she couldn't see the swords that were the focus and the purpose of all that dancing.

WEEKS INTO THEIR journey, this was the first sand that they had come to; and even this, she'd been told, was not the true sand, the drifting dry of the desert ocean, the *mul'abarta,* what Jemel called simply the Sands: only a wind-blown herald of what awaited them days further to the south.

"Look at it, Julianne," Elisande had said, scuffing at the trail with her boot, digging the sand aside to show glassy black lava beneath. "This is a dusting, no more. We could take an ox-cart over this, no need for camels. The sand just smooths the ridges here. You wait until you wade in it, until you swim in it, until you think you could sink and sink and never touch bottom . . ."

Well, she would wait, then; and not be afraid, though she thought her friend wanted her to be. *Anywhere you can go, I can go too*; and Elisande had been that way already, more than once. There were things ahead to be afraid of, Julianne knew that, and those she would fear when she needed to—but not the journey, no. Only what lay beyond the journey, what had caused them to travel this way . . .

THEY WERE TRAVELLING with a caravan for cloak, for safety, certainly not for speed. *If my father need speed,* Julianne thought, *if his cloak, his safety lie in our speed to reach him, then I have no father.* She wasn't sure about Elisande's ox-carts, there had been cruel ruts in the lava-bed before they reached the sand, that wheels must have balked at; but their horses had picked their way across that, and certainly they could have ridden hard across this ground, this demi-desert. Other parties had done just that, indeed, sweeping by the laden camel-train with cries and cracking whips.

But Rudel was master of their own small party, even Elisande had had to accept that; and when they'd met this caravan of northern tribespeople at a well on the margin of the lava plain, he had paid over silver and jewels from their small stock of wealth for the right to travel at its tail, to share its food and fires.

"News blows on the wind," he'd said, when Elisande—inevitably, Elisande—had challenged him, "and all the winds blow southerly from here. You know that, daughter. We have need of haste, perhaps—but our need for secrecy outweighs it. What we carry with us we must hide, for as long as we can."

And his gaze had fallen inexorably, inevitably, on Marron where that boy sat at a little distance from their fire, from themselves; and even Elisande had had no further argument to offer.

AFTER SOME DAYS with the caravan, Julianne thought that it had perhaps not been the wisest decision he might have made. To be sure, the rest of them could hide to some extent within the milling crowd at every halt, they could conceal their own origins beneath rough woollen clothes bartered from their new companions; but the quality of their horseflesh could not be disguised, nor emphatically could Marron's strangeness.

A boy who held himself apart, a boy who walked while his friends had fine beasts to ride; more, a boy who could not come close to any animal in the train without that animal backing or shying or bellowing its terror . . .

No, such a boy would stand out in any company. The greater the number, the more was he isolated against it. It might after all have been better to have travelled fast and few, to let the rumour fly ahead of them, *a party of riders well-mounted, and one boy who runs beside and never falters* . . .

They'd have needed a mount for Jemel, of course, better than the scruffy pony he rode now; but there were other beasts among the caravan they might have bought for him. Better to have spent their money thus, and gone ahead . . .

BUT THE DECISION had been taken, well or ill. Too late to revoke it now. Their immediate goal, the oasis of Bar'ath Tazore, lay only one further day's journey down the trail. There this trail ended, there they would part company with the caravan and strike on alone. They'd leave behind the questioning glances of even these uncurious folk, the murmurs that neither Rudel nor Jemel could understand; with luck, they just might avoid all company else, and outride the rumour.

She didn't expect such luck, but she could hope. There was nothing else indeed that she could do.

For now, while men and women and beasts rested under the sun's height, she sat and shaded her eyes against the glare and watched two shadows, two stick-figures dance and spin.

Marron, and Jemel. Two boys, and neither seemed to feel any need of rest. Jemel was scornful of this midday lethargy, promising them hotter days by far before they reached Rhabat; while Marron—

Marron, she thought, was ice-cold in his spirit now, and no external warmth could touch him; or else his blood was fire, and there was nothing any sun or fire could do to heat it further. Wherever the truth lay, he was inexhaustible.

And so the two boys fenced while others dozed. Properly they were men, she supposed, young men who had loved and killed and carried the weight of that with them always; but it was their youth she saw, in Jemel's anger and Marron's silent pain. She was younger by a year or so and had never had a brother, but sometimes she felt like elder sister to them both.

Sometimes not. As now, watching them at swordplay and flinching even at this distance from the ferocity of it: play perhaps but no game as she understood the word. Games should not be deadly.

THE SAND LAY thicker away from the age-worn trail, rising in billows that looked soft and were not. Hard-packed by time and their own weight, baked like mud by the occasional rains and the sun that came after, they made good ground to fence on, seemingly. Not so good for sitting, hot enough to scorch where her hand fell; she shifted uncomfortably, and yearned for shade.

And had it for a moment, as a shadow fell across her; she glanced up, and saw Elisande.

"Julianne. What are you doing?"

"Resting."

"You don't look very restful."

Julianne sighed, as her friend settled beside her. "Well, no. I was watching them," with a jerk of her head. "They don't exactly inspire ease in my mind. I worry about them both."

Elisande's face twisted in sympathy "We all do. I keep telling myself that it's good that they're together, that they find some comfort in each other; but I don't know . . ."

"No." The opposite might be true; Julianne couldn't tell, any more than Elisande. Jemel was a bitter companion, and she thought that it was not truly comfort that he found with Marron. Awe and fear she was certain of; more there must be, to make the one boy dog the other so determinedly, but when she was honest with herself she thought that neither found much comfort in it.

"Are they trying to kill each other out there?" Elisande murmured, after a few moments' pause to watch.

Julianne chuckled, dry-mouthed from more than heat. "Not them," she said. "Jemel would never do anything to harm the Ghost Walker, even if he was able; and Marron—well, Marron wants never to kill anything, ever again." Too many bodies in that boy's past, she thought; more than she'd seen herself, she thought, though he wouldn't speak about it. Nor willingly about anything, any more. Perhaps that was why he accepted Jemel's company where he shunned theirs: he was spending time with the one member of the party he could barely exchange six words with. Perhaps.

"Even so," Elisande said. "There can be accidents at practice, even with bated blades; Marron knows that." *That's how he got to be the Ghost Walker.* "Someone should stop them—"

And she stood up to be that someone, but Julianne gripped her sleeve and tugged her down again.

"Leave them. Marron wouldn't allow an accident. Supposedly, Jemel's teaching him to use a scimitar—but it's Jemel who's taking lessons. Marron's the master, even where he doesn't know the weapon. He's faster, stronger, a lot more careful."

"You call that care?"

"Sit and watch. You'll see."

Even from this distance, even with the tricks played by heat and light against her eyes, she'd seen; and so did Elisande, with a little unnatural patience.

"All right. He won't hurt Jemel, and he won't let Jemel hurt him. But someone should stop them anyway. I don't know about Marron's body any more, since he took the Daughter into him—but Jemel can't ride all day on a mouthful of water and an hour's fight at noon."

"Yes, he can. He's a boy. You let them be, Elisande. If you try to call a halt, they'll fight another hour just to show you."

Elisande snorted. "I'm not picking him up, mind, if he falls off that pony. And he will, sooner or later. He doesn't eat enough to feed a snake."

Neither did Marron, but that was a different matter. "Jemel's still grieving for the death of his friend."

"Hating, more like. And I'm the one that killed him . . ."

"No. It was d'Escrivey that killed him." They'd established that cautiously, obliquely, largely by dint of encouraging Jemel to spit his anger at the fire night after night.

"My knife that gave him space to do it, though. It's my burden, Julianne, let me carry it."

"So long as you don't try to share it with Jemel."

"I won't," though silence was clearly costing her; how much, only Elisande could know. "Jemel's teaching Marron to speak Catari too, did you know?"

"No . . ." It wasn't a mutual and enforced silence that drew the two boys together, then. "That's good, though."

"It is. And it reminds me, I'm supposed to be teaching you. Tell me what you see, Julianne."

I see trouble, and danger, and uncertainty—but she couldn't say any of that in Catari yet, and the lessons did at least help to pass the time. Even when the heat lay like a smothering blanket across her head, fuzzing her mind into stupidity. She took a breath—and even the air was hot, parching her throat and her lungs, doing her no good—and fumbled for words she could barely pronounce or understand, a language she couldn't think in.

And found shelter in that, a relief from constant anxiety. When she couldn't think, she couldn't worry either.

THEY TALKED ALSO as they rode, side by side and a little lag of the caravan proper, not to breathe its dust or the smell of it; but they talked only in Catari. Elisande insisted on that. Slow talk, then, and slipping soon into a weary silence. It was possible almost to sleep ahorseback under so much weight of sun, to slide into a half-doze and touch the borders of dream before jerking back and staring wildly for a moment, before realising or remembering what and who and where she was and so slouching in the saddle again and slowly, slowly losing grip . . .

WHEN THEY CAME to where they would camp that night, she thought for a short while that they were a day ahead of themselves, that they had come to Bar'ath Tazore already.

What else? This was her abiding picture of an oasis, from a thousand childhood stories: stars pricking through the sky above as darkness swept across it, just at the moment when the trail dropped into an unexpected valley, glimpses of green before the last light fled. And then the glimmer of fires below, to match the glimmers overhead; and a song sung from two dozen tribal throats to announce them to the watchers at those fires, to say they were peaceful folk and no bandits come to steal and slay; and cries of welcome from left and right as the path brought them down to the valley bottom, and then the shimmer of dark water ahead, a pool knee-deep to beasts and men both, and what could this be but an oasis . . . ?

Elisande laughed at her. "Oh, Julianne, this is a happenstance, no more. This is lava country, remember? The ground cannot drink the rain, and it must go somewhere; so it floods any dip or hollow it can find. Here is more than a dip, it goes deep and it takes a lot of water. And the water lingers in the shadow of the cleft, where the sun can't bake it dry in a day. What's left now seems like a treasure to you, but it's little to what was here before, and every mouthful your horse drinks reduces it further. In a fortnight, there'll be nothing; and what's green here will die back till the next rain come, and those who camp here will feed their camels on the husks and then look for somewhere else. No, my love, this is no oasis. Wait till tomorrow."

And so she would, though she was glad enough of this tonight: water to drink and to wash in, despite the animals who had waded and perhaps wallowed in it first, bathing dust and dung from their pads and hooves and hides. Perhaps adding a little water of their own, before they were done. She didn't care; it tasted better and far better than a warm and stale drink from a dubious goatskin.

This night as every night the six of them sat around their own fire, though it was made up of dung-cakes from the caravan's store. This night as every night a woman brought them food. Her headdress was sewn with silver rings and her arms clashed with bangles; she kept her face so low that Julianne was never sure if it were the same woman every night, or if the duty were shared around.

Tonight, it seemed, they were feasting: a plate of boiled meat and greens, and a basket of flat breads. Rudel reached for a fleshy rib, bit and chewed, chewed and swallowed; spat gristle into the flames and said, "Ah, well. All things are comparative. At least it's better than preserved eggs."

Jemel frowned. "This is good food."

"Then why don't you eat it?" Elisande demanded. Receiving nothing but a shrug in response, she scowled momentously and went on, "And you, Marron. Here . . ."

She folded two breads around generous portions of meat and vegetable and thrust them into the boys' hands, didn't serve herself until she'd seen both begin to eat.

Julianne hid a smile behind sudden activity, picking out what tender pieces she could find for the elderly Redmond. His broken hands were healing now, but were too badly damaged to manage such work without pain.

He thanked her kindly; she helped herself and then settled down beside him to eat, finding him far the most restful of her companions.

The meat was stringy; there was sand in the greens, and more in the bread. She worked her way through it till her jaw ached with chewing, and her lips were raw from the grit. It was hard to be grateful: hard to remember that they had eaten less and worse already, or that there would likely be shorter commons still in the journey to come. Sometimes, though—when she tried—she could still find some pleasure in this adventure, in discovering the pampered and privileged daughter of the King's Shadow fallen so far from grace.

No, not fallen—jumped, rather. Jumped and run deliberately from her secure and comfortable existence, for the sake of a djinni's word against her father's life . . .

She was also of course the Baroness Julianne von und zu Karlheim these days; she should be Countess of Elessi in days to come, and had run also from someone who offered more than security or comfort—but there was no pleasure in that particular memory. She jerked her eyes away from the fire, where they could so easily have seen his face form in the flames.

And looked instead at the ground before the fire, and saw instead how the air seemed to flicker with more than the flicker of the firelight. She narrowed her gaze and bent a little closer, and saw a black line drawn above the sand: thicker than a hair, finer than a wire, snagging her eye like a hook. It was there, and then it was not there; for a moment she thought *djinni* . . .

But then there was another, and then there were two at

once and she lost them both by trying to watch them both; and there had only ever been one djinni, and it had never played games with her this way. It had come, had done and said what it meant to do and say and then it had gone again.

So no, not the djinni; but—

"What *are* those things, do you see them?"

Surprisingly Redmond laughed, though there was a harsh and knowing ring to it that she liked not at all. "The insects? The Sharai call them sand dancers. Try to catch one."

She made a cup of her hand, and grabbed; and opened her closed hand to find it empty. And tried again, and failed again; and tried to snare one between her two clapping hands, and still failed.

"You could sit all night," Redmond said, stilling her with a touch on her shoulder, "and still come up with nothing. The Sharai say that they slip between two worlds, this and another, which is why they call them sand dancers. One reason why."

"I don't understand," she said.

"No. Be grateful."

She swallowed her irritation and said, "Well, I will try. Since you ask it. But what is the other reason?"

"They are killers," Redmond said. "If you set a beetle on the sand there, they would destroy it. If you set a nest of ants there, they would destroy them all."

THE DAY'S HEAT dissipated quickly; after an hour of darkness, they found themselves shifting closer to the fire. Except for Marron, of course, who apparently felt neither cold nor heat; and except for Jemel also, who felt or at least said that the nights were as warm as the days were cool. If he had another reason for keeping a touch of distance—as for example that he hated so much the place and the people they had come from, it was an effort to him not to hate them also, and he would not risk his knife too close to their throats—then he did not say so; neither if he had rather a reason for staying quite close to Marron.

Julianne felt that she had reasons in plenty for staying as far as possible from Marron, and yet she couldn't do it. As a Ransomer boy he had charmed her with his naïvete, and a little with his blushful beauty too; as a creature out of nightmare, slaying and slaying with a flicker of his eyes or a gesture of his bleeding arm, he had terrified her. She tried deliberately to remember that terror sometimes, to use his red eyes and his inexhaustible, inhuman energy as a reminder that he was not what he used to be. She wished that she could react to him as her palfrey Merissa did or any animal else, bucking and screaming; but it seemed that she could not. She still looked at him and saw the boy that he had been, in many ways the boy that he still was, only dreadfully burdened now.

And she was not even Sharai, she hadn't grown up eyeing the night's shadows for any hint of the Ghost Walker, while a hundred stories thundered in her head. No blame to Jemel if he'd chosen to run the other way that night or the morning following, if he'd kept all the distance he could between himself and Marron; but he was Sharai, and so he had not.

Also, of course, he'd not seen that skein of red that killed, that was the Ghost Walker's wicked will; all he'd seen of Marron was the eyes and the energy and the flesh that contained them, the silence and withdrawal. She thought that probably what he saw was also mostly boy. And boys will cling together, she thought, against girls or against authority, against the world itself . . .

WHEN THE FLAMES died to a glimmer among white ashes and the cold pressed in at their backs as the day lay heavy on their bones, they wrapped themselves in blankets and lay down two by two around the circle of the fire: the older men Rudel and Redmond, the girls Julianne and Elisande, the boys Marron and Jemel.

Except that Marron slept as little as he ate, and Jemel also. Julianne was accustomed now to seeing them still sitting silhouetted against the stars as she closed her eyes; she knew they would be up and about before her in the morning. She hoped tonight that all their long nights were full of talking, that the excuse of language lessons would teach them both to share their troubles; only then she thought of what each might have to say to the other when they could talk as equals, and rather wished they would not.

Something else to which Julianne had become accustomed: Elisande's being wakeful and watchful also, restless at her side. Wakeful for many reasons, Julianne thought, but watchful only over Marron.

Between them all, they made it precious hard for a girl to get any sleep herself . . .

BUT SLEEP SHE did, and wake she did, and watched them all through their morning rituals.

Jemel—who had kept to his Sharai dress and Sharai habits also—would walk some distance away and kneel, and pray towards the rising sun: alone, he said, because the tribespeople they travelled with were untrue in their words, following bastard rites. Elisande said that it was Sharai pride, that he thought himself superior; Julianne thought it another expression of his anger.

Marron made a great point of saying no prayers at all. No longer a brother of the Ransomers, no longer squire to a religious master and not at all certain what he had become, he would sit apart and do nothing until Elisande took him bread, and stood over him until he had eaten it.

Rudel had discarded his jongleur's garb for the anonymity of the simple clothes the others wore, but he still practised his juggling for half an hour every morning.

Redmond had been too much hurt in his hands and his feet to do anything active. He would sit over the fire, warming his bones for the day ahead, he said; his eyes watched them all, though, and his wise tongue soothed any quarrels that might be building.

Elisande saw to everyone's breakfast, though Marron was her special charge and her father Rudel her hardest, seemingly. They were the two most likely to stretch Redmond's peacemaking.

Which left Julianne to see to the horses, a duty she took on willingly, and more than ever so this morning. They were all of them friends by now and Merissa had always been special, a wilful and occasionally difficult companion but a confidante too when they were both young in Marasson, sometimes closer in her affections than any of her circle. Julianne had a building ache in her heart, as each day's journey brought them that much nearer to a certain parting. There was nothing she could do to prevent it, they could not take horses into the true desert nor keep them alive if they had tried to; but soon it would be another's hands that brought bridle and saddle, hopefully sweets and petting. Julianne had known too many hard separations in recent weeks; she wasn't sure that she could tolerate another.

She wasn't sure either that it was truly the loss of Merissa that grieved her so, but she was determined to think it. Otherwise she might still be crying herself to sleep every night over a pair of green-grey eyes, blond hair and a devastating smile . . .

So this one time more—and trying not to torment herself with the thought that it might be the last time—she fetched all the horses from where they foraged fresh greenstuff by the water's edge. She stroked their soft noses and pulled their ears, and promised them more and better eating that evening. She spent longer with Merissa, murmuring secrets that only the palfrey could hear and would not spread around. Then she burdened them one by one with saddle and harness, glanced around for her human companions and called softly to say their mounts were ready. The caravan was on the move already, filing up the shadowed path into the early sun's light above. Julianne would have preferred another hour's rest and then a fast gallop to catch it, but Rudel was firm about that, they must do nothing to attract attention.

No more than they could help, at least. Nothing, she thought, would keep the quiet tribespeople from gossiping at journey's end. Their best hope would be hardly to pause at Bar'ath Tazore, to trade their horses for camels tonight or tomorrow and be away before the rumour spread.

AND SO ANOTHER day of weary riding at a walker's pace, weary for herself and Merissa both: the horse was as restless as she was, sidling and jerking and tossing her head. As keen for speed too, Julianne thought, and a cool wind running. That they'd never find on this baking plain; when the breeze came it brought only more heat with it. Marasson summers were worse, though, not so purely hot perhaps but stickier and far more draining, and they'd both enjoyed the freedom of a gallop then.

This trailing of the caravan was nothing but dull, sucking at reserves of patience. As the sun rose higher, so conversation flagged. She covered her head with a fold of cloth to shade her eyes from the pale sky's glare, and focused her gaze between Merissa's ears. Marron was a shimmering dot away to the side, as ever. Jemel rode as close to him as he dared, which was not close at all; Rudel and Redmond rode ahead, Elisande at her side. Julianne worried about them all, in turn: Marron for the burden he carried or else the creature he had become, the thing that infested his blood had made the two indistinguishable; Jemel for his grief and loss and anger, which could not be allayed; Redmond for his physical weakness, the cruelties worked against him by the Ransomers' questioners; Rudel and Elisande for the gulf between them that she still did not understand, that they would not talk about, that should not so divide father and daughter.

Betweentimes she worried about her own father, whom she was travelling so far to find and to rescue, according to the djinni's word, though she did not know how. It had refused to tell her; sometimes, often, she doubted herself and her ability.

And when she was worrying about none of them, when she occasionally found space to think about her future, that too was nothing but worry and grief, a loss as great as Jemel's. Or greater, she dared to think sometimes, because it was her own choice that had caused it. She had deliberately fled the man she'd married, the one young man she would happily have given herself to for the rest of her days; she thought he would never take her back now.

And yet—despite boredom and discomfort and the ache in her bones, despite anxiety and sorrow and the ache in her heart—yet she was happy. Happier than she had been before, she thought, perhaps.

In the past, in Marasson, happiness had always been contingent: she was happy *but* her father was in Outremer, as he almost always was; she was happy *but* she was afraid of falling, and dared not climb; she was happy *but* she was to be married to an unknown lordling in a far-distant province.

Now all that was turned around. Her father was in Rhabat, in the hands of the Sharai, in danger; but she was happy. She was afraid of many things now, and afraid for many people for many different reasons; but she was happy. She was married to her lordling, and she had fallen desperately, dangerously in love with her husband, and had fled him for her father's sake for whom her love was far more complex and far less all-engulfing—and still, bizarrely, treacherously almost, she was happy.

She pulled her mettlesome mount into line again, for the hundredth time already today, and tried to understand herself. It might be the freedom, she supposed, that she so relished: to ride untrammelled—better yet, unveiled; these people did not cloak their women's faces—under wide skies, to sleep in a blanket beneath the stars with no other guard than her own and her companions' watchfulness. To make her own decisions, or at least to have an equal voice among the company. Perhaps. Or it might be the prospect of action, the chance to do what she felt to be right or necessary, to be more than a quiet voice sequestered in her lord's ear. She was afraid of making mistakes, afraid of failure, but still it might be better to try and fail than not to have the opportunity to try.

Perhaps.

Or perhaps it was simply to be riding into doubt and mystery with these particular few, these dubious and mysterious folk her friends. If friends they were. One at least she was sure of, Elisande who rode beside her and kept far fewer secrets now. The others still kept more of their own counsel than they shared with her. That was fair, though; so did she. It was only Elisande to whom she whispered the truths of her heart, and not all even to her. Some she held back, though the other girl had seen enough surely to guess at those also.

THE SUN CLIMBED to its highest and moved on, as they moved on beneath it. For the first time in many days, the caravan did not pause to rest despite the heat. There was no place, the endless plain offered no hope of shade nor water beyond what they carried in bags slung below the bellies of their beasts; even so, Julianne thought there was another reason today. Even these trading tribes must grow tired of the road, must press with added urgency when their goal came close, eager to arrive even an hour earlier than they might . . .

DESPITE THAT, SHE did not recognise the signs when they first appeared, she was only confused. The sky was green, and she thought that meant a storm. She thought it had to. In Marasson, when the sky was porridge-yellow and porridge-thick, even the animals sought shelter against the coming deluge.

None of that heaviness here: the sky ahead was green but

glimmering with it, like a fine translucent glaze on a good pot. It couldn't be rain, surely. She had heard that it rained even in the true desert, but not from such a sky. There were other kinds of storm, though; she had heard that also. A dust-storm, a sand-storm might somehow look like this from a distance, if a rain-storm looked like porridge.

Green, and glimmering like water as they rode through heat that made the air dance above the sand; and Elisande at her side but not so much watching the road ahead or the sky above it, much more watching her and smiling, smiling in anticipation . . .

At last the egg broke, she cracked it, and all but choked on her sudden rush of understanding.

"That's it, isn't it? That's the oasis doing that . . ."

"Bar'ath Tazore," Elisande confirmed, grinning. "Pastures of the Sky, they call it; but any oasis can seem so from a distance. The Sharai say that it's the generosity of their god, to guide them to water and good grazing."

"Do they?"

"Well, that's what they tell their children. Maybe it's what most of them believe. If you can read the mind of a Sharai, then you explain it to me. I spoke to a man once who said the mirage was all to do with light and reflection and the heat, but I didn't understand him either."

"You didn't understand him. Right . . ."

"Well, I can draw his diagrams for you, then you can explain that too. He was Sharai himself. Now watch, you're going to enjoy this."

DID SHE ENJOY it? She wasn't sure, that didn't seem quite the word. Elisande enjoyed it, no doubt of that—but Elisande again was watching her more than she watched the road or the sky.

She could hardly have seen, that moment when the air rippled and closed like a curtain, hiding the long stretch of the caravan ahead and blurring even the near figures of Rudel and Redmond to a single shifting silhouette; though even Elisande, even without looking, could hardly have missed that moment when the masking air shivered to a mirror. Briefly Julianne found herself staring at a smudged, wild image of herself, that hung perhaps an arm's length above the road, though it seemed to have a road of its own to ride on.

Whatever Merissa saw, with those large and wide-set eyes that could take in half the horizon at a glance, it must have been something other than herself. The horse snorted as though there really were some barrier drawn across the sand, something more real than the nonsense Julianne's eyes reported; but she didn't shy or startle, as she would have if she'd thought there were a sky-horse coming down to meet her, nose to nose.

She walked steadily forward and met that horse, nose to nose. Only when they touched did the image jar and vanish, like a reflection in water shattered by a stone.

And the curtain lifted, the air cleared, Julianne could see for miles ahead—and for miles ahead all she could see was green. The sky was sere blue again as it should have been all day; but where there had been yellow-white sand and the odd black lava outcrop all around them all day and nothing else to fix the eyes on, nor the mind, now there were trees and simple houses and more trees. There was pasture and cultivated land, and trees; and there were people moving among the houses, people and animals flowing this way and that through narrow alleys and wide avenues, and all the avenues were lined with trees.

Julianne chanced a glance behind, fearful of magic; at her back she saw the endless desert of the day, a vista of sand and occasional rock blurring too soon with the heat.

Here there was no blurring, and the heat was less too, she thought, though as yet they were only on the margin of Bar'ath Tazore and still a long way from any shade.

"Elisande? What happened there? Is there some kind of protection, that hides this place from those who mean it harm?" Some kind of priestly magic, she meant—though if there were, it should have hesitated long before it let them through. She thought that this little party carried harm very much within its shadow.

"No, none," Elisande said with a chuckle. "It's the mirage, love, that's all. The hand of God, or the hand of mystery that some men think they've solved. Unless it's desert magic, like the djinni. I don't know. It's desert charm, to me—and you're seeing some of it even before we reach the desert proper. That was the mirage; and this, Julianne, is an oasis. Forget that puddle where we camped last night . . ."

Julianne had forgotten it already, as she gulped at cool beauty with sore dry eyes, drinking and drinking.

THE OASIS LAY in a broad shallow bowl below them, though she hadn't realised they'd been climbing a ridge to reach it; that might explain something of how it had been hidden till now, though not all. Certainly it explained how she could see so much of it at a glance, even the great pool at its heart like a gleaming jewel set in a cloth of green. The trees were date-palms and there must be thousands of them, to make such a canopy. On the far side of the water, she could see the roofs of one grand building rising up through their cover; she'd like a closer look at that, though she doubted that she'd have the chance.

The caravan they'd followed so far was moving on already, but Rudel held his mount rock-steady, breaking that easy link. A sudden flight of birds drew Julianne's attention, the first she'd seen for weeks; it burst from the treetops, wheeled screaming above her head and then dived back out of sight. She turned her head to find Marron, standing away to one side as he always was. The older man was right in his stillness, he didn't need to speak; they couldn't risk taking that deadly boy into the busy traffic below.

BETWEEN THE DESERT and the trees, around the rim of the bowl was a broad band of rock and gravel that made for easy riding. Rudel led them that way with a gesture, as though he meant to circle the oasis and strike straight out into the desert again. Not possible if they meant to go further, but at least he wanted that option, Julianne thought, if things should go badly here: a quick escape through the heat-curtain and away to rethink, retreat or reroute. They could go back to the wild country, or else they could go west and find their way into Outremer again. Skirt Elessi—*please?*—but come to Tallis or Less Arvon and so sneak south, perhaps even as far as fabled Surayon, accursed Surayon which was home to Rudel and to Elisande . . .

Not that things would go badly here, of course. Why should they? Travellers seeking to change horses for camels could hardly be unknown at this oasis; they ought to be its lifeblood. Any border trading-post subsists on what passes through, and the rich trade here must be from Outremer to Rhabat and back again. She had heard that Rhabat had links with tribes and peoples far further to the east, strange empires with stranger goods to bargain with; she knew that silks and ivory came that way to the courts of Outremer and Marasson.

So there ought to be no cause for Rudel's caution, but she applauded it anyway. After so long mewed up in the castle at the Roq, desperately trying to get away and being balked at every turn, she favoured open spaces and no walls. Redmond at least, she thought, must feel the same.

WHOEVER LIVED IN the palace whose roofs she'd seen, whoever ruled Bar'ath Tazore favoured palm-tree walls to his territory. His people worked the land within the circle of trees irrigating the soil with a complex system of dykes that must somehow draw its water up from the central pool.

Long ago, Julianne thought, when the lava of the plain had been boiling rock, it must have flowed all around this bowl and found no way inside. Its cooling had killed all the surrounding land but left this living, fertile but isolated, a tiny kingdom only waiting for its king.

Eventually they came to a spot where the trees seemed sick, their great leaves brown and drooping. The mud walls of the dykes beyond were broken, the channels dry; nothing grew in the land around.

There was a simple hut between the dykes, one of many that they'd passed. The others had all been occupied, people busy among their crops or tending goats or preparing a meal in the doorway of their home, all of them pausing to watch the riders through the shadows of the trees. Here, though, the hut door was cast down and they could see black shadows within, no signs of life.

Rudel called back, "Wait," and guided his horse between the trees. He rode to the hut and called again, "Hullo in there!"

When there was no answer, he dismounted and walked inside.

After a moment he reappeared in the doorway, beckoning.

THE HUT WAS as abandoned as the land it served. It seemed strange to Julianne, as to the others; where viable ground was so sparse and precious, even death or disgrace should simply have opened the way for another family to claim it.

But the hut was here, and unclaimed. "We'll use this," Rudel said flatly. "There's no forage for the horses, but we've grain enough for tonight. Water we can fetch. The girls can sleep in the hut while we men stand guard outside, in turns. Marron must stay here, and Redmond too; the market will be too far for you to walk, old friend. The rest of us, though—if the girls will veil themselves, we can all go down and taste the life here, listen to the gossip and hope not to find ourselves the theme of it."

"I will stay with Marron," Jemel said, predictably.

"No. Please, Jemel, we may need you. There will be

Sharai among the traders; they will deal fairly with you, but not with me in this garb," with a gesture at the discreet plainstuff that he wore, "and I had rather not declare my true name here."

"I will stay with Marron." Jemel's words again, but this time it was Elisande who spoke them. She was perhaps simply being convenient, helping the young Sharai to choose her father's way; more likely, Julianne thought, she preferred not to walk with her father.

Jemel hesitated, before nodding reluctantly.

IT WAS A party of three, then, who left the hut and the horses and their friends, to find out the heart of Bar'ath Tazore. There were signs of a path, sun-cracked mud with a dusting of blown sand, running beside the dry watercourse; that led them shortly to another line of palms, and beyond it a sudden change, almost a different world. Here the air was full of birdsong and goat-cries, the smells of moisture and growing; the irrigation channels ran with clean water; beside the narrow path the ground was green with crops.

This land too had its hut, well-kept and busy; children stood gaping by the wall. A man rose from among the crops, muddy to the knees before his robe fell down to cover them. He had mud on his hands too, and held them self-consciously at his sides as he strode forward.

"What are you seeking, strangers?" He spoke in Catari, of course, but he spoke it slowly, out of courtesy, and Julianne was only a beat behind his words in understanding.

"The best way forward," Rudel said mildly. "I regret walking on your land, but we are newly arrived here, and do not know where we are free to go and where not."

"The land is the Sultan's," the reply was brisk and corrective, "and not my own. All land here is the Sultan's. Walk where you will. But the resting-place for travellers is on the further side of the oasis."

"Is it? Ah. I did not know." It seemed likely to Julianne

that he was lying, she thought he must have been here before; but he did it wonderfully well, so that even she
found it hard not to believe him.

"There you will be made welcome. Take the highway
past the pool, anyone will show you . . ."

"We have come a long way, and our beasts are tired.
We've settled them now; I think we'll not move on again
today. Unless the Sultan would object to our staying
where we are . . . ?"

"The Sultan provides water and a roof for all travellers," *in the proper place,* he was saying, *where they can
be watched.* Julianne understood him very well. The Sultan would indeed object to their camping where they
were, if he heard about it; and she was reasonably sure
that he would, that a child would be running the news to
the palace any minute now. "Where else have you found,
to halt?"

"Why, just here, through the trees," Rudel told him,
with an expansive wave. "There was a hut that seemed
abandoned, to give shade and shelter to our womenfolk;
and space enough for men and horses, if you wouldn't
mind our fetching in a little of your water . . . ?"

But the man was backing off suddenly, taking hurried
little steps that crushed his plants in their tidy rows. When
he was five or six paces distant, he lifted his hands in a
gesture of denial. "Keep away! Keep away from me and
mine . . . !"

"Well, if you wish it. Though we will still need water.
What is the matter, have we profaned holy ground?"

"Diseased ground, infected ground! Touch nothing and
no one, you are corrupt . . ."

He turned and hustled his watching family within the
safety of their hut, leaving the door only a crack ajar so
that wary eyes could follow what strangers did.

"Well. If we're corrupt, I suspect the Sultan would not
welcome us in his caravanserai; and just as well, I think.
We could neither leave Marron nor take him into com-

pany. But if that land truly harbours disease . . . Jemel?
What do you think?"

"I saw no sign of it. Nothing grows, but nothing has
water. Even the palms are thirsty."

"Mmm. We'll ask questions, I think, around the marketplace; but no one speak of empty huts, until we know.
There must be some reason why it was abandoned, the
land and the trees left to die. No one wastes good land,
where it lies so sparse . . ."

THEY HAD TO cross another man's fields before they
found a wider path, a wagon-road in a shaded aisle. That
led in turn to a broad highway which ran straight as the
spoke of a wheel, between fields and houses and directly
to the pool that was the jewel of Bar'ath Tazore.

The nearer they approached the water, the more traffic
they met and mixed with. No one asked questions of them
now, no one seemed to look at them twice; certainly there
were more interesting people for the old men squatting in
doorways or the children playing in the narrow alleys to
look at. There were men in rich dress on horseback or
camelback, cursing and cracking whips to clear a way
through the throng; there were servants in simple tunics,
running errands or carrying sacks or dripping water-skins.
There were black men in gorgeous robes, reminding Julianne of the slaves who'd borne her in the palanquin
from Tallis, though these were surely free; there were men
who might be slave or free who carried similar litters
here, which perhaps hid girls like herself behind their con-
cealing curtains. Other women walked as she did, some in
swathes of black with only their eyes showing, some in
gossamer veils and silks that clung like a shadowy second
skin to the body beneath, teasing and revealing.

Some of the riders were Sharai in tribal robes, whose
dark gaze found Jemel and then dismissed him, either for
his own tribal allegiance or his companions, or both. He
stiffened each time that happened, and his hand twitched

towards his scimitar's hilt; each time, though, he fixed his eyes blindly ahead and strode on.

Once, passing a large house with an inner court, Julianne glanced in through the open gateway and stiffened momentarily herself, before hurrying on. She gripped Rudel's sleeve and whispered, "You may think me mad, but I swear I saw Ransomers in there, Knights Ransomers . . ." Tall young men with light hair and sun-bronzed skins, at least, wearing white robes with black cloaks thrown over, and what else could they be . . . ?

"Outremer trades with the Sharai, child," he murmured, and she thought he was laughing at her, almost. "How else would the lords of the Kingdom have their silks and salt and spices? They meet often on neutral ground, places such as this. Some of the lords are brazen, some are discreet; a great many come, or send their agents. They come warily, though, and often with an escort of knights. Not the brothers, they are not permitted to dabble their fingers so close to heresy; and not I think from Elessi, if that's your fear."

That was the worst of her fears, to be seen and known; sought for, even, even here. She was reassured, but not completely. He added, "The lords come, but not their women, Julianne; keep a hand on your veil, and be discreet with your eyes." That gave her the excuse she needed. She walked closer in Rudel's shadow thereafter, and held her head lower, and wished that he would do the same. He came from a proscribed state, but still his face and beard had been seen widely throughout Outremer, in many guises; she dreaded a chance encounter that might carry news of her back to Elessi, and believed the God or fate or perhaps that damned djinni malign enough to allow it. Even to arrange it, perhaps . . .

THE GREAT POOL at Bar'ath Tazore must presumably have been a natural occurrence, but men's hands had worked it extensively, so that now it was a broad, wide rectangle, as deep and dark as myth in the centre but shallow at its paved edges; and shadowed by the inevitable palms. At intervals, steps led down into the water; the water-carriers filled their skins there while naked children splashed and shrilled, while men in decent loin-cloths immersed themselves in a ritual cleansing. Further out, squads of small brown birds ripped the air with their shrieking and the water with their beaks, drinking aflight and then darting, twisting, diving after invisible insects.

All along the nearest side of the pool was a noisy marketplace. Gaudy awnings shielded rank after rank of stalls from the sun; other traders spread their goods on a carpet or on the bare sandy ground. Julianne saw sacks of maize and millet, tables laden with still-dripping meat or piled high with vegetables strange in both shape and colour; she saw jewellery and carved ivory, bolts of silk and bales of plainer cloth; in one distant corner, she saw near-naked people squatting disconsolately or standing to be bargained for like any other goods.

Mostly, though, she was still watching faces in the crowds, watching for light-coloured eyes or sunburned skin, any sign of Outremer; and so it was she who first saw a small group of men gathered by the bole of a palm, men in robes such as the Sharai wore but that the robes were black rather than midnight blue. The men were silent, watchful; she met the intensity of one man's gaze, and shuddered.

Two of their number were squatted at the others' feet, seeming to play some simple game with stones; puzzled, she watched for a moment. Both set their stones left-handed, and there was something strange about those hands. It took a moment longer to register with her, but each man was missing the smallest finger from that hand.

Again, she tugged at Rudel's sleeve.

"Those men—what are they?"

He followed the nod of her head, saw them and turned swiftly away; Jemel was a little slower, and his eyes were wide and anxious as he hurried after.

"Who are they?" Julianne asked again.

Rudel said nothing; it was Jemel who told her, in his own language, and though she understood the words she still felt little wiser.

"They are Sand Dancers. Beware of them . . ."

2

Taking Rice

EVEN AT HIS loneliest, at his most frightened and depressed, Marron had never felt so alone as he did these days.

Always at his back, two ghost-voices whispered against the wind from the desert, the wind of his running: Aldo and Sieur Anton, friend and master, boy and man. Both had invaded his heart, his life, his bed; and now Aldo was dead—by Marron's own hand, yet: literally by his hand flung up, by the bleeding wound on his arm—and Sieur Anton was betrayed. Marron ran from the dead and the living both, and could not escape them.

And though he ran in company, almost in the company of friends, he could not come close to any of them. Where they were riding, it was their animals that shied at his approach; where they walked or sat or lay down, they lacked that excuse, and still they shied. Not meaning to, not knowingly, but still. He saw it in the flinch of an eye before the smile followed; he heard it in their firm, deliberate voices when they spoke to him, how determined they were to sound warm and welcoming.

Only Jemel was different, and perhaps Elisande—and Marron shied himself from both of those, for different reasons.

And so found himself unbearably alone, even in company; felt himself in another world, almost, isolated from those who moved around him, shadow to their substance unless it was the other way about.

In ways, of course, that was true. He did walk with one foot in another world. His blood beat with a strange inhabitant. He dared not wake that creature, but when he ran its strength was added to his own, when he fenced its speed led his arm—and always, always he saw at least a little through its eyes, or else it infected his. He saw the world through a red haze, though he saw by night and day far more clearly than ever he had before.

Actually he was growing accustomed to that haze, as he was to the seemingly inexhaustible strength and the furious speed and the immunity to physical pain. His soul hurt exceedingly, but never his body now. These gifts were all of them borrowed, not owned; owed though, perhaps, a payment in kind for his carrying a passenger in his blood. When he looked at a thing he could see its true colour, his eyes had adapted that much. Sometimes he almost forgot that red cast, he had become so used to it.

What he never could forget was what other people saw, whenever they looked at him. They saw the unnatural redness of his eyes, and even after weeks of it his companions had not learned to hide the disquiet that they felt.

AS NOW, AS Elisande came over to where he stood among the slow-dying palms, gazing back across the many miles that they'd covered: gazing north and west, towards the castle where he'd left Aldo dead and Sieur Anton abandoned, along with love and duty.

He didn't turn his head, he didn't consciously turn even his mind towards her, but he knew that she was coming. Almost before she did, perhaps; certainly as soon as she started to move his way. His hearing was as much sharper as his eyesight now. Only his mind was fogged and grieving, doubtful and distressed and not really able to remember why he was here, even, where or how this had started, which step it was that had set him on an inevitable pathway to destruction . . .

Destroyed was how he felt, despite his new-come powers; he was still Marron, and Marron had lost everything he valued, and was trapped now in a body he could not own and on a course he wanted neither to follow nor to leave.

He might have left regardless, although he knew nowhere else to go; he might have left days ago, weeks ago, if it weren't for Jemel and Elisande.

JEMEL HAD GONE away for a rarity, which made things easier, which made things harder; in the absence of that boy's watchfulness, here came Elisande, with her own.

With things also, for excuse; with water-skin and bread, with bowl and cloth.

"Marron, here. A long dry day for you, I brought you water . . ."

He tried to say thank you for memory's sake, for manners, and could not. Realised that she was right, his throat was too parched for speech; and took the skin and drank, and tried again.

"Thank you, Elisande."

She shrugged awkwardly. "You're stupid, you forget if someone doesn't tell you; and that Jemel's gone off, so . . . Will you eat? If I tell you to?"

He did think about it for a moment, before he shook his head. "No. I don't need to."

"You mean you're not hungry. That's not the same thing. You weren't thirsty either, were you? But you needed water. And you need food too, you were always scrawny but you're all bone now . . ."

"I'll eat when Jemel eats," which meant at dawn and

sunset, and scantily. Once he'd loved to eat, but now it was only a chore, chew and swallow with no savour.

"He's as bad as you are. It's a conspiracy of boys. I'll break you both, eventually—if you don't break yourselves first. If you'd eat more, then so would he—and he needs to, even if you don't. For his sake, Marron, you could make the effort. Well," taking the water-skin back and pouring into the bowl, moistening the cloth, "you'll let me bathe your arm, at least, and have a look at it. I know Jemel won't do that."

"There's no point, it doesn't change." Not even Redmond or Rudel could change it now, they'd both tried and they'd tried both together, though they'd said all along that it was hopeless. Elisande had tried and tried.

"I know," she sighed, "but show me anyway."

LIKE A RAGGED range of hills Marron thought his wound was now, if ever hills had been so brutal: thrusts and folds of scar tissue ripping across the smooth skin of his forearm where it had been slashed and torn and let half heal before it was torn again.

And torn a final time, and this time there would be no healing. Like a chasm sundering a range of hills, an open mouth of raw flesh cut through the scarring, fresh and glistening wet. It did not bleed, it could not hurt, but neither could it mend. New leather stitches were knotted through it to draw the lips together, to close it somewhat against filth and infection; those had not hurt either, but neither could they help. Marron had told Rudel so, he and Jemel together; the older man had grunted, had said, "I know," and had sewn the stitches regardless.

Each evening Elisande brought water to bathe the wound, and there was no purpose to that either, but he bore it patiently. For her sake, for her deep regret that was so clear and unscarred by the others' darker emotions: Julianne's fear of him, Rudel's distrust, Redmond's almost-envy. What Jemel felt, Marron was uncertain; he knew only that it was darker yet, and hungry.

Cool water washed across his arm, carrying away little particles of sand and grit that had lodged within the wound. It could have been soothing, if he could have been soothed by any service so small and meaningless. Cool fingers held firmly to his wrist; uncool eyes, dark and fiery eyes lifted to seek his face, hesitated, and then were distracted. Were almost glad, he thought, to find some other interest.

"What's this?" She reached with her other hand, the one that still held the cloth; he felt it touch his neck.

"I don't know. What?"

"There's a bruise . . ."

"Oh. Yes. A child threw a stone, I didn't see it . . ." He had already turned away, after straying too close to the tribe's small herd of goats. They had scattered in terror, and so had the children who drove them. One had been brave with a slingshot; he'd heard the buzz of the stone in the air, but understood too late to do more than twist so that it struck his neck and not his temple. It hadn't hurt.

"You should be careful," Elisande said anxiously: "If it had cut . . ."

If it had cut, the Daughter would have flowed out of him with his blood, a red mist, lethal in his anger; but he had not been angry, so the child would have been safe. What matter?

He said all of that, patiently. Elisande was still fretful, though. "Would it have healed, after?"

"I think so, yes." If he had nicked his arm again, to take the Daughter back. The open wound on his arm was the Daughter's gateway, in and out, sealed to that purpose. It might escape through any break in his skin, any window to the world, but there was no need to let it back in the same way.

The cloth dropped, to lie wetly on the shoulder of his tunic; it was her hand now that lay against his neck.

"You make an interesting companion," she murmured, trying to be teasing and falling short by a distance, her voice betraying her, "but—oh, I do miss Marron . . ."

"I'm still Marron," though none of them would believe him if she did not.

"You look like Marron," she allowed, and he could feel the effort she made to stay light, not to break completely. "And you talk like Marron too, sometimes, when I can get you to talk at all. Though you don't say the right things any more. But the old Marron used to fall asleep after a glass of wine and you don't, you hardly seem to sleep at all; and the old Marron would never have let me do this," and her fingers stroked his cheek, deliberately sensuous, "without the blood rising until he'd blushed himself to death. And you just sit there now and look at me, and don't react at all . . ."

That wasn't true, only that his reactions didn't show in his face any more. "Something else has charge of my blood now, Elisande."

"I know, I know. And—oh, Marron, I'm so sorry . . ."

He knew that, she'd told him time and again. That it was in no sense her fault, she knew. He might have blamed himself—or she might have blamed him, volubly, viciously—except that it had been no choice of his either, he hadn't known in the least what he was doing.

And so they were stranded here, nowhere further to go; and so they stood as silent as they always did, until she sniffed and tossed her head and took the bowl and left him.

Left him with the water-skin, half full still. Slowly, thoughtfully, he lifted it to his mouth and drank again.

WHEN THE OTHERS came back from the marketplace, Julianne was carrying a brace of black-feathered chickens and a bag of other purchases while Rudel and Jemel struggled with sacks of fresh and dried produce, as much as they could carry on one trip. They brought news too, as much perhaps as they could glean on one trip, more perhaps than any of them had wanted to hear.

"Sickness and miracles," Rudel said wearily, slumping to the ground as though the weight of the tale he bore had exhausted him. "That's all they want to talk about. Redmond, old friend, try if you can to make sense of this, for I cannot. People fell sick and silent, they say, dozens of them, with a dreadful wasting disease. The old and the weak turned their faces to the wall and died, and it seemed that the hale would follow them; there was no remedy that anyone could find. Until a holy man came out of Outremer, they say, a wild priest with the mummified hand of a saint in his possession. He preached the God in the market here, and the Sultan would have sent him forth or silenced him, I think, he has done that before; except that this holy man touched those who were sick with his saint's hand, and they were made well again. Others came to him with other ills, those lame or blind from birth, and those too he cured. He left here a fortnight since, and in his train he took all those his hand had touched. They followed him like slaves, it's said, with all their households too. We must just have missed this circus on the road. Have you ever heard the like?"

Redmond breathed once, in and out; and said, "No. If it had been one man healed, in another place and time, I might have thought about the Daughter," as he thought about himself, as Marron guessed, and what the Daughter might have done for him: *if any of us had to bear that thing,* Marron suspected was the constant burden of the old man's thoughts, *it should have been me . . .* "But as things stand, here and now—no, I have no answers for you."

"No. Well. The Sultan has declared them all apostate, who followed the miracle-worker; he says it was the work of devils, to deceive the faithful. He may be right, I cannot say. The people watch their health, and pray, and avoid the houses of those who were sick. They want their priests to purify them; their priests are as afraid as they are. Which is why we can rest here undisturbed, though our neighbours may spit at our shadows."

"Will they share their water with us?" Elisande demanded, practical as ever, awkward as ever in any exchange with her father. "We cannot drink their spit."

"I think we can take an allowance of water; they wouldn't pollute themselves to prevent it. If our doing so pollutes the water in their eyes—well, it's their problem and not our own."

"Unless they fetch out dogs to drive us off," Julianne suggested.

"What, and kill the beasts afterwards, for fear their bites may bring corruption back? I doubt it. No, we'll be shunned, no worse than that. And Jemel and I both doubt there's any true sickness here, that we might catch. I think you can rest easy in that hut, if not quite comfortably."

Jemel stirred, but didn't speak; they all knew what he would have said, that the hut was luxurious quarters next to what awaited them in the desert. Better than half the company had travelled that desert already, and knew the truth of it; Julianne would learn; Marron didn't care.

Marron was keeping his usual distance from the group, listening but saying nothing, little concerned by talk of disease. If it were true, it still couldn't touch him; the Daughter wouldn't allow it. And if it did, still he wouldn't care. His life was not his own. Sworn to Sieur Anton and forsworn shortly after, possessed now by magic, it would be no loss to him if he did die. Two, perhaps three of his companions would mourn him, he thought. No more than that, no one else in the world. Rudel certainly would be relieved; perhaps the whole world ought to be.

Elisande built and lit a fire by the doorway of the hut, fetched pots from their baggage, set Julianne to plucking the chickens and sent Jemel for water. He went unprotesting, with only one backward glance at Marron. When he was gone, Elisande produced a meaningful glance of her own. Marron made a gesture, *all right, I will eat. For his sake,* or for hers.

IT MIGHT HAVE been for his sake and Jemel's that she fussed so over her cooking, jointing the fowls and slicing vegetables, rummaging in Julianne's bag for salt and spices; it might equally have been to show her father what she could do, or else simply because she was weary of desert food.

Whatever the cause, she produced a savoury stew, serving it in wooden bowls as the sun set, with fresh bread warmed at the fire's edge. Marron sat and ate with Jemel, matching the young Sharai mouthful for mouthful. That much was duty; it was something more—perhaps only an appetite unexpectedly rediscovered, but he thought something even more than that—that had him standing, taking both his bowl and Jemel's back to the fire to be refilled. Elisande gave him a glad smile, to season the food the better. Jemel didn't smile, but he did accept the second helping, and before he ate it he did tap the rim of his bowl against Marron's in token of thanks or again perhaps something more.

And he didn't do as he usually did, he didn't murmur his dead lover's name over the food like a blessing or a vow renewed, a promise kept. Marron thought that was progress, an improvement, a definite step taken towards a private peace; he thought Elisande would have been pleased to hear of it, though nobody would tell her.

The stew was delicious, he thought, sucking at a chicken bone before tossing it neatly into the fire. At his side, Jemel did the same; their eyes caught, and this time Jemel did smile briefly.

RUDEL WAS DETERMINED that they should move on the following day. They would need to return to the market, he said, to buy more essential provisions; they would need

to take the horses to the livestock market on the far side of
the oasis, to sell them and find camels fit to tackle the
mul'abarta. Six beasts to ride, and two more to act as
pack animals initially, but also to keep in reserve against
disaster. Disaster was inevitable, he said, in the high
desert. They couldn't hope to come through it without loss;
if they lost no more than a camel or two, they'd be lucky.

Jemel twitched, and made a soft noise in his throat;
Marron glanced sideways at him, thinking that the Sharai
would once again be dwelling on his own loss, his love-
sworn partner Jazra who had died on the wall at the Roq.

Had died at Sieur Anton's hand, with Marron just a further pace away; had died with Elisande's knife in his side
also, and though it was the knight's sword that had slain
him, that other slim blade was guilty too, as was the hand
that had thrown it.

No one had said as much to Jemel, of course; no one
had spoken of it at all, or not directly. None of them was
stupid enough to cut loose the bindings on that particular
fury. But he must know some of the story at least, he must
have seen Marron fighting beside his master on the wall;
he might already have put a name to the knight who killed
Jazra.

There was no sullen louring in his eyes now, though, no
dark thoughts imprinted on his face; he was gazing at
Marron with a fierce determination. His hand left his side
and touched against Marron's for a moment, knuckle to
knuckle; it felt like a promise, an oath heard and witnessed, *whatever we may lose in the desert, Ghost Walker,
I will not lose you.*

Or was Marron misreading? He'd assumed that the
message was for him as Ghost Walker, that figure of myth
and magic, rather than for him as fleshbound boy and
journey's companion; of a sudden, as Jemel turned his
head sharply away, he wasn't sure any more.

But that made only one more question, one more doubt
to lie unresolved among the many others in his head. Marron was becoming used to those. Ever since his coming to

the Sanctuary Land, certainties had been stolen or worn
away, confusion had fed and flourished. Now he believed
in nothing, trusted nothing: not his own strength nor his
strength of will, not the oaths nor intentions of those he
ran with, not the God of his own people nor the god of the
Sharai. If he could have done it, he would have doubted
the ground beneath his feet and the sky above, the sun's
rising and the mirror of the moon.

Even in the dense dark that surrounded the circle of
firelight, though, and even with the horses' shuffling and
the murmur of voices and the cries of distant birds, he had
to trust his eyes and his ears both. An alteration in the
noises of the night alerted him; he lifted his head and
stared east and west, north and south.

"What is it, Marron?" Redmond asked, the first to notice.

"Men. Moving silently, two at each quarter . . ."

Rudel cursed and rose slowly to his feet, his hand on
his belt-knife. "If they're moving silently, how do you
hear them?"

"Their bones creak. But I can see them too," crimson
shadows in a starlit haze; the red cast to his sight seemed
to shine more clearly in the night, as his eyes did. "Shall I
point them out?"

"No, don't do that. They'll announce themselves, I'm
sure. Keep your weapon in its sheath, Jemel. We don't
want a fight, if we can avoid it." Rudel folded his arms
deliberately.

They were all standing now, Julianne stooping to help
Redmond to his feet; it was inevitably Elisande's voice
that murmured, "I thought you said we would be left
undisturbed here?"

"I thought we would be. I was wrong. Be quiet."

They waited, in a growing tension; at last, "One is coming forward," Marron muttered. "From the west there . . ."

From between the palms, a figure approached: a tall
man in flowing robes and turban, with a sword undrawn
at his belt and his hands spread wide in sign of peace even

before the firelight had touched him. Marron lowered his head, not to let his eyes betray the passenger he carried.

"Greetings," the man said softly. "I am Raben ib' Taraffi, and I have the honour to be chamberlain at the palace here. It is the Sultan's express wish that you should take your rice with him tonight."

It was a command, barely veiled as an invitation; Rudel nodded slowly. "Your master is most gracious. Is it his custom to offer hospitality to all travellers who pause here at his waterhole? Or to send his own chamberlain in person, to extend it?"

"No, it is not. Will you come now? You need not concern yourselves with your beasts or your baggage; my men will attend to all."

His men had stepped up out of the shadows now, forming almost a circle about them, armed and silent. The chamberlain made an elegant, sweeping gesture, *will you walk?*

Rudel said, "No lights? One of us is old, and others may be nervous in the dark, in a place strange to them . . ."

"Not strange to you, I think; though you have perhaps forgotten our ways? We do not carry torches, in Bar'ath Tazore. It is an order of the Sultan; we may not rival the stars. They give us light enough. Your friends should find it so, once the fire has died from their eyes. Till then, those with younger sight could offer an arm for guidance . . . ?"

MARRON NEEDED NO torch to see by, the stars were a glory. In fact, all the party seemed to see well enough; and Rudel, he thought, forgot nothing of others' customs. The older man had been bargaining, he thought, or making a point, trying to make them all out as strangers here. If so, he had missed his mark. Julianne perhaps was nervous, as he'd suggested; she busied herself with helping Redmond, though, and it was not for Marron to speculate which of those two offered more support to the other.

The chamberlain walked ahead with two of his men, two more walked behind. They could be an honour guard, in form at least; Marron determined to think so.

Jemel strode watchfully at his side. Marron murmured, "We have eaten already; the Sultan's invitation comes late. Must we eat again?" If so it would help Elisande, he supposed, in her campaign to force food into them.

Astonishingly, Jemel chuckled. "A little, yes. Taking rice is a Sharai custom, it means more than it says. We may feast with our sheikhs or other lords, but we go back to our tents to eat rice with our own kin before we sleep. To take rice with a stranger is to accept his protection, his hospitality for that night. The Sultan means that we must sleep within the walls of his palace."

Well, that would mean greater comfort in one sense at least, though greater cause for concern also. Julianne would be glad of a bed, he thought, and Redmond also.

Unless the Sultan's hospitality meant the Sultan's cells, or worse. It would be hard to keep his eyes hidden, even if the palace were kept as dark as the streets. He said, "Who is he, then, this Sultan? What do you know of him?"

"You should ask Rudel, I know little. Only that his family was of the Sharai, which tribe I have not heard; but they came to this place many generations since, and settled here. And built houses and took taxes from the traders, and they planted palms, they call him the date-king now . . ." Which made the Sultan no longer Sharai, so much was clear from the contempt in his voice. Marron wasn't clear whether it was the settling, the building, the taxing or the planting which was the worst offence. He only hoped that Jemel would govern his scorn, anywhere they could be overheard.

He wanted to know more, what kind of man the Sultan was, how he was likely to treat reluctant guests, whether he might delay or forbid their journey. Jemel was right, he should ask Rudel; that man had evidently been here before, though it was evident too that he hadn't expected to be recognised.

Rudel was walking almost in the star-shadow of their guards, though, almost on the chamberlain's heels: making a point again, Marron guessed. This was no time to be asking him questions. Elisande might know more than Jemel, but she was laggard, dawdling behind Julianne and Redmond, going so slowly that the guards who followed her were stumbling over their own feet as they tried to match her pace. They were frustrated, silently furious, barely holding themselves back from shoving her forward; she was normally so brisk, she must be making a point of her own. These were dangerous games, Marron thought, but he would not interfere.

THE WIDE AVENUES were quiet now; lights burned in the houses, sometimes a wash of laughter or loud voices leaked out, but there was no movement beyond the flight of bats and night-birds, clouds of insects, the occasional giant moth. Perhaps there was a curfew after dark; perhaps the people simply preferred their bright-lit homes to the dark of the streets. There might be thieves about or worse, to supply another reason for this armed guard.

Marron didn't believe it, though. All his stretched senses could find no human presence lurking in the shadows; if it was fear that kept the people withindoors, it was not fear of robbery or assault. Fear of the Sultan was his better guess.

THEY PASSED THE vast pool, the heart of the oasis. Its waters were still and restful, reflecting the patterns of the stars in crystal, clouded only by stirring masses of tiny nightflies and disturbed only when a great fish rose from the dark centre of the water to gulp at something on the surface. The marketplace alongside was quite deserted: empty stalls and folded awnings, not even a few bruised

leaves or a scatter of nut-husks left on the stone flags, not
a smear of wine or oil spilled. Such tidiness was unnatural, Marron thought, remembering the markets of his
childhood where men lingered late, long after the light
was gone, and no one swept or scrubbed until the following day. There were always pickings to be found on the
ground for beggars.

But there were no beggars here either. That was
strange, too. He wondered again what kind of man the
Sultan must be, to rule his territory so strictly.

FROM THE POOL, all roads led upward. The way they
took was another broad avenue, lined with the inevitable
palms. There were large houses on either side, but it was
the palace ahead that drew the eye now.

A wide blank wall closed off the further end of the avenue. There was only one narrow gate that he could see,
and that was guarded. Beyond the wall, beyond a fringe of
trees, lights burned in many windows; there seemed to be
several buildings within the complex, rising two or three
storeys to steep tiled roofs.

The chamberlain took them to the gate; the guards there
swung it open without a word, and stepped back to let
them pass through.

They stepped from a dry, chill, bright-lit desert night
into a garden. Heavy, damp foliage brushed at Marron's
arm; overhead, a tangle of low-hanging branches blotted
out the sky. The air was thick with competing scents,
scarred by the jagged cries of insects, soothed with birdsong.

The path under Marron's boots was a little slippery
with mud. He wondered vaguely if this were magic, if
he'd stepped into another world through that misleading
gate. Rudel ahead of him was blundering a little, with the
loss of light; Jemel took Marron's arm, his good right
arm, with a fingertip touch.

"What is this place?" he asked, in a hissing whisper. "I can see nothing . . ."

"It's just a garden," Marron murmured. "The trees hide the stars, that's all. There's light ahead . . ."

There was, although the path took a twisting way to find it. The chamberlain and his guards clearly knew every turn, and Marron could see well enough, but his companions were all but blind, fumbling and shuffling. Julianne took a grip on his tunic from behind, while she kept her other arm linked with Redmond's, so that he was guide to three until they reached the light.

For a moment, Marron thought that too might be magic, the moon ensnared in water; but it was man's work, no more than that. A creamy, perfect globe of glass was set on a plinth above a pond; inside the globe an oil-lamp burned, and the water shimmered under the weight of the globe's reflection.

Beyond the globe was a walled terrace; beyond the terrace, the palace waited.

THEY WAITED TOO, for lingering Elisande and her train of guards. A boy came past them, carrying a bucket and a scoop; as Marron watched, he took a dip of water and sprayed it into the foliage with a practised flick of the wrist. None of this was magic, then, it was only wealth. Great wealth, deliberately exploited to make a different world within the Sultan's walls. Once more, what kind of man . . . ?

ELISANDE JOINED THEM at last, playing with plucked fronds between her fingers. The chamberlain made a gentle gesture, *shall we proceed?* She made a lavish gesture in return, *by all means,* and scattered what she carried across the terrace at her feet.

As the chamberlain led them forward, Marron saw another boy scurry and stoop to retrieve each shredded frond.

THERE WERE MANY windows to the buildings that made the palace, but they were high and narrow, and barred with elaborate iron traceries. There seemed to be no doors. Marron remembered the narrow, guarded gate in the outer wall, and thought, *this Sultan is a cautious man, and comes of a cautious family.* With reason, though, most likely; Bar'ath Tazore was a jewel beyond price, and must have been the target of many an acquisitive eye. Even the nature of its value made it vulnerable. Not water alone had made this place so rich, but its situation, a crossing-point between two cultures. Without constant caravans, the passage of many men with goods to trade, it would be all but worthless; every man who came was a potential threat.

Which was presumably why they had been summoned here, to be examined. Though why a small party of men and girls should be judged such a risk, Marron couldn't guess. Even if Rudel had been seen and known, there was little in that. A wandering prince he might be, but by his own assertion he came from a peaceable princedom. His own people might not accept that, but the Sharai surely did . . .

Not Rudel was the danger, then. Marron reminded himself once more to keep his head low, and hope.

THERE WAS AN inner court, faced by all the buildings in the complex; all the doors were here, where they and their guards could watch each other. One was opened at the chamberlain's approach; the men who walked with him stepped back to either side. He walked within, and Rudel followed. Jemel's finger-touch urged Marron forward: his turn to act as guide now, with Marron's eyes so firmly fixed on his feet. He seemed to know it.

The Sultan might allow no torches in his dark streets, but the corridors of his palace were ablaze with light. Even the floor was dazzling, a gorgeous mosaic of many-coloured stone chips that glittered and seemed almost to spark as the chamberlain's robes swept across them. Briefly, Marron worried about the condition of his boots, whether he might be leaving muddy tracks. Then he remembered that he had more and far more to worry about; then he remembered the boy in the garden, whose only apparent role was to rush and tidy. There were sure to be others in the house. Perhaps if he looked back he'd see one at work already, down on his knees with water and cloth . . .

He didn't look back. Didn't look anywhere but down, relied on Rudel's heels and Jemel's touch to keep him walking straight.

He breathed through his nose, using scents as substitute for what his eyes were missing. The air had been moist and exotic in the garden, heady with too much perfume; in here it was easier, drier and spicier, less overladen. Someone had been burning incense, someone had brought cut flowers and boughs indoors. Closer, fresher, someone was nervous: he could smell sweat cutting through an aromatic bodywash that might have been meant to disguise it. Not Julianne: she was nervous, but she was also behind him and he was walking into this air, this information. Besides, when did she last have a chance to wash in perfumed water?

It must be the chamberlain, ib' Taraffi sweating cold this close to his master; and again, what kind of master could rouse so much fear in his most favoured servant, this mature and cultured and elegant man . . . ?

MARRON'S EARS WERE also busy, sorting and sifting. He heard the distant sounds of many people, guards, and servants and slaves at their many duties. More closely he heard a strange music, drum and flute, only that the flute wailed almost like a human voice under its incurable weight of sorrow.

The feet that Marron followed slowed, and turned; Jemel's hand on his elbow urged him to do the same.

Now the floor was tiled in blue and white, in intricate patterning; it was hard not to lift his head, not to see how far it stretched away ahead and to either side. All his other senses were telling him how vast this space was that they had entered, but still he wanted his eyes to say it for certain.

Not only broad, but high also; a hand-clap sang like a bell. The music stilled, and hurried, barefoot steps set up a whisper that took a long time to subside. The sounds of their own boots rang and echoed back like drumbeats all out of rhythm with themselves.

He could smell sweat here too, the sweat of a hard dance interrupted; but more, the sweat of fear again. There were perhaps two dozen bodies in this massive chamber, and most of them were fearful.

There might be a reason for that: he could smell blood also. And roasted meats, and cold meats, and breads and fruits and herbal drinks; but the blood had been recently spilled, and he didn't think it was animal. He felt the Daughter react to the tang of it, stirring within his own blood, and was certain.

THE CHAMBERLAIN BROUGHT them to the foot of a dais, overhung with carpets; it was high enough to make an awkward step up for the girls, but that they were not invited to take the step. They were arrayed, rather, stood in line two paces short, where they could be well looked over.

There were men on the dais, and men standing to either side; further off men and women mixed, Marron's nose—or the Daughter's use of his nose—could tell so much. Those were the musicians and dancers, and oddly, they were not afraid. All the fear was closer set about him, among the robes and perfumes of this rich court.

Ib' Taraffi dropped to his knees; Rudel emphatically did not, so neither did the others.

"Excellence, I have brought—"

"So I see." The voice that interrupted him was high and cool; Marron shivered at its touch. "A Sharai'—Jemel stiffened; Marron's turn to touch his sleeve, to warn him, *keep your temper, temper your pride in this place*— "and a full hand of the Patric. An odd company, where none of them has any goods to trade. Nor even decent clothing, it would seem—except the Sharai boy, of course, and he is Saren. Rudel, how does your father?"

"Well enough, excellence, I thank you for asking. When last I saw him, he was well enough. For a man whose age has softened his skull, I hear."

There was a smile in the Sultan's answer—a thin smile, Marron suspected though he did not look to see, a thin smile from a thin and dangerous man. "Did I say that? Well, well. He has charge of a soft country, perhaps he can afford to be so. Some cannot."

"These times are not soft for anyone, excellence."

"No. Perhaps not. When last we saw you, Rudel, you wore other dress in other company, and paid me the honour of a visit uninvited. Today it seems you prefer to travel in disguise through my territory, and camp in plague-spots, and keep me from meeting your friends. How is it that I have so offended you?"

"Excellence, the offence is all mine, and I ask your pardon for it. Our mission is secret, and urgent; I chose not to impose on your hospitality, for fear that the comforts of your palace and the pleasures of your company delay us. You have forestalled our intent; I wish I could regret that, but . . ."

"Well. The silver in the beard is new; the silver on the tongue, I see, is as smooth as ever. We will talk, and I hope you will not offer me any reason to delay you beyond this one night. First, though, you must name your companions to me. I am intrigued."

"A duty can be a privilege, excellence—but do you not recognise Redmond? He too has passed this way before, and tasted your generosity."

"Indeed, though he was in better health that time, if I remember. Your pardon, Redmond—my eyes were distracted by the beauty of your handmaid."

"More by the shadows of my age, I think, excellence," Redmond said, with a soft chuckle. "Though she is beautiful behind her veil, and not alas my handmaid. This child is Julianne de Rance, daughter of the King's Shadow."

"Lady, a delight to offer you welcome here. Your father of course I know; I had never hoped to see his daughter grace my house."

"Excellence, you are courtesy itself, but you know the delight is all my own. To be ushered from a hard bed to such a gracious house is a kindness quite unlooked-for." Her voice was tight, but her words matched these careful, neutral, meaningless manners exactly; Marron hoped she could sense the others' approval, and his also. "Nor am I the only daughter you should greet tonight; here is Elisande, who is Rudel's own child."

That, Marron thought, was wicked; but it served the trick. More effusive expressions of welcome, delivered crisply; more self-effacing rebuttals, in a tone that carried only a hint of Elisande's normally needle-sharp tongue.

"Father and daughter ride together, how charming. And the Surayonnaise, of course, are famously friendly with the Sharai."

"That is true." Rudel's voice once more. "This is Jemel, of the Saren as you have observed; he is our guide, as well as our companion."

"A guide, is it? You used not to need a guide, Rudel."

"Times change; the wise man takes assistance where he may find it."

"Truly. Jemel of what family?"

"I am of no family now, excellence," Jemel said shortly.

"Ah. You are Saren, of course. Which leaves us only with the shy boy at your side . . . ?"

Again, Rudel stepped in. "His name is Marron. He was once a brother of the Ransomers, but he has fled them; he travels under my protection now."

"And stands under mine, for so long as he stands within my house. But I will entertain no guest who has not looked me once directly in the eye . . ."

A rustle of silken robes, a bulky figure moving in the periphery of Marron's vision, stepping lightly down from the dais, coming to stand before him. No possible escape. A big, pudgy hand rising, heavy rings on every finger; those fingers strong beneath his chin, forcing his head up, not to be denied. Those fingers also smelled of blood; Marron wanted to wrench his head away, and did not.

A fat face trimly bearded under a jewelled turban, and everything about this man belied his slender voice. His dark eyes widened momentarily, as they met Marron's; then he breathed out slowly, and stepped back.

"Yes. I see why such a boy would flee the Ransomers. We must talk of this, Rudel, and also of your mission. But first, Redmond is exhausted, and in pain; all of you are dirty, and should rest. And yet I insist that you take rice with me, it is my custom and I will not break it for any friendship, old or new. How shall we resolve this? In a manner satisfactory to none, alas; such is the way of the world. However I choose, I must deny myself and insult you. But let us part for a little hour, too long for me and too brief for you; let my doctors attend Redmond and my slaves you all. Wash, bathe if you will, seek what comforts my poor house can offer; but then return, I beg you, and we will eat a little and talk at least a little more than that."

MARRON THOUGHT THAT Rudel might object, on the girls' behalf at least if not his own, although the Sultan clearly meant to keep him all night talking. They really had no choice, though, and Rudel only bowed a silent acquiescence as barefoot attendants in pure white gowns and turbans beckoned them away. One took Redmond's arm, displacing Julianne; neither made any demur.

Although he was gazing about him freely now, drinking in the decorated walls of the palace, the bowls of cut blooms and the pots of greenery, Marron didn't see where Redmond was taken, only that the old man was suddenly gone from the company. The rest of them were led to a suite of interconnected rooms, luxuriously furnished with couches and tables and beds; from a doorway at the far end, steam was leaking.

Julianne collapsed with a groan, stretching out full-length on a bed; Elisande touched her shoulder, laughing.

"Go away, let me sleep . . ."

"No, sweet, not yet. You heard the man. Up you come, and let me help you off with that scratchy stuff. Look, there's a hammam, concentrate on being warm and clean; and see, here comes a girl with fresh clothes, we can dress up after. *After* we have bathed . . ."

Briefly, Marron thought she meant to strip Julianne there and then; but a procession of slaves had followed them, and with Elisande's assistance two women soon had the other girl on her feet again, and were ushering them both through into the steam.

One of the male attendants made a gesture, inviting the men of the party to follow. Rudel laughed shortly.

"No, we'll let the ladies have their privacy, thank you. If you could bring us bowls of water, we'll wash out here. And change our clothing, gladly . . ."

MARRON HAD TOO many questions burning in his head, and there were too many of the Sultan's slaves too close, he dared not risk being overheard. One of those questions should be safe, though; he shared a great copper bowl of scalding water with Jemel, and as they splashed he hissed, "Why did he call us Patric, what does that mean?"

"It is the Sharai word for your people. I think it is because you call your God your father, is that right?"

Right it was when they prayed in the old tongue, as they always did; and "Pater" to "Patric" was not so far a leap. Marron grunted, and cast about for a towel. One was handed to him, by an elderly man—a man with blue eyes below his turban, and a skin that must once have been pale beneath its age-old tan.

"I have not prayed to the God for many years," the man murmured, "it is forbidden to us, and the Sultan is my father now; but yes, they call us Patric for that reason. Should I summon a doctor, lad, to look at that hurt on your arm?"

Marron blinked, to be sure the man had seen his eyes. When there was no reaction, only a patient waiting for an answer, he said, "No. Thank you, but it does not hurt." *Except my soul, and that is beyond the reach of any doctor . . .*

The man bowed, and stepped away; Marron reminded himself again not to ask any question where the answer might be important, if the Sultan's slaves were the Sultan's children. Good children always carried news to their father, and no language that he knew could be secret here.

WHEN THEY HAD washed, they dressed in cool, shimmering gowns that felt slippery against the skin, after the rough stuff they had worn before. For Jemel, who would have refused any dress else, there was a new Sharai robe which he could tie in his tribal style. Their old clothes were borne away; the neutral expressions on the faces of the men who took them suggested that they might be bound for a furnace. Marron tried to regret that, and could not. He owned little enough—and less that he valued, the sword Dard and a good knife, no more than those, and he hoped never to use either one of them again—but he would happily see the number of his possessions reduced further, if it meant not having to wear those clothes again. Even if it meant that they were dangerously beholden to the Sultan: what's given can be taken away, and a naked man is half a prisoner already, but Marron would run naked and grateful not to have to hide again, either his white skin or his burning eyes.

WHILE THEY WAITED for the girls to join them, they sat on couches and sipped at beakers of crushed iced fruit. And it wasn't a question, it was a flat statement and any listening slave must know it already, and his companions he thought would need to; and so Marron said, "The Sultan has blood on his hands."

"Show me any leader of men in these days who has not," Rudel countered.

"I mean new blood, I mean that he has killed today. Himself, not his executioner; and with his hands, I think, no weapon else. He had scrubbed his fingers with rosewater, but I could scent it still. And all the lords of his court are afraid of him, but his slaves are not . . ."

"Ah. Yes. The Sultan is a singular man, and he keeps a singular grip upon his people. It's no secret," with a nod towards Marron's caution, "that he doesn't keep an executioner; when he feels that a death is needed, he sees to it himself, and where it will have the most effect. If one of his lords had offended him, the whole court would have watched that man die; but I don't believe that he would kill a slave."

"What of the people outside the palace?" Jemel asked. "They are not Sharai, but they are said to have that blood, or to claim it. And yet they are all in their houses by sunset, the doors are closed, the marketplace is abandoned . . . Where are the fires, the songs, the tales? Where are the young men dancing?"

"I don't know," Rudel admitted. "They did dance, when I was here last; though that was long ago. Perhaps the Sultan grew displeased with it. His people obey him in the least particular, or he casts them out."

"And will he cast us out also?" Julianne demanded as she and Elisande came through, swathed and veiled in folds of falling silk.

"That I do not know, my lady," Rudel said, rising and bowing to her, teasing gently without mockery. His daughter as usual he ignored. "He might forbid us to go further, if he feels there is danger in it for him and his."

"Has he the authority to do that?"

"Within Bar'ath Tazore, he is master; well, you have seen that. Beyond the lip, then no, he has no authority at all; but his word here denies us camels, denies us food and water for the trip. He could deny us freedom too, and he might yet do that; he could imprison us or kill us, and answer to no one for it. Power gives him the authority he lacks by right."

"So how should we talk to him?"

"Truthfully, I would suggest. He knows more than you might think, in any case; half the world passes through this little point, and brings its news with it. He may play the ignorant tyrant, but he is not. He will know of your marriage, Julianne, and of your fleeing it; he will have heard rumours of that night, and of our party on the road. He may even have been expecting to see the Daughter come this way, though not perhaps with such a host as Marron. Nor will he have been idle this last hour; giving us time to rest is the least of it. If he didn't know before that the Ghost Walker was abroad in his territory, he knows now. There will be message-birds flying to Rhabat and other places; we have no hope of arriving unannounced. He will also be taking advice from his lords perhaps, his astrologers certainly. So step carefully, and say as little as you can; but don't lie to him. If he asks a direct question, answer it. And don't ask any on your own account, a clever man can learn a lot from what is asked of him."

"I knew it," Julianne muttered aside to Elisande. "It's

going to be like talking to the djinni again." And then, direct to Rudel, "Should I tell him about the djinni?"

"I think you must. It's hard to explain your journey else; and even the Sultan might be impressed by a djinni. We'll see. Are you ready to face him?"

"No." But she was rising, smoothing needlessly at the gleaming gossamer fabric of her dress before reaching for Elisande's hand. "If we must do it, let's do it now. Rice and cool drink and conversation, what could be more pleasant of an evening . . . ?"

"Eat with the right hand only," Redmond murmured, one last swatch of advice before they reached the corridor where servants waited, "and don't talk of weighty matters till the meal is done . . ."

WHEN JEMEL HAD spoken of taking rice with the family, Marron had thought he'd meant that literally, a bowl of cooked rice and no more.

Looking at Jemel's face now, he was sure of it. That was the Sharai custom, what was dictated by centuries of usage, what spoke to the nomad's soul.

Taking rice with the Sultan of Bar'ath Tazore, it seemed, was something else entirely: a noble custom corrupted, by Jemel's expression, a beautiful vessel broken.

The Sultan's rice was a precious mountain, a heaped and steaming dish of jewelled gold. The rice had been cooked with saffron, and was flecked with bright peppers and spice-pods, preserved peels, coloured shreds of smoked meat and fish, all gleaming with a buttery sheen. Around it was set a circle of smaller dishes containing boiled eggs, salted lemons, vegetables pickled in vinegar or drenched in oil.

This was on the dais, the divan they called it here, at the far end of the great chamber where the Sultan held his court. The first time they had stood before it, and been examined; this time they had been beckoned up by the man himself, and had arranged themselves upon his carpets, side by side with His Excellence and the lords of this small state. Slaves had brought and poured scented water above great copper vessels, so that guests might wash their hands; they had proffered towels; they had brought the giant platter in and all its attendant dishes, and had set them in the centre of the dining circle. Marron's mind had been distracted by those white robes they wore, too reminiscent of the Sharai boys burned at the Roq, their white tunics and the white shifts of the penitents which he had worn himself and dyed with other men's blood . . .

Following that thought, Marron looked at Jemel's face and saw his scorn again, and understood it; and so like all his party he was surprised by what that young man did next, and perhaps he was more surprised than most, although he'd spent most time with the Sharai, or the Sharai with him.

"Excellence," Jemel said, staring darkly while one of his hands clenched hard on the skirts of his robe, "will you hear my oath?"

It seemed as though the Sultan were startled also, the way his hand stilled in its reaching for a bowl of crystal fruits. He blinked his wide, deceptive eyes, and smiled as if at a victory won, and not a small one.

"If you wish me to," he said, "I must; it is my burden, to carry young men's oaths. Along with the souls of all my own people. But not till we have eaten, youth, I beg you."

"An oath should be made on an empty belly," Jemel growled. "There is little virtue in a well-fed man."

"But you have not yet taken rice with me; there is no obligation between us, till you do."

Jemel's fingers twitched, and Marron was briefly afraid for him; he thought he might do something extravagant and stupid, take a single grain of rice on his tongue and so insult his host in the same moment that he claimed his protection.

Sharai manners won the day, though. Jemel bowed his head, hiding his face as he accepted the Sultan's ruling;

diplomatic Redmond stretched awkwardly forward with his twisted fingers to scoop a handful of rice from the platter, and Elisande spoke lightly, gratefully of the comforts of the palace.

AND SO THEY ate, though they were not hungry; and so they spoke meaninglessly of what mattered not at all; and all the while they were only waiting for what must come later, Jemel's revelation and the Sultan's doom on their expedition.

Music was played softly in the shadows. Under its veil and the buzz of louder voices, Marron murmured, "What oath is that, Jemel? And why must the Sultan hear it?"

"It is the tradition. He claims to be Sharai, though he is not; there is no other sheikh here that has a better claim, at least, and this will not wait. Be patient, you will hear."

Marron thought Jemel could listen to himself, could show a little patience in this, above all could and should both talk and listen to his companions before launching himself into whatever private venture he had in mind. But there was no talking to him here; nor would any words have served a purpose, by his set face and his intense scowl. He meant to have his say, to swear his oath in public and before a prince of his people, or the nearest to it that he could find. If he wouldn't speak to Marron, he would speak to no one.

Nor would he wait past the niceties, the conventions of his culture. The food-dishes were removed, and he fidgeted but was silent yet; coffee was brought and served in tiny cups which were twice refilled, and still he said nothing.

As the slaves withdrew, though, the Sultan turned once more to Rudel at his right-hand side; and for the first time there was purpose in his voice as he said, "So now. You are far from your lands, my friend, and trying to whisper through my own, though your footsteps betray you. Tell me why."

"No!" Jemel shrugged off Marron's vain and belated touch, leaping to his feet to stand centre-circle before the Sultan. "First, my oath! It is my right, excellence, and your duty to hear it . . ."

The Sultan made a shrug of apology to Rudel, *forgive me, but young men will be impetuous*; and followed it with a gesture to Jemel. "It is your right, and my duty. Continue, then. Is it an oath of blood?"

"It is."

For the briefest moment, the Sultan's eyes seemed to say, *it would be.* But his voice said, "Let all bear witness, then, that I who am Sultan of Bar'ath Tazore and lord of the tribe of the Buresset as my father was before me, I who have taken this Jemel of the tribe of the Saren into my house and offered him the protection of my name, in the absence of his own lord I will hear his oath; and if he fail or forswear it I will take vengeance on his body, for the sake of his tribe's honour and my own."

Jemel bowed low; Rudel touched a hand to his forehead, as though he knew what was coming and despaired. Marron was simply bewildered, watching the young Sharai as he straightened, as he began to speak.

"Excellence, I am Saren, as you have seen and said; but here in your presence I will renounce my tribe and live outside their tents or any man's, until this oath I make now be fulfilled."

He unwound the silken rope that tied his headdress and threw it down, twisting the cloth instead into a simple knot to hold it. He drew his dagger and cut away the silver ends to the rope that was his belt, and let them fall; he tugged at his robes until he had unmade that particular style of wear that declared him Saren. His way would be hard in the desert, without a tribe to claim him as its own: that much Marron knew, though little more.

"Excellence, when I was Saren I was sworn blood-brother to a man, Jazra of my tribe. You know the strength and meaning of those vows. Jazra died at the castle of the Roq; he was first wounded and then slain, while I was

prevented from going to his aid. I could name the one
who prevented me, who made me break my vow; for our
peoples' sake, though, I will not. I could name the one
who wounded him, who broke his stroke and guard; for
her own sake, though, and for the sake of mysteries I do
not understand, again I will not. I can and I will name the
man who killed him, and this I swear: that when I have
done the service I am bound to now, I will hunt down that
man and challenge him, blade to blade and to the death,
for Jazra's honour and my own."

"The oath is heard and witnessed, Jemel of the Sharai.
Name the man."

"His name is Anton d'Escrivey, a Patric knight of the
Ransomers. This I have learned, and it is sure."

SURE IT WAS, Marron had been there on the walls with
Sieur Anton at the time. He didn't remember Jemel, but
he remembered the Sharai who had come close perhaps to
killing his master. Elisande's knife had taken him in the
side, and Sieur Anton's sword had finished him; Jemel
must have heard the name and worked out the truth of it
in these weeks of travelling, though his companions had
tried so hard to keep it from him.

Marron stared down at the intricate knotting of the rug
he sat on, and swore a private, secret vow of his own: that
he would keep Jemel at his side if he could and go with
him if he could not, and that one way or another—whatever way lay in his power, once he had learned where his
power lay and how to use it—he would cause this oath
also to be broken.

WHEN HE LIFTED his head there were other people in the
hall, though only he perhaps had heard their coming. They
walked softly, to the rhythm of the music, and they came
through a hidden door at the further end. That was what

he'd heard to alert him first, the snick of its lock sounding; then he strained to listen to their progress.

The others seemed oblivious, even Jemel, who dropped into place again beside him and gave him a stubborn, challenging glare. Marron just looked back at him, with all the advantages of his new eyes that no one could read. He wouldn't say anything about the men at his back, unless or until there seemed a need. They must be making their way behind the pillars that supported the gallery, all but invisible to anyone on the divan; some servant or guard must have shouted the alarm by now, though, if they were unknown or unwelcome here. And Marron thought perhaps there had been the faintest movement on the Sultan's face to acknowledge their arrival, though if so it was subtle beyond expectation for such an obvious man.

He was speaking to Rudel again, speaking of their journey; and now the thing was said, the truth was told, simple and direct.

"We are travelling towards Rhabat," Rudel said, "though we may not all go so far together. Redmond has been a guest of the Ransomers, and he still feels the effects of their hospitality; well, you have seen, and your doctors have seen more. Him I would like to see safe in Surayon, but I must take him this long loop from Outremer, to be sure. I also want to watch over these young people, as far as possible in their journey."

"Indeed. The young can always bear watching. And why do they travel to Rhabat?"

"Marron because of what he carries, that he does not know how to guard or use; there are those who can teach him, there. Julianne because a djinni sends her."

"A djinni? Which djinni would that be?" His voice was not—quite—incredulous, but the question stung none the less; and it stung Julianne into answering for herself.

"It said its name was Shaban Ra'isse Khaldor."

"Then I think we must believe it, my lady Julianne. The djinn do not lie about such matters." He sounded impressed, despite himself.

"I had heard that the djinn do not lie at all?"

"Yes. I have heard that, also. Why does Djinni Khaldor send you to Rhabat?"

It seemed she was taking her attitude from the djinn, because she did not lie at all, even by omission. "I am uncertain, what it truly wants. It said to me that I must go where I am sent, and marry where I must; and it sends me to Rhabat, though I am married already. It said also that I would find my father there, and that he would be in peril, but that I might save him. Though it might be better if I did not, it said that too."

So much information, so much honesty: the Sultan took a while to mull it over and weigh its value. The men on the floor of the hall were quite still now; a servant had lit a burner, now that the meal was over, and a waft of incense hid even the hard, dusty smell of them from Marron.

"There is a gathering, at Rhabat," the Sultan said at last, trading truth for truth. "I have heard that much. Hasan passed this way a week since," *after his failure at the Roq* he did not add, nor need to, "and he was on his way there, to meet with tribal leaders. I will not go myself, I have my charge and am not free to travel," which likely meant he hadn't been invited, Marron thought, "but you will find it busy. Perhaps that is your father's work?"

"Perhaps it is," Julianne agreed neutrally. "The King's Shadow does the King's will; he does not discuss it with me."

"Neither with me. He can be as mysterious as the djinn. Why one of them would send you from your husband, and on such a long and chancy journey—well, it may be that we will both learn the answer to that, in time to come. I for one will not delay you, when such powers are pushing at your back. Indeed, I will do what I can to haste you on your way."

"That is generous, excellence," Rudel said gruffly.

"No, not generous. Sensible, I feel. I had as soon see such a party move on quickly from my land. One of your company, though, may not need to go so far as he thinks. There are those here who can test what he carries, and teach him the proper use of it . . ."

And now there was movement at Marron's back, as those men strode out into the centre of the hall. He saw sudden anxiety on Rudel's face, fear on Julianne's; he heard the rasp of steel as swords were drawn, and felt Jemel stiffen at his side. A touch of his hand on that young man's knee was enough to still him, though.

Marron stood, bowed his head to the Sultan, and turned to face whatever had come, for surely it had come for him.

3

Company for the Road

IT WAS ELISANDE'S profound conviction, based on a lifetime of observation, that men were by nature perverse.
The only exceptions she allowed were Redmond and her
grandfather, who were both of them kind, sensible and
wise. Her father was the prime exemplar of her belief:
leave Rudel to make a decision, any decision that mattered, and he would be sure to choose wrongly.

If anything, boys could be worse than men; after a few
short weeks of knowing him, she thought that Marron was
worse than any boy she'd met. Give him the chance and
he'd not only do the wrong thing, he'd do the stupid
thing. The most stupid thing that it was in his power to
do . . .

As now, when four armed and deadly men had arrayed
themselves in a semicircle across the floor of the hall;
when he had friends on the divan there who would do
their best to shelter him from any threat, two at least who
would die for him if necessary; when he had a terrible gift
in his blood that could counter any enemy, the mere sight

of which should be enough to still any man who understood it.

Marron stood, and she thought he would back away from the danger, into the circle of his friends.

He walked the other way, to the edge of the divan, and drew his sword; she thought then that he would touch that to the wound on his arm and free the Daughter, only to show it, to have it seen and known.

He stepped down from the divan, and walked to meet those four lethal blades with only his own to answer them.

Stupid, *stupid* . . .

She jerked and tried to rise, to go after him; and was held back by her father's strong arm, his clamping hand about her wrist, his hissed whisper, "Sit still!"

"But—"

She still had one hand free, she could work one of her throwing-knives out of the harness beneath her bodice and maybe drop one man with it, give that stupid boy better odds to play against . . .

Except that Julianne took hold of her other arm, and muttered frantically, "Elisande, aren't those Sand Dancers? We saw them in the market, I don't know what they are but Jemel said to beware of them . . ."

Right, Jemel knew best what Sand Dancers were, and how deadly; and Jemel was only sitting there opposite, watching while the Ghost Walker, his friend Marron went down to meet their silent challenge.

"Yes," she said to Julianne, "Sand Dancers is just what they are. See those robes, those mutilated hands? They have mutilated hearts too. No one can hope to fight four of them, not even Rudel, and," grudgingly, "Rudel is the best and the smartest and the sneakiest swordsman I've ever seen. Marron needs help, and between the two of you, you and Rudel are preventing me from giving it . . ."

She had time for the speech, because Marron seemed to be speaking to one of the four, in his slow and careful Catari. Or slow and distant, perhaps, because he'd seemed so detached from them all since the Roq; but he couldn't be distant or detached now, his life hung like silk against a blade's edge. One twitch and it was cut and gone, if those men truly meant his death.

Which they would, for sure. Red eyes or no, unhealing wound or no: they had seen convincing frauds before. They would kill him to test him, and if he died and was true, no matter. The Daughter would be there, for the first who dared to claim it; there would be another Ghost Walker this night, one of their own, seen and acclaimed . . .

"Child, be still," Rudel said again, into her ear. "In this, even you cannot interfere."

"But he could have stood back and shown them, one drop of blood, no more; doesn't he *know* that?"

"He knows. He chose another way. Why can you never trust?"

"Because my trust is always betrayed," she said bitterly, furiously. Rudel caught his breath, and then released her; Julianne had already freed her other arm. She did draw her knives, both of them, but kept them hidden uselessly in her sleeves, only for her own comfort. Rudel was right, for once; she had no place in this. Marron had made his choice, and must live or die by it.

Stupid, *stupid* choice . . .

MARRON AND HIS opponent had finished their talking, it seemed. Each took a step back, and now all blades were raised in earnest. The soft, insidious music faltered and fell silent; she was glad of that. This dance needed no accompaniment, and Marron should not die to the beat of an alien tune.

It was his good sword he carried, the straight Patric blade that he called Dard, not the scimitar he fenced with against Jemel. She was glad of that, too. It felt right to her, although she knew something of how complex his own feelings were about that sword.

Steel glinted in the light of many lamps; steel whispered, grated, sang to other steel. This truly was a dance, that made its own harsh music. It had grace and strength and a distressful beauty, and the wonder of it was how well Marron knew the steps, and how he seemed to lead all four of his adversaries although they were men grown and he was still so very much a boy.

She'd seen him fence day after day with Jemel and yet hadn't realised how fast he could be, how certain in his body. It must be the Daughter, she thought, taking strange control. The Ghost Walker was not invulnerable, very far from that; but hard to kill, yes, that was the tradition. Now she could see why.

Marron spun and blocked and thrust, and leaped away; and he made those four deadly warriors look wooden, like poppets jerked by strings. Again and again he could have killed one, and did not.

Julianne beside her let out a breath she'd been holding, and whispered, "Tell me what they are, these Sand Dancers?"

"They are men sworn to a brotherhood," Elisande replied, without taking her eyes from the dance, "sworn to serve the Ghost Walker, if he should come. They give a finger to their god, in witness; and they live apart from the tribes, in little groups together. For centuries now, they have lived with each other and their vows and nothing more. Now the Ghost Walker has come again, he stands among them, and they are trying to slay him . . ."

Trying, and failing; and yet not dying as they ought, because Marron had made vows also, and would not kill. So many high oaths he'd broken, and yet this, this newest and least of all his promises he clung to even in the teeth of death, although she yearned for him to break that also, to find some value in his life and cling to that instead.

IT COULD NOT last. A slip, a misstep, a jarring screech of steel sliding on steel—she waited for any one of those, knowing what must come after. Because they were not

wooden poppets, those men he fought, they were not
novices, although he made them seem so. They were masters, overmastered; but in the end he could not hold them
all, unless he killed them. Which he would not do, and so
in the end they would kill him, though they could never
earn such a victory. It was written in his body, on his skin,
in his determined will.

Except that what is written can be scratched out, or
written over; and she was not alone in watching men by
lamplight and seeing ghosts, shadows cast by future suns.

The Sultan stirred, and stood; his lords followed his lead,
and guards stepped up from the divan's sides. He gestured
them all back, and strode forward to loom above the mêlée.
Elisande too had to scramble to her feet, to see around him;
but Julianne had done the same, and Rudel after. Only Redmond was left sitting now, and one kindly merchant prince
was stooped above him, offering an arm to help.

Well, he wouldn't want to miss this, would he?
Elisande thought bleakly that it was only the rush of idle
scandal-seekers to an execution, wanting to be sure of a
decent view. She hefted her knives again, and yearned to
bring them out and use them, as she'd used one of them
before. But the echoes of that one time were with them
still, in Jemel's oath against Sieur Anton. She dared not
imagine what vengeance might follow if she let fly at a
Sand Dancer in the perfect moment of his vow, Ghost
Walker at his scimitar's point . . .

The Sultan, it seemed, was less anxious about disturbing other men at their devotions—but then, the Sultan did
not throw a knife. His heavy body was girdled round with
a robe of dense embroidery, tied with a simple sash; as far
as she could see, he did not have a knife to throw.

Instead, he seized a massive crystal vase of flowers
from a pedestal at the divan's corner, and threw that.

HE HAD A fine eye as well as great strength of arm and
shoulder, or else it was a lucky cast: the vase tumbled as it

flew, strewing blooms and water across the circle of the fighting men before it smashed to the floor in their midst, shattering into a thousand pieces.

Fragments skittered wildly across the tiles. Marron and his adversaries had been startled into stillness by the great falling shape of the thing and its glinting, spinning facets; now each of them jumped backward, skipping foolishly to avoid those vicious shards.

The near-formal symmetry of the dance had been destroyed; they seemed uncertain suddenly, lost in confusion. The Sultan clapped his hands twice for their attention, and stepped lightly down from the divan.

"Enough!" he cried. "You have seen that you cannot slay him; you have seen that he could have slain you. All of you, and with some ease. Is that not enough?"

"We are men," one man replied, the same man that Marron had spoken to, his blade still deliberately unsheathed and ready. "Men may be slain by other men. Even Sand Dancers die. He handles his weapon with a rare touch, but it means nothing."

"And his eyes?"

"There are herbs and powders, that can redden a man's eyes . . ."

"Not as his eyes are red, to the iris. You know that. But very well, for certainty's sake, let us test him here, under the eyes of all. If he is false, he dies."

The Sultan stooped, and there was an unexpected grace even to his bending; he picked up a shining piece of crystal, delicately between finger and thumb, and beckoned to Marron.

"I regret this, lad—but for certainty's sake . . . ?"

Marron stepped slowly towards him, taking his sword in his left hand and rolling back the sleeve from that arm. He was barely out of breath, though all his skin was flushed; Elisande saw that there was blood on his blade. Even his care hadn't saved his opponents from some harm, then. He was untouched, so far as she could see; hence the necessity of this.

The Sultan gripped his wrist, gazed for a moment at the vivid red of the open wound on his forearm, and then pricked at it gently with the sharp edge of the crystal. Blood oozed out and the Daughter with it, a red haze like smoke rising into the air. As it thickened, so Marron's colour faded.

"Now, is this enough?" the Sultan demanded.

"It is." The Sand Dancers dropped swiftly to their knees and laid their weapons down, the hafts all toward Marron. The first among them went on, "Ghost Walker, we have waited an age to serve you . . ."

"I do not want your service," Marron said distantly, gazing into the swirling cloud of mist which had almost a shape to it now, was almost a creature with eyes and shell and claws. "How if I had done this first, before we fought; if I had turned it against you, as I could. How then?"

"Then you would have died. Had you used it as a weapon, knowing what it is, you would have demeaned it and disgraced yourself; there would have been nothing we could teach you. And there are archers, in the gallery above. Even the Ghost Walker cannot stand against arrows."

Chagrined, Elisande squinted up into the shadows under the doming roof. Yes, there they were, a man on either side though with their bows unstrung now, their hands clenched on the gallery rail as they stared down. She should have known, she should have thought to look; those perhaps she might have dealt with, if the need had come. She was good at throwing knives to a height . . .

"No. Though I knew they were there." His thin voice drew her attention back to himself; with the Daughter released he was all Marron now but whittled, skimmed, shaved of any excess. No energy, no humour. Pain, she thought, a great deal of pain, and not only from his arm that never healed. And his eyes were natural now, their simple tender brown, and they looked as weary as the rest of him. "I used it before, as a weapon," he said, honest as he ever was. "I killed dozens. If that offends so greatly, use your arrows; I'll abide their judgement."

And be glad to do it, she thought angrily; she thought he'd welcome death, like a stranger's kiss that bespeaks a new friend. She tried to shoulder her way through to reach him, but Rudel was ahead of her, and so she checked.

Her father put an arm around Marron's shoulders and murmured, "Take it back, lad, enough have seen it now."

The nameless near-creature in the air there lost its form, flowing into smoke again; the smoke seeped into Marron's wounded arm, against the run of blood; the boy's eyes were red again and his skin was quickly pink, and no more blood dripped to the tiles at his feet.

Rudel hadn't shifted from Marron's side, nor his hand from Marron's shoulder; now he said, "His Excellency the Sultan is quite right; you need not come with us now, all the way to Rhabat. What you need is here, with these."

If you can endure it he did not add but should have; perhaps only Elisande heard what was not spoken. Almost sure that only she—or perhaps she and the Sultan both, but no more—heard something else, but for certain it was there: *if you cannot, if you die under their strictures, well, that may be for the best.*

"What he needs," Elisande declared, pushing through to his side regardless of her hateful father, "is peace, and rest."

"That he may not have," the Sand Dancer responded, the only one she'd heard or seen to speak yet. His face was a skull, bone-lean, desert-drawn: she'd known such men before, admired and detested them both at once. This one she thought she might simply detest. "He is the Ghost Walker; it is not in his fate to know peace. Rest is waste, and we do not waste God's gifts. The bearded one speaks truly, though. We do not go to Rhabat."

"And neither should you, Marron." That was Redmond, joining them, leaning on the arm of an attendant. "If counsel is being taken there, your presence would only throw it into confusion."

Marron stood silent for a moment, before his bright, fiery eyes moved from Elisande's face to find Jemel's.

"I will go where my friends go," he said calmly, irrevocably.

It was a visible shock to most of his listeners, almost a rebellion; and she loved him for it.

THE OLDER MEN—the Sultan, the Sand Dancers, Rudel and Redmond too—all wanted to argue with him, but he would not, he was implacable. Elisande seized the opportunity gifted to her by his stubbornness, to break up this difficult gathering. Julianne was all but falling asleep on her feet; it was no effort to take her arm and guide her towards the door. On the way, she could conveniently pause for a word with the slave who supported Redmond, to suggest that that old man needed his bed more than a wakeful night of talking, talking. And Jemel needed less of a hint than that, only a glance and a jerk of her head, *bring him too, before they back him into a corner and bully him into following their will rather than his own.*

The Sharai nodded, and moved to Marron's side. His devotion she could trust, though she was still not sure she understood it; she slipped her arm around Julianne's waist and urged that tall, sagging girl forward, towards their quarters.

THE SULTAN'S INFORMATION had been excellent: there were three bedchambers in the suite, with two beds set in each. Whether Redmond would claim his, Elisande was uncertain; she thought the slave would take him to the doctors first, and they might choose to keep him under their watch tonight. His hands and feet all had healed crooked—*lucky to have healed at all,* she thought, thinking of Marron, and suppressed the thought bitterly—and they hurt him constantly, that much she was sure of. There must be drugs, to ease the pain and help him sleep; she hoped that the doctors would have wisdom also, to see what other harm had been done him that he didn't talk about.

She guided Julianne to the furthest chamber, next to the hammam. No steam now, the fires had been let die; come the morning, though, she dreamed of another bath. Likely it would be her last, until they reached Rhabat. No more luxurious guesting: only the desert now lay between them and journey's end. If Rhabat should prove to be any kind of ending, and not just a place to pause in a longer journey. *Go back to the Sharai, Lisan of the Dead Waters. They will bring you a gift of questions.* But she was not going to think about the djinni's sending now, she was not . . .

Thinking of Rhabat instead, remembering the last time she'd guested there—though it was hard to think of Rhabat and not of the Dead Waters—she stripped Julianne ruthlessly and bundled her into one of the beds. Covered her over with a light cotton sheet, blew out the lamps, turned yearningly to her own bed—and allowed herself to do no more than sit on its foot, still fully clothed, and waiting.

Blessedly, it was not a long wait. She gazed around the darkened chamber, seeing how starlight glimmered through the traceries of a high shuttered window; then she heard footsteps, the sound of male voices murmuring. Young voices: not Redmond, then. Jemel had done what she'd hoped for, had fed Marron's mulishness with an excuse to escape the browbeating of his elders.

She didn't go to them, there was no point. She only sat and listened as they took possession of the next chamber, sat and watched as the light died in the doorway; sat and held her breath and listened to the silence that followed, and prayed that both boys might be sleeping.

Then she undressed, as quietly as she could manage, and slipped into the bed. Closed her eyes, and felt weariness engulf her.

AND DID NOT sleep, she could not; but lay and listened to the slow rhythms of Julianne's breathing, and tried re-

sentfully to match it with her own, in case there should be
some sympathetic magic in the beat.

There was none. She gazed at the ceiling, where the
window had laid a pretty pattern of light; she thought it
ought to move as the moon moved, but it did not. That
puzzled her, until she saw another pattern on the floor,
that did creep slowly across the tiles. Of course, moonlight would not shine up onto the ceiling; there must be
some other source out there, fixed low, like the globe in
the garden.

She tried to focus her mind on that, but it was all distraction. At last she allowed her true concern to take command, to lift her out of her bed. She checked on Julianne,
one last needless delay, and then padded barefoot and
naked as she was through the connecting doorway into the
boys' chamber.

There was more light in here. Jemel—it must have been
Jemel—had put out most of the lamps all through the
suite, but he'd left one burning in the furthest chamber,
for Rudel's sake if he should return before dawn. Not yet:
that light made a pale glow to show the way through,
should she wish to venture further.

She did not. Jemel, again Jemel must have opened the
screens across the window; a soft light fell in to show her
Marron's head on a bright silken cushion, where he lay
deeply asleep.

He was all her anxiety, tonight more than ever before.
She went to stand beside him, gazing down almost in
wonder to see his face so relaxed, his native beauty breaking through the strains that rived him moment by moment
when he was awake.

How long she stood there rapt, she couldn't have said:
only that the spell was broken by the sudden glimmer of a
reflection on the wall behind his bed. She glanced round,
startled—and saw Jemel sitting up with a drawn blade in
his hand and his arm cocked, poised to throw.

She lifted her face full into view, and spread her hands

slowly wide; he nodded, and slid the knife out of sight beneath a pillow.

And stood up quietly, throwing his coverlet aside, unconscious of his nakedness or as unconcerned as she was; that was Sharai custom, natural to him and taught to her. He gestured and she followed him to the window, then up onto the ledge and through to a place where they could talk without either disturbing the sleepers or being disturbed themselves.

IT WAS A courtyard, closed in by palace buildings on all sides; but it was another garden also, dense with growth and harbouring a tiny pool at its centre where another of those globe-lamps glowed to light their way. The air was heavy with perfume, cool and damp and pleasant against her skin. She saw a door in one of the walls, but that was closed; all the windows that overlooked the court were shuttered, bar the one they'd climbed through.

Jemel's eyes too were shuttered and secretive, as ever. She meant to unlock that reserve, she was determined to do it; tonight could make a start, and she had the key, she thought. She gazed at his lean body, seeing white scars against dark skin, and asked, "How did you get him to sleep so, did you beg a potion from the Sultan's doctors?"

Jemel smiled faintly. "No. That would not work; what he carries in his blood would not allow it. But even the Ghost Walker is not immune to others' skills. He needs to rest, to dream a little; I led him there, with the *sodar* my father taught me. Do you know the *sodar*?"

Elisande nodded slowly. The *sodar* was almost magic, she thought, though everyone who used it swore that it was not. It varied from tribe to tribe, from family to family within each tribe; sometimes it was song, sometimes a chant, sometimes simple speaking but always touching too, a gentle massage to the rhythm of words. She could use it herself in a clumsy way, all but untaught. She had experienced it many times from her childhood on, from the days when she would allow her father to touch her; it had always seemed like magic, that easy drifting into sleep, guided by a loving voice . . .

She thought of Jemel's fingers on Marron's skin, the murmur of his voice insinuating into Marron's muddled mind, and tried to feel nothing but grateful that the Sharai had achieved what she could not. The result was all that mattered, she told herself firmly, Marron's peaceful sleeping; she struggled hard to believe it.

"Thank you, Jemel. That was a kind touch." *To us both,* she meant, and he seemed to understand. At any rate he nodded, as though accepting that she had the right to thank him for a gift given to Marron.

She crouched down beside the pool, and dabbled her hand in the near-luminous water; a shift of shadows, and an invisible fish rose to nibble at her fingers. She smiled, and lifted a palmful of water towards the stars, and let it trickle teasingly down her arm.

Above her, Jemel said, "I have learned why the city is so quiet after dark."

Bar'ath Tazore was hardly a city, she thought, hiding her smile; except to a Sharai boy, clearly, for whom three tents would make a town. What on earth had he made of Rhabat?

"Why's that, Jemel? And how did you learn it?"

"I spoke to the Sultan's slaves. They said there is a curfew now, from dusk till dawn. It was the sickness, it brought such fear with it; and the miracles that followed, they were fearful also. Most people kept their houses when night fell; but others went out in bands, and slew those they blamed for the evil, or burned them in their homes with families and servants and all."

"Don't tell Marron that," Elisande murmured. He was so tender still, about his stable-boy friend who had been put to death by fire at the castle.

"No. I would not." They shared a glance of mutual understanding; she thought perhaps they were the only two who could.

"Go on, then. What else did the slaves tell you?"

"The Sultan called a curfew, to stop those killings. He said that they had more to do with blood-feuds than diseases, which was true. He said that the sickness was not the work of men, but of demons; and the healings too, he said, they were not miracles but curses. Those who had followed the holy man had been deluded, and were outcast for abandoning their people.

"There were some who disputed that; there are some still, though mostly they keep quiet now. One did not, a Patric priest who had been let live here for generations, to minister to those of your people who come to trade. He preached against the Sultan's ruling: he said that he had seen what he had seen. The Sultan put his eyes out this afternoon, that they might not confuse the man further. That is what Marron smelled on his hands."

Julianne shuddered; the night seemed suddenly colder, and less welcoming.

"You should go back to bed," Jemel said, surprising her.

"Yes. I will. But—" But sleep felt as far away as ever, or further; she had more to worry over now. "Jemel, will you, would you perform the *sodar* for me too?"

"I would, and I will," he said; and surprised her again by taking her hand, to lead her back to the window. Her feet stumbled a little, in the long grasses underfoot; she clung to his strength, and thought that his public oath had somehow mellowed him, that he could be kinder now that they were all witnesses to his sworn revenge.

BACK TO THE chamber, with his hands to help her in through the high window; she fell gladly onto her bed, lay on her belly and felt his firm touch on her tangled hair.

He came from a people who whispered their *sodar,* it seemed; his voice was a soft sibilance, a flow like running water, like his fingers that flowed all down the run of her spine. She couldn't catch the words, they were too liquid, a quicksilver chorus, fish in a river, not to be distinguished one from another or any from the water that they swam in, his hands against her skin; she thought she heard more voices than his one, as her mind submerged.

SHE WOKE TO laughter, and the tickle of cool fingers on her neck. Emphatically, that was not Jemel.

"Wake, laze! The men want to bathe before breakfast, as we do; but they will not share with us, so we must hurry . . ."

And Julianne snatched back the sheet that covered her, that emphatically she had not used to cover herself last night.

Obediently Elisande rose, and walked towards the hammam. Julianne shrieked, and threw the sheet hurriedly around her.

"Grief, girl, there are no doors to close here! Or hadn't you noticed?"

Marasson manners: Elisande knotted the sheet complaisantly about her body, and gave her friend a smile. Julianne wore a white robe, simple but decent dress for men to see her in.

"It'll come off in a minute, love."

"Even so. Do you want Jemel to blush for you?"

That was clever, that she'd noticed enough not to say *Marron,* as she would have done before. Still, Elisande hid another smile. Julianne had a deal to learn, before she left the desert. Elisande only hoped that Sharai ease with nakedness would be the hardest lesson, though she doubted that.

JULIANNE WAS EASY enough once they were within the privacy of the hammam, with none but female attendants to see them. Hard enough to see anything clearly, through the billowing steam: but Elisande saw her lolling on her back on a marble bench, hugging one knee to her chest while her hair hung down in damp tendrils.

"Oh, this feels so good . . . Will you rub me down, Lisan?"

"I will if you call me by my name. Not otherwise."

"Elisande, Elisande my sweet . . . Mmm. Yes. Harder," as Elisande took a rough towel to sweat-slick skin. "If we are to believe the djinni, your name will be Lisan; I was only practising for the change."

"The djinn are not famous for their invention, Julianne; I have been called Lisan before. It's the Sharai version of my name, easier to their tongue. But let's leave it to the Sharai, shall we?"

"Surely. Jemel doesn't call you Lisan."

"Jemel doesn't call me anything." Except friend, perhaps, after last night; though she wouldn't care to count on that.

"No. He's very sparing with names, isn't he? I suppose you'll tell me that's Sharai custom again."

"Sharai manners, yes. Names are potent, you don't bandy them about unnecessarily. And Jemel is very much adrift still, one among strangers; regardless of his private troubles," *his dead lover, his oath,* "he doesn't have the knack of being friendly. Best thing is just to leave him be."

"With Marron. Yes. I do. The djinn follow Sharai manners, though, you told me that; and the djinni named you. Lisan of the Dead Waters, it said . . ."

"And it said your name would be greater than your father's," she countered.

"If I fail not. I know. We'll see, won't we? Perhaps I'll fail, whatever it wants me to do. I've done the getting married, and I seem to have failed at that," mournfully, trying to hide her true mourning behind a joke, not well enough to carry it off, though Elisande applauded the ambition. "So what are the Dead Waters, Elisande?"

"A lake, an inland sea beside Rhabat. The water is so salt you cannot drink it, nothing can live in it, it's dead.

And more, inhabited by some evil, according to story. It stinks; I lay no claim to it. Roll over."

"Ow! Don't pummel me—oh. Actually, that feels good. Don't stop . . . So what did the djinni mean?"

"I don't know."

"Shouldn't we try to find out? Before we get there?"

"Julianne, you can't interrogate a djinni! Besides, it's gone away."

"I'm not so sure. And the Sharai are part of the story also, we can interrogate the Sharai . . ."

"Oh, yes? Which tribe, which family? Someone is to bring me a gift of questions, whatever that means; but you ask the wrong questions of the wrong people, and the djinni can go play in the sand by itself, they'll slit your throat and mine besides for bringing you."

"So what do we do, then? What can we do?"

"Nothing. Go to Rhabat, sit patient, wait. Patience is a virtue anywhere; in the desert, or among desert people, it's a necessity."

"Tell me about the desert, then. How far is it to Rhabat from here?"

"Never ask how far something is, sweetheart. As well ask how far it is to the next new moon; nobody measures that way. They count journeys in days, not in miles."

"Well, how many days is it?"

"I don't know." She ducked, grinning, as Julianne threw a sponge at her. "No, listen. For a pigeon carrying a message—and there will be birds with messages, don't doubt it—not long at all, a few days, no more. We're not birds, and cannot go their way nor at their speed. There is a slow road, a water-route that skirts the *mul'abarta* and meanders like a river from well to well. We might go that way, though it would not be safe. Your name and style will attract attention; if you have enemies, that road is where they'll look for you. Rudel certainly has enemies. And Marron is worse: half the Sharai in the wide desert would come to look on the Ghost Walker, if they knew where he might be found."

"What else can we do, then?"

"We can travel quick and chancy, taking as straight a line as we can manage and keeping well away from the camel-trail. The desert is dangerous, though, and so are its people; that's why we need Jemel, for guide and guarantor among the tribes. He knows the ways of sand and rock better than we ever will, and he is at least Sharai. And tribeless now: that will help, although he did not mean it to. No one can claim a blood-feud with an outcast, though few will offer hospitality. The Patrics—that's you and me, love—are almost welcome here and tolerated on certain routes for certain purposes, but we are forbidden to wander at will in the *mul'abarta*. Even we from Surayon. Rudel has a reputation, and so does your father, but even so we need Jemel to make our excuses for us. And he still may not be enough."

"And if he is not?"

"Why, then we have Marron. Trust me, love, Marron will always be enough."

If they always had Marron, if the Sand Dancers didn't cut him out of the party, as was certainly their intent. Rudel and Redmond would put up no resistance, unless losing Marron meant losing Jemel also. Elisande thought it would; she thought one of the two older men should have realised that, at least. She was disappointed in Redmond, for being so obtuse.

THEY TOOK THEIR time in dressing while the men bathed, indulging the sheer pleasure of it, this one last chance of diaphanous silks, vivid embroideries, servants to help them with the intricate folds and veils.

When the men were decent they all ate together in the largest chamber, finding an array of food and drinks laid out that made Elisande wish they were true guests here, and for longer than just one morning. More practically, she wished for bags and flasks to take with them what they could not manage now.

"If this is breakfast," Julianne said, slicing cheese cheerfully at her side, "no wonder the Sultan is so portly. One such meal a day will do me . . ."

"Hush, and eat," Rudel said repressively, with a glance at the silent attendants. "Eat as much as you can; one meal a day may well be our lot, in a few days' time."

Quite unsquashed, Julianne pulled a face at him, which made Elisande giggle around a mouthful of sweet fruit-bread.

They all took the wisdom of Rudel's injunction, though, and stuffed themselves to groaning. Even the boys ate well, Elisande was glad to see, without need of her nagging. Marron looked better than she had known him, she thought, fresh after his bath and well-rested, almost forgetful of his burden as he murmured quietly with Jemel. That would not last, it could not, but it was welcome none the less.

WHEN THEY WERE done, the slaves began to clear the remnants of their meal; almost immediately, the Sultan's chamberlain appeared in the doorway.

After polite greetings and ritual questions as to their health and sleep and general contentment, which they answered equally ritually, he said, "My lord has asked me to fetch you to the stables, if such a thing would please you. Will you come?"

Of course, they would come. They rose, brushing crumbs from their fine garments, and followed. Julianne took her usual duty at Redmond's elbow, though even that old man seemed fitter this morning, a tribute to the Sultan's doctors.

Elisande walked behind with the boys, as if only to avoid walking ahead with her father. She felt a great temptation to imitate her friend and tuck her arm through Marron's, but did not; instead she said, perhaps a little wickedly, "Jemel, I have to thank you for your *sodar* last night."

"You slept well?"

"I did. But you know that, you saw . . ."

She'd hoped to raise a question from Marron, that much at least; all she managed was a curious glance, though she thought he might ask the Sharai about it later. She gave him a bright smile to feed his piqued interest a little, and let be.

IB' TARAFFI LED them through the palace complex, and out into a wide flagged court where they found the Sultan himself standing in the shade of a fringed parasol, held up by a gorgeously dressed black page. He greeted them magniloquently, asking the same questions as his chamberlain, but never taking his eyes from a string of half a dozen camels that were parading in a circle before him. They were fine bull beasts, decked out in jewelled golden harness that detracted not at all from their own quality; each was ridden by a small boy, no more than seven or eight years old by the look of them. They wore identical clothes, and all had a similar cast to their faces: fearful under their master's eye, Elisande thought, and hungry with it.

"You must forgive my passion," the Sultan said, "but this is the racing season, and these are my pride. All bred here, in my stables; I know the stars and lineage of each."

And he proved it, stepping from one to the next as their riders drew them to a halt and greeting each beast by name, stretching up to stroke a high-arched nose or slap a tawny neck while the camels coughed or bellowed or stooped to snuffle at his robes. He beamed, clearly seeing each response as a gesture of recognition and affection. Elisande, who knew something of camel nature, was less than convinced. But at least none of them spat in his face, or tried to bite him; and they were exceptional animals, there was no disputing that.

"He breeds the camels," Julianne muttered in an undertone, "but where does he get the children, does he breed them too? They're tiny . . ."

"He'll buy them," Redmond replied, equally quietly. "Peasant children from their parents, nomads from raiders. There's perhaps more prestige in having a Sharai boy aback your camel, but not much. Being light and wiry is the only useful qualification; you don't need brute strength to sit a racing camel."

"What happens when they grow too big?"

"There's always work. In the stables, the palace, the fields . . . The Sultan cares for his slaves, don't doubt it. He wouldn't cast them out, though they'll likely never know anything like these glory days again."

"They don't look glorified, they look plain scared."

"Only of falling or losing control, of disgracing themselves in front of him. Believe me, they're not frightened of the Sultan. They have no cause to be. We're the ones who should be nervous now."

"Why so? He said he wouldn't delay us . . ."

"He's had a night to think about it, he's had a long night of talking with Rudel; and he has been known to change his mind. This isn't just a parade-ground, Julianne, it's an execution-ground as well. Ask Marron."

Indeed, Marron's nostrils were flaring even where he stood right at the back of their group, and his face was tight with tension, losing half the advantage of his night of sleep. Elisande didn't know which she resented more, the effects of this place on the boy or those of Redmond's words on their friend. Unnecessary, she thought, to have brought them here; if the Sultan felt that he needed to make the point so crudely, he was less subtle than she believed. And stupid of Redmond, to spell it out for Julianne. Just healthy male detachment, no doubt, but that girl worried too much already. The last thing she needed was extra fuel for her anxieties.

He should have known that—no, he must have known that, he saw the world too clearly to miss what was so obvious to Elisande. Which meant that he'd said the thing deliberately, for deliberate effect, for purposes of his own . . .

Julianne could be detached too, though, or at least she could play that game. She didn't flinch; she smiled, indeed, and said, "Perhaps we should sell ourselves into his service, if it means he'd treat us kinder. What would you say I was worth, Redmond?"

"Diamonds. Diamonds beyond number—"

"No," and that was Rudel, interrupting. "Not diamonds, old friend, your eyes are rheumy and play you false. Diamonds are for my daughter; she will have the hard heart of truth, and tell it too. Pearls for you, Julianne: pearls of every colour, pink and cream and black. Pearls are not so forthright, they're beautiful but subtle, disguising, deceptive. A many-layered thing, a pearl is, and you never can see to the heart of it. Tell me, do all girls resemble their fathers so much?"

At least half of that little speech was aimed at Elisande, if not directly said to her; she was ready to explode with indignant denial, except that Julianne spoke first and stole her air and her father's also.

"I think perhaps they do; though your daughter at least knows the colour of my heart, Rudel. Hush now, here comes the Sultan."

ODDLY, THE SULTAN came directly to Julianne. He took her hands and bowed above them, smiled down into her clear eyes and said, "Forgive my lingering over an indulgent pleasure, my dear, but you I think will understand; I fancy you have your own similar attachment, is it not so? You will want to see how my people have acted, in your stead . . ."

Keeping a grip on one wrist, he led her a few paces forward and made a gesture with his free hand; across the court, one of three dozen stable doors swung wide, and there were figures moving in the shadows within.

Julianne's frown of puzzlement vanished in a moment;

Elisande deliberately relaxed the tension in her muscles, and took her hands away from where she'd stowed her knives no more than half-hidden at her waist. She'd quite forgotten about their horses, what with all the turbulence of last night and her uncertainties about the road ahead. Julianne, of course, had not.

"Merissa!" In a moment of sheer childishness which she would undoubtedly blush for later, Julianne pulled free of the Sultan and fairly ran over the flags, skirts flapping and hair flying loose, veil coming awry.

Merissa it was, but not Merissa as she had been when last they'd seen her, her coat dull and gritty and her mane tangled for lack of proper grooming, her head hanging with weariness after the long trail. This was a proud, high-stepping aristocrat with two lads to attend her, as she deserved; sunlight gleamed gold on her russet flank, all her coat was bright with recent brushing. Jewels in her harness glinted as they caught the light.

The Sultan gave Julianne a minute to kiss the palfrey's soft nose, to hug her neck, to whisper endearments in her flicking ear; then he walked across the court to join her, his page scampering behind with the parasol. Elisande followed, her curiosity overriding manners; she wanted to hear what they said to each other.

"Excellence, this is, this is more than kind in you, to take such care of her . . ."

"Not at all. You are my guests; it was my duty to see to all your beasts, but my privilege in this case. It is not only camels that catch my eye. This little lady is a princess, she graces my stables as you grace my halls." He reached out to stroke Merissa between the eyes, a tribute which she permitted; her blatant condescension made Elisande bite back a grin. "If you will permit it, lady, I have a proposal to make. You cannot take your horses into the desert, which you know; let me hold them here for you, and I will provide you with camels in their stead. Under my eye they will be treated as they ought; my people know better than the market traders, what a princess requires for her comfort. These boys raced camels for me," he added, his voice so neutral that for sure he had overheard Julianne's earlier hard questions, "before they grew so large; they will give her the same attention they gave my beasts before."

Julianne did blush at that, adjusting her veil too late to hide it; but then she laughed, and said, "I'm sure they will. May they ride Merissa, as well as pampering her? She's too feckless to race, I fear, but she likes a run; and they're light boys yet, they'll not be too heavy for her."

The lads gawped at her, gawped hopefully at their master; all he said was, "Someone must exercise her, certainly. Such a beauty must not stale in a stall. Will you trust her to me?"

"Gladly, excellence. It would be a great relief to me, to know her so well set up. I've been grieving over the loss of her; it must happen, but if I may give her to you, I can be much more easy in my mind . . ."

"Leave her; do not give her. She shall be another guest, until you can reclaim her. And the same for all your mounts," the Sultan said, making a grand circle and bowing to the whole party; the men had come up quietly to join Elisande, Marron as ever hanging back, not to come too close to the animals. Jemel as ever was at his side. "I have empty stalls, and lazy boys aplenty."

Elisande caught Jemel's eye and flashed him a grin around her veil, delighted at the thought of his scruffy pony sharing the luxury of the Sultan's stables. He smiled back, which she counted a minor triumph.

"You are the soul of generosity, excellence," Rudel said cautiously, "but I am reluctant to dip so far into your debt. We do not know how affairs may fall out, at Rhabat; it may be a long time before we can come back. Nor do I think that racing bulls would make the ideal companions for a difficult journey."

The Sultan snorted, and clapped his hands together; a boy ran to open a gate that led to another court. Another string of camels was brought through, each with a lad at its nose-rope. Females all, Elisande noted, and all mature beasts.

"This is Sildana," the Sultan murmured, going to the first of them, whose coat was a shimmering white. "She has been dam to three of my finest racers, and will breed again if you return her. If not—well, these things fall out as God orders them. You are here, and in need of good beasts; I need to see you gone. We will do this, Rudel. Here is Caret; she is full sister to my greatest hope this season . . ."

And so through all the string, each one named and flattered: a mount for everyone in the party—except for Marron, of course, no mount for him—and two besides to carry packs or riders if necessary.

"There is some food in your own luggage," the Sultan added after each camel had been introduced, "but I will give you more, plus whatever else is needful for the journey. Fresh clothes, at least, and a little gold to smooth your travel."

"Excellence, this is far more than we had looked for—"

"I know it. You looked for me to forbid your going further, did you not, Rudel? And so I might have done, I would for almost any other of your kind; I do not love to see Patrics pass beyond my borders into the Sands. There is little trust between our peoples, and good cause for that. But the son and granddaughter of the Princip of Surayon make a special case, as does the daughter of the King's Shadow; and then there is Marron. For any one of you, I might have done as much; for all together, I dare not do otherwise. There is something momentous in your party, that lies beyond my judgement; this talk of the djinn makes me fearful, as does the sight of the Ghost Walker. Go to the council at Rhabat, and let the sheiks there make what decisions must be made. I cannot send my blessings with you, but I will do what I can to ease your journey. My concern is for my people here; they are restive since that cursed healer came. I keep them peaceable by day and penned in at night, but I want no further disturbance."

"That is more than fair, excellence," Rudel said quietly. "We will take your gifts gladly, and go on today; we ask no more."

"That is well. One thing further, though: go by the traders' route. It will take you longer, but the way will be easier; and the tribes too are restless. Hasan wants war with Outremer, and there are few who speak against him. They will look less kindly than I do on a party of Patrics, if they find you loose on their land."

Rudel bowed, but said nothing; after a moment, the Sultan turned to Redmond.

"You, old man—you should not go with them. My doctors say so, and they are right. Stay with me until you are well, and then I will give you an escort to see you safe to the borders of Surayon."

"Excellence, I agree with your doctors, and with you. I will go home happily, if I can persuade one other to come with me." Redmond turned to Julianne and went on, "Child, lady, heart's daughter: these others our friends have all some experience at least of the road to Rhabat, or else a pressing need to go there—"

"As does Julianne," Elisande broke in, ready as ever to come to her friend's defence, needful or not. "There was a bidding laid on her, we have told you of it," *don't you remember, old man?* "She's only fulfilled one half of the instructions, thus far." *Go where you are sent, and marry where you must*—and she'd done the marrying because she had to, she'd been forced to it, and now she was running from her new-wed lord and looking for her father. Whom she would find in Rhabat, by the djinni's word. By her face, she had no plans to turn aside.

"That should not have been spoken of," Rudel grated, ready as ever to stress his daughter's faults. There was none to hear but the Sultan and his page, though, and the Sultan had heard it all last night. Elisande glared, and was entirely ignored. "Julianne, I would be glad to know Redmond in your company on his way to Surayon, and you would be very welcome there. Your father could find you as conveniently in that place as any other, once we tell him where to look . . ."

"I expect that's all very true," Julianne said briskly, "and all very wise to boot; but I was told to go to the Sharai, and I will go. Besides, I was also told that he would be in danger, and that I could save him. If I wait for him in Surayon, I think I might wait a long time, and waste it anyway."

Rudel stiffened, and his eyes darted rage at Elisande. She moved not a muscle, gave him not so much as a twitch of the head that he might read as meaning *no, not me, a lucky hit, no more, a cruel chance; I have told her nothing.*

"A girl should go where she is told to go," the Sultan said lightly; it was impossible to tell which way he intended them to understand that, whether he thought she should obey the djinni or these men.

"And so she will, excellence." Elisande slipped her arm through Julianne's, deciding to claim his support whether he were offering it or no. "We were both of us sent on this journey, and we two will see it to an end."

"Or die trying."

"Indeed, excellence. The one, or the other. We are quite determined."

"Stubborn, I should have said. And wilful, and foolish, and—"

"—And so well supplied of your generosity that we have the finest chance of seeing Rhabat, girls and old men and all," Julianne completed for him. There were famously risks in interrupting an arbitrary ruler, men had lost their tongues for doing so; but Julianne was a girl, and a guest, and the daughter of a powerful figure. Elisande didn't so much as nudge her in a belated warning to be careful, she only smiled and listened and thought she couldn't have played it better herself as Julianne went on, "Redmond, I am sure that His Excellence is right, that you ought to stay and rest and then go home; but you know and I know that what is right is not always what is needful. If there is a council of the Sharai at Rhabat, and if there is a chance that the voice of Surayon will be given audience at such a council, then you know and I know that your wisdom should inform that voice. The Sultan has named me stubborn, and he is right in that also. I will go, for my father's sake. If it costs you pain, I am sorry; but I hope that my stubbornness and your understanding together will persuade you to travel with us, for the sake of all our peoples. With our companions to lead us and these magnificent beasts to carry us, I am sure we can come through safely."

It was a clever speech precisely weighted, clear-sighted and politic, deferent both to Redmond and indirectly to Rudel; it had what must have been its intended effect. Redmond sighed and bowed, while Rudel nodded his head.

"I am afraid I will slow you all," the older man said, and little doubt of it, "but that cannot be helped. If I can ride a horse, as I have, then I can ride a camel; and I can travel the traders' road. It may be true what you say, that there is need. And the Sultan's doctors have given me a measure of relief. So be it, then. You are a hard creature, Julianne; but these are hard times, and we must suffer them. I will come with you."

Julianne kissed his cheek gently, in gratitude or apology, both; Elisande wanted to do the same, but instead looked around to follow the Sultan's sudden gaze, to see who or what had drawn his attention.

And saw, and recognised the inevitability of this even as her spine chilled at the sight, even as the Sultan spoke.

"Your party will be a little larger than you had anticipated, perhaps. I have no voice in this, they answer no command but their own. They will see you all safe to Rhabat, though, if the Ghost Walker goes so far."

Everyone turned, at that; Elisande sensed their various puzzlement or doubt, quickly dispelled by understanding as they saw what she had seen, the Sand Dancers standing in a group in the shadow of the palace wall.

She watched Marron's face change, and Jemel's also; she watched how the Dancers moved forward with a slow dread grace, seeming to bring that shadow with them; and she swore a silent vow that whosever possession the boy might ultimately fall into, it should not be theirs.

4

Singing for a Stranger

AT THIS DISTANCE she thought they looked like statues, monoliths, black silhouettes that seemed to own more potency than their simple size would suggest. Hazed by the heat, they flickered and jerked in her sight like those deceptive, disturbing insects they were named after, unless the insects were named after them; sometimes she thought they'd vanished altogether, only that they came back before her eyes had really registered their absence.

And yet she knew that they stood monolithically on the sand, still as statues, moving not a muscle. And among the Sand Dancers, at the focus of their little convocation, stood Marron: stiller than any except that the skin around his eyes would twitch with effort, that much he couldn't prevent.

Julianne knew all of that because the first day and the second day she had gone close to watch. No one had seemed to mind, and she'd been curious; bored too if she were honest, keen for any distraction to while away these noon-tide hours when it was too hot to ride and too hot to sleep.

After those first two days she'd kept her distance. Curiosity was sated, and she could only bear so much of watching a friend fail and fail at something that might matter beyond her ability to reckon its worth. Besides, this too was boring, though it was an agonising boredom. They would stand unmoving throughout the hours of rest, the Dancers in half a circle around Marron at its heart; only the one man would speak and perhaps Marron would reply, but only to say, "I can't. I am trying, but I *can't* . . ."

He'd say it in Catari, but that much at least Julianne had learned.

THAT MUCH AND a deal more, actually, just as Marron had; though she thought he was the quicker pupil or had the better teacher or more application than she, unless having the Daughter in his blood somehow gave him an advantage in this too, as it seemingly did in swordplay. At any rate, he seemed fluent now when he spoke to Jemel, while she was still fumbling for the right words and her grammar made Elisande smile more often than Julianne quite liked.

Her friend was her back-rest just now, as she was Elisande's; but the other girl was restless, shifting and twisting to peer over Julianne's shoulder, to watch that same motionless group of men.

"Do you want to go and see?" Julianne asked at last, in careful Catari.

"Want to? No. But your back's too hot to lean on, so we might as well move; and there's nothing else to look at . . ."

Julianne understood more than the words, she understood her friend also, better perhaps than Elisande would want her to. The whole world was too hot, her back was not to blame; walking would be hotter than sitting still. But she stood, and waited for Elisande to do the same; and took her friend's hand in hers, and together they walked away from the roadside and across soft sand towards Marron and those unmoving Dancers.

Standing up, she could see now the one figure that had

been missing before. There were the tall still figures, men and boy, who might have been statues; and there just a short distance off was the shorter, more squat shape of one young man sitting in the poor shade of a low dune, though he might have been a rock. He moved as little as the others, which meant not at all.

That was Jemel, of course, keeping as close to Marron as it was safe to come. It was towards him the girls chose to walk, not quite directly towards the group. He might not welcome their company, but they would welcome his.

SOME DAYS BEYOND the oasis, they had left the lava field behind at last, at a ridge of broken hills; there was gravel now beneath the hard-packed sand of the road. That was all the difference that Julianne could see, between this and their previous journey. The sun was hotter, or seemed so, but the Sharai robes they all wore were cooler than the clothes they'd had before. In truth she was disappointed, and a little angry. She'd expected real desert, high dunes and short water and only an intimation of a track to follow, no traffic. Instead they clung to this well-travelled route, met caravans coming and going, camped each night by a populous well. It was easier for Redmond, that was sure, and she supposed easier for her also; riding a camel was an uncomfortable art that she'd been slow to acquire. All her body ached, although Rudel had led them in steady stages and never pressed the pace.

What angered her, beyond her own weakness and inexperience, was that she saw no need for the camels, and felt cheated because of it. She could have brought Merissa after all, she thought, and so have had no need of sores or suffering. She felt that she'd been promised a hard road, and had not found it.

NOT SO FOR Marron, nor those who cared most for him. The Sand Dancers had claimed that boy, and he lacked the

will or the knowledge to deny them. They walked with
him while the others rode, and at times of rest they drew
him away and tried to test or teach him. Jemel had been
forced out, kept at a distance; the same was true, Julianne
thought, of Elisande. At least she seemed as resentful, as
jealous almost, as the Sharai lad so obviously was.

As now, when he could do no more than sit stone-still
and bear witness, and neither did they dare go any closer.
He greeted them, for a wonder, though only in a grunt and
a Catari grunt at th⸱⸱ unfair to expect anything more, perhaps, when he w⸱ ⸱ visibly bound up in the show before
him.

They settled down at his side, in what thin shade his little dune could offer, and gave their attention to what was
gripping him.

MARRON STOOD, AND the Dancers stood about him;
but only in half a circle or a little less than that, a few
careful paces back.

Marron held his left arm stiffly, painfully out from his
side, and bled slowly onto the sand.

In front of him, that thing that Julianne still thought of
as the Daughter twisted slowly in the air. Trying to please
him, Julianne thought, trying to be what he wanted. She'd
have liked to dismiss that thought as fanciful, and could
not. Certainly it was not shaped as she had seen it before,
insectoid and deadly, a killing shadow; now it seemed
more like a window or a looking-glass, she thought, its
cloudy mass drawn out into a frame with only the faintest
skein of red across the centre.

The man who was first among the Dancers, whose
name she had learned—though not from him—was
Morakh, that man was speaking softly. She couldn't hear
what he said, only the murmur of his voice; Marron could
hear, though, and his face was tight with strain. The
Daughter shifted like smoke in a breeze, although the day
was utterly still; for a moment a clear space seemed to

open at its heart and a hard golden light shone through, almost tangible even under the sun's fierce glare.

Julianne's mind tripped, sending her back to a cave, an impossible brightness, dark terror that had snatched at her own stupidity. She jerked her head hard away from the memory, and was grateful to see distracting movement among the Dancers.

One of the men had reached into his robe and brought out something living, something that wriggled and squirmed in his hand.

"Sand-rat," Elisande muttered at her side. It looked like a plain rat to Julianne, sand-brown perhaps but a rat none the less; squinting, she saw that its kicking back legs were longer than a rat's.

She heard its thin sharp squeal, saw it fly; saw it as a dot of darkness as the man tossed it carefully towards the gleaming light where the Daughter—or Marron, it was hard sometimes to distinguish between them—had opened a way into another world.

That way snapped shut, though, a moment before the tumbling creature reached it. There was a soft, implosive sound, and silence after; more blood than Marron's sprayed across the sand.

Marron cried out at that, and his voice carried his grief: "How do I make it hold its shape?"

"Strength of will," they heard Morakh reply, impatience sharpening his tone enough for it to reach them. "It owns you, at least a little; you must make it serve you instead."

To judge by Elisande's soft snort, that girl doubted Marron's strength of will as much as Julianne did. He had been owned entire by the Ransomers, and then by Sieur Anton; and then, yes, for a little time by the Daughter. Less so now, she thought, or wanted to think. Marron's life had become more complex, though not of his own desire; likely he still wanted to give his soul away, if he could only make the choice. Certainly the Dancers wanted to possess him, and believed they had the right, but there were others too who would make a claim. Jemel, for one; and Julianne thought that she could name another.

"Again," Morakh said. "You must learn to command it, as you command yourself."

"He never has," Elisande murmured distressfully, "he doesn't know how."

SO IT SEEMED, as they watched Marron fail, and fail again; as small creatures died to mark each failure, and each death upset him more. Elisande muttered, and fidgeted uselessly; it was Jemel at last who stood and walked boldly into that group of men, unslinging his water-skin as he went.

"Enough!" he cried. "Marron, call it back now, and drink. We have a long road before nightfall, and Rudel will be eager to get on . . ."

Morakh moved scowlingly to block his way, to deny him; but Marron had already nodded and stretched his arm out, to take the Daughter back into his blood. He seemed grateful for the interruption, as Julianne was herself. There was no entertainment in this, only a brutal fascination.

"That's a brave boy," Elisande said, her voice all regret, as though she blamed herself for lacking the necessary courage. "Rudel would be pleased with him. If that meant anything to Jemel, though I'm glad to say it does not."

Both halves of that were true. The Dancers worried Rudel, their influence over Marron worried him more; Jemel had his own reasons for everything he did, and they were none of them Rudel's.

"Come on," Julianne said, rising and offering her arm to Elisande. "Let's get back to those accursed camels. On the way, you can explain to me again how it's possible to sit in that saddle all day and not raise blisters . . ."

THE CAMELS WERE couched by the side of the road, high-necked and haughty with deceptive eyes, long-lashed and seductive. Julianne's own beast—or at least the one she rode, she would never claim possession, nor want to—was the white, Sildana, whose proud lineage the Sultan had first proclaimed. That pairing had been at his insistence, beauty to ride with beauty he had said, a compliment she couldn't refuse; she was sure now that a devil had inspired that choice, that this particular camel was the least-fleshed, the hardest-boned and the most wilful of them all.

They exchanged glares, she and Sildana, promises of later pain. Then men moved, rising from where they'd been resting in their camels' shade, Rudel and more slowly Redmond.

Rudel said, "Where are the others? We should be moving on," and as usual he spoke across his daughter and yet to her, implying that the delay was somehow her own fault and no one's else.

"Jemel is coming," Elisande said shortly. Marron and the Dancers would follow in their own time, that was understood. The unspoken accusation was simply ignored; Elisande collected her riding-stick and went to the string of pack-animals, to begin the lengthy process of loading them up and persuading them to their feet.

Despite all these weeks of travelling together, despite the many hours of quiet and private talk, Julianne still hadn't discovered what it was that lay so bitterly between Elisande and her father. There had been chances aplenty, and many times she'd felt the question lie upon her tongue, but each time she'd put it aside unasked. She wasn't accustomed yet to having so close a friend; and even in the best of friendships, she thought, some secrets were too dangerous to share. She was frightened of making herself equally vulnerable, of hearing Elisande ask in return how she really felt about Imber, and about leaving Imber. It was a question she wasn't prepared to answer, for fear of discovering the truth within herself, whether she spoke that truth or no; and so she did not ask, and Elisande did not tell her. She only showed her again and again how a warm and instinctive girl could be cold and hard and unforgiving, if she felt she had reason enough. Which was a useful lesson, Julianne thought, and one she might need later, though she dreaded the opportunity to apply it.

SHE HELPED ELISANDE lade the pack-beasts despite her aching muscles, heaving sacks of rice and flour with an ease that she certainly hadn't known before, and an economy of effort that she'd consciously acquired under the hot sun. Jemel came before they were finished, and lent his own hands to the task. Julianne could almost have resented that, except that she knew now that among his own people he wouldn't have done it, he'd have felt demeaned to work with women. More than her body was being changed by this trip, she thought.

All possible work done, even Elisande mounted now and Rudel manifestly impatient—manifesting it by pacing his camel in tighter and tighter circles on the road, while he glanced back and up at the sun and back again—she left the string of pack-beasts to Jemel and approached Sildana with a reluctance that was so passionate it was almost loathing.

There were minor skills to camel-riding, and those at least she had learned. She untied the hobble that bound foreleg to thigh with a single twitch of her wrist; she lifted her stick and settled into the saddle in a single movement before the animal realised its freedom; she tucked her right foot under her left thigh in that curious one-legged posture that was obligatory, it seemed, though whether for practical reasons or only for proper style she was still unconvinced.

Tap of stick on Sildana's flank and the camel rose, hindquarters first and already roaring. Julianne swayed back and then forward for balance, hoping for some grace, knowing that her companions were watching. All too soon, she knew—and her sore muscles and chafed

skin were already reminding her, lest she forget—she'd
have passed beyond all thoughts of grace or style: she'd
be shifting her weight constantly from buttock to agonised
buttock, she'd be changing her lead leg more often than
her mount did and groaning more often also, though hopefully not so loudly.

If it weren't so constantly painful, she was sure there'd
be pleasures in riding like this, so different from horseback. The slow rocking motion reminded her of boats, of
her early adventures with sails and oars on the great river
at Marasson. Elisande told warning stories of men being
lulled into sleep on a long trek and falling from their
mounts, being lost in the *mul'abarta*; those she could almost believe.

She looked about from the height of Sildana's back and
spotted dark figures keeping pace across the sand, Marron
and the Dancers taking up their usual station. Looking
ahead was harder, Sildana's head got in the way; but there
would be nothing interesting to be seen in any case, only
the men on their camels and the endless hours of the unchanging road. She had Elisande at her side for company,
teasing company for sure once she started to fidget. Julianne sighed and tried to settle grimly into her discomfort, knowing that there would be no break now until
sunset.

And was proved suddenly, startlingly wrong, by the
sounds of running footsteps and jabbering voices just
where the road turned around a low hill. She glimpsed
milling figures ahead, Rudel's camel twisting out of line
as it met a pack of men on foot. Elisande grunted and
plied her stick, to drive her own mount forward; Sildana
followed without Julianne's needing to lift a finger.

There were five or six of the men, camel-drovers by
their dress, and that they had abandoned their animals
only underscored the panic that was obvious in their gestures, their high strained voices and their wild eyes.

They spoke Catari, too fast and shrill for her to follow
yet. Rudel was trying to calm them and his agitated beast

both at once, and succeeding at neither. It was Redmond who produced an unexpected bellow, to still the scene; into the quiet after, Elisande's voice fell like wisdom.

"Who is first among you? Let him alone speak, and tell us what your trouble is."

"He is dead," three voices answered her, "and a ghûl has eaten him."

No trouble understanding that, despite the chorus. The words resounded in Julianne's head, dragging up echoes of memory: another road, another delay, another encounter with power freed from story. That too had left blood in the dust; it had also and directly led this party here, and it led them still. Briefly, she was afraid. If there was such potency in these meetings, who could say in what direction she might not be flung now, and for what purpose?

That was nonsense, of course. A ghûl was not a djinni. And the djinni had waited especially for them, for her; while the ghûl it seemed had killed and gone, and this would not be in any sense a meeting or a confrontation even if she were allowed to witness it, which likely she would not be. Rudel would forbid it . . .

But there again, here again came an echo of before, Elisande wickedly forestalling her father as she had previously forestalled Sergeant Blaise and all Julianne's retinue of guards on the road to the Roq.

Wicked it was, and consciously so, but not done out of mischief. Elisande's face was grim as she pulled a dagger from her sash and cried, "A ghûl? Ride, Julianne—let's see if you can make that camel run . . ."

SHE COULD, THOUGH she hated the graceless jouncing of it and the insecurity, the constant fear of falling, almost the expectation. She bumped and gasped, clung to head-rope and saddle-horn, plied her stick determinedly in Elisande's wake and didn't look back even at Rudel's bellow, "Wait! Both of you, wait till I . . ."

He would take a minute longer to be free of his beleaguerers; Redmond would be slow to follow, as he was slow in everything except his mind; Jemel had the leading of the pack-string, and would be delayed by that.

Their road was clear, and Elisande for one must be rejoicing inside, however set her features. Even Marron and the Dancers were too far off to follow this tale or to interfere in its telling, her making. Any opportunity to defy her father was a godsend; this was defiance and action both, a hard ride under hot sun, burning fever below a burnished sky. This was how the Sharai lived, she'd said to Julianne with envy the salt on her tongue: slow days and sudden moments, idle as a big cat is idle, only ever a breath away from fury. It was how they lived and how they expected to live, how they loved, how they prayed, how they fought. The world was harsh and dull and repetitive, day on day and year on year, with no seasons to mark how the years passed. Pain and fear were events as much as joy or discovery; in that landscape they stood out just as boldly, and were welcomed just the same. The Sharai raided for the thrill of it more than for camels or honour; the death of their own was only a little less bright or less to be cherished than the death of an enemy. Anything, Elisande had said, to break the monotony.

They'd both had a taste of that monotony, on the road: protected, unchallenged, bored. Even Julianne's saddlesores had at least provided distraction. Now she was tasting a little of the antidote, the sharp brassy tang of terror. There was a ghûl ahead, a killer that had killed already this day. By its reputation—her nurse in Marasson had told stories of ghûls and her friends had told others, cruel tales of blood and fell deeds and the victory of the dark— it would be glad to kill again, and yet again. And here they rode towards it, two girls with knives and nothing; and yes, she was terror-stricken and she thought her friend was mad and she was mad to follow; and yet her blood sang and her throat yearned to, and for that little time she could have been Sharai and glad of it, if truly their lives were lived like this.

BUT THEY CAME around the rise of the hill, she and Elisande, and neither of them Sharai; and there was no ghûl to meet them, no work for their blades or their working, cursing mouths.

Dry mouth, in Julianne's case: abruptly dry, and that nothing to do with hard riding or the heat. Nor with the fear, released by the stillness of the road ahead, no sign of any fabled creature crouched snarling over its kill, no sign of anything that moved.

Rather it was that stillness that sucked her dry, certainty that followed doubt. She had not consciously doubted the drovers, perhaps, there hadn't been time; but men in a panic will run and not look back, will report their nightmares as truth observed. Men of the desert would see a ghûl's attack and flee, and say perhaps that it had eaten their master because that was what they knew of ghûls, what they had been told as she had. It didn't need to be true.

Men of the desert knew more than she did, though. What was true was what she saw, she'd been trained to believe her own eyes and none other; and what she saw now was the long run of the road, and a terrible stillness at the limit of her sight. She could see nothing clearly beyond the stretch of Sildana's neck, what with the jolting of the camel's speed and the dazzling glare of the sun, and Elisande ahead; but for sure there was some darkness that stained the pale road, a shadow of confusion, and for sure there was nothing there that showed any sign of life.

They came closer, too close; and still Elisande did not slow her mount, and so neither could Julianne. Not till the heavy smell of death rose to greet them, and then it was the camels' choice to slow, to halt, to stand and groan a few short paces from catastrophe.

Elisande slipped out of the saddle then, and so did Julianne; Elisande hobbled her beast quickly, and so did Julianne.

Elisande walked slowly, softly forward and so, reluctantly, did Julianne.

THEY WALKED AMONG tumbled bales and bags; bright cloths and spilt foodstuffs were strewn across their path. On either side of them camels lay dead in their harness, slumped and vast and angular, their heads askew amid vivid pools of blood where their throats had been ripped out. The stench was vile, every breath was blood and she choked on it; but that was far, very far from the worst of this. Almost she turned her head to look more directly at the slaughter that surrounded her, only to avoid looking further, to where one more shape lay fallen in the road.

That shape had been a person once, so much was undeniable. Now, not. Now it was only rags and bones; rags of dark cloth that might once have been less dark, rags of flesh that must once have made a living, thinking man.

More recently, that flesh had made a meal for some ravening monster. A ghûl she'd been told, and so much she was prepared to believe, sight unseen. No mortal animal could have done this, could have killed and eaten such a weight of meat and then killed and killed again, and yet have vanished in the time those terrorised men had taken to run less than half a league . . .

She stretched up, glad of the excuse, and took a slow, measured look at the land around. Broken hills of rock and shale and shadow, ever-wider stretches of sand between; she could have seen further from Sildana's back but gazed more intently now, and found that she'd been wrong before, when she thought that nothing moved or lived. There were shadows that shifted, there were shapes, silhouettes against the sky. Lions, ghûls . . . ?

She shuddered, and had to squint and shade her eyes to be sure. Only camels, broken away from the train and fled before the killer reached them. Of course, with that many drovers, there must have been many more camels than the half-dozen or so that lay dead here.

As she stared and stared, seeking more reassurance than her eyes or her logic could provide—or else only seeking comfort, looking away to prevent herself looking down and seeing again that mess of ruined meat almost at her feet—she heard the pounding hurry of riders at her back, which must be Rudel and Redmond following on. Jemel too, most probably, leaving the string behind. She heard them check some little distance off, she heard them dismount as she and Elisande had done, unwilling or unable to force their camels in among the dead; then she heard other, softer sounds, men running over sand.

She turned at that, to see Marron approaching fast, outsprinting the Dancers. They had their swords drawn, he did not. She saw him meet the invisible wall the camels had balked at, the stink of so much death; she saw how he balked also, how his blood rushed to the call of what was spilt here, suffusing all his skin. She saw how his right hand clutched at his left arm, as if to hold his own blood back within that ever-open gate.

The Dancers ran around him, and came on. Julianne's eyes remained fixed on Marron, where he stood transfixed. She waited for the inevitable, for someone to go to him; she wouldn't be the only one who'd seen.

A small figure rushed past her and scurried to his side, and almost Julianne could smile at that, despite the devastation all around. Not a Dancer, and not Jemel; it was Elisande who took his arm and turned him, led him away, talking softly in his ear as they went.

"WELL? WAS IT a ghûl?"

"Oh, yes. Did you doubt it?"

"I have never seen a ghûl-kill before."

"Nor I, that I know of. A ghûl kills in the shape that it takes; it might be a woman, with a knife. This was not. But look here, the trail it left. See?"

"Are you sure those are ghûl-tracks? A man might ride an ass, on this road. Or there might be wild asses in these hills . . ."

"I have never seen an ass that went on two legs, Rudel."

Julianne ducked her head quickly, to hide her sudden smile. She'd never suspected Morakh of possessing a sense of humour. Rudel snorted his self-disgust, and said, "What should we do, hunt it down?"

"We will follow the trail," Morakh said, with a subtle emphasis that clearly meant *we the Dancers* and no one else. "I do not expect to meet the ghûl, but the effort must be made. You should stay, and help to clear the road. Bury that, with what rites you please; the men will return for the strayed camels, but they will not touch the kill. Wait for our return, when you are done. We must consider how best to go on from here."

Julianne thought it would be best to go on quickly, and watchfully; it didn't seem to her to need discussion. She would have no voice in whatever decisions were made, though, she knew that. Rudel seemed a little startled, to have his own authority so ignored; just as well that Elisande hadn't overheard. There was no point adding further fuel to that particular fire.

THE DROVERS DID come back, slowly and warily, bringing the party's string of baggage-camels with them. They were willing enough to drag the dead animals off the road once packs and harness had been cut free, but as Morakh had predicted, they wouldn't even approach the body of their dead master.

Jemel took a short-handled spade from the baggage and went a little way into the sand, to dig the best grave that he could manage. Rudel was thoughtful and detached, Redmond too weak to help, Elisande still busy with Marron, two distant figures on a hilltop; Julianne appointed herself to assist. She gathered rocks to make a cairn, both to mark the grave and keep scavengers from digging up the bones. Building a heap close to where the young Sharai was digging, she said, "Tell me about ghûls, Jemel. I only know what my old nurse told me, tales to scare a naughty child . . ."

"Ghûls can scare a grown man," he grunted, flinging sand. "And should do. They are deadly."

"So are the djinn; but—" *But I have met a djinni and been more angry than scared, though Elisande tells me that was ignorance and not wisdom.*

"If a djinni were a man, a ghûl would be a jackal: mean and vicious, with no thought beyond its belly. But a jackal is a scavenger; ghûls kill. They can kill with terror, as today—I have not asked what shape it came in, but it was fearful. You have seen what its jaws did. They can kill with guile also. Sometimes they take the shape of a woman, to deceive a traveller. By God's grace they cannot change their feet; always they go on asses' hooves. That you should watch for, if you meet a woman alone on empty ground. They are fond of ruins, graveyards, places such as that. This one may haunt the road awhile, if the Dancers do not slay it or drive it off. Good hunting here, for a ghûl."

That was evident, though it had killed the camels not for food, only for the joy of slaughter.

IT WAS JEMEL too who wrapped the body in its own torn cloak for decency, who carried it—alone, altogether too light a burden—to the narrow grave and laid it there. The others gathered then: Rudel and Redmond, even Elisande and Marron, to Julianne's surprise. The boy was again flushed with blood, though there'd been little enough left in the corpse for his own to react to. He came none the less, with Elisande gripping his hand in silent support. Not at all to Julianne's surprise, Jemel moved immediately to stand at Marron's other side.

Redmond spoke, from the head of the grave: chanted

rather, and swayed slightly to the rhythm of his own beating words. A prayer it sounded like, in an old and formal style of Catari that Julianne could barely identify, let alone understand; but she could name it none the less. This was the *khalat,* the death-rite that would sing the slain to paradise; without it, his soul would haunt the ground he died upon. Julianne had heard the *khalat* whispered three times in Roq de Rançon, when Elisande had tried to free the spirits first of the man she'd helped to kill, then of all the Sharai who'd died that night, and then of the dozen boys who'd died the night following, burned in the preceptor's auto-da-fé.

Voices answered Redmond: Rudel's and Elisande's, Jemel's, not Marron's and of course not hers.

The last part of the rite, though, that she could watch and copy, understand and join in. They each took a handful of sand and sprinkled it over the covered body; and as pale grains scattered over dark robe like salt over meat— but no, she didn't want to think about meat, it was only sand on sodden cloth and nothing more—each one nicked a finger on a blade, gave a drop of blood to the dead and said a few words, private thoughts for private sharing here under the bright sun, under the shadow of a stranger's death. They spoke in Catari still, to honour the departed, and Julianne was pleased to find that she could follow it.

Redmond spoke of the Catari vision of paradise, a place of soft air and sweet water, birdsong in gardens; she thought of Bar'ath Tazore, an oasis in a desert, and thought that if she had grown up Sharai in this harsh land—or simple Catari, conquered under the harsh rule of her own people—that would be her vision too, a place of pleasure after the release of death.

Rudel spoke of journey's end, rest after hard travail; Elisande of what was good in travelling, the lessons of experience, the getting of wisdom. Only Jemel spoke of the ghûl, and even he managed to set shock and anger aside, to find some good in a horrific death: "He gave himself to the beast, to save his men. They say he threw himself into its jaws. To choose death for your friends' sake is high honour; to do so for such as they, for servants and vassals, is beyond my praise."

Julianne waited, but no one moved, though no one looked at her. At last she drew her knife and touched point to fingertip, squeezed out a drop of blood and let it fall. She drew a breath to follow and said, "I do not know what is common or right to say, at such a time; and we none of us knew him who is dead here," indeed she didn't even know his name, and wasn't sure if anyone had heard it. "But Jemel says he died bravely, and him I trust; Redmond says he is in paradise, and him I trust. Rudel and Elisande say that his journey was worthwhile, and his peace now well-deserved. The only sadness, then, is that his family is not here to see him buried and hear him praised; I will stand for them, if I may. I have nothing to say of a stranger, but I can grieve his death."

Elisande kissed her. Still no one moved, they were only waiting; there was one more to speak.

Marron said, "He is dead, and I, I did not kill him; that's all I can offer him. Not my blood." *For the God's sake no,* Julianne thought, *not that!*—and thanked the God that Marron had that much sense, at least. "This is dead ground we leave him in. Nor can I open any door to where his soul is now, if anywhere . . ."

And he turned and walked away, and there was a long moment's pause before Jemel and Elisande both hurried after.

Rudel lifted his head, to watch them go; he said, "I hope that boy is right, that he did not kill this man. Myself, I'm not so certain."

Julianne didn't understand that, but the grim expression on Rudel's face made her shiver none the less.

THE DANCERS RETURNED before she'd finished shovelling sand and stacking rocks to build the cairn above the grave. Small help she'd had in that: Redmond had stayed but said little and did less, Rudel had taken a turn with the spade but then excused himself to go and speak with the drovers. Elisande and both the boys were distant figures, holding themselves apart.

She might have resented that—Marron was tireless, the other two were not saddle-sore as she was—but was surprised to find that she did not. Hard work, stretch and sweat was better than the cramping discomfort of her seat on Sildana's back; and it made her feel useful, which was rare on this journey. It also kept her from thinking too deeply, which was also rare, and equally welcome.

But the Dancers returned: a twist in the horizon's shimmer like a flaw in a glass, and then a single broken line of black that marched like killer ants, like the killers that the Dancers were. Rudel went to meet them. For a moment that vision of rapacity stayed with Julianne, so that she wanted to call out, to cry him back.

They brought nothing but their predicted failure with them, so far as she could see. Certainly none of them carried the head of a ghûl as trophy or reassurance, proof that they had slain the monster. When a ghûl died, did its corpse keep the shape it had died in? Might they have come swinging a woman's head by the hair, claiming that it had changed to deceive them—and would they have been believed, if they'd done so? Not by the drovers, she thought, who had seen the ghûl in some more dreadful shape. Rudel and the others would have wanted to see the asses' hooves, to be convinced. Herself, she simply felt glad that the ghûl's trail—or the Dancers'—had not crossed a solitary woman's path this afternoon. She thought those men might have swung the sword without looking for tracks in the sand, or the feet below the robe.

She watched them coming closer, the discipline of single file broken now by Rudel's walking beside Morakh. The discipline of single-mindedness might be broken too, she thought, seeing how those two argued. How Rudel gestured, at least, angry or emphatic or both; how Morakh only walked steadily with his hands hidden in his sleeves, but his head's jerk, his jutting beard's stiffness spoke more loudly than his voice.

As though the Dancers' arrival were a signal, a summoning—unless it was the argument that drew ever-eager Elisande, the hope of seeing her father worsted—that little group of Julianne's friends came down from the hill to join them. To join the debate, as well; as did Redmond, making only a perfunctory sign to her that must have been intended as a sketchy apology, *I'm sorry to leave you with your work unfinished, but . . .*

Seeing the conclave gather without her, now Julianne was resentful. She slammed rocks together, hoping that the noise she made would make her point also, refusing to look and see if it were noticed; she built the cairn as best she could, high enough and strong enough to withstand storms and digging animals, she thought; and then she walked across to where her companions were gathered. As she went, she ostentatiously slapped her hands together to shake off sand and rock-dust.

And went unnoticed or was deliberately ignored, one or the other; and realised that once again dispositions were being made, her future was being decided without reference to her. Now that she could and really did resent. That it was in part her own special friend who was doing it only fed her vexation further.

"Julianne and I," Elisande was saying, "will come with you, Morakh. Whatever others decide." "Others" in this context clearly meant her father; a disdainful twitch of the head in his direction underscored that. And no doubt that was the only reason Elisande was taking such a stance, to be in opposition to her father; and even so, Julianne had had more than enough of hearing what she would or would not do, of never being asked.

"Oh, will we?" she asked, in a voice that had lashed princes and earls before this. Elisande was a princip's granddaughter; Julianne didn't expect the girl to flinch, exactly, but she meant to make her mark. On Elisande's hide, if necessary. "And where is this, that we will go with

Morakh? And why must we divide, what decision is it that will take others elsewhere? Why must our plans change at all? We are delayed, perhaps, but not by half a day . . ."

Morakh and the Dancers stared at her; more than one turned his head towards Rudel or Redmond, expecting to see them discipline her, teach her where her duty lay, in obedience to men. She snorted and turned the same way herself, expecting answers when Elisande gave her only a look that was half stubbornness and half appeal, *back me up in this . . . ?*

"It is suggested," Rudel said neutrally, "that this road should no longer be considered safe: that we should therefore leave it, and take the harder but more direct route across the Sands, across the *mul'abarta.* I say that this is an overreaction, and that we are in any case safer on the road than away from it. My daughter is pleased to disagree with me."

As ever, in every meaning of the phrase. Julianne nibbled at her lip where it was chafing in the heat, glanced at Elisande and then at Morakh. This must have come from him, so . . .

"Morakh? Why is the road unsafe? One has died here, but we are warned now, we can be watchful . . ."

"Can you watch against a creature that may shadow any living thing, that takes what image it desires? Can you distrust every man and every woman on the road? A ghûl will haunt a place where it can feed in safety; a road such as this, where people come and go but no one guards, it will haunt until it is killed or driven off. We could not find it, but it will be here. Also, it might not be accident that we so nearly met it first."

"How not?"

"It might be hunting one of us," and his mouth did not, but his eyes said *Marron.*

Rudel had said almost the same thing, by the grave. This time she asked, "Why?"

"The Ghost Walker would draw such a thing from half the world away."

Again, *why?* She saved her breath, though; he had clamped his lips together behind his beard and turned his back, a little disgusted with himself perhaps for having taken so much talk with a woman.

Redmond picked up the thread, and made an argument of it. "If Marron draws the creature, he will draw it into the desert also, and we will be no safer. Less, perhaps."

A dismissive gesture of the head, and, "In the Sands we are alone; whomever we meet, man or woman, is an enemy until they prove themselves a friend. An animal is prey. In the Sands, simplicity is guard."

And on the road not so: life was complex and unpredictable, everything was shaded, appearance deceived. It made sense, in a way.

But, "I cannot cross the *mul'abarta,*" Redmond said.

"No." No argument there, from the Dancer or from anyone. Julianne had not travelled in the true desert yet, but even she knew that much. "You can go to Rhabat by the road," Morakh went on, "alone or you can take the women with you—"

"No," instantly from Elisande, leaping in before Julianne could gather breath to get there. "Where Marron goes, we go."

Which was interesting, no part of the djinni's charge laid on them, but no surprise to Julianne. Nor to Morakh, though by the look on his face it was more than unwelcome. The Dancers were unfussy about veils, to the point where both girls had virtually discarded them, using them only as the men did, to mask their faces against the gritty wind; it was the entire presence of women that revolted the Dancers, against which their naked faces were no more than an irritant, a speck of dirt in an open and poisoned wound.

"I think it is foolhardy to leave the road," Rudel said, glowering, "but similarly, where Marron goes I will go. Perhaps Marron himself should say, where he will go . . . ?"

At least that one was easy for the boy. He looked

around at the Dancers, at Jemel, at Elisande, and said, "I do not care much, where I go; but if we will be safer in the Sands, then perhaps it might be wise to take that route."

"Marron, you betray your own ignorance with every word," Rudel countered: "No one is safe in the Sands. The Great Waste, your people calls them, and with good reason."

That was a mistake; Marron's face closed down. "I have no people," he said, his voice harsh and broken suddenly. "Not there," with a jerk of his head to the west, to Outremer, "nor there," to the south, to Rhabat. "Nor these either," the Dancers, "and not you, Rudel. I go where my friends go; if they choose the Sands, then so do I."

His friends only chose the Sands because he did, to go with him. Sometimes Julianne thought this whole mission was like that, a quest to nothing; it was hard these days to remember the djinni's warning, her father's peril. She was the one with the most need to reach Rhabat; the rest she thought followed each other, and it was only chance that took them all in the same direction. Chance and stubbornness. Elisande went to watch Marron and to spite her father, more than to support her friend or to obey the djinni; Rudel went to watch Marron and his daughter both, Jemel to watch Marron only, deferring even his vengeance to that end. Redmond—Redmond was old and hurt and should be going home. He was the only one of sense among them, she thought, ready to quit their company sooner than ride the *mul'abarta,* but still he was going to Rhabat. Not so much sense after all . . .

"So be it," he said then, strength of will overriding the weakness of his body, or he wanted them to think so. "You follow your paths, and be careful; I will take the slow road, and be patient. I will organise these frail folk," the drovers, "and bring their master's goods in with me. They will loot them all, else. I have played the merchant too often to see that with equanimity, it offends my soul."

"Old rogue, you were a thief before ever you were a trader."

"Even so. A thief reformed, which means the most rigid of men." Redmond and Rudel grinned at each other; Elisande growled in her throat.

"Rigid as that one will be rigid soon," she snapped, jerking her head back towards the fresh cairn, "if you travel alone. Those frail folk will slit your frail throat, Redmond, and take their loot regardless of your corpse."

"Not they. They'd be afraid of my ghost."

"And might meet it even if they do nothing. You need more than a companion to watch your back; you need a healer to keep you upright through the day. Do you think I don't know how much strength you've been taking from Rudel? How do you imagine you're going to manage without it?"

"Poorly, I confess. So come with me, Elisande: you and Julianne both. She can watch my back while you stand in for your father, lend me your youth and resilience . . ."

"I do not have the skill," she replied tartly, without a hint of regret. "You know that. Take Rudel. Neither of you is needed, in the Sands."

"None of you is needed in the Sands," said Morakh, with simple blinding truth. "For the sake of the Ghost Walker, because we are his servants, we will take those he names to come; but none other. Fetch up the camels now, it is time to prepare. If ghûls sleep, I have never heard it. We should be far from this road by nightfall."

IF JULIANNE HAD thought that leaving the road would be a simple matter and leaving Redmond the only difficult part of it, she was swiftly disabused. Two of the Dancers walked back along the road, searching it seemed among the baggage discarded in the panic of the ghûl's attack; the others unloaded everything from the pack-camels, and began to slash open the cords that tied the food-sacks.

"What are they doing?" she demanded of Elisande. "Surely we're going to need that, more than ever?"

"Of course. We'll eat nothing in the Sands, bar what we can hunt or glean or carry. But can you carry one of those flour-sacks?"

"No, but the camels . . . Aren't we taking the camels?"

"Yes, we're taking the camels. Camels die, though, sweetheart; sometimes you have to let the camels die. Sometimes you have to kill them, or else die yourself. Never take anything into the desert that you need but can't carry on your own back, because you may well have to do that."

"Elisande—just how dangerous is this journey now?" Not a stroll, of course, not a pleasure-trip: but if those dour Dancers judged it safer than keeping to the road, then it couldn't be so very bad. Could it?

"Julianne, my love, this is the most dangerous journey of your life, the most dangerous adventure you've ever undertaken. Believe that. You must believe it, or you will endanger us all, even more than we are endangered already."

No. She would believe many things, she would believe everything that Elisande had ever told her, but not that. She closed her eyes and remembered falling, *falling and falling, and in the dark too*—her life had hung by a stretching thread during that endless fall. Nothing here could push her close to such an edge again . . .

And yet, when she opened her eyes, she saw not her friend's determined face urgent with its message, nor the busyness about her on the road: only the desert, the *mul'abarta,* the Sands. Grey dust and gravel underfoot, golden dunes building just a little walk away; building and building, a rolling sea of sand broken only by hills like rocks and darkening with distance so that what was far away—what she looked at now, what held her eye— was red under the burning sun and shimmered like a dreamscape, moved momentously towards her like the sea . . .

"Hush now and watch," Elisande said. "These men know more than I ever will; we can both of us learn by watching . . ."

EACH OF THE Dancers carried water and flour in evil-smelling goatskins, pressed dates in a wrap of rags. Julianne had noticed that already, though they'd been using the company's general store of food and not their own. Necessarily, she supposed, each man's rations must be enough to see him through the desert, at least from one well or one oasis to the next, as they had no beasts to carry more. Unless they did use pack-camels on a long march, they might be forced to do that, although they would not ride. She knew so little about how the Dancers lived . . .

She would learn more in these next days, that much was clear. Obedient to Elisande's command, she watched them now as they transferred flour and dried fish from sacks into scavenged skins.

"Why not the rice?" she asked, seeing how they left some sacks untouched.

"It takes too much water to cook. It's water that matters now, Julianne. We can live hungry, on a handful of flour a day—and wait till you've eaten desert bread, it's a revelation—but thirst is the killer."

"Dried fish will make us thirsty . . ."

"The fish is for the camels. We'll find little forage for them; it may be that they have to eat before we do."

INDEED THEY FED the camels with all they had of green-stuff, before they left the road. Redmond had taken brisk charge of the drovers, as they returned one by one with their strayed camels; those beasts were laden high now and tied nose to tail, a caravan ready to march.

He was satisfied but sombre, anxious about his friends' more perilous journey; he tried once again to persuade the

Dancers that there would be less danger on the road. Safety in numbers, he pleaded, now they were alert against the ghûl; so much greater risk their way, not the ghûl alone but all the possible mischances of the desert too, especially with those who were strangers to it . . .

"We will watch them," Morakh said. "The Sands are ours; we know where evil lurks, and can avoid it. The ghûl will haunt the road—they do not love the desert, nor the Dancers. I have killed a ghûl before this. You stand at greater risk than we do; be prepared."

Redmond sighed, and conceded. Then he said a slow and private farewell to each of the companions. Julianne couldn't hear what more than farewell he said to any of the others, but to her he murmured, "This is an adventure—more than your father or any of us had hoped for you, child. Enjoy it when you can, learn from it whatever you can; but above all come safe through it to Rhabat, and bring your sister with you . . ."

Soul-sister he meant, she understood him perfectly; and kissed him before he could her, and gave her promise to hold fast to Elisande.

She watched him give messages—the same or similar, surely, what else could he say?—to Marron and to Jemel, though both boys flinched a little from his words. Then Redmond mounted his camel, threw his arm in a wide gesture that ended with his riding stick pointed firmly to the south, and called much the same thing to them all: "Go straight and safely to Rhabat, and meet me there!"

Julianne twisted her head aside, wrenched suddenly by the loss of him when she thought she'd been managing so well; and so she happened to see Morakh's face before he could control it, and she had a moment to wonder why mention of Rhabat should make him smile so when he was not a man who smiled, when he himself had said that the Dancers did not go to Rhabat . . .

Then he caught her gaze, and turned away; and the blaze of the sun stung her eyes where she'd stood in his shadow and not realised it.

5

The Pillar of Lives

MARRON FELT THAT he had been remade for this exactly:
the heat underfoot and in the air to match the heat in his
blood that surged and pulsed in sunlight, that was very
much a creature of the Sands and nothing at all of what
had once been his; the slow endurance of the days to
match the slow endurance of his body, that could run
grimly all day and all night too if he willed it so, and there
seemed so much to run from; the dark robe that cloaked
him, the dark figures that surrounded him to match the
shadows that swathed his heart, the dead and the betrayed
he'd left behind him.

He had been remade, he thought, to be the Daughter's
host and nothing more, no vestige of himself.

He thought he should resist that, but it was hard to do.
The sun drained him, the stars sucked at his soul, the
desert was alien and endless so that he felt utterly lost
within it; the Dancers were with him constantly, allowing
him no privacy. This was how they wanted him, only a
vessel, a doorway to open at their word. It was his abiding

failure to do that which served as a reminder that he was still Marron after all, still a boy with a history and sometimes a touch of hope.

Elisande knew something at least of what was happening to him, and tried to help. Whenever they paused to rest, at the sun's height and at night, she brought him food and sat with him while he ate it, talking of the world they'd left, of Outremer, or else of Rhabat where they were headed; she asked him questions too about his childhood, though he was finding it increasingly difficult to remember that. And the Dancers were always there, always listening as they plucked at bread with their maimed hands, condemning her with their silence.

Jemel sought Marron's company less often now, or less obviously. He had taken the string of pack-animals as his duty, which kept him at the tail of the line of riders and kept him busy at the halts. When he did try to come closer, he couldn't breach the wall of Dancers that enclosed Marron. They had rejected him, and the bruise was sore yet.

IT HAD BEEN their first night in the Sands, that Jemel had made his declaration. He'd left Marron's side without a word, and had taken a flat stone to the Dancers' fire; had sat in their circle without invitation, and laid the stone on the sand before them like an offering.

Confused, intrigued, Marron had followed him a little way over, just close enough to see and hear what had passed.

Jemel had spoken to Morakh, as the leader of the band; had said, "You serve the Ghost Walker; so do I. I would like to swear myself to your brotherhood, to be as you are, wholly committed. Give me grace to join you in your service . . ."

And he had laid his left hand out on the stone, with the fingers spread; had taken his knife from his sash and set the edge against the lowest joint of his smallest finger; had looked to Morakh for the nod of permission.

And Morakh had said no.

Had said, "No, you may not. I know you, tribeless; I know that you have sworn another oath, which touches on another life. This corrupts you. And I also doubt your desire for the Ghost Walker's eye; your intent is not pure, it defiles him and you. We will have none of you."

Jemel had hesitated, and Marron had thought for a moment that he might have cut anyway, regardless. But the young Sharai had sheathed his knife and nodded, had risen and walked away without another word.

He had walked away from the fires then, out under the blazing stars, alone; and when Marron had followed, Jemel had sworn at him spittingly and turned his back.

HE DIDN'T TURN his back now, but neither did he come close; only lurked, gazed from a distance and tended his animals obsessively to keep himself from gazing longer. Even Elisande could find no way to reach him. That was one tool, one weapon she used to keep some kind of grip on Marron, feather-light and failing though it was: Jemel's detachment made it easier for Marron to slip into numb acceptance of the Dancers' will, but Elisande's anxiety about the Sharai could pull him back where his own could not. Pull him back a little, at least, though not far and less far every day . . .

The desert made strong things weak, he thought, and not only bodies. He could watch the bonds between people fraying as the Dancers' robes frayed at the hem, where they pulled threads loose to make tinder; some he thought might flame suddenly and shrivel as those threads did when a spark caught them.

Rudel, he thought, might scorch every hand that reached to touch him. The older man rode with a constant glower, making plain his distrust of the Dancers and his disavowal of every decision made since they'd left the road. He argued as always with his daughter, but now also with everyone else. If there'd been another Patric man in the party—well, any Patric man bar Redmond, who was so much missed—they'd have come to blows by now. More than once, he'd nearly come to knives with one Sharai or another.

It was the desert doing this, Marron thought, remembering the wise and witty jongleur whom Rudel had been in the castle, courteous and diplomatic and endlessly patient. The sands blew in, and made gritty what had once been smooth; clean and solid structures deformed in the heat. The desert separated people from themselves. He'd have been more frantic than fretful, bitterly concerned, if only it hadn't separated him so far from what was Marron, what was capable of concern . . .

Instead he only watched and saw it happen, and wondered what would happen next. He felt himself some kind of witness on this journey, observing and remembering, all but untouched by the pain and the anger, the fear and the scorn the others bartered between them. As he was by the journey itself, the long toiling miles of it, as they were not.

Since he could not do what he was meant to do, he was as useless to the Dancers as he was to his friends. They guarded him not for his own sake, but for what he carried. He was their talisman; they meant him to be their tool. He watched them also, and listened where he could, though they used a private language between themselves that he couldn't quite follow. It seemed somehow to snag at his understanding, teasing him like a face behind a veil, allowing him glimpses that always fell just short of recognition. He thought perhaps the Daughter could understand it; a man who could use the Daughter as it was meant to be used could perhaps use it for this also, to open a doorway into comprehension. All he could do was mark it up as another minor failure, of a piece with what was greater.

When the Dancers spoke with his own people, though, he needed no translator. Even when they spoke Catari: he was as fluent in that now as in his own tongue. He thought again that that was the Daughter's doing, mostly, although Jemel's had been the hand that drew the veil back.

He had overheard—from a distance, the Daughter's gift; sharpening his ears as all his senses—the first time that Rudel had questioned the route they followed, more west than south; he had heard Morakh's reply, that the tribe holding the land to the south was no friend to the Patric. Dancers could travel freely anywhere among the Sharai, and Jemel perhaps, now that he had forsworn his allegiance. For their own safety, though, Rudel and his party must skirt this territory . . .

"We of Surayon have a special dispensation," Rudel had growled in response. "I have never been other than welcome, to any tribe."

"Times are changing," Morakh had said. "Even Surayon is in Outremer, and so accursed. Hasan has drawn the tribes together in this, and word of the Ghost Walker will be spreading also; our people will see that as a sign. You would find yourself less than welcome now. You can go your own way, if you choose; but if you go with us, you must trust our choices."

Rudel trusted nothing about the Dancers, that much was clear, but he had said no more that day.

This day, though, they'd climbed a rocky bluff above a wadi, and now their only course was west and nothing but west; the steep fall down to the wadi was overmatched by cliffs to the south. They walked atop a wall, leading the slow camels; by the midday halt, Rudel's doubts had mounted into fury.

"This is useless to us!" he stormed, in full hearing of the whole party. "There's no break to these cliffs, where we might take the camels down. We should go back, and strike south straight away. I'll risk the Ashti or any tribe else, sooner than wander like some lost soul in the *mul'abarta* till our food runs out and we lose all trace of water. Our mission is urgent, Morakh, and imperative."

"You will risk the tribes, even when they are risen against you? Good. Will you also risk the ghûl?"

"The ghûl? What ghûl? We left that days ago, by the road. That's why we came this way, at your insistence . . ."

"I was wrong," Morakh said simply. "I had misunderstood it, perhaps—though it behaves like no ghûl I have heard of. Something drives it, more than hunger; it may have smelled out the Ghost Walker, and be drawn to him. It has followed us, at least, since we left the road. We have found tracks; last night I saw a shadow skirt our camp."

"Why have you not said, before this?"

"What point? We know the danger, and we guard against it. So long as you trust no strangers and keep your swords to hand, you will be as safe as you can be. It will not attack a group alert, as we are. This is neutral ground we stand on, sacred, forbidden to the tribes; if the tribeless one were still Saren, we could not have brought you here. The ghûl may be afraid to follow, where God has walked; I do not know. But if you go down, how will you know what chance encounter is a woman drawing water on her own land, and what is a ghûl eager for your blood?"

It seemed a fair question, though Rudel gave no fair answer, only a snort and a dubious glare. "Next time you see a monster's tracks, I would appreciate it if you showed them to me."

"As you wish."

"In the meantime, can you say how we will find our way to Rhabat? This sacred crag of yours is leading us far astray . . ."

Morakh's face darkened at what might have been a blasphemy of tone, what might be a case of knives against this rud-skinned Patric; but there was perhaps a law against the spilling of blood in high and holy places, or else he was uncertain of his ground, or more peaceable than he appeared. "Be easy," he said shortly. "The ridge rises to a flank of hills tomorrow, where a track comes down to the open sands again. From there, due south and perhaps a week's travel lie the Dead Waters, and so Rhabat. Are you content?"

"When we stand in that place, I will be content."

"Even so."

A gesture that was not the graceful bow of Sharai convention but a deliberate mockery of it, and so an insult; Rudel's turn to flush. But he said nothing, and he kept his hand far from the haft of his dagger. Marron felt that he should be grateful for so much self-control; only that the Daughter was singing high and pure in his ears and had been all day, louder and more strident every hour, and tugging his mind further still from any human sympathy. He rather thought the Daughter might have liked a little blood. Perhaps this place really was holy, and that was what it responded to; perhaps it only felt its power more, its slow victory over what had been Marron, and so exulted.

Marron felt its power more, that much was certain. The higher they climbed this ridge, the clearer the air, the further he could see across the Sands; and all he saw was sand and rock and shadow, and all of it reddened by the Daughter's bloodied eye, and that he thought was his life now, what was left that he could call his own: barren and dry and overcast by an eye and a will that was not his own at all.

SWEPT BY THE wind of centuries and scoured by what sand the wind could lift up from the plain below, the bare rock was smooth beneath their feet, even the bare feet of the Sharai. Marron was forbidden to go shoeless, for fear of a cut; the girls chose not to. Elisande had said, "I have done that, when I was a hoyden; it took years to be rid of the skin I was left with, like dried leather, I could strop my knives on it. I did. Now I am a lady, I prefer to keep my feet soft and pink and sweet of my perfume . . ."

Even Jemel had smiled. Julianne had collapsed in giggles; only Rudel had schooled his face to stillness, and even he had seemed to take a little effort over it.

Rudel also wore his boots beneath his robe; Marron thought he kept spare knives sheathed in them. But then he thought so did Elisande, now she was a lady . . .

The rock was smooth but awkward; that same wind that had abraded its harsh edges had cut it also into uneven steps, up and down. Where the camels could be ridden, progress was still slow. Marron ranged ahead, with his constant companions the Dancers; a couple of them had gone further still, scouting or hunting, though he thought their bows would find little meat on this denuded height.

Morakh walked beside him, but for once was not speaking of the Daughter and how to control it. Neither had he forced Marron to the test, to yet another failure at the noon break. That was the first time in days. He had perhaps been distracted by the argument with Rudel; that was perhaps unfortunate for him, for his cause, with the Daughter seeming so alive in Marron's blood this day, its shrill song jagged in his ears. Himself, he was only glad of the respite.

Gazing ahead, he saw the two Dancers as dim dark shadows in the eternal red, tiny shadows, too far away for normal sight to find. He watched them moving, and then he saw them standing still, waiting as it seemed.

He walked on with the others, and they waited. After a while, when they were sharp and clear to his adapted eyes, he saw one of them stand tall and gesture stiffly, his arms making signs in bright light.

Marron pointed, needlessly; Morakh had seen already. He stepped up onto a high rock, wind whipping his robe as his arms whipped the air, stabbing forcefully. The distant Dancer shaped a sign in response, and then stood still.

He has found something . . . He wants to show it to us . . .

Possibly anyone with clear sight and an abstracted mind could have understood such basic signs; possibly that touch of familiarity, that sense of a veil lifting in the wind to show the face beneath was no more real than a mirage. Possibly. But Marron felt the Daughter fizzing throughout his body, and couldn't truly doubt it. The Dancers' spoken language might still be shadowed even up here, he wasn't sure, but their language of signs was open and accessible for him to read.

He said nothing, though, he only followed as Morakh hurried forward.

THAT NARROW WALL of rock had widened into a broad shelf by the time they reached the waiting Dancers. Ahead, at the furthest limit of Marron's sight, a line of shadow lay across the horizon, first glimpse of those hills that Morakh had promised.

A dusting of sand gritted underfoot; in places here it had pooled like water in dips and crevices too deep for the wind to rake clear. The Dancers were standing by one such dip, where level stone was interrupted by a run of sand before the stone thrust up again.

The sand had been smooth, and would be smooth again; already particles were flying in the wind, whipped away, the sharp edges of the tracks eroding as Marron watched.

The tracks of an ass's hooves, except that there were only two, spaced as a small man might space his feet if he were hurrying, a small man or a woman . . .

"Shield those from the wind," Morakh snapped. "Rudel will like to see them."

MARRON COULDN'T WAIT for the riders to come up; this shelf might be broader now, but it was still no place to terrify an animal. He withdrew to a prudent distance, and sat with his back against a rounded pinnacle of rock. He could see well enough, and hear too; he heard the whisper of the camels' feet on sand and rock as they approached, he heard the questions passed from rider to rider, the silence that fell after as they saw their answer.

He heard the thud of Rudel's boots hitting ground, his stomping paces forward. In the next moment of silence, that moment where Morakh might perhaps have spoken— *see, unbeliever?*—and did not, he thought he even heard the insuck of Rudel's breath as that man stood and gazed down at the ghûl's prints in the sand.

"What, even here? I thought you said that it followed us?"

"So it did."

"And now it is ahead. How did it come here? Nothing has passed us, and we were camped at the foot of the climb all night. You watched, and so did I. Did it fly up, is it a harpy now?"

"What is a harpy?"

"Part woman, part bird. A woman with wings."

"And claws," from Elisande, never content to hold back at any meeting where her father had a voice. "Harpies snatch."

"A harpy now, why not?" Morakh said, with an exaggerated shrug. "A woman with wings, it can be that if it chooses. If it has the idea in its head. They are stupid creatures, but they can take an idea and hoard it like a treasure . . ."

"Harpies come from stories," Elisande objected, "not from truth."

"So. The ghûls listen to stories when they can, or so the stories say."

"I meant I don't believe in your harpy." Her father's harpy, rather. He had blatantly not meant it as a serious proposal, but it had come from him, and so she must reject it. "It must have come some other way, got ahead of us in yesterday's travel. Or there are two of them, why not? There could be two?"

Again, Morakh shrugged. "There could be two, there could be many. We could be hunted by ghûls, though I have never heard that they hunted in a pack before. It could have taken goat-shape and climbed up from the wadi, perhaps . . ."

He gestured north, but that bluff was too far now, they couldn't see how steep it fell away. No one volunteered to ride across and look; some at least were thinking of a ghûl, crouched out of sight and waiting . . .

"It is here," Morakh went on. "That matters. Not how it came."

"So what do we do," Julianne asked, exposed by her nervousness, "go back?"

"No. If it hunts us, it would follow; if there is another we would meet it, perhaps where we could not fight. This is better ground than this morning. We will go on; we know it is ahead, we can be watchful. And we, we Dancers know this way, as the ghûl may not. We will lead you in the dark, and so deceive it."

"And if it takes some form of life, something monstrous that can see in the dark?" Rudel demanded.

"Then it will not be deceived. It hunts us anyway; we lose nothing. And if it sought to attack, there is nothing that can see in the dark, in the Sands, better than the Ghost Walker. We would have warning."

"Marron can neither walk nor watch all night." Jemel, objecting fiercely, where Marron might have expected Elisande.

"Do not be foolish, boy. He can, and so can we. Even the women can at need, though we will not push them so far. If the ghûl come, it dies; if not, we have a better chance to evade it, if we keep moving at least some hours of the night. At moonrise, there will be light enough to cast strong shadow. You know this, you have seen. We do not truly need the eyes of the Ghost Walker, our own are good enough."

Then how will you evade the eyes of what tracks us? He was too far away to ask, and too little interested; a night march would be welcome, a welcome change from common nights. He needed little sleep now, and the Dancers spoke to him in shifts while he was wakeful. Sometimes he lay down and pretended to sleep, only to escape their whispers, but that was small improvement. Hours of tedious discomfort on hard and stony ground were as nothing to the timeless, endless parade behind his eyes: what he had done; what he had not done, what he would doubtless do and not do in the long ache of shame and sorrow and self-disgust that would be his life to come, however it come out . . .

THEY RODE ON, leaving the ghûl-sign in the sand for any later traveller to read, if travellers came before the wind had finished its deletion. Marron strode on, no need to run; he could lead the camels and outpace them walking, where they were so cautious. He'd like to outpace the Dancers too, but they were constant as his shadow, and as fast. If he chose to run, they'd match him up here as they had on the sands below. He might outrun them on a road—he didn't know how fast he could run now: faster than before, though, that much he could count on, as well as very much further—but not on uncertain ground which they knew and he did not.

One thing he did know, though, or seemed to: he knew where they were going, although what waited there was a mystery to him as all this land was. Or perhaps not where they were going, but where the Daughter wanted to go, at least—he could feel it, no longer a passenger but something stronger, more demanding, impelling his feet forward. The wadi had turned away to the north, so that this was a high plateau that they walked on now; there was no visible path, nothing to hold him to the line of the southern cliffs except Morakh's promise of an eventual way down, and the knowledge of Rudel's intent to take that way. Whenever he tried to wander, though—and he did try, if only to test himself or the Daughter, to challenge this compulsion—the song in his ears grew harsh and discordant, his arm throbbed and threatened worse, his legs grew heavy as though he waded through water that flowed against him. If he only paused to look back at the following riders, even so small a resistance was difficult, almost painful.

Soon he abandoned any rebellion, and simply set his eyes and his will directly ahead. That was easy; for a wonder even the Dancers fell back, or rather allowed him to forge on alone. The wind was dry and clean, the heat lifted as the sun lowered, he could walk and walk and never tire of walking.

Due west he went, leading or being led, both; the range of hills on the horizon grew slowly, marking an end that they would not reach on this march. He wondered what would happen tomorrow, if the route to the south opened before the Daughter was done with calling or driving him west. He must betray one or the other, and he had betrayed so much already . . .

He thought it likely that he would leave his friends, or force them to follow him; he could neither leave nor deny the Daughter. But that was for tomorrow to resolve. Today, tonight he had nothing to do but walk.

Briefly, as the sun set directly in his sight, he thought he saw the shadow of something tall against its brilliance, a tower or a pinnacle of rock; momentarily he thought it was a needle, seeing a flash of fire through its rooted eye.

Morakh hailed him then, from some distance back. Marron turned, and saw the Dancer's arm move in a gesture that anyone could have read, *wait there, until we come*. That made sense; even the Ghost Walker should not walk alone in the dark, however certain he felt his path to be. Not where a ghûl might be lurking behind any rock. He was surprised they'd let him come so far on his own, even in daylight. Would the Daughter be a match for a ghûl? He didn't know, and didn't want to discover.

He might have asked Morakh when the Dancers caught up, but did not. Neither did he ask about that needle of rock, though its image still burned behind his eye. His curiosity was a small thing, all but smothered under weightier concerns. Nor was Morakh an easy man to question, or a natural confidant. If he could have walked with Jemel or Elisande, he might have tried their knowledge, but that was impossible while they rode.

The party closed up with the sudden fall of night, the riders coming as close to Marron and the Dancers as their animals could bear. For an hour they went by starlight, and slowly; desert stars threw strange shadows underfoot, though they were bright enough even for mortal eyes. To Marron's they were a gorgeous blaze, a veil of scarlet fire thrown across the sky.

When the moon rose they could make a faster way across the uneven rock, and did for several hours, until Rudel called out that the girls were swaying in their saddles. A snort from Elisande might have disputed that, but Julianne at least confessed it. So they made camp in a bowl they found, a little dell of rock where the low walls offered at least some shelter from the wind and gathered sand offered a softer bed than stone, if not much softer. They made no fire that night, despite the chill of air and ground; they must harbour what fuel they had, Rudel said. Morakh said nothing to that, but agreed that it would be foolish to set a light that might attract any eye that sought them.

They organised watches in stints for what remained of the night: Rudel and Jemel, and then the Dancers, two by two. No one suggested including Marron, though he didn't expect to sleep. The Dancers of course would watch for his protection, which was perhaps some hint how he might—or might not—survive an encounter with a ghûl; Rudel and Jemel both he thought would watch him, as much as they watched the rocks and the shadows and the sands below the cliffs. Both would have their reasons.

And both, all of them might be right, he thought, to keep more than half an eye on him, if only to cry the alert if he tried to slip away while others slept. His feet might take him, he thought, even against the wishes or the instinct of his mind. His feet, he thought, were barely under his command now; if his attention wandered, if his thoughts did drift into the margins of sleep . . .

Even now, wide-eyed and focused as he was, his feet had brought him to the far western lip of the hollow where they camped. Nor was it his feet alone that were drawn so, to the edge of rebellion; his eyes strained westward, seeking he knew not what, but finding—or so he imagined—a thread of dark caught between land and sky; crimson thread against scarlet cloth, a night thread that might well be a needle by day, tall enough now that it didn't need a red-ochre sun behind to make it show.

When he looked back to call or gesture one of his friends up to say if they could see it too with human eyes unfiltered, it cost him an effort to turn his head even so much, so little from their westerly path; it cost his eyes a genuine pain, a stabbing hurt that was worse for being so unexpected. He'd thought himself immune to pain now, he thought the Daughter drank it, except when he opened his arm to let that creature out and pain flowed back to fill the space where it had been.

Besides, they were busy down there, making camp and setting watches, feeding the animals, feeding themselves. Soon no doubt Elisande would come to feed him, and he could ask her then.

So he stayed where he was and as he was, eyes and thoughts all bent to the horizon and more interested now in that needle, that stood so exactly in their line of travel. It could be coincidence, he supposed, a way-marker and nothing more; but this hunger in the Daughter was nothing random. There was an object, a place it yearned for, to which it meant to drag his body whether he would or no. And that hunger had grown so quickly through this day, surely it meant that they were coming close . . .

Elisande did bring him food, cold and leathery bread from that morning's bake. He tore at it to soothe her, and asked to test her eyes for his reward. She frowned, squinted, stared; said, "I'm not sure. Perhaps, I think I do

see something, like a pillar, a pinnacle . . . ? Silver in the
moonlight, but what isn't . . . ?"

Which, as he had not said what he would have her see,
was satisfaction and answer enough.

"Why don't you ask the Dancers?" she asked, glancing
round her suddenly, registering his solitude and seeming
as surprised as he was. "If there's anything there, they'd
know it."

"That's why I don't ask them—because if there's anything there, they must be prepared for us to ask, and
would you trust what they told you?"

She tilted her head and gazed at him thoughtfully, a little sadly. "We've all changed, and are changing," she said.
"Except Rudel, obviously. But you—ah, you're not the
same boy at all, and I do miss that Marron. Too much wisdom isn't good for you. You're young yet, Marron, despite the age of that thing in your bones; can't you be a
little foolish sometimes? Just for me?"

He opened his mouth to say that he was, that he had
been, and recently so—but remembered just in time that
he'd been with Jemel then, which he thought wasn't what
she meant at all.

And here was Jemel, coming up with the smell of
camels hot and heavy on his clothes and skin, though the
smell of boy was stronger. Marron hoped he'd adjust soon
to such intensity; he didn't think he could live for long in
so enriched a world. Perhaps that was why the Daughter
made him feel so detached from it, so uncommitted. It
was only his friends who caught him, held him back.

Jemel came, and Elisande left; Marron chewed bread in
silence, then pointed to the horizon when Jemel was
equally silent and asked what the young Sharai could see.

"A tower, or a pillar of rock," was the immediate answer.
"A tower, with light at its door?" To be sure, a star's gleam
showed through the eye of the needle; even to the sharp
eyes of a Sharai, it could look like a lamp at a doorway.
"But I have never heard of anything such, in the Sands. The
hermits are all dead or fled, and none of them built so high.

If some madman had made himself a desert hold, we should have heard, the Dancers should have told us . . ."

"So they should," Marron agreed. "Perhaps they don't know of it. Don't mention it to them, Jemel, not tonight." If it were new, they would be shamed by their ignorance, and doubly so by his finding it out; they were his guides in this their world, and even the Ghost Walker should not lead here. But he did not believe that it was new. He thought that they knew it, whatever it was; and whatever it was, they chose to march towards it through the dark. He thought that might be no accident.

His feet burned to be moving, to get on. Due west, and directly toward the needle. He thought that might be no accident either.

EVEN THE LITTLE distance down from the lip of the bowl and towards where his friends sat in a chilly huddle, where the Dancers sat in another, where Jemel stood uncertainly between—even those few short paces were next to impossible. He walked or tried to walk against a fierce will, against the solidity of air, as though a gale blew directly against him although the night was still. Standing had been hard, like standing in a tugging stream, a torrent; it hadn't hurt. This hurt.

A few grim, determined, stumbling steps were all that he could manage by himself, and all that he was allowed to try. Jemel came back to him, almost at a run; Elisande started up with a soft cry, gazed at him—at them—and subsided slowly.

"What is it?"

"Me. It's just me," *as it always has been.* "Best if I sleep apart tonight," as he always did only higher, further and the only way that he could go. The camels agreed with him; although they had been couched on the far side of the hollow, it was none the less too close for them, they were grunting and restless, lying still only because they were hobbled too tight to stand.

"Best you sleep," Jemel said sourly, "I care not where. And I with you; you must not be alone tonight."

Marron didn't argue. He turned and floated back up to the ridge, feeling that he hardly need set foot on the earth; the absent wind would carry him west, the wind that blew in his mind and only there, unless some shred of it whispered also among the Dancers.

Stopping was not easy, but he did stop; he had Jemel at his side and could grip his arm for steadiness, for the little time it took to take control again of his feet.

In order to tempt them no further, he sat down, setting his back against an outcrop and gazing, gazing west, gazing at the needle.

"This will do," he said, drawing his robe about him as though he meant to sleep. "How long do we rest?"

"Until dawn, you. I have the last watch, before."

"Then lie down, and sleep."

Jemel did, like a servant at his master's feet. Marron scowled, and shifted a little further off. And turned his eyes and his mind to the needle, squinting through the red-hazed night, trying to see what he could not quite make out, trying to understand what he could not grasp either out there or within himself.

Closing his eyes was useless, turning his head or his thoughts aside was impossible. He thought it would be a long night, although they'd marched through half of it already.

HE THOUGHT SO, and was wrong. Barely two hours had passed before there was a cry in the night, and the grate of steel; Marron heard nothing more than that, until he heard the sleepers waking, calling to each other and to the watch, running to see.

Running east; Marron stayed where he was. Jemel started to go, then checked and came back.

"What has happened?"

"Hush . . ."

Distantly he could hear Rudel and Morakh questioning one of the Dancers, who had stood on watch; who had seen a moving shadow in the moonlight, as it might have been a woman slipping from rock to rock and stealing closer. He'd thought it best to cry out, to wake the camp; he'd known it best to draw his scimitar. A man only ever had one chance to slay a ghûl . . .

Marron relayed that, and Jemel's own scimitar hissed from its scabbard. "Indeed; and the dark is no time for an arrow. Shall we move?"

Marron nodded, but his feet stayed rooted. He was fairly sure they'd move, yes—but not to hunt the ghûl. Jemel perforce stayed with him, as self-appointed companion and protector only ever reluctantly relieved by Dancers; when Morakh came to do that duty, Jemel at last found cause and courage to challenge him.

"Well? Did your man see true, is there a ghûl in the rocks?"

"We found tracks that were not ours, nor yet a goat's: something two-legged and hoofed, it seems to be. We would see better in daylight."

"Undoubtedly. And it would seem we must wait till daylight, before you go to follow those tracks."

"By daylight," Morakh said after one slow, controlling breath, "we hope to be far from here. No one can sleep now, and we will be safer moving; let the ghûl follow us. We can rest in the day, when we can see what moves around us. Do you see to your camel now, boy. I will watch the Ghost Walker."

Jemel snarled, but that was sheer temper. He slammed his weapon back into its sheath and ran off, to where other members of the party were indeed busy around the camels.

Marron turned his back to the scene, standing fully exposed on the lip of the hollow, his eyes once more drawn to the needle that he saw as darkness, that others saw as light. He didn't think he stood in any danger now. Indeed, Morakh made no move even to touch hand to sword's hilt, to be ready to draw. He stood with arms folded, watching Marron, watching his stance, watching the direction of his eyes.

"How far is it?" Marron asked.

"Not far. Not far at all."

They might both have been speaking of something else, or else of different things entirely. Somehow, he didn't think so.

NOT FAR AT all: he'd known that in any case, he'd have known it blindfold or blind. His eyes were his least informant. Every beat of his heart, every yearning muscle in his body, every bone, every hair on his twitching skin told him that it was not far, it couldn't be. There was no pain now that they were moving, but the compulsion was momentous. He felt more than inhabited, he felt possessed; the Daughter sang in his ears like the demon it was to his old masters, Church and knight. It was a tide and not his feet that carried him forward, once more leading alone. He didn't watch where he walked, he didn't need to, though the ground was treacherously uneven; he wouldn't be allowed to fall. Neither did he so much as glance back. Again, there was no need. He could see them, almost, without looking, they were shadows in his mind: the Dancers arrayed like a wall at his back, the riders on their beasts in line behind. Rudel had stood the first watch, had had no sleep at all; Marron could sense how he dozed on his swaying camel, how his head sagged and his thoughts drifted. He was the only one, Marron thought, whose eyes had not yet found the needle. The Dancers knew of it already, had been looking for it, surely; he had himself shown it to Jemel and Elisande; she would have warned Julianne, but surely not her father. Whatever it meant, if it had meant lethal danger she still would not have told her father.

THE PLATEAU DIPPED, or the hills rose ahead of them, both; whichever, the needle was lost behind a slope that

intervened. Their way still led directly toward it, though.
Marron had no doubt of that. He reached the foot of that
slope, and started up; as the camels' stride altered to meet
the climb, he felt Rudel rouse and stir. He would see nothing but the hill now, until they breasted it. Marron could
do nothing to alert him, even if he'd been certain of the
need. His body was no longer his own; he was no more
than a passenger now, borne along by another's will, as
the Daughter had been all these weeks. He thought perhaps he ought to be frightened, but was not. He seemed to
have lost that ability too, to have lost everything that had
made him Marron. Elisande had said that or something
like it, more than once. Now, suddenly, tonight he seemed
to have lost all that had made him the Ghost Dancer also.
There was so little left of him, only a bare thread of
awareness swamped by haste and thirst for something that
was not water, and he couldn't even fear the finding of
it . . .

HASTE INDEED UP the flank of the hill: he was running
now, running to beat the sun; he didn't look back to see,
but knew that all the sky behind him was paling, from rich
indigo above through lilac to a shimmering pink. Ahead it
was dark yet, but the needle not; he could see the tip of it
suddenly, touched with early light. Not so sharp now, not
this close: it was broad and textured, built of dusty stone.
And it rose as he climbed, it towered over his head and he
still couldn't see the eye of it, only more and more of the
shaft, so that it seemed to stab higher and higher into the
sky.

Again he thought he should feel frightened, and could
not. All he could do was run; and did run, and so came at
last to the crest of the hill, just as the sun rose at his back
so that his own shadow ran ahead to find and strike, pure
through the eye of the needle.

A great arch that eye was, three times his height and
half of that in width, cutting clean through the massive

base of the needle where it stood on this high promontory. His feet faltered, the singing in his ears died to a murmur, all rush was gone and his body was his own again, now that he was here. He could tip his head back and gape, and wonder why; and now, yes, at last he could be afraid.

The needle was not a tower, it had no doors or windows. He had known another tower like that, but this was different; there was no hollow space inside, he could sense that, he could feel the incredible mass of rock that made it. Small rocks it was built from, no single piece greater than a strong man could carry; he thought that might be important. Many, many rocks, each crudely shaped and precisely placed: there was no mortar to bind them together, each was gripped only by the solidity of those around and the weight of those above. The wall of it was rougher than any masonry he'd seen; he thought he could climb right to the top, to the tip, there were cracks enough for hands and feet to find, if only he dared to touch it . . .

He did not dare, he wouldn't even go closer than this, still its own height's distance; this hilltop was broad and flat, and the needle—pillar? monument?—stood at its centre, set back from all sides.

Marron heard the Dancers come up and stand about him, like a wall still, to divide him from his friends. Like a curving wall that embraced him, almost, that gave him no more choices than the Daughter had before: he could stand where he was and look at the needle, or he could walk towards the needle. Bodies blocked him at either side and behind, left him no route else.

He stood still, and went on gaping.

Soon the camels came, snorting and blowing and keeping their distance, from him and the needle both. Even before they breasted the hill—and even shielded as he was from the sight of them, by the Dancers and his own back turned—Marron felt that same awareness of the pattern of their thoughts. It wasn't much that he could glean, but he knew some seconds early that Rudel was furious, and frightened too. Frightened for him, he thought—or frightened of what this place might mean or do to him, that was more than what he might mean or do on his own.

Some seconds early he was with that knowledge, but not many, and nowhere near enough to be useful. The camels came, and Rudel's was the first among them now, and breathing the hardest. It sidled unhappily across the rocky ground; its rider slid down unheeding, left it unhobbled as he stormed across to the Dancers where they guarded Marron, seemingly from him.

His riding-stick flailed the sand and stone at his feet; even in his anger, though, he was giving sidelong glances to the needle. Marron could feel that too, without being able to see past the bulk of the Dancers' bodies. He thought it was a mistake, to show fear or weakness to these men. They would be merciless.

"This . . ." Rudel began—and stopped, spat over the hill's edge, drew a breath and began again, more temperately. "This is the Pillar of Lives." A statement, no question about it.

"It is."

Marron still thought it was a needle and he the thread, plucked and drawn.

"If I had known your path would lead us here, I would have forbidden it."

"It is not yours to forbid. We go where the Ghost Walker goes."

"And the Ghost Walker goes where you lead him. Well, we are here—but we do not stay, do you hear me? I lead the Ghost Walker now, and we return to the cliff-edge and seek a way down to the Sands. You can follow or not, as you choose."

"It is not ours to choose, nor yours to lead. The Ghost Walker goes where he will . . ."

"The Ghost Walker goes nowhere," Elisande's voice, sharply cutting across, "until he has eaten, and rested. This seems no bad place," though her voice seemed to hesitate and lost its certainty for a moment, and Marron thought that her eye too had been snared by the needle then. "We can stay here and watch all sides for any sign of the ghûl. I will make a fire; its smoke will announce us, but . . ."

"You will make no fire here," Morakh interrupted brutally. "Do you think this is a jaunting-spot? You stand on holy ground, girl, and you will respect it." And his hand was on the hilt of his scimitar, as though to enforce that respect.

"What is this place?" Marron asked quietly. "It sucks at my soul . . ."

"You are the Ghost Walker; this is your place of power. That is what you feel. What you carry was created here, given its life and purpose; you have brought it home."

"And that . . . ?"

"That is the Pillar of Lives. We made it, we the Sand Dancers, through all the generations we have waited; it is the rite of acceptance to our brotherhood, that each new postulant bring a stone from elsewhere, climb up and place it in the Pillar. We build slowly, but what we have built endures."

So many stones, so many thousand stones; so many lives, and how long had this thing been a-building?

"Is it finished?" he asked, in a whisper. Morakh only smiled. Of course, it was not finished. The Ghost Walker was here, to be sure, the Daughter had returned from its exile of centuries—but for how long? He might be hard to kill, but he would die regardless. No one could say what would happen then. Or before then. The Ghost Walker was an infidel to these men; they might have refused Jemel the chance to join them, but Marron thought they would still go on recruiting. Or accepting postulants, that seemed a closer way to say it.

"Tell him about the oaths you swear," Rudel urged, not pleasantly, "as the other part of the rite. When you cut your finger off, in witness of your earnest."

"Those oaths are none of his concern. Nor yours."

"Oh, I have heard them; and they concern me greatly.

As they should him; and how can they not be his concern? He is the Ghost Walker."

But he is infidel, Morakh's face said; his lips said nothing. Rudel it was who said, "He said before the Sultan that they were sworn to your service, did he not, Marron? That is true, but it is not the whole truth. The Sand Dancers are sworn to serve you by sword and fire, till all unbelievers are harried from the land of God. You are meant to lead them in this venture. That is so, is it not, Morakh?"

"So it is foretold."

"You see what this means, Marron? They are your private army, and your bodyguard—but only so long as you will lead them against Outremer. Against your own people, Marron . . ."

"Are they my people? They cast me out, and I fled them . . ." That wasn't quite right. *They cast me out, and I fled him . . .* But the truth was still there, a kernel to the words. Words were only a dressing, and could not numb the pain of what was true. Whether he was traitor or betrayed, no matter; treachery, two or more, several treacheries lay between him and his people now.

"You are the Ghost Walker," Morakh said and suddenly, rarely touched him, gripping his wrist in a hand that was hot and hard despite the dawn chill in the air. "You have no people but ourselves."

Themselves or his friends, perhaps. Not both. And one of his friends was Sharai and one was Patric, and who could choose between them?

"You are a small army," he said, "to set against Outremer."

"There are more of us. Not enough, for that battle; but you need not lead the war, you need only fight within it. The prophecy speaks of a gathering of all the peoples of the Sharai, and it says the Ghost Walker shall be one among them."

"And if I say no?"

"Then you are not the one foretold, or now is not the

time. But there is a gathering of the tribes at Rhabat, Hasan has called the leaders there; and you go to Rhabat, you said, though we do not. We will wait, we will gather also; and after the conclave we shall hear what has been said, and what you have chosen."

And if he had chosen wrongly, they would perhaps decide that the Daughter rested in the wrong body; and so he would die, beneath their arrows if they could not kill him with their swords . . .

Well, so be it. If they offered him the choice today, now, one path with his friends or another with the Dancers, he knew which way he would go: neither to the left nor to the right, but straight ahead and alone, through the arch in the Pillar of Lives, the eye of the needle . . .

His own eye still hadn't strayed from that massive monument to patience and belief. So many lives lived out, first to last, in waiting for what had not come; he marvelled that Morakh and his brethren could be as calm as they were, discovering their miracle in their own generation. Morakh's hand was still about his wrist; now the Dancer lifted and turned it, so that Marron's sleeve fell back and the ever-open wound was revealed. A blade appeared in Morakh's other hand, a long fine poniard that Marron had come to know well.

"Now," Morakh hissed, "now you will learn, boy. You have been slow, and stupid; here, it cannot be denied . . ."

"No!" Rudel tried to push his way through to them, but two of the Dancers gripped his arms and held him fast. His voice rose, almost a gabble: "Marron, listen to me! Whatever you see happen, remember that this thing leads to death, to uncountable deaths if you let them take you down their road. Remember the stables, at the Roq . . ."

Marron had not forgotten the stables; he carried Aldo with him always, a terrible pain in his heart, and the guilt of what had come after. But Morakh's blade slid neatly between two of the leather stitches, a sharp prick of pain; his blood rose to meet it, and the Daughter followed.

This time it did not float in the air before him, waiting

for his inadequate control. This time it flowed, it ran like water, much as he had run to fetch it here. It ran straight to the arch in the pillar, and there it spread itself like a veil, like a curtain between stone and stone, between sky and sky.

It clung to the rocks above, the rocks on either side, the rock below; and then, like a curtain rent asunder, it rippled and tore from the centre, from top to bottom it spread itself apart, it opened like an eye.

Through the needle's eye, Marron found himself staring at a golden country, under a golden sky. The same landscape he saw, or thought he saw, only that now it glimmered and shone.

He took one slow pace forward, and then another; and heard Morakh's soft approval. "Good. Will you go, boy, will you lead us through?"

His arm hurt unbearably; he gripped it in his free hand, pressed it to his chest despite the stickiness of blood, and felt no relief. Would he go? He had no answer, except his eyes' focus and his feet's slow shuffle.

Suddenly, though, there was something more to look at, between himself and bright gold. It was a shadow, a figure, a man: a young man, much like himself.

And that was Jemel, who had his own answer for Morakh. Before Marron could stay him, he strode ahead, all purpose. When he came to the open iris that was the Daughter, he barely hesitated, taking just time enough to glance back once and meet Marron's gaze; there was a message in his eyes, perhaps, except that Marron could not read it.

And then Jemel stepped through.

6

With and Without Him

JEMEL STEPPED THROUGH, and stood for a moment in two worlds, one bare foot grounded in each.

The one foot stood in shadow, the accustomed chill of desert stone at dawn, unwarmed as yet by desert sun; the other reached over the eddying red line that marked the doorway—careful, careful!—to touch gold and feel the instant strike of warmth through leathered sole and numbed bone, as though he trod on hearthstones or the slab floor of a hammam. Except that the floor of a hammam is damp always when the fires are lit, and the air is damper; and here the golden rock was as dry and dusty as the grey, and the air was dry too when he gasped it in at the shock of that warm touch.

The two airs mingled in his throat, the bitter cold and the bitter warm, and he might have gasped again if he weren't coughing.

And then momentum had carried him through, and he stood entire within the golden light of that other world.

No glancing back, not now, although he yearned to;

they must not think him fearful of this, those men who had refused his brotherhood. He lifted his eyes and his head, straightened his back and walked forward, through the arch and out under an opalescent sky, and even that had a shimmer of gold to it.

Only then, as he stood looking at a landscape that was not his own, as he struggled to build walls in his mind against the sudden press of fear that he was still determined not to show, only then did he think how strange it was, that there'd been an arch on this side to walk through. The Pillar of Lives was a work of man, which inhabited man's world; those who had built it had had their reasons. What reason could there be for anyone—anything—to erect its like here? Unless there were a law of symmetry between the worlds, and whatever was done in one must be mirrored in the other. But men were busy, always busy, and it would so debase those who lived here, to copy mortal labour to no purpose . . .

So he turned although he had sworn not to, not to let those watching think him frightened; he turned to see what point there was to a pillar here, and what he saw threw a shadow over his eyes, although there was no sun to cast it.

He saw that it was men who copied, who struggled vainly to imitate their masters. He wondered if any Dancer, if any one among the early Dancers had stood here and seen as he did, or if it had only been some dim-heard echo, a sense toward a greater truth that had driven them to raise their Pillar. Or if they'd been instructed to, perhaps . . . ?

He stood beneath a God-sign, he thought, a testament to power and a call to worship. Almost, he fell on his knees. Certainly no man had made this thing; that was inherent, there were no men here, save him. But it seemed to him also that whoever had made it, they'd done so in praise or promise; not for themselves, surely no creature could think itself so mighty . . .

It was a pillar, as the Dancers' was; but theirs was

rough, blunt, unfinished in every sense. This was a leaping spire, smooth and slender, a blade of golden stone thrusting at the pearl-gold sky. It towered higher far than ever man could build; Jemel didn't want to guess how tall it was, nor did he ever want to see anything taller.

He looked back at the archway, and perhaps that shadow hung still across his eyes, because it was hard to see through to the land, the world that he had come from. He saw the red shimmering outline of the way from there to here, but beyond what he saw was grey and dim. There was ground and sky, a bare line of hilltop to distinguish them; a ball, a dull globe hanging, and that must be the sun; between that and this a shadow, moving . . .

A faceless shadow, a figure closing, looming; Jemel's hand touched the hilt of his weapon. The Dancers might hold this as sacred ground, forbidden to those not sworn to the Ghost Walker; they would not recognise his oaths, nor share theirs. They had said he was defiled. They might be right, he had no eye to judge himself; but he would fight for his life, if they sought to take it . . .

The figure blurred momentarily, becoming more vague than a shadow, even; and then it was through, and there were no shadows even under the arch, and it was no Dancer who had followed him.

He breathed out explosively, a moment of relief chased hard by wondering. He took his hand away from his scimitar, but stood still, only watching as Marron turned to face back the way that he had come. He made no gesture, but there was suddenly a veil of red across the arch, no way through for the Dancers or anyone else.

Jemel waited, frowning as he saw how slowly Marron moved, how he hugged his wounded arm to his chest, how his face was twisted with pain. It was an effort not to go to him, not to offer strength against his weakness; but even an ordinary man must be allowed his pride, and Marron was the Ghost Walker, and Jemel could still find it in himself to fear that name.

So Jemel waited, until Marron had come to stand be-

side him; then, "You could have taken it back inside yourself," he said quietly. "That would have eased the pain."

Marron smiled tightly. "I was afraid it might not come,"
he confessed. "It fought so hard to be there, to do this . . ."

"And yet you could make it close, to be a barrier and
not a door."

"Yes. It seemed easy, now. I can understand it; but can I
command? I don't know."

"You are the Ghost Walker. There is more than that,
which you may command."

"Perhaps. The Dancers serve me, they say—but will
they obey me, even as much as the Daughter does? Again,
I don't know. Nor if I want them to. I never sought servants, Jemel . . ."

"This I know." His own smile was as thin as Marron's
had been, and as hard to make, and perhaps as full of
meaning. Of course he knew Marron had been a servant
himself, to his Church first and then to a man, his knight,
Sieur Anton. Given his will, Jemel thought, he'd be doing
that service yet. His soul craved to follow, not to lead.
There was no dishonour in that; proud as they were, quar-
relsome as they were, the Sharai understood rank and
duty, none better. Marron's choice of master was another
matter, and an issue between them, one they could not
speak of. *Not yet*—but soon, he promised himself. Soon,
they must. *For Jazra*—and for himself too, Jemel
couldn't deny so much. His future perhaps hung on that
conversation; aye, and perhaps Marron's too, Ghost
Walker though he be.

And, of course, Sieur Anton's future also . . .

But not yet, not now. Now, at last, the place where they
stood was having its effect on Marron, as it had already
on Jemel. He was all young man suddenly, and all Patric,
no hint of the Ghost Walker about him; he seemed mis-
dressed in Sharai robes as he stood and stared about him.
At the glittering golden ground they stood on, the great
stretch of hills before them, the paler sky that was yet shot

through with hints of gold like a dim reflection of the land below.

"Look back," Jemel murmured, "look up and see what the Dancers seek to build, how short they fall . . ."

Marron did look back and up, at his injunction; and gasped, and staggered perilously close to the steep fall of the slope. Jemel flung an arm around his shoulders, and held him firmly until he was sure of the other's balance against his wound and weakness; and kept his grip even after he was sure, reaching with his other hand to take Marron's wrist and turn it into the light. There was a heavy wet stain on the dark robe, and all the skin of the arm was streaked red.

Jemel watched the wound pulse, and said, "This bleeds more than usual, far more than a dagger's prick should cause. It hurts more, also. Yes?"

"Oh, yes. Since I came through." Marron's voice was vague, detached; his eyes were still on that towering monument, gazing up and up. "What is that thing?"

"Some work of the djinn, or their servants. I do not know. Only that the Dancers would like to make their own, and cannot."

"No. No man could . . . Jemel, where are we?"

"In the land of the djinn. It is said to be the source, the true land, and ours only a crude clay shadow. I do not know. At least ours is alive. Even in the heart of the Sands, there is life."

"And is there none here? Someone made this," with a gesture up at the great spire.

"The djinn, or something lesser of their kind. The Sharai say that if you do not die, you cannot live."

"The djinn die."

Jemel laughed, surprising himself. "They don't expect to."

"But they do, they can be slain. And their kind. I heard that you killed an 'ifrit . . ."

"Yes." With an arrow blessed to the task; he and Jazra both had carried one, a rare gift from a rare imam. Now

Jazra's was lost, and his he thought might find a baser purpose, if ever he saw a certain white-clad knight and could not come close enough for sword-work . . .

A knight whom Marron had served, before he was the Ghost Walker. And if Jemel had not slain the 'ifrit, if he had left it to kill Julianne, then so much would have fallen out differently. Certainly he would not be here now; he would neither know the knight's name nor be bound to his former squire, as he was bound, though Marron seemed not to know it and the Sand Dancers had forbidden him to take their oaths and make it public.

He crouched, and sifted golden dust between his fingers. It was warm to the touch, as the air was warm, though there was no sun to heat it. If the Sands had been made in imitation of this, he thought, that was a great making, and yet it had failed. Their yellow could not match this gold, nor their coarse grains its silky texture; they were hot only by day, and brutally cold by night. And yet men could live in the Sands, if they only knew the way of it . . .

"Men cannot live here," he said, continuing both thought and conversation. "Nor anything that has flesh, or needs water." He could not pray here either, though it was dawn in his own world and he owed that duty to his God. He thought perhaps that God needed men, a world of men; this bitter, beautiful landscape held no mystery except its own creation. There was no place for worship here.

"We are here, and alive."

"For how long? We should go back."

Before we are noticed, by something that even my blessed arrow cannot slay was all he meant, but Marron cast a glance at the archway and the shimmering red curtain that blocked it and said, "Yes. Before there's trouble, between Morakh and Rudel . . ."

There would always be trouble, Jemel thought, between Morakh and Rudel. Trouble between Morakh and Marron might be harder to allay. It must come, though. The Sand

Dancer had seen his dream turn real—and his dream had turned out to be a Patric boy who would not kill. Trouble must surely come of that; and when it did, Jemel meant to be there, to set his scimitar and his body too between them. Marron was more than one man's dream made flesh, and Jemel would not see his own dream perish on a fanatic's blade.

Marron walked back towards the arch, leaving a trail of blood in the sterile dust to mark where he had been. Jemel went to follow—and hesitated, and turned back. He scanned the ground quickly, saw what he was seeking and hurried to gather it up. It was hot against his skin, though not too hot to handle; and heavy, heavier than he'd expected by its size, though not too heavy to carry. He held it two-handed against his chest, and took one last look around at this empty, wondrous land before going over to where Marron stood watching, waiting, wondering.

"Why do you want that? And should you take it?"

Jemel shook his head, to both questions. The one was easily answered, Marron should know, and if he did not he would see soon enough; the other was impossible to answer. What did Jemel know, what did any of them know about the rules that governed the two worlds, this and their own? If the djinn were jealous, possessive— well, no doubt they would make that known. Again, soon enough . . .

This time Marron made no gesture that Jemel could see, but the red haze that blocked the arch drew itself apart, like diaphanous curtains opening to an unfelt breeze. Marron stepped through and Jemel followed, stumbling unexpectedly, almost brushing against the lethal scarlet border that shaped that gateway; what he carried felt suddenly hotter and heavier, a burden greater and more perilous than it had seemed in its own country.

He bore it through, though, hugging it to him, masking it almost with his loose sleeves; and paid little attention to what Marron was doing, drawing up his own damp and bloodstained sleeve to take back his draught of smoke and danger, what he called the Daughter. That was unexpected, deliberately defiant, denying the Dancers any access to the land of gold; but Jemel had his own concerns, and for once Marron was not the most urgent of them.

He stepped out from under the arch, and turned his eyes to the rough stone wall of the Pillar of Lives. Eyes and touch: he could—just—grip his burden one-handed, freeing the other to test the solidity of that wall. He tugged at several of the stones; none moved, although there was no mortar to bind them together. Good.

At his back he could hear loud voices, Rudel's and Morakh's, an argument. He ignored it, slipping what he carried inside his robe and drawing his rope girdle tighter to hold it. It burned against his skin, but not enough to blister. This deed of his must have consequences, he was sure of that; what they would be, he could not predict. It was necessary though, a private avowal and an act of independence, perhaps of rebellion, as his oath before the Sultan had been.

He set both hands to the wall, lifted one bare foot and worked it into an open crack, began to climb.

He was some way up before he heard a voice, a girl's voice call his name. He didn't look down, even when Morakh hailed him in fury; he just kept his eyes focused on his next handhold, his mind fixed on climbing. He had spent half his childhood clambering up and down cliffs as steep as this; his only concern was the awkward weight against his stomach, the urgent need not to let that either pull him off-balance or—worse—slip free and fall to ground, and make a nonsense of his ascent.

Higher and higher: there was a breeze up here but not strong enough to worry him, warmed already by the sun but not enough to challenge the heat of the thing within his robe. He'd thought that might cool after its transition from world to world, but he'd been wrong; if anything it was growing hotter yet. He dug his feet deep into a crevice, detached one careful hand to touch and felt its energy even through the wool of his robe. No time to rest:

he'd best get on, he thought, before it burned for true. Before it scorched the robe to flame, and himself also . . .

And so up, and further up. Spot a hold, reach and grip; he watched his hands and let his long toes find their own anchorage, never looking down. So it had been the night they had attacked the Roq; so it had always been. It was unusual, to say the least, such a talent among the Sharai; the tribes generally avoided the heights, or any fixed settlement. But then he was—no, he had been Saren, and the Saren were an unusual tribe.

At last even his muscles were aching, and his arms were trembling through to his shoulders. He'd travelled far since the cliffs of his childhood, and he was out of practice for such a climb—except for that one terrible night at the Roq, and then he'd had Jazra at his side and Hasan to lead, the promise of glory and the dread of shame uniting to overcome any weakness in his body. No longer. He would never see Jazra again this side of death, he would never follow Hasan again; today there was only his own fierce will to drive him on.

Drive him it did, until one hand and then the other found the topmost edge, and clung. One final effort, and he hauled himself up and over.

Briefly he lay flat on his back, breathing hard, his skin slick with rare sweat and his burden a searing weight below his ribs. He felt unmanned, all but overmastered, and was glad that none below could see him like this. Especially, that one below could not see him so . . .

Soon, though, that same implacable determination that had brought him this far drew him to his feet, although his legs shook and he felt dizzy and unbalanced. He still didn't look down, nor around at the wide country of the Sands; he kept his head down and fixed his eyes firmly where he stood, on the summit of the Pillar of Lives.

This was a place of myth among his people, almost as much so as the land of the djinn, where he had stood only a few minutes previously. It lacked any of the wonder of that place, though: only a crude circle of stones, with a

long drop below its rim. As with the walls, there had been
no attempt to level off the summit; indeed, the Pillar had
not yet reached its final height. The centre stood two or
three courses higher than the edge, where the last few
dozen men to join the fraternity of Sand Dancers had laid
their individual rocks.

Which was why he had come this far, why he had made
that climb. Denied the chance to share their vows and
their brotherhood, he had brought a rock of his own regardless. Theirs had been gleaned from the desert; his he
had fetched from the land of their aspiration, where he
and none of them had walked.

He reached into his robe and drew it out, cruelly hot
now and shining more brightly here than it had in its own
country. For a moment he stood right on the rim where his
friends—and his unfriends—could see him, held it high to
show them what bright thing he carried; if any were uncertain, Marron could tell them. Then he stalked proudly,
defiantly to that raised centre and treated it like a pedestal,
like an altar almost, setting his rock to stand higher than
all the others, in the place of pride and honour.

It was a statement at the least, perhaps another oath,
though even he was beginning to doubt quite what he was
swearing to. He stood and gazed at it a little while, feeling
more muddled than he had expected, less triumphant; then
at last he raised his eyes and gazed about him.

And he who had grown up with far views was transfixed again by a view, the second time this morning. This
was a place of wonder after all, only that the wonder lay
not in itself, but in what it commanded.

He could see for days, by the Sharai way of measuring.
Not so far to the east, where the low strong sun defeated
his eyes; but eastward lay no lands that mattered, only the
margins of the Sands where they were claimed by tame
tribes, peoples who would allow a merchants' road and
the passage of unchallenged strangers. To the north and
the west were lost lands, where once the word of the
Sharai had been the word of law—and would be again,

that at least he was certain of, that was inherent in any vow he made—and he thought he could see them all. That purple haze which made the far horizon, he thought that was Outremer as the Patrics called it, as he was learning to. All the wide country between there and here he could see, and he thought he could overleap it in a bound.

Hasan had thought so, and had tried to make it true, with his doomed, disastrous expedition against the Roq. Jemel wondered if ever Hasan had stood here, if this was where the idea had been born; or did Hasan see the world always from such a height, in such breadth and detail? Did he perhaps have a Pillar of Lives in his head—and did he count the lives that fell from it, as he reached and overreached?

Thinking of Hasan, Jemel turned to face the south, where the true Sands lay and Rhabat at the heart of them. He saw ochre instead of gold, and thought he would never see true gold again unless he walked again in the land of the djinn; but ochre was enough, he thought, where it meant the rolling dunes and sweeping plains of his own dry country. From here he could see how broken that country was, the grey of rock upthrusting and the black shadows of sudden scarps; distantly he thought he could see a gleam of water. If true, that must be the salt sea, the Dead Waters that were once more a place of myth and legend; if so, then there lay Rhabat also, where Hasan was or was headed, and so was he if Marron's intent held good. So were they all, except that the Dancers did not go to Rhabat . . .

Thinking of Marron and the Dancers, he strode confidently back to the summit's eastern rim and looked down. He didn't mean to wave, exactly, nothing so childish, but he would like to be seen as himself and for his own sake, not as the answer to a question, what he carried. Also, he wanted to see. Morakh and Rudel had been arguing; that was no surprise, but he'd like to see how that had fallen out, who stood with whom, whether Marron had been

•

drawn in or had become the cause of another argument, perhaps.

Maybe so. It was hard to be sure from so high above, when so many of the party wore the same dress; but the air was clear and his eyes were sharp, and he thought he would know Marron at any distance, from the way that boy moved, the way he held himself. He thought that was Marron, the small figure moving swiftly away from the Pillar and down the hill, as swiftly almost as he had climbed it as the dawn came up. He might well be taking himself away from an argument, whether or not he was the cause of it.

If so, then that was very likely Elisande who followed him, scrambling down the slope with bags swinging loosely from her shoulders: empty water-skins, Jemel thought, a reason or probably an excuse. They'd be more than lucky to find water anywhere up here, but they could spend a long time searching, or claiming to search . . .

Certainly those were the Dancers, that small huddle of black-robed men directly below, where he could spit on them if he had not been too careful of his body's water, if he had not done more than that already. That was equally certainly Rudel, the broad-shouldered man who stood apart from them; which left only Julianne, and it took only a moment for him to find her among the camels, keeping her distance from all arguments.

Satisfied, he sought Marron once more. Elisande had all but caught him up; indeed he paused and waited for her, probably at some screech that Jemel couldn't hear. She flapped her bags at him, and gestured: *Morakh says there's water over there, we may as well fetch it, rather than just storming off in a rage,* or else *Look, I brought these, I said we'd look for water, there's a path down there looks as likely as anything and they won't expect us back for an hour . . .*

There was a path, of sorts: a goat-path perhaps, though Jemel had seen no other sign of goat or any game since they'd climbed above the level of the Sands. The Dancers

surely didn't come here often enough in their separate
troops to wear a path across the rock; and if it were only
beaten sand that marked it out, then a week's winds would
shift or bury it for ever . . .

Slightly puzzled, rather more curious and almost
alarmed already—Jemel was of the desert, and what was
unusual in the desert was always a caution to the wary—
he looked ahead of them, further down the path than they
could see.

And saw movement, and saw too what it was that
moved, or thought he did.

And was bellowing a warning that same instant, lifting
his hands to make a trumpet-mouth to carry the sound far;
and whistling and waving, and dancing almost on that
great height, doing anything he could think of to attract
the attention of either one of them.

Marron heard, of course he did, nothing happened that
Marron could not hear with his alien ears. His head turned
and tilted, Jemel could see a pale blur beneath the hood
that was his face; Marron no doubt could see a great deal
more.

But all Marron saw, it seemed, was his friend capering
on the Pillar's tip, solemn gesture over and *look at me!* He
lifted an arm, to say that he had looked and seen; Elisande
waved both arms extravagantly.

Jemel cursed, tried to shout words and knew they were
not reaching even Marron across the breeze and distance.
The Dancers had a code of signs, of gestures; but Jemel
did not know it, and couldn't think how to sign *danger!* in
any common way that would be understood.

Those below were all staring up at him with no more
understanding, making no more effort to understand.

He saw the two Patrics turn away, and go blindly on;
and gave up his wild shouting and crouched, took his
weight on his hands on that extreme edge, lowered his
legs over and began to climb down.

If you chose to call it climbing. Even in his wildest
days, he'd never made such a descent: skidding and slid-

ing, barely holding on, letting his weight as much as his skill carry him down the near-vertical face of the wall. They'd called him "Spider" as a boy, before he'd earned his name, but spiders were more careful. And spiders had rope, which he did not.

He might have died a dozen times or more, when his fingers missed their grip or his foot failed to find a ledge to lodge on. He had no balance and no sense, only desperation in head and hands and heart as he went slipping catastrophically from one juddering moment's halt to the next, with a long slither in between. He should have died, it was impertinent to God that he survived, he thought after.

Survive he did, though, even the last uncontrolled tumble that had him sprawling at Morakh's feet with all the breath knocked out of him, his palms skinned and hurting now as his toes were also, which he hadn't felt before. There was blood on his face too, sticky and stinging, and he had no idea what had happened there.

"You have profaned what is holy to us, tribeless. I forbade you—"

"Morakh, listen! Ghûl . . ."

"Ghûl? What do you mean, ghûl? There is no ghûl."

He seemed very sure, for someone who had seen and shown footprints of the ghûl only yesterday, whose man had heard and seen it just last night.

But Jemel's sighting was more fresh, and urgent. "Where they are gone, the Ghost Walker and Elisande. I saw it, waiting for them . . ."

"What did you see?" Rudel demanded, gripping his elbow and drawing him ruthlessly to his feet.

"A ghûl. No. A woman. Perhaps. Something in women's dress, but its shape seemed wrong, and the way it moved was not human . . . Oh, go! Run! They have not met it yet . . ."

"The boy is dreaming," Morakh said. "Or seeking to distract from his offence. It cannot be . . ."

"Why not?" Rudel snapped. "We have been plagued for days with ghûls and rumours of ghûls . . ."

"Well, perhaps so. But if there is a ghûl, the Ghost Walker will destroy it."

"Has anyone told Marron how to destroy a ghûl?"

There was a silence; then, "He does not know?"

"How should he? This is not his country . . ."

"We will go. Immediately . . ." And now suddenly there was almost fear in Morakh's voice: fear of Marron's dying, Jemel thought, and he not being there to receive what he most desired. That man might have sworn to serve the Ghost Walker, but he was not content with his service.

The men left at a sprint. Jemel tried to follow, but all his body was sore and bruised, and his legs would not hold him. When Julianne came hurrying over she stayed him with ease, her woman's body a support he clutched at shamefully.

"What is it? I could not hear . . ."

"There is a ghûl, they are walking straight towards it . . ."

She gasped, but still did not release him, though he struggled against her grip.

"You cannot follow, you are hurt. And bleeding . . ." Her hand touched his forehead, and came away stained. "The camels . . . ?"

"Yes! The camels, quickly . . ."

She had to help him, even over that little distance. The beasts were couched and hobbled, but this at least he could manage, tugging at the tie and dropping into the saddle, plying his riding-stick furiously until his mount was on its feet and running, though it roared its displeasure.

With Julianne at his back, he drove the camel down-slope to where that path began, winding away north between buttresses of rock high enough to block their view. They could hear the men ahead, calling loudly; no answering shouts came back. Jemel beat his mount to greater speed, bending low over its neck to watch the path; there was a clear track in the sand, marked by nothing but the booted and bare feet of his companions. He thought how a wily ghûl might have laid just such a trail for temptation's sake, trusting its disguising robes to sweep away the signs of its own hoofed feet. Were ghûls that wily, that intelligent? Not of their own nature, by all the stories that he had heard, but there was something more than natural in the way that their party seemed to have been hunted by these creatures . . .

They caught up with Rudel and the Dancers, sweeping past to round another high outcrop. Now at last they had free running for a distance, and a glimpse of two small figures a long way ahead. Too far: Marron and Elisande had almost reached the jutting rocks where he had seen the lurking thing that had alarmed him. He yelled, a high whooping call that made them stop, and turn. He waved his stick wildly, and called again; they hesitated, and began to make their way back towards him.

His cries had alerted the ghûl also, if ghûl it were. Something emerged from those rocks, only a few paces from his friends. It still looked a little like a woman, but that was its clothing only; even from so far higher up and further away he hadn't been deceived, and was not now. He had thought ghûls better at disguise than this. Perhaps they were, when it was needful; it could have nothing on its mind now except attack.

Attack it did, in a great leap that had its hood falling back from its head, revealing a long head like a horse's, except that no horse had ever had such a mouth, gaping wide and toothed like a lion. Nor such arms, long and clawed and reaching, flailing toward Marron . . .

He heard its coming, of course, and twisted round to face it; and had his sword out to meet it, barely in time. A low slashing cut made it jerk back; it seemed to grow taller, letting its last pretence fall away.

Jemel heard Julianne's gasp of relief behind him, and realised that she was confident of Marron's swordsmanship, even against such a nightmare creature as this. Well she might be; but no more than Marron, he guessed, did she know how a ghûl might be killed. Or not killed, which was what mattered more.

If he could only hold it off, though, until Jemel arrived . . .

Jemel shifted his riding-stick to his left hand, drew his scimitar and wished for a horse, and spurs. A horse can be brutalised into a sudden burst of effort, though it may die as a result; a camel, not. A camel treated too harshly will slow rather than speed up, may balk altogether, and he'd already belaboured this one to the point of risk. He fixed his eyes on the conflict ahead, and prayed.

The ghûl was all demon now, the robe ripping asunder as its back swelled into monstrosity. Elisande screamed; when the creature's head turned towards her, she flung one of her knives. Jemel saw it glitter in the sunlight, saw it embedded deep in the ghûl's throat. A clever play, and one that might prove enough, if they would only back off now, if she would only cry a warning to Marron, call him away . . .

But Marron saw the creature stagger towards Elisande, its long arms reaching. She tried to run backwards, her heel caught a jut of rock and she fell sprawling in its path. Marron leaped to straddle her body, and showed his reluctance in only a moment's hesitation before he drove his sword hard through the ribbons of cloth that still clung to the ghûl's chest. It should have been a lethal stroke; Jemel groaned.

The ghûl recovered in an instant. Its one arm swiped across its own neck, knocking the dagger out; its other slashed at the stunned Marron, tearing through cloth and flesh alike, opening his shoulder to the bone.

It was unlucky, matching mistake with mistake. More than blood ran from the wound; a soft smoky shadow formed between man and monster. Marron could slay it now, with a thought; or Jemel was closing fast, Marron must have heard his approach. If he would only hold still and wait, all would be well now . . .

Marron did neither. He had only a moment to choose, and he chose a third way. The dim scarlet shadow stretched itself into a frame, a doorway with a shimmer of gold at its heart; and Marron bent, scooped Elisande up in his one good arm and stumbled through that door.

Jemel screamed his name, too late; and cursed, and tried to ride his camel in a hectic plunge through at his back, and was too late again. The frame shrank and disappeared, seemed to be sucked into a vanishing point of gold, and Jemel was left facing the bewildered ghûl.

Well, this at least he could do as it should be done. He swung his blade once, ferociously, hewing clean through the creature's neck. The head fell and rolled, the body slumped; this time it was truly dead, and Jemel's camel danced away from its corpse.

HE SLIPPED TO ground, letting the beast wander as it would till Julianne collected it; he stood gasping, sobbing almost, staring not at the awful remains of the ghûl but at the bare patch of sand and rock where Marron had been, and Elisande.

Rudel reached him first. The older man took his blade gently from nerveless fingers, wiped it fastidiously on a rag of the creature's robe and returned it to him with a gesture that was almost a salute.

"That was well done, Jemel."

"It was useless, I came too slowly. Any of you could have done as much, anyone who knows. They are guileful, but not great fighters. Will he come back?"

"The ghûl? Not now."

"Not the ghûl."

Rudel sighed, as though he'd known exactly what Jemel had meant, and said, "I do not know. He was hurt, yes?"

"Yes. Badly hurt, perhaps."

"Then not soon, perhaps. Not here. Would you? Not knowing what had fallen out, with the ghûl? He has Elisande with him, she will tend the wound. When he is fit, they will likely travel a little before they chance returning. If nothing disturbs them, where they are . . ."

"Travel? Travel where, where will they go?"

"South, I would guess. If they can find the south, without sun or stars to guide them. They know we are headed for Rhabat; they should go in the same direction, and cross back into this world when and where they think it safe . . ." Though his voice betrayed a little doubt, as though whatever he thought they should do, his daughter would be sure to do something other.

"He was safe. With me. I would have killed it for him, or he could have destroyed it himself . . ."

"He doesn't like to kill," Julianne said wearily. She'd hobbled the camels, and came now to join them. "Didn't you see what it cost him, to try? When Elisande fell? And then, when that didn't work, of course he wouldn't use the Daughter, except to escape. He wouldn't have used it in any case. Why didn't his sword kill the thing, though, Jemel? When yours did?"

"It was a ghûl."

"I know that."

"Then know this, it's important. You have to kill a ghûl with a single stroke; a second only restores it to life again."

"*What?* That's ridiculous . . ."

"It's true, Julianne," Rudel confirmed. "Well, you saw. Elisande's knife wounded it badly, might have killed it, given a little time; but Marron struck again, and it was as though the creature had never been touched by either blade."

"I confess, I saw it. But how . . . ?"

"Magic," from Rudel and "God's will," from Jemel, both speaking together. They glanced at each other, but neither so much as smiled. Jemel made a small, polite gesture; Rudel bowed, before continuing.

"God's will, the Sharai say; they are a fatalistic people, they tend not to ask why or how such things happen. That is the way of the world, and they live within it; that is enough. Those of a more enquiring disposition say that creatures of spirit bend themselves only reluctantly to the limitations of flesh, and will stretch those limits in every way they can. Even to the point of a joke, 'slay me once, I'm dead; but do it twice and back I come again . . .' Myself, I do not believe that ghûls have a sense of humour. Remember that they are shapeshifters, like all the spirit creatures; again, you have seen. If they can do that, if they can change the body they inhabit, they can heal it also; so you must slay them instantly, and give them no chance to recover. As Jemel did. By the time a second stroke falls, they're already altering, shifting, flowing to meet the effects of the first; and so the second is useless, and seems almost to heal the damage dealt by the first. That's my belief, at least . . ."

Jemel frowned, shook his head, would have argued; that was not what he'd been taught, nor what he had seen. But Julianne got in ahead of him, with another puzzled question.

"Creatures of spirit, you said. But the 'ifrit was a creature of spirit, and its body melted into smoke or dust, when Jemel killed it. This does not . . . ?"

"Never confuse ghûls with 'ifrit, child. The 'ifrit are closer to the djinn, they do not inhabit this world naturally; when they come, they take what form they like, and when they die they dissipate, as you have seen. Ghûls are bound to this world; they can shift their shape, but what spirit they have is yet contained within a vessel of flesh and blood. That remains, when they are slain. You could say that they are servants to the 'ifrit; they share at least the same evil nature, though they follow their own desires and none other, but they are by far a lesser order . . ."

His voice trailed off, as he turned to watch what Morakh was doing behind him. The Dancer was bent over the ghûl's severed head and busy with his knife, cutting something out of the creature's mouth. When he straightened, he showed it silently to his companions, and then came across and thrust himself in between the two Patrics.

"This one at least was true servant to the 'ifrit," he said, and held out his hand for evidence.

In his palm Jemel saw a pebble, slimed with the ghûl's thick blood but gleaming gold beneath the stain. It should be hot, to judge by the way Morakh shuffled it around with his fingers.

He and Rudel only stared at it; it was Julianne who asked, "What is that?"

"It is a stone from the land of the djinn," Jemel said when neither of the older men replied; it was small cousin to the rock that he had brought through the arch himself, though he said nothing of that. "I do not understand what it was doing in the ghûl's mouth?"

"It was embedded in its tongue," Morakh told them shortly.

Julianne frowned, and shook her head. "I still don't understand . . ."

"Such things are potent in this world," Rudel said, barely glancing at Jemel. "Among the spirit-kind, they can be overmastering. The 'ifrit are said sometimes to use a ghûl this way, to set a token from the other world within its body; then its will is subordinate to that of the 'ifrit and it is forced into service, to do its master's bidding. I have heard tales that tell of this, though I have never seen it before, nor ever heard that the tales were true. I would never have thought to look for such a thing . . ."

Jemel grunted his agreement; he too had heard the tales, and had thought them only storytelling. He faced Morakh and said, "You cannot have seen that; I did not, and it was I who slew the creature. How did you know to look for it?"

"The creature's behaviour seemed strange; this is no normal hunting-ground for a ghûl, so far from any road or village. Only we Sand Dancers come to this place, and we are no meat for their tasting. Nor are they ordinarily crafty enough to lay a false trail. So I thought to look for this, and so I found it. This is my country; I at least can tell fable from truth."

Jemel bridled; this was his country too, and he would not be scorned. Especially by such a one, at such a time; after he had lost Marron and slain his first ghûl, he deserved better on both counts . . .

Before his hot tongue could say so, though, or say anything, Morakh had said something more.

"Besides," the Dancer said, "I have seen this before. And the ghûl was silent in its attack, where normally it would have been screaming; so that I knew where to look for the stone."

"Seen it before?" Rudel challenged. "Seen it where, and when?"

"This is not my first ghûl," was all that Morakh said, as though he had read some or all of Jemel's thought upon his face. He said it near-contemptuously, as though putting down a boy who had thought to claim some honour. Jemel's scimitar twitched in his hand, but Morakh had already turned his back and was speaking to his younger brothers in their own coded tongue.

Jemel burned for a fight, a true fight, to assuage the ache of loss in his heart. Marron had been his talisman, no substitute for Jazra—never that!—but a powerful charm, a lodestone on his own account. In his sudden absence, Jemel was struggling under a double grief, the old and the new; and he had seen Marron hurt, which felt like his failure. He needed action, to blunt the pain of it. Killing the ghûl had not been enough, too easy and too soon over; Rudel's praise had been a sop, no more, and all this talk was nothing but distraction. He would have loved to set himself against Morakh, blade to blade, for the implied insult. But even a tribeless man sworn to a Patric's protection has his honour, and he would not attack even his greatest enemy from behind. Besides, Rudel's hand was clenched now around his wrist, to hold his sword-arm down. The older man's eyes carried a message, *we are one party yet, and have no time for petty quarrels.* Jemel gritted his teeth, nodded a reluctant acceptance of that wisdom, and forced his muscles to relax.

When Morakh turned back to face them, though, he did so swiftly, and his own scimitar came hissing from its sheath in the same movement. Jemel cried out, startled, and flung up his left hand, his only hand that was free; he felt the bite of steel in his fingers, and the sharp shock of pain that followed after.

Rudel bellowed, drew his long sword and closed with Morakh. That was a private combat that swirled away across the sand, too fast and too far for Jemel to follow. He shook his head against a sudden dizziness, and looked to find the other Dancers.

They were five men, swordsmen all, and they faced one girl. Julianne had a knife in each hand now, but little good those would do her. She knew it, too; she was backing already, against their inexorable advance.

Jemel thrust himself forward, exulting almost despite the odds; this was what he'd wanted, what his soul had been crying for, the chance of battle to allay his guilt and all else that he was burdened with. Never mind that it came from among their own number and inexplicably, without warning; never mind the deadly reputation of Sand Dancers. Now he could fight, he could kill or die or both. If he killed and killed well, he might with luck see Marron again, if Marron lived; if he died and died well, he should with luck see Jazra. That was enough.

A blade came at him from the right; he met that edge to edge and felt it skitter off, turned quickly to beat back another from the left, and still found time to wish that he had said his prayers today, that he stood in good grace with God. Gambling was forbidden, but he had seen men gamble, he understood about odds. He did not think that Rudel would defeat Morakh, and come to help him here. One wounded boy—his long sleeve covered his left hand and he'd had no chance to look at it, but it hurt terribly and he could feel blood running—and one girl, against

five Sand Dancers? He thought this was his death-hour,
his and Rudel's and Julianne's also; he didn't understand
it, but he thought his bones would lie here to bleach in the
sun, and only hoped that one at least among the Dancers
would have the kindness to say the *khalat* for him, if not
for the Patrics.

Gambling was forbidden, but he thought that all men
gambled, with every choice they made that changed their
life or others'. He had gambled on Jazra, and had won and
won until he lost him; they had both gambled on Hasan,
and had lost the world in each other. He had gambled
again on Marron, and seemed likely to have lost him too,
to death or Elisande. Now he flung his life down as men
fling dice, to chance or God's decision. Not to skill: if
skill alone decided this, then there was no breath of hope,
fight as he might.

A blade to the left, a blade to the right; he parried them
both, glitter and kiss and the grating hiss of steel on steel.
Still only the two, though: they were playing with him, he
thought, and not for honour's sake. The Dancers were
Sharai, but they kept only those customs that were useful
to them. When they chose to kill, they would ordinarily
kill without honour or mercy, in defiance of all teaching;
and two of these men had bows. He and Julianne should
both be dead already. They had chosen swords, though,
and three were hanging back. Jemel thought perhaps that
they remembered the humiliation of their bout with Marron in the Sultan's palace, when he could have slain them
all and did not, time and again did not. This was perhaps
their revenge for that, to slay the Ghost Walker's chosen
companion but to do it slowly, to take turns to nick and
wound until the sand was sodden with his blood and he
was emptied of it . . .

Determined at least to nick them back, not to die with
his blade clean, he closed with one; battered his scimitar
aside, saw what seemed to be an opening, and thrust—
into empty air. A moment before his point must have met

and cut cloth and flesh and bone beneath, the man was simply not there.

Briefly, Jemel was shaken to his roots, all his certainties trembling on the point of collapse. Then there was a guttural laugh at his back, he twisted round—and saw two Sand Dancers where there had been one, and both of them were grinning coldly.

And that was right, of course, that was why they were so deadly. One reason why. They were masters of their weapons also, no one could dispute that; if they served the Ghost Walker, they meant to do so with war and slaughter. But they had this talent, this magic, this gift of God they called it, to be in one place and then suddenly in another, without seeming to move between the two. And so they were named Sand Dancers, after the little insects that seemed to do the same—unless the insects had been named after them, he wasn't sure—and so Jemel thought that he would certainly die today, when they were tired of their gaming with him.

Well, he would play along; there was nothing else he could do, and besides, his blood was raging. He felt mocked, degraded as a man and a fighter; and worse, when they made no effort to raise their weapons against him. He slashed at one in a tricky feint, lunged at the other; the one merely laughed at him, the other was not there when the scimitar sought him.

Cold steel touched Jemel's neck and withdrew, leaving blood to trickle warmly down his back.

And so the fight went, if fight you could call it. Jemel spun and leaped and sweated, focused his fury, used all his knowledge and training and a lifetime's guile, and still could not lay edge or point on either man. They danced about him, here and there and further off, and never moved their feet. Only their swords moved, and only to prick and prick again.

Beyond them, beyond this circle of his rage and frustration, Jemel caught glimpses of Rudel and Morakh still fencing, though Rudel had blood in his beard now and

seemed to be weakening, only warding off the other with
slow, heavy strokes. Those would grow heavier and
slower yet, Jemel knew, as the sword's weight grew in his
exhaustion, until at last he could not raise the blade at all.
Then Morakh would have him—but again, Morakh
should have had him ere this. Rudel too was being toyed
with, Jemel thought.

Fuel to his fire, though that burned hot enough already
and was pointless. He could not kill what he could not
touch; and he could feel the weight of his own weapon
now, which he had not earlier. Oh, he was bitter, and
would die so, no doubt; but not give up, not that. So long
as he had the strength to swing his sword, swing he
would. They must tire of sporting in the end; he only
hoped that would be before he was too tired to fight.

He had all but forgotten Julianne, forgot certainly to
keep himself between her and the Dancers. So it seemed
had they forgotten her, or else discounted her; one of them
worked his vanishing trick once too often or too care-
lessly, appearing again right in front of her, but still facing
Jemel.

When Jemel turned to close with him, half minded to
shriek at her, to tell her to run to the camels and flee, he
saw that man crumple suddenly, and fall. For a moment
he was nothing but confused, until he saw the knife-haft
that jutted from the Dancer's spine. He yelled his joy instead, and wheeled round to fall upon the other.

His brother's death seemed to enrage that man, so that
he would play no longer. Sword met sword's edge, and
now Jemel could fight at last; and never mind that he had
more than one to fight, as those who had been standing
back came running forward. He blocked and parried and
stabbed, exulting; his turn to dance, to shimmer and twist
across the sand, to be somewhere else than at their
swords' points. Even the pain in his hand was a blessing
suddenly, a burning-point that helped him to focus. He
still thought he could not win, but there was honour in his
imminent death now, it would be no mocking jest. If he

could make one kill before he died, he would go to paradise rejoicing . . .

The chance came sooner than he'd dared to hope. He faced three Dancers side by side, and had to fall back from their probing blades; but something ripped through the air, glittering, light made solid. One of the three checked suddenly, the one in the centre, and Jemel saw a strange growth jutting from the shadow of the man's hood. He fell, his hood slipped from his head; there was a knife sunk deep into his eye.

The other two Dancers were more startled even than Jemel, or took a moment longer to recover. A moment was enough. He leaped and slashed, and opened one from throat to belly before he could even see the blade's approach, let alone gather his thoughts to work that vanishing-trick.

The other did flick out of sight a moment before Jemel's scimitar found him too; but when he reappeared he was some little distance off, beside his remaining brother. That one was stringing his bow; Jemel turned his head to find Julianne, and saw her tugging her first knife free of the Dancer she'd stabbed. He snapped, "Help Rudel! These are mine," and plunged towards the archer.

Arrived in time, if only just; the man was pulling an arrow from his quiver. Jemel's sword harried him into dropping his bow; defenceless, he was gone, but his bow was left behind. Jemel faced the other, who had no stomach it seemed for single combat; he too disappeared.

Jemel scanned the ground around and saw them both, standing on an outcrop: not far, but no danger either at that distance. If they came back with swords, then he'd be ready; meantime he looked urgently for his companions.

Rudel seemed all but finished, using his sword two-handed now, only blocking Morakh's thrusts and backing, always backing. But there was Julianne, knife in hand, arm cocked to throw; Jemel saw her cast, and watched the weapon spin through the air. Her aim was good, only that the distance was too great for her skill; it was the haft and not the blade that struck Morakh clean in the head. The blow seemed to stun him, though, so that he staggered; now Rudel could step forward, and swing with a tremendous effort.

Morakh recovered his wits a moment too soon. He had no time to bring his blade up in a parry; like his brothers before him, he melted out of sight and Rudel's blade met only air.

And then there were three on the outcrop, and three on the sands below. Jemel made his way warily towards his companions, more watchful still after there were suddenly none on the outcrop. If the Dancers came again, they could come without warning, and from any side . . .

Only the breeze stirred the sand, and Rudel's heavy breathing was the only sound he could hear until Julianne broke her stillness, hurrying to the older man's side. Her arm supported him, until he could sink onto a low rock; but it was to Jemel that she addressed her question, "Have they gone . . . ?"

"Who can tell? You tend him, I will stand guard. Or perhaps you should guard us, you killed most . . ."

"Did she?" Weakly, from Rudel.

"Two. And you she saved."

"I know it. Thank you, Julianne. And well done."

She made a face, reluctance warring with modesty; it became her well, Jemel thought, that moment before she busied herself with stripping back Rudel's robe to see how badly he was hurt.

"You did well yourself," she said, grunting with relief; he was marked many times, but they were all small cuts, few deeper than a finger's width.

"He was biding his time. And making sure that I knew it."

"Why did they attack us? And that, that thing they did, that disappearing act—how . . . ?"

"One at a time, child. There is water in my bag, here; tear strips from the hem of my robe, if you need cloth. I think they attacked us because we were unnecessary, with Marron gone; they had only endured us this long on sufferance, for his sake. And we had seen their holiest site, perhaps profaned it."

"They are Sand Dancers," Jemel added. "They live to follow the Ghost Walker, and kill Patrics." *And renegade Sharai,* but he did not say that aloud. Perhaps he did not need to.

"As to the vanishing—ouch!—there is more than one magic in this land, and the Sharai have their fair share of it. You have seen a little of what your people can do, at your wedding in the Roq; I have seen more than that. I have seen a great deal more, among both peoples, and learned from both. In Surayon, we use what we can find; we have to. I had never seen quite this before, but I knew of it. The Dancers have spent decades, centuries, developing the arts of combat; what more useful than to fold space together, to be here one moment and there the next? It's all knowledge, all depends on understanding how the world is made. Also, it is a fragmentary imitation of what the Ghost Walker can do, walking between worlds; they think it honours him, or them . . ."

Julianne would be some minutes, Jemel saw, washing Rudel's wounds and binding up the worst of them. His hand hurt him; to distract himself, he wandered off to where the bodies of the Dancers lay. They would each of them have been carrying water, flour, dates; those would be useful.

Rummaging one-handed among the robes of the fallen, he found a bag that puzzled him, that seemed to contain two short, fat sticks. He worked the mouth open, and tipped the contents out; stared for a moment, then slowly understood. Scooped them up and carried them back, to lay in the sand before Rudel's feet.

He straightened, saying nothing. The bearded man gazed, and nodded.

"Morakh said he had seen such a thing before, that stone in the ghûl's tongue. He did not say when; a few short days ago, I guess to be the answer. This needs thinking on . . ."

"I don't understand?"

"Julianne, these are the feet of a ghûl. See the ass's hooves? Those are no ankles of an ass, above. That one that killed the merchant on the road, they lied to us, when they said they could not find it; they must have tracked it down and killed it. And kept the feet, and made those tracks they showed us, to force us on last night and bring us here, to where they thought that they could control Marron. They were wrong; that boy answers only to himself. Leave me now, and see to Jemel. He is more pale than you are, and hurt worse than me. I don't think he can stand much longer . . ."

He could not; he was sinking already, under a sudden dizziness. He barely felt Julianne's hands on his sleeve, drawing it back to expose the hidden hand; he could hardly force his eyes to focus, to see how bad the damage was.

Still, blurred sight was enough to show him the joke of it, sweet irony that forced a painful laugh from his throat. Morakh's scimitar had sliced clean through his smallest finger, so that it hung now by only a sliver of skin. The other fingers were cut, but none so deeply. Those he would keep.

It was Morakh who had forbidden him the Dancers' vows, the sacrifice of a finger and a stone set on the Pillar; Morakh who had brought them here and shown Marron how to open the gate between the worlds, so that Jemel had set a stone—and a potent stone—on the Pillar regardless; Morakh now who had completed the ritual.

Jemel smiled, against the swirling darkness of the world. God worked in His own way on His people. The oath was made, and witnessed; Marron would come back, and Jemel would follow him. It was written, in blood and deed. There were no choices now, for either of them.

7

Days of Gold and Thunder

ELISANDE THOUGHT THAT terror was an oil, which meant that time simply couldn't get a grip on her.

When the ghûl had sprung out at them, after the first heart-stopping moment it had seemed to move so slowly, they should have had all the time they needed to fight or flee. And yet for her it had been like moving through oil, instead of air; her thoughts raced, but her body was left behind.

When she had screamed and flung her knife, it had seemed to drift, to hang almost like a banner on the breeze, it took so long to strike home. When she'd fallen, she'd thought that she was floating; when Marron had overstood her with his blade in hand, her tongue had been too thick and heavy to shape the words she needed until it was too late, creeping sword had pierced crawling monster and the thing was made well instead of slain.

If they'd had time, she could have warned him—but however slow their bodies were, words had been slower still to come.

The Daughter had risen out of Marron's ruined shoulder, and even that had seemed leisurely to her; and Marron's hesitation had taken an age, long enough she'd thought for the ghûl to devour them both, though not long enough for her to drag herself to her feet.

Then he'd shaped the Daughter into a door, and hauled her through; and thank the God her mind had still been running fast, not numbed into stupor by her first sight of the place he'd brought her to.

Because Marron at least was not thinking now, he'd done that; boy-like, all he was doing now was react. The first thing he did, of course he did, was to close the door that he'd made, to keep the ghûl—and others too, maybe—on the other side of it. He let that near-solid frame fold in on itself till it was only a heavy, shapeless waft of smoke. It looked thicker, stronger here than it ever had before; and that was perhaps a blessing, it might have given him a moment's pause.

At any rate, the second thing he did was to set her on her feet and hold her so, until she found her own balance; which gave her just time enough to realise what he intended next, and to prevent him.

She clapped her hands over the bloody ruin of his shoulder, where the ghûl had gored it, just a moment before that dense streak of smoke could reach it.

Marron screamed and jerked away, but just had wit enough to jerk the Daughter too, so that it rose high in the air above them. Then he stared at her, and said, "If that had touched your skin . . ."

"I know." She would have died, he couldn't have prevented it. Perhaps she too had only been reacting—*girl-like,* she thought, with a touch of grim humour that she didn't share with him—though she'd rather think that it had been a gesture of absolute trust, that she'd been certain of his quick response. "But, Marron, you can't take it back through this," lifting one hand towards his shoulder again but not touching this time, not to hurt him further.

"It would stop the bleeding . . ."

"Yes; but it would stop its healing too. You know that. It'd be like your arm, you'd have two open wounds that would never close again."

He shrugged, one-shouldered, and gazed at her, huge brown eyes in a face that was white with pain. "I could live with that." *As it is, it may kill me, soon or later . . .* He didn't need to say that aloud. And he could be right; it was a dreadful wound, she could see white bone beneath the torn flesh and the pumping blood. He could bleed to death quite quickly, or else it could fester and poison slowly; she'd known a man die from the simple prick of a thorn.

But that man hadn't had Marron's advantages, nor Elisande at hand when he needed her; she had come to his bedside too late, when his whole arm had been putrid and her skills too little to save him.

"You'll have to endure the pain a little longer," she said softly, "you can't take the Daughter back till the blood stops flowing. But that at least I can do for you." That and more, if she could work at all in this strangest of landscapes, where all her talents and knowledge might come to nothing.

That she didn't believe, though; she felt herself strong and potent, more so than usual, just as the Daughter itself seemed to be more potent here. She tucked her shoulder under Marron's good arm and guided, half-carried him to a rock that was warm to the touch, as the air was warm, and the ground beneath her booted feet. He could at least sit down; she didn't think he could stand much longer. All his skin was slick with a chill sweat; pain and blood-loss between them were draining him faster than she cared to think about.

She still had one knife remaining to her; working quickly, she used that to cut away the ripped shoulder and drenched sleeve of Marron's robe, peeling them carefully back from ruined flesh. For all her care and his courage, still he gasped; she took a moment to touch his cheek with tender fingers, leaving it printed with his own blood, the marks of her concern. Then she slashed a swathe of cloth from the hem of her own robe and shrugged off the empty water-skins she'd been carrying till she found the one that was hers beneath, husbanded through the long night-ride and still full.

She soaked the rough dark cloth, and swabbed at Marron's wound. Here she had to be unkind, ungentle; he sobbed under her touch, but who knew what filth a ghûl might carry on its claws? Not she; and though the Daughter was said to be sovereign against poisons, she wouldn't trust what she didn't fully understand. Better to be certain, to do the work herself.

When she was sure as she could be that the wound was clean, that water and blood between them had carried off all dirt, she threw the cloth aside and laid both hands against the wound. She closed her eyes and concentrated her mind, shutting out all thoughts else and drawing on everything she knew, every power that she possessed; then she pressed hard, pulling rags of flesh together as best she could, forcing the wrenched and twisted joint back into shape.

This should have been cruel, but was not. She heard Marron gasp again, but only in surprise; she felt the cold flesh warm beneath her tingling fingers, as she channelled healing strength through them and into him.

At times like this, when she was so focused on another's body and wellbeing, it had often seemed to her as though her thoughts followed that flow of power, out through her fingers and under alien skin. Today that effect was amplified beyond measure; she felt almost like another Daughter herself—though she flinched from the word, she hated to think of herself as anyone's daughter— as her awareness seemed to leave her own body and slip into Marron's. She could sense, almost see the damage that the ghûl had done, although her eyes were shut; she could feel how torn vessels closed beneath her touch, how stretched tendons drew tight and firm again, how shattered bone itself started to rebuild. Above all, she bathed in the glow of healing well begun. Almost she wanted to pass out of her body altogether, to leap that extra little distance and flow entire into Marron to visit his heart and all his other organs, to sidle into his head and try to read his thoughts as well as she could read the processes of his flesh and blood . . .

Almost, but not quite. She retained so much sense, at least, to resist that call at the last and draw back instead, forcing her eyes to open and her hands to fall away. Staggering, gasping, she needed suddenly to sit herself, and did so at his side. Her turn to sweat, she found, pushing her fingers through tangled, sodden hair.

When she lifted her head, she found him looking at her; but she'd known that already, she had felt it even through that enveloping exhaustion.

"How is it now?" she asked, only to have some passage of words between them; she knew how it was, she had seen it from the inside.

"Better. So much better, I can't believe . . ." He tried to swing the arm to prove it, and yelped instead. She amazed herself by laughing at him, though it was a hoarse, hard little bubble of a chuckle that hurt her throat in its rising.

"Steady. It's not mended yet, only started. It'll be a long journey."

"Even so. I didn't know that you could do such things . . ."

"Neither did I," she confessed. "It wasn't me—or only partly me. Partly it's this place, there's a power here . . ." More powers than one, she remembered; she glanced upward, to see where the Daughter still hung above them in the sky. "You should take that back now, it'll kill any pain you feel and maybe help the healing, I don't know . . ."

She didn't know either if she could work even here on a body that contained such a creature; she'd had no success before, on Marron's arm. But if need be he could release it again, and let her work on him while his blood was pure, untainted. While his eyes were brown . . .

When he didn't move, she reached to do it for him: lift-

ing Marron's bare arm—just a little, not enough to make
him cry out with the pressure on his shoulder—and taking
her dagger again, pricking lightly between the stitches of
his old wound and squeezing until the first drop of blood
appeared. There should have been no more than that, he
had lost too much already. A drop would have been
enough, a pin-hole sufficed. But it spurted, even through
the tiny cut she'd made, and she felt Marron jerk with an
unexpected pain.

He looked up and the Daughter flowed down like a
scarlet thread, insinuating itself into his body. The run of
blood died as swiftly as it had begun; his terrible paleness
receded, and so clearly did his discomfort, as he gazed
with an oddly detached interest at the results of her work
on his shoulder.

As did she. There was a great ragged gash, and the
edges were open still; no miracles, even here. But the
blood had stopped running, there was no open gateway
now out of which the Daughter might have slipped un-
called-for. And the flesh was pink, the bones she knew
were rightly set, and knitting . . .

"I must bind it up," she said, "to keep this out," this
fine warm golden dust that covered the rock they sat on
and the ground below. What that might do in a wound, inside a body, she couldn't begin to guess. "And we'll make
a sling to hold it, you mustn't use it yet or you could tear
apart what's just begun to mend . . ."

His face twisted, at a memory she couldn't share; she
could guess at it, though, and hurried on.

"I'd like to know what's happening back, back in my
world,"—she couldn't say "our world," not quite; with the
Daughter in his blood Marron was a bridge between that
and this, and seemed to belong in neither—"but . . ."

"No," Marron said, decisive for once. "You need not
worry for the others; Jemel will kill the ghûl."

"Will he?"

"Oh, yes." Utter certainty in his tone, and almost a hint

of pride. "He was behind us, when we came through. He will do that."

"Well, he should know how, at least. I'd like to be sure," *as sure as you are,* "but we can't tell what we'd be going back to. I don't think you should let the Daughter out again, anyway, not for a while. What I've done felt good, better than I'd expected; your body needs a chance to heal properly, though, and it'll do that best if you're free from pain. The Daughter can do that for you, at least . . ."

It could give him the strength to travel in this country, too; and that was what she wanted most, now that they were here. She was concerned for their companions— well, for Julianne, at least, and of course for Jemel—but after being flung so abruptly away from them, and so far, it was hard to feel involved in that small struggle. What she felt rather was enchanted; as though she'd been gifted a glimpse of wonder. It would be cruel to wrench her back into that company of secrets and doubts and mistrust, when she was suddenly here in this place of mystery and myth. And with Marron, the two of them together and alone, as they had never been before . . .

She pushed herself to her feet, looked around and saw a low scarp of rock just a little distance off. She left Marron—and marvelled that she could do that, even for a minute, but did it none the less—and walked over to the foot of the scarp. Set her hands on it, and found that it too was warm, as all this world was warm; lifted her eyes to the peak, and began to climb.

She was still weary in mind and body both; this was no great ascent, but still it was an effort to push and drag even her light weight up to the summit. She wanted to see, though, more even than she wanted to rest. She knew where they were, in the land of fable, but she needed her eyes to confirm it. Knowing wasn't enough. Neither was touch, that warmth that pervaded everything; nor taste and smell, though the air both smelled and tasted uniquely different, rich and flat at the same time. *Unbreathed,* she thought, and smiled at herself for thinking it.

There was hearing too, of course, and she could hear nothing but her own hard breathing; she'd heard silence before, though, the deep silence of the Sands at midday when nothing moved, when even the air was still. It was strange, but not strange enough. She burned for a long sight of this mystical country, and all she'd seen thus far was a close view of dust and rocks. Golden rocks, to be sure—but still, not enough.

And so she hauled herself to a height, not a tremendous height but the best that she could manage just now; and when she got there, sweat stung her eyes so that for a little while she could see nothing but a blur. She rubbed at them, and staggered where she stood; caught her balance with a wild swing of her arms, and looked about her.

Now she could see for miles, for days; days of hard travel they would be, too, but she yearned to make them. Softly gold under the soft light, the land stretched before and below her like a glimmering image of the Sands, except that she thought that the Sands were an image of this. A crude image too, more coarsely made of ruder stuff and patched by shadow, which this land was not . . .

Puzzling over that, she glanced upward, and realised suddenly that there was no sun in the sky. How could that be? And would there be a soft and starless night to follow day, or was this land unchanging even in its light?

Well, an answer to that would come in time. For now she turned in a slow circle, feasting her eyes; or turned half a circle, rather, and came to a dead stop. Where in their world the Dancer's Pillar had been raised on its high hill, here a gleaming blade of stone leaped up, too high almost for her mind to fathom.

She gaped, recognised that she was gaping, and closed her mouth with a conscious effort. Completed her circle quickly, wanting no more wonders and glad to see none; and dragged her eyes down to find Marron where she had left him, sitting on his rock. With his head lifted, she saw, watching her . . .

That was enough, and more than enough. She scrambled back down the scarp in what came close to a headlong tumble, was almost indeed a fall; arrived at the bottom with sore fingers and scuffed boots, dust in her hair and hurry in her feet.

She ran over to him, running into his gaze all the way like a girl who ran into a hard, hot wind for the sake of something precious at its back. When she reached him, she sank breathless to the ground just a little touch away from him, the distance that red eyes could keep a girl; and she said, "Have you seen it? That, that . . ."

She didn't have a word, but she could point: *that* way, what should be north by her memory of where they'd been in the other world. She'd always had a strong sense of direction, and she was relieved to find that it felt like north here too, though there was no sun to confirm it. At least the two worlds seemed to map each other.

Marron nodded, more distracted she thought than wordless from amazement, as she was. It couldn't be seen from here, the scarp was in the way, but of course he'd seen it. That had to be where he and Jemel had come through before. She wanted to ask what it was, what on earth it might mean; but how would he know?

Instead she busied herself with making bandages, improvising a sling to hold his arm. He'd have to go barechested, but that should be no hardship, even for a pale-skinned Patric; the warmth was better than pleasant, it was delightful, and he couldn't burn where there was no sun.

That was another reason, she thought, why they should stay and journey in this world and not their own. The others of their party would move on, south to Rhabat; if she and Marron tried to follow over the Sands, he would blister and sicken of sunstroke without a robe to cover his head and back. Here they could do it safely, if they could find their way . . .

Except that here there was nothing of this world that they could eat, and no water they could drink. If there were water at all, she wouldn't risk it; nor allow him to do so, despite the Daughter's internal watchfulness. Perhaps they should hasten back after all, hope to catch the others before the party abandoned them and moved on. She was only looking for excuses to stay, after all, and here was a better reason to leave . . .

"Marron? Would you like to go back? It would mean more blood for you, a little, and more pain"—*a lot,* she thought, and perhaps more blood than she was saying, perhaps more than he could afford—"and we don't know what we'd be going back to; but you could, you could check on Jemel," a low stroke, she knew, but refused to blush for it, "and we'd have supplies and company. And a known route to follow, though there may be trouble on the way. We wouldn't just be striking out in the dark . . ." Or *in the light,* if this place knew no darkness.

She knew what she wanted, but she didn't know what was best; it was a genuine choice she offered him, and if he'd said *go back* she would have gone, and never challenged the decision.

But he gazed at her with those strange, inhuman eyes she could not read, and said, "We'll do what you want, Elisande. If it's safe for you. What supplies do you need, that you have not got?"

"We both need food and water," she said, trying to obliterate the difference between them, and only seeing him smile at the attempt. "I have one skin that is full, these others that are empty except for what drops we can squeeze from them. I also have a bag of flour"—Dancer-like, in the desert she carried her survival on her back always, even where there were wells and pack-camels and friends and all—"and flint and tinder, but no firewood. We will need a fire, to cook the bread; I don't think we'll find anything that we can burn." It seemed to her that except for what came up out of the earth, oil and tar and coal, anything that burned must once have lived; she thought that nothing lived here. Except the djinn, of course, and the 'ifrit. Neither of those, she thought, would feed a fire.

She seemed to have persuaded herself, against her own intent; when he said nothing, she sighed and said, "We'd better go back, I suppose." And once gone, they were gone for good, most likely; she didn't expect to have this chance again. She couldn't ask Marron to bring her through on a pleasure-jaunt, it cost him far too severely.

But Marron surprised her with a smile; he said, "How far do you think we have to go?"

"I'm not sure. They said Rhabat was a week's journey; but that was on camelback, and through the Sands. I don't know how fast we can travel here, on foot . . ." They could go as directly south as the land would allow, no need to seek for wells when they couldn't drink the water; she felt a flicker of hope which blossomed into flame, a burning desire when he reached down with his good hand to lift a large rock that lay on the ground beside her, that she'd been resting her elbow on.

Marron turned it over with an easy flick of his wrist, and said, "I don't think we need fire, Elisande. I doubt it ever gets cold in this land; and as for cooking bread— well, touch. Touch lightly . . ."

She did, the swiftest brush of her fingers; and still she had to snatch them back and suck at them. Warm like everything on its upper surface, it was scorching hot on its underside; lay a dough on that and he was right, it would bake through in minutes.

"We still don't have much, either flour or water . . ."

"Not much, no—but enough, perhaps. I don't need much, and nor perhaps will you. Less than you would in the Sands, in any case, with no sun to roast you. And this country lends me strength, as the Daughter does too; it may do the same for you, when you are not so tired."

Indeed, she felt stronger already, stronger far than she'd expected after the exhaustion of healing him. They shouldn't take the risk, even now her good sense told her to go back and join the others; but he was offering her the chance to stay and she lacked the will to resist him.

She lifted her head and gazed into those fierce eyes, seeking the gentle soul behind and not finding it, as ever. Sure of it none the less, she laid a hand on his knee and said, "There must be dangers here, that we can't foresee . . ."

"Yes. But we can flee them, if we must, as we did the ghûl. You want to stay, Elisande; don't work against yourself."

She sighed, for pure contentment. Adventure, exploration, new wonders to discover, and all of it in his company, which was adventure and exploration in itself; there was risk, of course, but that only spoke to her soul the louder. Hunger and thirst she'd met before, and survived them. If they met worse, or stranger—well, that was the quality of the world, and some part of what she sought.

Was she too tired to begin now, as she ought? Perhaps she was only too happy to move; she could begin in any case, or rather take another step on a journey already begun. She sat entirely still and said, "Marron, you've changed so much, so quickly. You used to be simple, but these days I can't predict you at all. There's the Daughter, of course, but it's more than that. What's happened to you?"

"I killed my friend," he said, his voice flat with honesty, "and left my master; I betrayed my people and my God. I killed more than one friend, I killed many. With a monster that I took into my body. How could I not be changed by that, by all of that?"

Elisande sighed again, for the opposite of contentment, for him; and laid her head against his leg, and waited to feel his hand touch her hair. Waited in vain and ached for him, that he could not make so easy, so human a gesture, and was content none the less, although she understood herself little better than she did him.

TIME PASSED, THOUGH she had no way to count it unless she'd counted the beats of her heart, which she had not. At last, because he would not stir, she had to. She pulled herself reluctantly to her feet, and allowed herself one swallow of their precious water; offered the skin to him, and felt some relief when he only shook his head. His abstinence had distressed her for weeks; now it was a blessing.

"We should start out," she said. "There's a long way to go." And she'd never been less prepared for a journey, nor looked forward to it more.

He nodded, and rose; glanced about him and turned unerringly towards the south, or so her own senses told her.

"You must say," he said, "when you need to rest. I think I could go for ever."

That was a glimpse of the old Marron, almost, the boy who would exhaust himself without knowing it; only that the old Marron would never have thought to say so. Elisande hid a wry smile inside her hood, and waved him on.

THE HEALING HAD drained her, a short climb too soon after had exhausted her; it seemed though that there was something restorative about unbreathed air, or adventure, or shadowed but much-desired company. Once started, she felt like Marron that she could walk for ever.

Unlike Marron—perhaps—she wasn't fool enough to believe it; but there was enchantment enough in the simple act of walking here to bury all her doubts. Unless it was simply the fact of being here, or the fact of being with him . . .

Certainly it wasn't the landscape itself that struck her so with rapture. She had been in many places, both natural and man-made, that were more beautiful to the eye, once that eye had grown accustomed to the golden sheen that overlay everything here. She had walked in lands that were wilder, and far more dramatic. This was dead country, or seemed so. There was only the absence of any sun in the sky or any shadow under their feet to speak of the

strangeness of where they were; only that towering monument, that blade or needle or pillar of stone, to speak of
the powers that dwelt here, and that was behind them. A
glance back could find it at any time during that first day,
like a finger to mark where they had started their trek, but
she glanced back seldom. It wasn't even useful as a guide,
to say how far they had walked; it was too big, she
couldn't read the scale.

Besides, that first day, she didn't care how far they'd
come nor how far they had yet to go. She was entranced
only by the journey, by each separate moment of it. To
step where perhaps no human had stepped before—and
she walked at Marron's side to be sure of that, or as sure
as she could be, not to walk in his footsteps—and to see
what perhaps no human had seen before: that was enough,
or nearly so. To share that walk and those sights with this
damaged, dangerous, delightful boy: that was plenty for
Elisande, it was all the thrill she craved and more. She
didn't need towering cliffs and thundering falls, nor yet
gardens with gorgeous blossoms and overpowering
scents. She had known those and loved them, drawing
them soul-deep with every sense she had; but she loved
this better.

THERE WAS NO path, there couldn't be, where no creature lived to make one; neither djinni nor 'ifrit would
leave a track where it passed. Unless it chose to, she supposed—and then only if it could form a physical body in
this world, as it could in the other. She remembered the
djinni she and Julianne had met, how it had avoided any
contact with ground, the touch of anything more solid
than the dust of the road—and the flesh of a boy's arm,
that too, but that not by its choice—and decided not to expect djinni-tracks here.

There was no path, but a way was easy to find. It must
have matched the way their friends would be going, she
thought, down from the heights of the Dancers' Pillar to

the great Sands below; except that here the pillar they left behind was so much greater, and what they came down to was softer, kinder country, and so much less than the Sands.

The way they went pitched steeply downward, but the dust was firmly packed, and where the slope fell sharply there was rock aplenty jutting through, to give good footing beneath their boots. She worried a little for Marron at first, for fear that his strapped arm would upset his balance; it was wasted worry, though, she saw that soon enough. He went down the incline like a mountain goat, taking it almost at a run, leaping sometimes from ledge to narrow ledge. She followed more cautiously, watching his progress always with one eye and hoping that he laughed as he leaped, that he could find some fun in his wild descent. He was too far ahead too quickly for her to be sure, but she did hope.

Reaching the foot of the drop at last, she found him waiting for her, a kindness she had almost not dared to hope for. For Julianne and the others, this would be burning sand and a long hard road ahead, veering constantly off their true direction from well to necessary well, each one claimed by jealous and likely hostile tribes. For her and Marron, not so. There was only that hard-settled dust stretching before them in rolling dunes which were broken rarely by an upthrust of the rock beneath. Their way lay straight before them, due south. The dangers of the Sands, both human and natural, she knew; the dangers of this place she could only guess at, and she would not trust her guesses. No point in anticipating them, then. She set herself at Marron's side and strode forward, eager to leave her light prints beside his, and never mind if no one ever saw them, she knew they were there . . .

THEY WALKED AND walked, and saw nothing that moved except each other, bar an occasional light rippling in the dust under a vagrant breeze. Mostly, even the air didn't move. Nor did the landscape change except in detail, the shapes and numbers of the rocky scarps that lifted above the level of the dust. Elisande had seen the Sands in many different faces, dune and gorge and gravel plain; she never had seen such a view as this. As the stories said, though, she did think that this was the original; that the desert she knew had been hacked out of coarse clay and rubbed into rough shape by a clumsy thumb, in brute imitation of what was here.

What was here and endless, or so it seemed. Sometimes she thought that they were not moving at all, or that the land carried them backwards at the same speed that they progressed; that was when she counted rocks, or took a rare glance behind her. In fact, by worldly standards, they were moving fast; those hills they'd come down from were a ridge of dusky gold on the horizon, that monument that had looked for a while so like a pillar holding up the sky—unless it was a blade that threatened it—had fallen to a line, an ink-stroke on parchment, its impression lost with distance. This far away, her eye could pretend that it was closer, not so big . . .

They were moving fast, they had come far: too far, too fast on just a mouthful of water. And yet she wanted no more; she wasn't thirsty at all, wasn't hungry, nor tired now. She swung along easily beside Marron, aware that he was holding himself back to her pace, that left alone he could have run and run; and into the silence that had held them both for a long time now, she said, "Is this how it's been for you, all these weeks? While I bullied you to eat and drink, and rest?"

"Yes," he said, "except it's stronger here. I think I really could go for ever . . ."

Well, and so he might; she could not, though she felt it. She would be sensible, she would call breaks and longer halts—but not yet, not with this next dune to mount. The landscape could and should grow dull, she thought, and yet it had not; every dune-top gave a slightly different view even if it was a view of the same thing.

It was Marron in the end who pointed out the changes that were coming. She could almost have been resentful, except that change was wonder too. Everything in this world was new, untried, intriguing . . .

"Look," he said, "those must be hills ahead. And the sky is growing darker."

True, and true. At least those must be hills if they were as like as they seemed to what lay behind the travellers now, a narrow ribbon of darker shade set between ground and sky. Not the hills that guarded Rhabat or their equivalent, not yet and not for a while yet; but there were ranges throughout the Sands where the land lay in folds and creases, and in those more primitive structures the two worlds seemed to match each other.

Also, the sky was undeniably growing darker; though she was glad that he had said it that way, not *night is falling*. This was no night as she understood it, the sun setting to the west and darkness rising in its absence in the east. All around the wide horizon—and she turned in a slow circle to be sure, to confirm its strangeness—there was a subtle change of colour, as though the sky were an inverted bowl with a rim of glaze darker than its body.

They walked on and watched it deepen further, watched it rise until the sky was altogether black on the horizon, fading through grey and still gleaming golden-white only at the apex, directly above their heads.

Marron stopped abruptly, atop yet another in the long march of low dunes. "We should find a place to rest," he said, "before the light has gone completely."

"I don't need to rest." Which might or might not be true, she might only have inherited his foolish mantle, along with some at least of his restless energy; what was true was that she simply didn't want an end to this steady walking. There was some magic in it, more than the abiding strength of her legs and the fascination of the place; she felt as though she'd left all anxieties back in the other world, and she could stay free of them so long as she kept moving. A long night's lying still—and she was sure that she would not sleep, she could find no trace of quiet in her—could bring them back, could send her thoughts probing relentlessly across the gulf to seek what she could not find; or worse, just have them spinning hectically around and around, tangling in the mess of her own desires and doubts . . .

Marron smiled. "We would lose each other in the dark," he said. "There'll be no moon to find each other by. Besides, we both should eat, hungry or not. And rest too, weary or not.

She didn't believe that he would lose her, his eyes and hearing were both so unnaturally sharp now. Nevertheless he was right and she was wrong, twice over; she was not used to that, and didn't like it. Sourly, she grunted her agreement and followed as for the first time he led away from their straight path south, off to the shelter of one of those sudden islands of rock among the dust. Not that they needed shelter, or not from wind or weather; there had been none of either, bar those occasional light zephyrs that stirred the air a little but had no presence else.

Shelter from watching eyes, perhaps, but there'd been none of those either, or none that either one of them had seen or sensed. Still, there was comfort in walls, even if it was only a single wall of rock at their back; better that than camping entirely in the open. And in fact Marron found a shallow gully in the twilight, a slot where they could lie sheltered on two sides and exposed only on one. Less light in there, only a notch open to the opal sky, and that was dimming; light enough, though, to show her a number of rocks fallen loose. Warm seats they would make until it was time to lie down, if time had any meaning here that she could judge. It didn't seem to; night—if this was night—had come before she was ready for it, after she'd trekked so far that she should have been worn out long since. And dry, and starving hungry, and she was none of those, she felt fresh as morning.

And was probably deceived, or so she told herself. Firmly. Marron turned a large rock over with his casual strength, and she burned her fingers brushing off the dust to find where it was flat; there was already too little light to see well. She tipped a measure of flour out of her bag, too little it should be for two young appetites at the end of such a day, though it seemed too much to her. She added a little water and this time used her knife to mix them quickly into a dough before the flour scorched.

When she smelled smoke, she flicked the dough-cake over with the point of the knife; when again her nose told her that it was starting to burn, she lifted it off and tore it gingerly in two. It was almost too hot to handle, though Marron seemed not to notice as she handed him his share.

"I'll eat if you will," she said gruffly.

"Oh, I'll eat."

And he did, and so she had to, although the crust of the loaf tasted like cinders in her mouth and the inside was still wet and somehow rancid. She choked it down, necessary fuel, and unslung her water-skin to rinse her palate; the water was blood-warm and rank, tasting of ill-cured leather. She took less than she'd meant to but still more than she wanted, and passed the skin to Marron. He drank even more sparingly than she had.

There was nothing to do then except sit on her chosen rock and lean her spine and shoulders against the towering wall behind her, regretting just a little that he had chosen a separate rock from her. She tilted back her head and watched as that little notch of sky darkened overhead, till it was as black as the rim had been earlier. No moon, as Marron had predicted, and no stars either; only an all-encompassing darkness. It wasn't quite a dead black, though, just as the white of the day-sky had not been a pure white; this like that had a pearly sheen to it—she had seen black pearls as a child, and had yearned to possess their beauty—and was shot through with glimmers of gold.

Still, it was black enough, it sufficed. She could see nothing. She held her hand a short inch from her face and could not make out a single finger: Marron was a sound of breathing in the stillness, nothing more. This was just what she'd been dreading, an engulfing shadow that would let her mind slip free and so torment her; she didn't think she could endure hours of it, even assuming that it lasted only hours. She had no real reason to suppose that light and dark followed the same rhythms here that they did in her own world, only a desperate hope; and that hope itself still left her facing a nightmare time, without even the benefit of waking.

She did what she could to meet it. She lay down on the dust of the gully's floor, which should make a warmer and a softer bed than she'd known for a while; it showed no hint of cooling. She settled herself as best she could, closed her eyes like an obedient child at bedtime and waited, hoping, praying almost that her body had deceived her, that in truth it was as weary as it ought to be, and so would slide gently into sleep and take her with it . . .

WHICH IT DID not, and she was not in the least surprised. She lay striving after sleep, and could not achieve it. After a while her eyes opened of their own accord, and she stared upwards until she could just barely distinguish the black of the rock from the iridescent black cleft of the sky. That seemed to ripple with faint light for a moment, as though a golden twist of air had passed across it. She sighed, hoping that weary eyes were playing tricks on her; and forced them closed again, tried to squirm more deeply into the soft dust, and went chasing once more after an oblivion she could not find.

IN SUCH A darkness, she didn't need to lift or turn her head to know that she had no chance of seeing Marron; equally surely, she knew that he was not sleeping, nor trying to sleep. His breathing betrayed him, as did every slightest movement of his body where he sat yet on his rock, just a few short paces from her. Cruelly alert to him, she lay and listened to his wakefulness, as she was certain that he was listening to hers. She raged against the stupidity, until his patience had outwaited hers; then, fighting against honesty with all the guile she could find in herself, she called to him softly.

"Marron?"

"Yes, Elisande?"

"Please, I can't, I can't sleep. I love this country by daylight, but in the dark it frightens me. It's so strange, and we know so little about it; I keep imagining monstrous things. And thinking we deserve them, we shouldn't be here, we don't have the right. Even you, you don't possess what you carry, you don't have any claim over it. The djinn would be so angry, if they found us. Or 'ifrit might come, and they are terrible . . ."

"Do you want to go back?"

"Into the Sands, blindly, at night?" If it was night in the Sands—but never mind that doubt, it was no use to her now. "No, that would be foolhardy. I just want company, that's all, and I can't see you. I hate being this helpless," and that at least was true; she was no Julianne, trained to rely on wits and tongue. "Would you come and lie beside me? Just where I can touch you? You should lie down in any case, you need rest as much as I do, even if neither one of us is sleeping . . ."

There was a moment's pause, she heard the silence of his breath and doubted her own wisdom mightily. Then he answered her without speaking. She didn't know if even his eyes could find her in this blackness, but his ears were sharper than hers; he walked swift and sure-footed to her side, and lay down to share her dust.

Almost to share. He lay close, but not close enough: an arm's reach away, and an arm was all that he offered her, reaching across the space between them to lay his hand on her wrist. She wasn't having that. She rolled over and nestled against him, her head on his good shoulder and all her short body pressed against his.

He stiffened; she flinched inwardly, but wouldn't pull away. Again she had no resources but her voice, and used it as best she could.

"How's your hurt, are you in any pain?"

"No. I don't know how it is, I don't feel it. I expect it's healing."

"I should have worked on it a little more, maybe; but that would hurt you, because I don't think I could do it unless you let the Daughter out. That thing overmasters me . . ."

"I wouldn't let you," he said, surprising her one more time with his firmness, so far from the biddable boy he had been. "It exhausts you, to do that; you must husband your strength."

"At least I might have slept," and she forced out a chuckle through a tight throat. "You're not comfortable, though," and now perhaps was the time for honesty, now that he'd come this far; at least, she hoped so. She was all out of guile. "Why not, if you're not in pain? You're very tense . . ."

"I'm—not accustomed to this," he whispered, "to lying with a girl."

Neither lying to a girl, seemingly; she was grateful that he hadn't done that. Once she'd thought that he wouldn't know how to lie, but he'd had to at the castle, again and again. Maybe all boys had the talent, even those who'd never used it. Girls, she was sure of. But no need now, he'd matched her honesty with his and she felt on safe ground suddenly.

"I know that, Marron. Don't worry about it, just relax. Forget that I'm a girl; I'm your companion, that's all, and it's good to stay close. There must be danger here, although we have not met it yet; we depend on each other, we have to learn to trust. With our bodies, too. The Sharai don't worry about bodies, and neither should we . . ."

And as she spoke she rolled again, she straddled him and sat back on her heels; and laid her hands on his neck and pushed him down when he tried to rise, left her fingers on the pulses of his throat and began to hum.

"What is this?"

"The *sodar*. Be easy. You met Jemel's, in the Sultan's palace; now meet mine. It will guide you into sleep."

"It was you who said you could not sleep . . ."

"Because you would not, fool," she whispered. "Be still, be easy . . ."

She slid her fingers through his hair and over his bare skin; she sang low and husky as her father used to do, she worked this little magic and barely dared to think that it might work. Likely the Daughter would work against her, here as elsewhere. But here all their little magics seemed to work, faster and stronger than in their own world; it took only a brief time before she felt the tension flee his body, heard his breathing slow, felt his head topple gently to the side.

And she stayed where she was a little longer, not singing now but touching, her hands falling still on his chest; and she sighed one last time that night and lay down close beside him, wishing almost—almost!—that Jemel was there, to say the *sodar* for her in her turn.

But maybe what she had said to Marron was truer than she'd meant, because his sleeping lulled and contented her, and it was not so very long before she slept herself.

NOR SO VERY long before she woke, or so it seemed; only that there was a line of light all around the bowl of sky, and it was starting to creep upward into the lustrous black.

She turned her head, and saw that Marron was still well asleep; and smiled with a wicked cheerfulness, no doubts in her head this morning as she reached for her knife.

Its prick woke him, as it must: too late. He gasped at the pain that followed, and she bit her lip hard; but she kept her hand steady on his chest and her eyes on his, see-

ing how they faded from fiery red to puzzled brown as the
blood flowed out of his arm, and the Daughter too.

"Why . . . ?"

"Because I must see to your shoulder, I don't trust your
reports; and that only gets in my way. I know it hurts, and
I'm sorry. Now keep that thing out of my way, and lie
still . . ."

She was all brisk efficiency this morning, and—without
the Daughter to give him confidence, perhaps?—he was
all compliance. She set her hands on either side of his
half-healed wound, and closed her eyes to see the better.

Good. Better than she'd hoped; healing was well
begun. If the Daughter didn't help, at least it didn't interfere. She had no need to waste her strength on him today;
just a little warmth, a little gentle encouragement, and she
withdrew.

"Take it back, then. Quickly: the less blood you lose
here, the happier I'll be. And it might attract attention, it is
half of this world, as we are not . . ."

Again he obeyed her, and she saw his eyes flood with
scarlet. Before he lost the habit or the Daughter stole it
from him, she said, "Breakfast, before we go on. Turn that
rock again, would you?"

He did, and she found the upturned surface hot: hotter
than it had been the night before when it had been upper-
most and nothing more than warm, but not so hot as the
underside when Marron had first lifted it. This heat wasn't
inherent, then; it welled up quite slowly from below, and
dissipated into the air. She wondered how hot a cave
would be, a mine, a sink-hole . . .

She baked bread again, and this time—by virtue of
slower cooking, and also of her being able to see—managed to produce a loaf that was baked through and hardly
burned at all. Eating was still an effort, she had no appetite and didn't see the point, and besides the taste was
no better than it had been the previous night; but she'd
eaten worse bread in the desert, and forced herself to it for
Marron's sake, because he would not without her lead.

Sleeping against his unprotected bones last night had impressed upon her just how skeleton-thin he was. He'd lost weight, she thought, since they left the Roq; and he'd been skinny enough before, a carcass entirely without meat . . .

A mouthful of water each, and at this rate their supplies would last them to Rhabat and beyond; and so they set out walking.

THAT SECOND DAY they came surprisingly soon to the range of hills they'd seen the previous evening, and climbed without effort. The rise was steep, but nothing like the savage heights she'd met in the Sands, where a difficult scramble up might lead only to an impossible crevasse, forcing a harder retreat and perhaps a day's detour. Admittedly she'd generally been encumbered with camels then, who were not made for mountains; but even so the land here was far less brutally torn, and offered little resistance to their passage.

The only trouble they encountered was one low cliff that lay directly in their way. They might have gone around, at the cost of an hour or two; but the rock offered plenty of handholds, and Marron said, "I can climb this, if you can."

"Easily. But should you, with your arm . . . ?"

"I will not need it. One hand is enough."

He proved that, all but skimming up the face of the cliff, barely seeming to grip even with the one hand. She waited below until he was safely over the top, envying him his confidence but still slightly regretting the doubtful boy he used to be; then she made shift to follow.

She'd taken on harder climbs in Surayon for sheer pleasure, learning in the company of friends and later going alone, driven to it, wild child pitting herself against the rock. No one climbed for pleasure in the Sands, but even there she'd felt a grim determination sometimes that had forced her higher than she'd needed to go, and a sense of triumph after at having overcome.

Here she hoped for pleasure and was well on the way to finding it, halfway up the cliff and already anticipating the top, intent on climbing as smoothly as Marron had if not so fast when she was stayed, frozen almost by a sudden touch of wind against her face, and a voice that was not Marron's.

A voice that offered no greeting and no warmth, no hint of humanity; a voice that chimed instantly in her memory, *djinni,* and had her clutching hard at holds that seemed abruptly perilous, as this land was perilous, which she had almost managed to forget.

"It is unusual," it said, "to find a child of the earth within our lands. To find two is not unprecedented, but it is perhaps worth a remark."

It sounded to be close by her ear, and yet a startled glance in that direction showed her nothing, unless there was perhaps a light disturbance of the air. Nothing more, nothing to give her eyes a focus. She hung on, both to the rock and to her reeling thoughts; drew a breath and held it, thinking hard, before she spoke in reply.

"Spirit," she said, fighting to sound calm when she was not, when she was anything but, "believe me, the circumstances that brought us here were no less unusual. We would not have ventured here from mere curiosity," which was a lie direct, but hopefully the creature that addressed her would not detect that. "We fled a ghûl, that might otherwise have killed us both . . ."

She hoped, she prayed almost that it was a djinni she spoke to, and not an 'ifrit. She had no way of telling, except that it had said "our lands," and this country was always said in stories to be the land of the djinn. All she was certain of was that this was not the djinni she had met and spoken with on the road to the Roq, and later at the castle; the voice was indistinguishable, high and sexless, but that other would surely have called her by her name if it had found her thus, and perhaps have made some reference to their previous encounter, or else to Julianne. It had betrayed a rare interest in their doings; this one, not.

"Indeed," it said, not even rising to the bait she'd laid, that mention of the ghûl. "It will have been your companion who brought you here; I sense a power in him, that you lack."

"Yes. The Sharai name him the Ghost Walker; he has that within him," and never mind how he'd come by it, or how he made it work, "which can open a gateway between the worlds. But he has been hurt, and so I thought it better to journey here awhile, before we venture back."

That was an apology, as best as she could frame it, and also a plea for permission to go on. She dared not ask directly; the djinn were quick to assume a debt, and to demand payment. Why else was Julianne headed for Rhabat?

"I am unconcerned with his hurts, or with yours. Nor does your presence disturb me, as it will not endure. You will find, though, that the 'ifrit are very much concerned."

"We had hoped to avoid the 'ifrit, spirit."

"No doubt you had. Human."

Was that a warning, was it telling her to beware the 'ifrit? She couldn't ask; even in this precarious position, her fingers aching and ready to slip and her feet none too secure, she had enough presence of mind to avoid the question. If it were a warning, though, it was unnecessary; of course she would beware the 'ifrit. At her first sight of one, however distant, she'd have her knife into Marron's arm whether he was ready for it or not. That assumed, of course, that she would see an 'ifrit and know it for what it was. She couldn't see the djinni . . .

On the other hand, the djinn were said to have an inner eye that could read something of the future; perhaps it meant that they would meet 'ifrit, however prepared she liked to think herself.

It was possible to be too clever, even when exchanging dubious compliments with a djinni. Her fingers did slip suddenly, so that she had to make a wild grab at the rock-face and barely managed to hold on.

"Forgive me, spirit," she gasped, "but I'm going to fall . . ."

"My forgiveness would not seem to be necessary," it replied. "You cannot injure me, by falling."

She gritted her teeth, held back a sharp retort, and began to climb again, with cramped muscles and a deal more care than she'd used earlier. She thought the djinni had gone, hoped that was true; persuaded herself definitely that it was, before her hands at last closed on the lip of the cliff and Marron was there, stooping to grip her wrist and haul her up with one swift tug.

For a moment she only sat at his feet, breathing hard; then she said, "Did you see it?"

"See it? Perhaps. I heard it come; a noise like rushing wind, but small. Not quiet, only small. I saw a zephyr, that hovered by your head. And I heard your conversation. You shouldn't fear the 'ifrit."

"Marron, it makes good sense to fear the 'ifrit. Sit down, we're not moving on for a little while. I'm blown." The truth was, she was trembling so hard she thought her legs might not hold her if she tried to walk. It made good sense to fear the djinn also, especially so here in their own land, and she strove always to be sensible . . .

"I do not think they would be let harm me," he said, settling down beside her, "and that protection is yours too, you know that."

"The ghûl harmed you, remember? Oh, not to death, and you recover fast," *with my help,* "but if that claw had found your neck, nothing could have saved you. And that was just a ghûl. How will you stop an 'ifrit, if it has no solid body here? How would you have stopped the djinni, if it had sought to kill me? Just a breath of wind, how can you cage that?"

She might be wrong about the 'ifrit, she very likely was. They were subservient to the djinn, a lower order— surely there must be some distinction between them that would be clear even to human eyes? Marron knew less than she did, though, and she had to persuade him somehow out of that dangerous confidence. The Ghost Walker was traditionally very hard to kill; but not immortal, never that. Even the djinn were not immortal . . .

"Mind," she went on slowly, following that thought, "what it said at the end there, 'you cannot injure me, by falling'—do you think it meant there was some other way I could injure it, or we could? I'm sure it meant more than the joke. Khaldor laughed at us more than once, but I don't think this one had a sense of humour."

"I don't know what it meant," Marron said. "After all you've said about the djinn, what's the point in trying to outguess it?"

"Because it's easier than trying to outguess a boy," she muttered darkly, gazing at him through narrowed eyes. "And it might be important."

"Anything might be important. Or nothing might. Come on," and he rose smoothly to his feet, bent and pulled her up after him, "let's at least finish the climb and see what's to see from the top. You can rest there, if you need to."

She didn't need to rest, or not from her exertions; but she looked at the slope that still rose for some distance above them, she gazed pointlessly at the sky to try and guess the time when there were no signs to show her, and she tucked a hand under Marron's girdle at the back.

"You'll have to pull me," she said; and felt his laugh more than heard it, a chuckle that twitched at his spine, followed by a shiver that was entirely silent.

ANYTHING MIGHT BE important; they came at last to the high point of this ridge of hills, and found that of course it was the highest that they'd climbed, they could look down on the peaks of all the others.

At first, though, they looked further down; even before they looked at the view, they looked at their boots and what they stood on.

The hill must have been higher yet at one time, it couldn't have been made this way; but the whole of its summit had been flattened, levelled, cut off perhaps by a shearing blade, and the exposed rock polished to a mirror's shine. In the gloss of that polish they could see faint images of themselves, reflected above the rock's gold.

If there were a purpose to it, they could neither see one nor divine it; but the work was on such a tremendous scale, so much more than men could achieve, it rang a bell of memory in both of them.

They turned to face the way they had come, and squinted against the pearl-white gleam of the sky, which seemed brighter or more concentrated at the horizons; Elisande thought that she could just make out a faint hairline, like a crack in the rim of the bowl. Marron said that he could see the needle clearly.

There was that, and there was this; both were vast, majestic, incomprehensible. They turned again, and walked almost reluctantly across the great floor they stood on. Something perhaps should be dancing here, but not they.

"It's stupid," Elisande murmured, "but I feel so exposed here, as if we never were before. Which is ridiculous. Do you think all those little winds that blew the dust about yesterday were djinn?"

"Yes," he said.

"Me too. But even so. I feel like we ought to skirt around the edge, like servants . . ."

"Do you want to?"

"No."

And so they did not; but she did take Marron's hand as they crossed the centre of this place, whatever it might be, and she thought the tightness of his grip was not entirely for her comfort.

THEY CAME TO the further side, and stood looking. If anything, the southern face of the hills was gentler than the northern; they could walk down with relative ease, she thought. And then the long sweep of a plain, simple going again; and beyond that, dusky with distance, hills again. But running from the hills, absolutely at the limit of her sight even from this high aspect, she thought there was a line of cloudy light that shone back dimly what the sky had given it.

"Marron, what's that there, can you see? It's not the horizon, it's like a hazy bar of light beneath, but I can't make it out . . ."

"It's a bar of light," he said, and almost earned himself a fist in the ribs before he went on. "There's no more detail than that, that I can see. As you said, it's hazy. But I saw something like such a thing before, once. When Aldo and I took our Ransomer vows and travelled from the monastery with Fra' Piet, to take ship to come to Outremer."

"Well? What was it?"

"It was the sea," he said simply. "I'd never seen it before, I hadn't thought that anything could be so big. But we first sighted it at dawn, from a height, from a great distance; and it was a gleam that ran the sun's light along all the horizon, and nothing more than that. It terrified me; for a moment I thought it was the God, sending fire to bar our way. Perhaps I should have listened to myself . . ."

"No. Oh, no. You shouldn't be frightened of a lie, even one you tell yourself." She gripped his good arm with both hands and hugged herself against it, for what comfort she could give, if it could reach him.

"The sea was bigger," he said, his face still fixed to the south though his eyes had lost their focus, "but it looks the same. Can there be a sea in the desert?"

There could; there was. And here too, apparently, and close enough to be in sight already . . .

"The Dead Waters, the Sharai call it. That's journey's end, Marron. We'll go back to our world there, and try to find the others before we all go on to find Rhabat."

8

Blood Heat

JULIANNE SLIPPED AS her feet broke through the crust of hard-baked sand to the soft, sliding stuff beneath. She fell flat on her back, and was dragged a little distance across the scorching, gritty surface; she rolled effortfully onto her stomach, and lost a little more skin off her elbows before she managed to haul Sildana to a halt. She'd learned to knot the rein around her wrist, for just these occasions; she tried to be grateful for the lesson, as she struggled to her knees and saw fresh blood on the leather. Better to bleed, she told herself forcefully, than to watch her camel race away along the dune one more time, and have to sit in an embarrassed huddle on the sand while Jemel fetched the beast back.

He was below her now, still in his saddle, holding back the baggage-string with every appearance of patience while he waited for her to regain her feet. She did so, furiously, and began the slow trudge up again, hauling Sildana in her wake. She thought there was some witchery in the Sharai, that he could ride these slopes even with three spare camels tied to his saddle-horn. She wasn't alone in her failure there; Rudel also had to dismount and drag his mount after him.

If there were witchery in the Sharai, though, there was sheer devilry in their camels; unless it was some great joke of the God—or their god, perhaps—that had made the only animal that could bear burdens in the desert so ill-designed for the work. Camels had great strength and great stamina, they could go for days on a mouthful of food and no water, as these had had to do; but they were precious poor on slopes. And the Sands, of course, were full of slopes: where there weren't hills or crags, there were always dunes.

These dunes, though—these were evil. Even Jemel had looked anxious, faced with the massive reality of them: dunes like hills themselves, lying east to west and so cutting straight across their path. They had too little spare water, too little time to make a detour that would run to days; nor was thirst the only danger, though it was perhaps the most immediate. There had been signs of recent usage at the last well they'd found, two days ago: fresh tracks, and camel-dung not dry yet. They'd been lucky thus far, Jemel said, but the borders between one tribe's lands and the next were always closely watched. If they crossed too many, they couldn't hope to hold their luck. Detours, by their nature, would have them crossing borders . . .

And besides the tribes, hostile or otherwise, there were also the Dancers. Morakh and his surviving companions, perhaps others also. Their absence was a constant threat, weighing on everyone's minds. There had been no sign of them since the fight below the Pillar, which lay days behind them now; but that meant nothing. Rudel said that their vanishing-trick and its reverse, their sudden appearance from empty air worked at close quarters only, they couldn't cover any great distance that way; he said also that they were masters of the desert, which she knew already. Jemel said that they could follow a trail that the wind had buried a week before, that they could walk into a guarded camp by daylight and be seen by none. She hoped that was legend more than truth, but knew that it would be wiser to believe him.

Not tribes nor Dancers nor water were her immediate concern, however. She drove herself onward, up this endless dune, cursing sand and camels and their journey indiscriminately. She had learned in recent days to swear fluently in Catari, but now was not the moment; she stuck to her own tongue, as though to stress to Sildana, her other companions and the listening Sands that she was alien here, no part of this their world. And that they were all equally at fault, equally guilty that she was here, and driven to such profane cursing . . .

Rudel, she knew, had been startled by her coarseness the first time he'd heard it; she'd been a little surprised herself, in all honesty. She hadn't realised how much of the waterfront had sunk into the diplomat's pampered daughter, during her more wild adventures in Marasson.

Step by slow step, she fought grimly against the clinging sand, the struggling camel, the bone-ache in her exhausted legs and the roiling, miserable fury in her head. Step by barefoot step, or as good as, only rags wound around her feet now to save them from the worst of the blistering heat that the sand soaked up by day. She'd abandoned her boots when Rudel did, when there seemed to be more desert than foot inside them, and that grating cruelly on already-sore flesh. Her soles weren't ready for this, they weren't tanned hide like Jemel's; but neither were Rudel's. The two of them doctored each other at every halt, working with a barely moistened cloth—spit-moistened at first, only that now neither one of them could raise the spit—and then rubbing in a meagre allowance of camel-grease, that Jemel swore would help to toughen them.

Privately, Julianne suspected that of being a Sharai joke. The grease stank abominably rancid, as Jemel had sworn their feet did while they still wore their boots, when they tugged them off at each day's close. Sharai humour, she thought, was like that; and certainly Jemel flashed her a brief grin as he played baggage-master each time, producing the pot and watching—from a cautious distance—while the two Patrics worked it in with careful fingers.

On the other hand, it might be desert-wisdom and no joke at all. There was little laughter to be had on this trip, and Jemel was least likely of the three of them to waste precious supplies; even rancid camel-grease must have its uses, she supposed, and wasn't to be frittered away in foolish mockery. So she decided to believe that this was one of those uses, and hoped each night that the following day would prove it, that what skin was left to her feet would have become miraculously harder. She didn't want Sharai horn soles, only a polite gesture towards that, a diplomat's imitation . . .

And didn't have it yet, and so suffered in her feet as elsewhere; but slogged on, hissed abuse at Sildana and jerked cruel-hard on the headrope when the camel balked, and so came at last to the summit of the dune.

Found Rudel resting on his haunches, offering an excuse she would gladly use but did not need; had he been halfway down the opposite slope, still she would have stopped here. If it had meant Jemel's riding by and her being left completely alone, still she would have stopped, she had to.

She couched Sildana—and even that took effort and use of her riding-stick, just to force the contrary animal to rest—and dropped into her shadow, resting her back against the camel's flank. Sildana turned her head and hissed at the liberty, another failing of the breed, that they had no idea of teamwork. Julianne ignored her. Never mind that the sparse white coat was hot and rank and full of sand and grit, badly in need of a grooming; still it made a cushion for her head, a support for weary bones.

Rudel made a sympathetic gesture towards her, and tugged his own camel down in imitation. He stayed where he was, though, some little distance off in his body and a great deal further in his mind. In another world, perhaps, Julianne thought. She'd foolishly imagined that he might make an easier travelling-companion, with his daughter gone; instead he had become withdrawn, morose and snappish, the last thing they needed at such a time.

Jemel rode up between the two of them, leading the spare camels and gazing down with that air of forced patience which he wore so superciliously that she wanted to throw something at him. Nothing to hand, though, except a knife—which was extreme—or else a handful of sand, which was pointless. The sand was everywhere already: in the food, in the water, in their clothes, in their mouths and on their skins. Under her skin, she thought sometimes, and working its way in deeper, till it would clog and saturate every organ of her body. Certainly she had sand in her mind already, causing her thoughts to stick and tangle instead of flowing smoothly. It had even invaded memory and dream, and that she resented most of all . . .

Jemel would dismount in a minute, she knew, with an expressive sigh at being cursed with two such feeble cohorts. He would sit his camel for a while first, though, just to emphasise the point, young man's arrogance and his people's arrogance commingling; also, though, he would use its height to advantage, to survey the surrounding terrain.

What point? she wondered dismally. She knew what he would see: dunes. Dunes behind them, two of these monsters marked already with their trail; and more dunes ahead of them, only ripples on the surface of the Sands perhaps but a terrible time foretold. A girl could drown, she thought, among such ripples . . .

"Tell me how many more to come?" she called, in the husky shadow that she was learning to recognise as her own voice. "If there are more than two, give thought to my shroud. Another three would kill me."

"No," he said. "Another day would kill you, I think— but perhaps you need not worry about that."

Puzzled, she squinted her eyes to try to read him against the sky's glare. He was sitting fixedly, gazing to the west, along the line of this dune-top . . .

"What is it?" Rudel demanded, rising swiftly to his feet. "Company?"

"Yes. Five riders."

"Sharai?"

"Of course."

Of course, indeed. Who else?

"Can you tell their tribe?"

"From here? No. They should be Tel Eferi. The Tel Eferi do not tolerate strangers on their lands. So it is said, at least. I do not know, I have never met one. There were none among the party that Hasan led against the Roq . . ."

And that was telling, Julianne knew. That war-party had been as much symbol as invasion-force, designed to teach the Sharai that they could fight shoulder to shoulder with sworn enemies, blood-feuds set aside in pursuit of a greater goal. It had failed against the castle; whether it had failed in that other aim also, whether more had been broken against the hard walls of Roq de Rançon was yet to tell, or to be told.

"Must we fight again?" Julianne asked, more in resignation than in terror. They had fought six Sand Dancers, and won; perhaps they could repeat the miracle.

It seemed that they would have to try. Jemel said nothing, but his hand went to the haft of his scimitar, and his face was tight and grim and saying much.

Foolishness, to suppose they could win such another fight. Oh, he would fight, his face said, and be confident of her and Rudel at his back; confident too of their deaths, all three of them. It would be waste and nothing but waste, his face said, no honour in it for either side, but it would happen none the less.

Now, she thought, they needed Marron, they needed the Daughter; and why hadn't he and Elisande come back to them, after escaping the ghûl? She'd asked herself the question repeatedly, and her companions too; but all their

answers were guesswork. She could guess privately at her
friend's desires, and wonder if those would outweigh the
calls of friendship, the needs of the group; but the decision had surely been Marron's, and he was a mystery to
them all.

Lacking him and the quick evasion that he could offer
them, she turned instead to his less potent substitute, their
only other magic-worker. "Rudel? The people of Surayon
are skilled at hiding, you have hidden your entire country;
can you not . . . ?"

"Hide us?" he finished for her. "No. I have not the
Dancers' skill, alas," and he was always secretive even
among his friends, about how Surayon had been Folded
out of sight or finding. So was Elisande, and no blame to
either one of them for that; even friends could betray,
without meaning to. "Neither, of course, have you; nor the
camels, and we could not abandon them. No, we have
been spotted, and must face the consequences. There is
perhaps something I can do, though, to avoid a fight we
cannot win. Do what I tell you without question, without
pause; in the meantime be calm, be patient . . ."

Well, that she could manage. She rose to her feet, and
was glad to see Jemel slide down from his camel, at
Rudel's urgent gesture. At least they would look peaceable, unchallenging; though how much good that would
do them was questionable. By reputation, the Sharai could
be generous and welcoming to strangers discovered on
their lands; they could also be swift and brutal. Jemel was
clearly expecting no generosity and she had no reason to
doubt his assessment.

They were in Rudel's hands, then; and Rudel had been
distracted for days, and had shown no gift of magic when
they had needed it most, in the fight with the Dancers. A
gift for swordplay he had, undoubtedly, but he himself
gave that no credence now. She touched the handles of her
knives where they were thrust into her girdle, and prayed
that they might stay there, though she had small hope of
that.

Small hope of anything, in truth, as she watched Rudel rummage in a saddlebag and pull out a gaudy but battered leather scrip, part of his jongleur's equipage. He slung that over his shoulder, and she thought it inappropriate and deadly against the midnight blue of his robes; what better way to declare himself a stranger, mocked up as a Sharai? She thought she might never see his living face again as he turned his back and walked away from her, from them, towards the approaching tribesmen. Julianne could see them now, five dark lines they seemed to be in the heat, swaying gently as they grew; and against them one tired man with white in his beard. With talents too, true; but those talents she'd seen and most applauded had been with voice and mandora, in his guise as a jongleur. His wonder-workings had been less impressive. He hadn't been able to lead them either into or out of the Tower of the King's Daughter in the ways that he'd intended. True, both Marron and Redmond, even—reluctantly—Elisande had said that he had great strength as a healer; but he hadn't been able to heal Marron. He hadn't tried to heal her feet, except with water and grease. He said they must toughen naturally, that his interference would only pro-long her pain as he made them soft again; of course she believed him, but even so . . .

When he had left companions and camels both some distance behind him, Rudel stood still and lifted one hand to his face. She couldn't see, but she thought he would be scratching at his beard as he did when he was thinking hard, when he was uncertain. Then he flung both hands high, in what might be seen by peaceful folk as a gesture of peace and greeting; others might read it as a prohibi-tion, a forbiddal, *come no nearer.* Julianne held her breath, wondering desperately what he intended to do.

Jemel grunted at her side, and said, "At least he has a beard."

So did Jemel now, or at least a dark growth of stubble on chin and cheeks; they had no water spare for shaving.

She didn't see the point. "What, will they respect his age?" It didn't seem likely.

"No, but he has a wild look about him, and all the Sharai respect a shaman."

That assumed that he could demonstrate the abilities of a shaman; anyone could grow a beard. Even Marron had shown a scattering of fluff before he left them so precipitately; she'd meant to tease him about that, and hadn't found the opportunity. Julianne chewed her lip, and waited.

Five shimmering shadows resolved themselves into five men on camelback, riding in line abreast. At first she thought that they wouldn't even pause when they met Rudel, that one of them would dispatch him with a single swing of a blade, without a word exchanged between them. By the way he sucked air through his teeth, Jemel expected much the same.

But they drew rein together and halted neatly, as though one man, one thought commanded all. Excellent discipline; she thought Rudel would approve. For herself she was surprised, she'd thought the Sharai more individual. Perhaps they kept a harsher discipline here, in the harshness of the Sands. One man spoke, and Rudel answered; too far away for her to hear what was said, but the tone of their voices carried. The Sharai had challenged, Rudel had snapped a response.

Oh, let him keep his temper, now if never again . . .

It seemed that he had, it seemed that he was in doubt, though his voice surely would deny it; he appeared to be chanting now, to judge by what sound came back to her, but that betraying hand had lifted to his beard again, to tell her that he was in doubt.

No—the other hand, she realised suddenly, the left. It looked wrong, even from a distance, from the back; men have their unconscious habits, and never break them. She'd never seen him scratch his beard left-handed.

She'd never seen smoke rise up to wreathe his head either, thin grey wisps that tangled like rising, writhing serpents in the air above and drifted slowly, slowly into fragments and nothing on the breeze.

A sudden silence, as Rudel ceased his chanting; it lasted as long as the Sharai's startlement, was cut by the sudden sharp edge of their fear. One man cried out, another hissed what might have been a prayer for protection. All twitched at their camels' reins, caught between backing and wheeling, creeping and charging away. Nothing else, clearly, was on their minds, confronted as they were by a man whose head was smoking.

"A juggler's trick," Jemel muttered.

"Yes—but think, Jemel. If these people are as isolated as you say, if they don't even mix with their own kind, if they forbid strangers on their land—when will they have ever seen a juggler?"

Rudel brought his hands together in a sharp clap, high above his head. Julianne saw, but didn't hear; the sound of it was lost in a fierce crackling noise like dry timber burning, as smoke poured out between his fingers. Briefly, she thought she saw bright sparks between his palms, contained lightning.

Two of the tribesmen's camels shied, and bolted downslope; one rider fell, the other clung to his mount's neck and barely kept his seat. The other three, she thought, were only in control still because their own instincts matched their beasts'; all had twisted around and were galloping now, back along the dune-top as they had come except much faster now, and crying to each other as they went in high, hoarse voices, men and camels both.

Julianne wanted to laugh, but dared not. It wasn't truly funny, danger and likely death averted by a simple trick. Rudel came storming back to join them—smelling strangely acrid, but quite unscorched in beard or hands—and his scowl was warning her, she thought, *no reaction, not a sound*; camels could not or would not run too far downhill, on slipping sand.

Those who had fled that way were still in hearing. Indeed, the unmounted one was dangerously close. His tracks showed that he had run a little, or tried to; she knew how impossible that was. He was not trying now. He was standing still, watching them; waiting, as it seemed.

Waiting for his brothers, of course. They were of one tribe, and would not leave him now. One—back in control already, of his mount and of himself: she was impressed—was going after the strayed camel, which had not bolted far; the others were leaving the dune-crest and riding down in single file to join their fallen man.

Which meant that they were riding back towards Julianne and her companions, or nearly so. They *were* impressive, she decided. One moment of superstitious panic, anyone could be allowed that; but they had mastered it so quickly. Too quickly: they were too soon themselves again, and deadly still . . .

Deadly still was how they stood, she thought, and how their camels stood beneath them, when they were together and the fallen one remounted; deathly still was how she stood herself, and those about her. Even their camels were quiet for a change, long heads on long necks turned to stare where they themselves were staring.

So much stillness, so much silent watchfulness on both sides, it was unbearable; someone had to break it soon, or she would. She would break altogether, she thought, and run screaming, the worst thing . . .

Well, no, she wouldn't. She wasn't even tempted, not seriously. She just wanted something to happen; what was hardest for her was being able to do nothing herself, being dependent on others.

At last something did happen, inevitably, it had to; and it was of course the worst thing that could happen in such a case, given that she wasn't going to run screaming.

One of the tribesmen touched his camel into slow movement and came riding up towards them, with the others following in his train.

"Well," Rudel murmured, "a little conjuring was never likely to be enough, once they rediscovered their courage.

It should buy us some talking-time, though. Jemel, you stand quiet, whatever they say; their pride drives them, so you must sacrifice yours. Julianne, be ready. Whatever I ask of you, be ready . . ."

ONE BY ONE, the Sharai came up the slope at an angle that brought them to the crest of the dune just a little beyond fighting-distance. That had to be deliberate; Julianne tried to be grateful.

The one who had led them back was an elderly man, with more white in his beard than Rudel had. He had scars too, though, to remind her not to make assumptions. His body under his robe looked as lean as whipcord, and as tough.

Rudel stepped forward alone, as he had before; when he lifted his hands, all the Sharai flinched. This time, though, he only spread them wide, in a gesture that could surely only be read as peaceful. Except that such a warlike people might have read it as weakness, Julianne thought, first time around; now, though, after Rudel's display of seemingly mystical potency . . .

Now that elderly Sharai spoke almost deferentially to him, certainly without any hint of aggression in his voice, though his words were still a challenge.

"We of the Tel Eferi do not welcome strangers on our lands; we guard our borders even against those of our own faith. You seem to have one such with you, though his dress declares him tribeless. Very well; he is of no account. Neither is the Patric girl. You, however—you are a shaman, and a Patric also. That is strange to us. It is death to trespass, and we are not afraid of your magic; but we would know why you have come, and where you are bound."

"I am not afraid of your death, Tel Eferi," Rudel replied—*and let him interpret that as he will,* Julianne thought, silently applauding. "My purposes are my own, and I will pursue them, whether I trespass or no. I will tell you this, though, that we are bound for Rhabat, for the council of tribal leaders that has been called there. Your own sheikhs may have chosen to answer that summons, or to ignore it; I neither know nor care. If you seek to stay us, though, you will suffer for it. Let us pass unhindered, and your rewards may be as great."

"I have heard tell of this council—but not that any of your kind have been summoned to it. Who are you, Patric?"

"My name is Rudel, and I am a prince of Surayon; but that is unimportant," though it had some effect, to judge by the way the Sharai muttered together. "What matters more is that I and my companions were leading another there, who is of great importance. We have been separated, but I hope still to find him before we arrive."

"This other, who is he? And why should he need your guidance?"

"He is a boy, a Patric like myself, who could not find his way unaided; though he has found his way into another land entirely, and chooses to stay there awhile. Do not you stay us, Tel Eferi. We are the chosen companions of the Ghost Walker, and he is one of us."

Again that hissing mutter among the tribesmen, this time accompanied by snorts of contemptuous laughter; their leader said, "I do not believe you," and his hand strayed to the scimitar in his belt.

"I can show him to you," said Rudel. "Will you believe your eyes?"

"Perhaps not, if they try to tell me what cannot be true. Who knows what lies a sorcerer may not tell? Your arts are demon-born, and there is no truth in them."

"What does a Tel Eferi know of truth?" Another voice, sudden and harsh; and that was Jemel, striding forward in fury. "No more than a scorpion, who lurks beneath his stone and stings any hand that touches it! The Ghost Walker is among us, this man has seen and known him; so has this girl, who is like him a prince among her people; and so have I."

"Well. It has a tongue after all, if no tribe. Or none that it will admit to, at least; and perhaps it is wise in that . . . ?"

Julianne thought, dreaded rather that Jemel would draw his scimitar in reply to the insult, and so doom them all; instead, startlingly, he laughed.

"Tel Eferi, I have a name, that I am not afraid to share even outside my friends. I am called Jemel, and I was of the Saren; but I have been called to a greater service since. Even you may perhaps have heard of the brotherhood of Sand Dancers; even you may know that they forswear tribal allegiance, and follow only the Ghost Walker wherever he may lead. I have not had time or chance to change my dress for theirs; but I have laid a stone on the Pillar of Lives, I have sworn my oath on its summit, and—"

And he lifted his hand, his left hand; and his sleeve fell back, to show the crusted stump where his finger had been cut away. Only that morning Julianne had removed the dressing she'd bound it with, to let it heal cleanly in the air. There was a moment's silence, before the Tel Eferi said, "My name is Wali Ras, and I am familiar with Sand Dancers."

"Then you know that on this matter, I would not lie to you. What this man has said to you is true."

"He said that he could show me the truth of it; yet he said also that the Ghost Walker walks in another world . . ."

"That is so. He chooses to walk with the djinn at this time. What this man can show you by his skills, I do not know; but it will be no demon-picture, that I swear to you. If it be the Ghost Walker, you will have my word that he shows you true."

"So be it, Dancer." The old man couched his camel, and stepped free; at his back the other tribesmen stayed silent, mounted, even now a guard against treachery and an unspoken threat.

"Jemel, that was very well done, though you had me

frightened for a moment there. Julianne," Rudel was speaking rapidly in her own tongue, "I regret this, but you must act my serving-girl, and the work will not be pretty. Fetch me the brass pot from the baggage, and be quick."

It was more a ewer than a pot, an ornate rice-bowl although they had no rice; Rudel had meant it for a gift, to any sheikh who offered hospitality. Now he had another, she guessed a darker purpose to confront these men who had offered nothing so courteous.

She fetched it as she'd been bidden, with speed and silence and the best air of servility that she could manage.

"Good. Now, we must lose one of the camels; it would be well to choose the weakest. Jemel will hold its head for you; I will hold the bowl."

It would be well to choose the weakest, but he was leaving the choice to her. Her eyes strayed to Sildana, and she was sorely tempted; they would be more impressed, surely, by the sacrifice of a white beast, and such a fine one . . . ?

Good sense overruled vengeance, though. She hesitated only a moment, before walking to what had been Elisande's mount and quickly unstrapping its burdens. That animal had an ulcerating sore on one leg, and was suffering in this hard scramble over the dunes. Jemel came after her, grunting his approval; she whispered quickly, "Is this wisdom?"

"No," he murmured, straddling the beast's neck and gripping its chin, forcing its head back against its struggles, "it is the act of a madman, and so may save us all. All shamans are mad, they know that . . ."

Rudel took the bowl from her, and held it poised below the camel's throat; Julianne pulled out one of her knives, glad of the edge on it and only praying that it would have no worse use than this today.

She laid the blade against taut flesh, gripped her wrist with her other hand for support and drew it back in a single stroke as she had seen the butchers do in the market at

Marasson, using all her strength to slice as deeply as she could.

Hot blood gushed and Rudel caught it—most of it—in the bowl, though they were all splashed as Jemel wrestled with the bucking camel's body.

At last it slumped, and lay still. They stepped away; Rudel carried the brimming bowl over to where the old man stood impassively watching, and set it carefully on the sand.

"Wait till the surface is still," he said, his voice soft and authoritative, "and then look. Look carefully, and with honesty." Then, changing tongues again, he went on, "Jemel, you must look too, to confirm what he sees; but turn your head away when he is done. Julianne, it would be best if you did not look at all."

Perhaps it would, though she didn't understand why; but she made no promise. She had promised herself to her young Baron Imber, and had torn herself away from him next day; she meant to make no more promises that she might not be able to keep.

Rudel knelt beside the bowl, murmuring softly in a new tongue, a third tongue, one she could not follow although the sound of it struck resonance in her mind and heart. He stretched both hands over the dark, reflective surface of the blood, then lowered them till his fingers touched it.

When he took them away, there were no ripples; the liquid seemed suddenly solid as glass. Glass coloured blood-red, ruby-red—but with a golden gleam at its core, she saw, as Rudel breathed on it. A gleam that grew, she saw, that seemed to pour up from the base of the bowl until the red was washed away by fierce-glowing gold.

It was like staring at the sun, she thought, blinking and turning her head away. The old man's gasp pulled it back, though, and she was suddenly glad she had not made that promise.

The bright glow had died within the bowl, although the image there was still golden. She gasped herself, seeing the image move: or seeing the people move within the image, rather. Two people, and she knew them both . . .

Marron and Elisande she saw, walking together in a landscape of gold: for a moment she almost thought they walked hand in hand, and her heart twisted for her friend's sake. But no, they were only side by side; though that was wonder enough, to see them like this. She wanted to apologise to Rudel for ever doubting his power, and of course could not. It was not the place of a servant girl to speak first to her master. Besides, he would not know of her offence, unless she first confessed it.

Though he might have guessed, she thought, seeing how he looked up briefly from the bowl to frown at her— but no, he had told her not to look and caught her staring, that was all. She turned her head ostentatiously to the side, saw how all the tribesmen were gaping at the bowl, and felt excluded, resentful. Why should all these men have licence to view his magic, and she not?

"Is that he?" the elder tribesman asked, stooping low over the bowl as if to imprint the scene on his mind, his voice breathless with wonder at more than the miracle of Rudel's showing it to him.

"It is." Rudel confirmed it, and Jemel also.

"How is it possible? A Patric boy . . . This is not the prophecy."

"Even prophets cannot see the whole of the truth; not even the djinn can know exactly what the future holds. It is a mystery to us all, why Marron has been chosen to bear this burden, or what will come of it or him. If he were chosen. It might be sheerest luck. For good or ill, though, that boy has that gift in his possession, in his blood . . ."

If it were a gift. Julianne thought it was a poison, or a curse.

"And see," the Tel Eferi whispered, "see where he walks . . . You show us marvels, shaman," though there seemed little to her that was marvellous about that golden landscape, bar its colour. "But enough; I will look no more. Such sights are not meant for mortal eyes. Who is that who walks beside him?"

"She is my daughter," Rudel said flatly.

There was bewilderment on the old man's face: was she perhaps another wonder-worker, a Patric girl-shaman and hence fit companion—perhaps—for a Patric Ghost Walker? He didn't ask; Rudel's tone had forbidden the question, and he seemed to have enough respect—or fear might be a better word than Jemel's, Julianne thought— not to force the issue.

This was still his tribe's territory, though, and his own people stood witness to his words; his pride required him not to show fear, even of a fearful man. He drew himself up and said, "You hope to find him again, you have said, this side of Rhabat. How will you achieve that, shaman? Can you too open a way between the worlds?" *Are the laws and prophecies so debased, that a Patric magician can do what we cannot, when what we have waited for so long comes not to us but to a Patric boy . . . ?*

Rudel laughed shortly. "Not I. I should have said, I hope that he will find us. Or perhaps the hope is mutual; it is certainly no stronger than a hope. We were parted suddenly, without the chance to make plans. But he knows our route, south to the shores of the Dead Waters and so down, and over the hills to Rhabat. A boat would be easier, but there are no boats that I know of . . ."

"No man sails the Dead Waters, shaman. No living man," and the Tel Eferi chuckled dryly, unpleasantly. "So. He knows your route, you say; do you?"

"South," Rudel repeated. "I have not travelled these lands, but a true line south must bring us to the Waters."

"A true line south will bring you to a crevasse you cannot cross, unless your powers allow you to fly its span. You and your camels. Come. I will allow you through our lands, for the sake of the news you have brought us; but I will show you the shortest way that is safe. Do not stray from it."

"We need water," Rudel said mildly.

"Then you will travel the speedier, to find it beyond our borders. Our wells are our own. Take a line east of south; there are crags beyond these dunes, and you must climb where they are kindest . . ."

The old man stumped across the sand, pointing with his riding-stick; Rudel followed him, and Jemel also. The tribesmen's camels paced behind them; Julianne was left alone, abandoned. *Just a servant girl,* she reminded herself sourly.

Well, servant girls didn't have to be responsible; and no one was looking, so she could . . .

She turned her eyes back to the bowl, wanting only to watch her friends wander in the wonder of that other world, no more than that, and not at all seeing why she shouldn't.

The image was gone, though; there was no gold now, only darkness. She bent low above it, trying to see if the blood had turned liquid again, with Rudel's power gone from it; she saw only her own reflection, and sighed mightily for the loss of magic.

Her breath misted the surface, and that glow came again, starting as a spark deep down. She gasped and drew back, too late; the spark blossomed like fire, driving out the dark. It was a gentler glow this time, softly golden, with no hint of dazzle to it; Julianne dropped to her knees, entranced.

When the bowl was filled with light, she saw a picture forming. Three figures, standing: the central one was a girl, long dark hair and a deep green robe. Julianne recognised the dress a moment before she knew the face; it was herself, and that was the robe she'd worn to marry Imber . . .

There was a man standing on either side of her, and she was holding a hand of each; they were both standing with their backs to her, but she still knew one of them. That tall figure with the blond hair that shone so, the youth of him clear even from a rear view: she didn't need to remember the green velvet that he wore—though she did, it was branded deep in her memory, never to be forgotten—to know her husband.

The other man was a mystery, shorter and black-haired, dressed much as she was now, in the midnight blue of the Sharai.

There was movement in the image suddenly, that picture of Imber turning and bending, and herself turning to meet him, stretching up; she caught a glimpse of his soft short beard, and saw herself kiss him deeply.

Felt it too, a tingle of memory on her lips, though he'd never kissed her as his image did. Only a dry and fleeting touch of his mouth against hers, with all the complement of the Roq as witness; but that again was a brand she bore, ever fresh and hurting.

She saw him straighten and turn his back again; saw herself turn the other way, towards the other man; saw him too meet her mouth to mouth in a passionate kiss.

This time the beard was black, though equally close-cropped. She could see no more of his face than that, bend and stare as she might, as she did.

And then startlingly, shockingly, there was a hand swooping down from the periphery of her vision, scooping up the bowl and lifting it, hurling it, sending it rolling far away down the slope of the dune. The blood poured out of it in a great wave—and it was only blood, no more than that, a dark liquid stain that soaked quickly into the sand.

She stared up at Rudel where he stood looming over her, his face set tight. For a moment she thought he was raging, and she almost quailed where she knelt before the force of him—but no, it wasn't anger that gripped him so, not fury that had drawn such violence from him. Perhaps he wanted those watching tribesmen to think so, that he was only livid at his servant for meddling where she should not; in truth, she thought, he was afraid. Afraid for her, for consequences . . .

Well, he wasn't the first to fear so, and nothing dreadful had come to her yet. There had been strange outcomes to her wilfulness, unexpected outcomes, this journey was one and her hurried marriage she supposed was another; she remained whole and healthy—in her body, at least: heart-whole she was not—and it seemed she remained wilful also. None of her adventures had proved a lesson in obedience. Not even that one in childhood that had broken bones and courage both, had left her terrified of heights . . .

She rose to her feet as gracefully as she could manage. She would have faced Rudel eye to eye, but for her knowledge that they were observed; she kept her head submissively low, spoke softly, and only her words were firm.

"I know, you told me not to look—but how could I not? As well tell me not to listen when you're shouting, or not to think . . ."

"What did you see? When I was gone? I know what was there before."

"I'll tell you—but not now. Later. When we're alone." The Tel Eferi showed no signs of understanding them, but ignorance was easy to pretend to.

"Very well. You should not have looked, though, child. I had my reasons to say so."

"Which you did not explain to me." Indeed he still hadn't, though she had a feeling for them now, perhaps; she thought she would rather not have seen herself so brazen. Or so torn . . . ?

"There was no time; there still is none. Later, we'll talk." And he turned a contemptuous shoulder to her, for all the world like a man who has not chastised his servant as much as she deserves, but will not do more in front of strangers.

AND SO SHE was left with her head aspin, wrenched away from a vision that she didn't understand. Ordinarily she'd have told Elisande, they'd have talked it through together; though ordinarily she wouldn't have needed to tell Elisande, because the wretched girl would have been right

there pushing her face in beside Julianne's, in the flesh if
not in the picture.

But Elisande had been in the picture already, pictured in
another world entirely and in other company, very much not
here to talk to. There was Jemel, but he was no real confidant of hers at the best of times, which these were not; the
sight of his precious Ghost Walker ghosted off to walk in
someone else's company had flung him into a fit of the sul-
lens, and he would willingly talk to neither of them.

And then there was Rudel. Who had promised her a
talk, but not yet; who was wise in his experience, and remarkable in his talents; who was her friend's father, and
also to Elisande the most despised of men, for reasons
that Julianne had still not contrived to learn. She could not
confide in him, until she knew the truth of what lay between them. She would feel treacherous to her friend to
do so; besides, it might simply be unwise. Despite all appearance, he might not be a man to whom it was safe to
unburden her soul . . .

Not for the first time, she wished fervently for her father's company, almost more than she wished for
Elisande's, or for Imber's. And could have none of them,
or not yet; and so set her eyes and mind grimly to the
journey, at the end of which she could at least hope for
two out of the three.

Down the steep dune, alternately coaxing and yanking
the splay-legged and stubborn Sildana; up the next, at an
angle now that made the slope a little easier, though not
much. All the way, she was conscious that they had acquired a shadow, a black smudge on the skyline, following their slow progress at a cautious distance. Being sure
that they knew he was there, she thought; and riding these
impossible dunes as easily as Jemel did, which only added
injury to the insult of his so-obvious presence.

THE DUNES BROKE at last, as they had been promised,
like waves against a rocky shore. A band of ink rough-

washed on the horizon resolved into high basalt cliffs; they had again been promised a way through, though, and found it swiftly. A break among the crags became a path, the first sign of human use they'd seen on the land for days. Here she could ride, thank the God. Sildana tried to knock her off a time or two, lurching suddenly against the rock walls that squeezed close on either side; but Julianne had ridden difficult horses all her life, she was well-versed in countering such tricks and plied her stick with cheerful abandon to drive the camel on. There were tufts of sandy hair, she noticed, caught in snags of rock along the way; Sildana wasn't the first to try this. At one tight angle where the path turned sharply, where no one could blame a camel for rubbing against the rock, she saw how the basalt had been worn away to a smooth curve, though it was knife-sharp above. How many years, how many centuries of traffic would it take, she wondered, to erode the rock so far?

THAT NARROW AND twisting path, shadowed even under the high desert sun, debouched eventually onto a high shelf, a sweep of sand-dusted rock that offered a long view to the long-sighted. Julianne squinted, and thought she saw a glint of light on the far horizon. Jemel shaded his eyes with his hand, looked long and steadily, and finally gave them a promise not of journey's end, but at least of the final push towards that end.

"I can see water," he said, "a desert plain of water . . ." There was awe in his voice, even though he must have seen it before; this was not his first time coming to Rhabat. Likely—no, certainly—it was the greatest body of water he'd ever seen or dreamed of in his life. The sea would be a myth to Jemel, a myth misunderstood, mispictured in his mind. This little lake, this pond was more than enough to outmatch it.

This little lake, this pond was what they called the Dead Waters, and Julianne wished she had another name for it. That title resonated too strongly with the djinni's high voice, Elisande's mysterious future. Though she was glad to see it, none the less. It gave hope of Marron's returning, and Elisande's beside him; it gave hope also of her father. Or at least it brought the djinni's prediction closer, that time when she could save her father from great danger. *Though it might be better if you did not—* she remembered the djinni's words exactly, and shrugged them from her. Whatever its intent, whatever its doubts, it had gifted her this chance, and she would take it. If she were able . . .

They paused to drink, though the water in their skins was foul now, and to chew a little on what was left of that morning's bake of bread. The water might be foul, but the bread was almost worse; she pined for proper food, and found herself yearning for the evening. Jemel had butchered the dead camel, before leaving its corpse to wither in the sun; he had left most of the flesh also for the Tel Eferi to take it if they would, but he'd brought enough that they were sure of meat tonight and every night until they reached Rhabat.

"We might have rested," Rudel said, "until the sun was lower; but—"

He signed to the rear, with a jerk of his head. When she looked around, Julianne saw a shadow at the path's mouth, their Tel Eferi tracker silent on his camel.

"Julianne, can you ride in the heat, this once? It would be wiser in any case, we should press on until we can find water . . ."

Oh, she could ride in the heat, if they could; the sun was not her concern. She nodded firmly, and then spoiled that decisiveness with a question that would have betrayed her to these two, even if her voice hadn't quavered in asking it.

"How do we get down?"

Jemel had ridden forward, right to the shelf's edge; he called back, "There is a path. Not difficult, it cuts to and fro across the cliff-face . . ."

Not difficult for him, perhaps. She dreaded it already, from his report. But she must go down, she must go on; even if they'd been allowed to rest here, it would have been only a temporary respite. And as she must do it, she might as well do it now.

"Jemel, you lead," Rudel ordered, "with Julianne behind you. I will bring up the rear. I would guess this to be the Tel Eferi border, I don't think we'll be followed further, but if I'm wrong he still won't press me too closely."

That was neat; it set her where she could feel safest, if not safe. She said no more, but touched Sildana on to follow Jemel. He seemed to ride his camel straight over the cliff; only his bobbing head beyond assured her that there was indeed a path.

It seemed more like a goat-track when she found it, plunging suddenly downward. He was already at the corner where it turned back on itself for the first time, the first of many; she saw its zigzag progress dimly, swimmingly, already dizzy from the great fall before her, hundreds of feet it seemed before the path came down to solid ground. She swallowed hard and nudged her mount forward, hoping that Sildana would have a head for heights, and praying that she'd have the good sense not to act stubborn or wilful until they reached bottom.

SEEMINGLY, SHE DID. She picked her way as delicately as any nice-mannered pony might, as sensibly as the most candidly frightened girl could wish. Even if she were being candid only with herself: if she were riding with her back straight and her head up, arms high in classic style, headrope in one hand and stick in the other. She was, she knew, fooling no one—not herself, not Jemel before her or Rudel behind, and certainly not Sildana. That beast could smell her terror, she was sure, she could see the wide nostrils flare to seek it out; and smelling, knowing, the creature had made the decision and walked as if on eggshells, making almost a show of how she placed each foot with pretty care.

During those long, long minutes, Julianne fell entirely in love with Sildana.

ABJECT FEAR HAS a cold hand that grips internally, that squeezes a chill sweat from the bone's marrow, then chases it through frozen muscles and out onto shivering skin. This was nothing new to Julianne; she was barely conscious of the waste of her body's water, it was so familiar. And it meant so little to her. She didn't look down, not once, leaving Sildana to find her own way, or to follow Jemel; but still that dreadful drop hung in her mind's eye, sucking at her. She had no thought to spare for how she was sweating.

Until she reached the foot of the cliff and let Sildana amble to a standstill while she shuddered, while her companions waited patiently a little apart from her, giving her decent space to recover herself.

When she had done that, when she could be aware of herself again, she became aware of how she was suddenly and strangely dry: dry of mouth, which was not unusual, but quite dry of skin also, where she had been, must have been, remembered being clammy such a little time ago.

She took a deliberate breath, and tasted heat at the back of her throat. She'd thought she'd been hot before, when she rode out of the path's shade onto the shelf above and into the full glare of the light; she'd thought that fierce, until the first sight of the way down had chilled her. Now, though, she felt the sun's weight on the back of her neck, and all but buckled under it. This was the true Sands, the Sands that Jemel had promised her, and Elisande also; the heat lay on the land as fire lies on coals, a thing in itself and almost tangible.

Absurdly she shivered, one more time, though this at least she was not afraid of. She ought to be, she knew, it could kill her as surely as a fall; she'd be wise to find some fear in herself, but could not. She'd trust her life to either one of her companions, anywhere in any desert that the Sharai claimed as their own; here, with both together, she felt entirely safe.

Safe and exhilarated, briefly; she grinned widely and wordlessly at Jemel, as he came riding over.

Did he smile back, did he understand? She couldn't tell; he wore his hood low and a veil across his face.

"Here," he said, his voice muffled by the cloth. "Put up your hood, so," and he reached to do it for her. "And you must adjust your robe also, or you will lose too much water to the air. Like this," and he gestured at his own dress.

She looked, tried to imitate how he had adjusted the robe, and could not; her fingers felt light and awkward, barely attached. She fumbled with the ties, tugged at the hems and only made matters worse. In the end he had to lean across from his saddle and do it for her. However bronzed his skin and however shadowed, she was still certain that he blushed as he did it, fumble-fingered himself when they touched her bare skin beneath the robe.

"You have seen the high dunes, and crossed them," he said, as though it were a rite of passage; perhaps it was. "You have seen the crags, and passed through them. Now you meet the plain, and the heat of the plain. Now we ride."

"What about water?"

"You ride, Julianne. Leave us to worry about the water."

SO SHE RODE. She felt their worry—the heat stole in like a thief to lay itself against her like a lover, a thief of love; and like a thief it stole all the moisture she had in her, drying her like a husk so that she had to keep sipping and sipping at the skin she carried, although she could barely swallow the foul liquid—but she could not share it. She'd been told not to, indeed, and for once she practised obedience, if only because she had no choice. It was enough simply to ride, to breathe; thinking was too much to ask in that draining, enervating heat. Worrying lay far beyond her reach. She couldn't even worry about Elisande and Marron. Like these that she rode with, those two were survivors; they'd all meet again. By the Dead Waters, or else at Rhabat . . .

The Dead Waters were far away, though, and Rhabat was further. Between lay this endless plain, this air that stifled, was almost too hot and dry to breathe. A fine sand drifted through her veil, gummed her eyes and choked her throat; again she was driven to her water-skin and forced to swill her mouth around before she swallowed, tasting every last nuance of the rank water. She'd have preferred to spit, but she had—barely—enough desert-wisdom to resist that, though her face twisted with the effort, cracking the mask of sand that had accrued like a second veil across her skin. She would even have preferred to ride without drinking at all, to endure the shrivelling thirst that puckered her lips and seared her tongue and throat; she had to breathe, though, and so she had to rinse and swallow, making a meal of the sand that threatened to clog her airway.

The sun burned her eyes whenever she cracked them open against the sand's seal, but they were too dry, she was too dry altogether to allow them to water. She longed to bathe her face; she did surreptitiously moisten a corner of her veil and use it to wipe the worst of the crust away, but it was dry a minute later when she reached to do the same again.

So she rode blind, often with her eyes closed, gratefully learning once again to trust Sildana. Here on the open desert the camel's behaviour was impeccable, as though all her earlier stubbornness and aggression had been protest at that demeaning, easy country she'd been forced to endure. Here she carried her head high, alert to every breeze and whisper, every change of light; her long, long lashes shielded her big eyes from sun and sand, her body rocked from side to side in a gentle, lulling motion as she paced steadily behind Rudel's mount, as the hours passed and she never broke stride, never jolted her nodding, drifting rider . . .

JEMEL'S STICK CRACKED across Julianne's shoulders suddenly, not hard but stinging, jerking her out of her dreams. She glowered at him where he loomed beside her, a black silhouette blocking the sun; he said, "Do *not* sleep in the saddle. Look about you."

She looked, and cried a protest, almost reeling from the sheer force of the light that struck up at her from all sides, glaring, blinding white.

"Salt-pans," he said shortly. "If you sleep, you may fall; I may not see. By the time you recovered your wits enough to stand and look for us, you would not find us. Better to stay awake, and live."

She nodded her understanding; she couldn't speak, and wondered that he could. A leather throat, or some Sharai trick of folding the veil, something he hadn't thought to show her, that could keep out this insidious sand? She must ask, when she had a voice for it.

Meantime, he was right. She worked her sore shoulders against the roughness of her robe, as a reminder. Even if Sildana felt her fall and stopped to find her, to allow her to remount—she would do that, Julianne was convinced, carried away by this new mood of affection and trust— Jemel was still right. In such a dazzle, she'd be disoriented from the moment of her falling; Sildana was no bloodhound, she needed sight and sound of her companions. Between them they could lose both men in a minute, and never find their trail.

So she fought the doziness that came with heat and inaction and the steady sway of the miles passing underfoot; unable to distract herself with views and still too numbed to think straight, she rode side by side with Jemel, forced a thin voice from her throat and set about extracting his life story. She gathered quickly that this was a terrible breach of good manners, as well as of desert convention: he muttered sullenly that a small party in unknown and possibly hostile territory should always ride in line and apart, to allow a better watch. She persisted, though; for her it served several purposes, not only focusing her mind but strengthening her newly fluent Catari and also satisfying her perennial curiosity. For him, her probing seemed as uncomfortable as her abandonment of good practice, or more so. He wriggled physically under her questioning, and his answers were as evasive as he could make them. She thought perhaps he was unused to being interrogated by a girl, as much as he was clearly unused to touching one.

Still, she learned more than she had known before, and more certainly than he had wanted her to know. And she came through the salt-pans and the gruelling heat of the day, albeit with a fried brain and a water-skin that was slack and nearly empty. When Jemel abruptly reined in his camel, yelled ahead to Rudel and pointed with his riding-stick to where a long tangled shadow lay across a low dune, she even managed a smile at the patent relief in his voice, in every line of his body.

They all three turned aside from their steady southward progress, to investigate the source of the shadow. It turned out to be what Jemel had clearly been certain of, a small patch of thorny scrub, pale and dry but forage for the camels none the less. And more: Jemel crouched and began to dig among the roots of the scrawny plants, digging like a dog, hurling back double handfuls of sand.

When he'd burrowed down the full length of his arm, he sat back with a grunt of satisfaction; Julianne saw damp sand clinging to his fingers. Disbelievingly, she peered into the pit. Slowly, sluggishly, dark and dirty water was welling up around the exposed root-system.

They took turns to lie on their bellies and scoop up sparse and precious handfuls, sucking the warm and gritty liquid from their fingers as though it were finest sherbet.

While her hands were still damp, Julianne scoured her face with them, for what little relief that could bring to skin that was chapped and sore beneath its crust of sand.

"We'll go no further today," Rudel declared. "There's another hour's riding by the sun, but we could ride half the night and find nowhere better to halt. Come the morning, that hole will be half full of water, enough to see us through tomorrow."

"And the camels?" she asked, urgent with her new concern.

"Will have eaten this back to the sand, and be fine. They won't need water for a day or two yet. Though we'd be wise to cover it over, or they'll drink it regardless."

Indeed, they were already questing towards the pit, scenting moisture; Jemel drove his back with a hard heel to the nose. Julianne tried to be gentle with Sildana, to guide her away with voice and touch; Sildana's response would have left her face a scarred ruin, if the bite had been just a little quicker.

It took two, they found, to guard the water. The camels couldn't be hobbled safely away from it until they'd finished grazing, and they were slow eaters in any case and worse today, taking a dry and thorny mouthful, chewing stolidly and turning towards that scent of water as they chewed, having to be beaten back to their meal.

"Where does the water come from?" Julianne asked, as she shared that duty with Rudel. "You couldn't dig such a hole anywhere else in the Sands, and hope to find water . . ."

"No—though there is water, often, where you would not think to look for it. These plants look like shallow-rooting scrub; they are not. They reach deep under the sand, and when they find water—after a rain, say, or if they chance on some hidden source in the bedrock—they draw it up while they can. They need little day by day, though, and when they find it, they find plenty; so they have learned to store. They spread it through the sand around their roots, low enough that the sun won't burn it off; and so they sip it as they need it, and never go thirsty."

"Until we come, and steal it."

"Ah, but the camels are cropping them back to the stalks, so they'll not need the water. They'll live, and grow again. We have not harmed the roots . . ."

"Rudel?"

"Yes?"

"What harmed you?" Whatever it was, it must be deep-rooted; and she'd never have a better chance to ask. "You and Elisande, I mean? You're her father, but you're so cold towards her; and she, she seems to hate you . . ."

"Hate me? No. She thinks it hate, perhaps, she calls it so, but she's wrong. It's not hatred, it's blame. Though as Elisande practises it, I grant the two are easily confused."

Half an answer was more than she'd ever got from the girl, Rudel had turned his back, a sign perhaps that the conversation was over, but Julianne decided to press her luck regardless. "She blames you for what?"

"For her mother's death. You know how hard that is for a girl, Julianne, how deep it cuts. Elisande finds it useful, I think, to have someone to accuse."

"I never knew my mother. She died when I was born."

"Ah, that's right, of course. I had forgotten. Perhaps you never felt the lack of her, in that case? Elisande was less fortunate."

Julianne hadn't ever seen herself as fortunate, growing up with a succession of nursemaids and chaperones; but now was not the time to argue. She bit back a sharp retort and said simply, "Tell me."

He sighed softly, and for a while she thought she might get no more answer than that. Then his slow voice began, "Cireille was young, and bright, and beautiful of course; one of that rare kind, a laughing spirit who sees no evil in the world until she meets it. Then it can destroy her . . .

"Cireille loved me, past hope or reason; and I her. I wanted only to protect her—to protect them both, after our child was born, our daughter. I was thankful that they were in Surayon and so well hidden, safe from all the world outside.

"At the same time, though, the same knowledge terrified me. Surayon is everyone's enemy. The other states of Outremer work against us all the time, testing our defences, seeking a way inside. They would destroy us if they could, the men who lead them would burn every living creature they found within our borders. And the Sharai—well, we have friends among the Sharai, but they too have their fanatics. Those would burn the Outremer entire, and us with all the rest.

"So I sought to keep my country and my family secure. I spent more and more time beyond our borders, travelling in Outremer and among the Sharai. You have met me as a jongleur; I have had other faces at other times. Always, though, I was a spy. Sometimes more than that, a secret diplomat: the Church denounces us, and so the princes must, their power is shored up by the Church, but Surayon has yet a few friends who see the benefits of our ways and do not believe the slanders."

He fell silent briefly, and Julianne wondered if there were more to his journeys, that he was not telling: if he had not perhaps been an assassin also at need, or something other that he was ashamed to say.

He shook his head, though, as if in answer to a question that she had not asked; and went on, "Cireille mourned, when I was gone. She worried incessantly for me, but it was more than that. She was a simple soul, and her life was entirely bound up in us, in me and Elisande; she felt herself incomplete in my absence. I was her criterion, or half of it. She loved our daughter too, but not enough; she needed both of us, to thrive. And I knew that, though I tried hard to deny it. I tried too hard, and too successfully. We were both of us obsessive, in our way: she for me, and I for her protection.

"And so I left, and left again; and managed somehow not to see the damage that my leaving did. Every time I returned she was thinner and more pale, and that much more joyful to have me back. I focused on the joy, and ignored what else was plain to see.

"Each time I left she plagued me with questions, how long I would be gone, when she should look to find me coming home. She demanded promises; I made them lightly, as any lover does.

"But then of course there came a time when I broke my vows to her, when it seemed more important to me to stay away. I was gone a year or more, serving the Duke of Less Arvon in his court and watching his army build. He wanted Surayon, not us but the land; he had a quarrel with the King's son who was Duke in Ascariel and did not like the weakness of his border, where we were. The shadow you cannot see is always more frightening than the one you can. It preyed on his mind, that we were there but hidden; he feared that we might make compact with the Ascari Duke and pass his armies through, to fall on Arvon all unseen and unexpected.

"So I played courtier longer than I should have, longer than I'd promised. I made a quiet peace between the two states, without either duke realising what I was about till after they were friends again; and I confess, I enjoyed it. I missed my wife, my daughter, of course I did; no news could reach me, and I dared not take the time or the risk to visit home. No—I did not take the time. Let me be honest now, as I was not then. It was no great risk, and no great distance either; I could have afforded both. But I did not, until my task was done.

"My task as I saw it, then. I was self-appointed; I had gone to scout, with my father's blessing but not his instruction. I stayed by my own choice, judging it more important than to spend time happy and idle with my family.

"When at last I did ride home, I went expecting another merry reunion, no more than that. Oh, perhaps a little scolding, that I had stayed so long; but Cireille would understand, I was sure, when I explained the importance of what I had achieved.

"But I came back to a house in mourning. Cireille had

pined in my absence, and died for lack of me. They tried to tell me she'd died of sickness, a wasting disease that none could cure; but I pressed the doctors and the servants both, and learned the truth of it. The longer I stayed away, the more heartsick she'd become; she believed alternately in my death and then in my betrayal of her, when she heard through others that I was still at the Arvonian court and playing the Duke's fool. She thought I had some reason to stay, some pretty lady who had won my favour. And so she faded, and so died the month before my return.

"Elisande was eight years old, and had endured every moment of her mother's suffering. She had endured her mother's fantasies too, and believed them, as she must. No child can see true, at such a time. Besides, they were true, in all but detail; the court's intrigue was my mistress then, and sang closer and louder than my wife.

"Ever since, she has held me to blame for that loss; and she is right. She uses it as an excuse to behave foolishly. There is more at peril here than an inexperienced girl's shoulders can bear; she acts like a child, always, and so I treat her like a child still. Again, no doubt I can be blamed for that. I know it makes her worse. I have made peace between nations, but I cannot make my own peace with my own daughter; it reflects poorly on my skill and my judgement both. I know all of this, you need not say it. But I will not have her acting as my conscience and my constant critic, thrusting my guilt at me at every turn; and I will not willingly see her destroy the security of my country, by her wilful adventures. She is neither as wise nor as strong as she believes herself to be. Enough now, Julianne. She is your friend, I know, but so I hope am I. Do me a friend's kindness, and question me no further."

And yet you love her, Julianne thought, watching how he reached out to strike a camel's probing head away, harder than he needed, *and so you follow her, when she strikes out wild; and so you keep her by you when you can, despite the pain she brings you. And so you worry*

*about her when she slips your guard, as now, when she is
away in a perilous land with a perilous companion . . .*

How much had it cost him, she wondered, to slay that
camel and seek her image in its blood, when he could not
know if she were living or dead? It must be better sometimes not to know, to have the freedom to hope; he knew
that better than her, he must carry the memory of it with
him always, all that time his wife was failing in his absence, in his ignorance . . .

She had a better understanding of him now, and of her
friend also. She wondered if Elisande had more reasons
than one to keep her hair cropped as she did, boy-short.
To be sure, it had helped her in her travels, to pass as a lad
at a distance; but what was also sure, she did not favour
her father in looks. Perhaps when she grew it long, she
had some look of her mother. If so, it could be an unexpected kindness in her to wear it short, not to remind him
too closely of lost Cireille; or it could be another punish-
ment, more subtle and more cruel, *you killed her for me,
and so I will not carry her likeness in the world, I will not
give you even so much satisfaction* . . .

She sighed and pushed Sildana back from their precious ooze of water, barely remembering to duck in time
as long and yellowed teeth snapped back, in a miasma of
foul breath.

9

Water of Life

STUPIDLY, ELISANDE HAD begun to think that this country could hold no more surprises.

She barely saw any more the golden, shimmering sheen that overlay everything from the sky above to the dust underfoot; her eyes had adjusted so far that it seemed nothing but normal now. Likewise the constant warmth in the air, the dust, the stone—she'd ceased to notice that at all except when she cooked bread, morning and evening, and even then she took it quite for granted.

And so as they came closer and closer to the reflection or the source of what in her world was called the Dead Waters, she thought of it only in terms of those Waters that she knew, close by Rhabat. If she'd been asked the question, if she'd been forced to think, she would perhaps have said that the water here would be golden, yes, of course, as it all was, all this world; also that it would be warm, hotter than body-warm, pleasant perhaps to bathe in but dangerous to drink.

Chased even further, she might possibly have added

"dead" to that list. Golden, warm and dead as all this land was. If the Dead Waters were well named—and they were: she had stood boldly at their margin, had dabbled her fingers in the blood-warm shallows and sucked them after, had tasted bitter salt and darkness, which was entirely her idea of death—then here where nothing lived that grew or ate or had a body to it, here assuredly the waters would be dead . . .

She'd never thought to see them steam, to see them seethe and hiss and bubble like something that lived in itself, even if it could not harbour life.

SHE STOOD ATOP the low rise that had hidden the sea till now, all but the cloud of steam that rose above; she had to struggle to find her voice at all, and then again to keep it light and jocular.

"Well," she said at last, "I don't think we can call them the Dead Waters here, do you?"

"Do you think you would live, in such water?" Marron countered quietly.

"Not me, no," *and maybe not even you,* "but something should, surely? Something must. Unless it's the water itself that lives," giving voice to the thought that most disturbed her.

"No," he said, and she thought she was almost being laughed at. "It's hot, that's all. As the rocks are, heated from below. I expect all open water steams, here. This goes deep, though, and so it boils. Nothing more than that."

She gazed across the vast sea that had no horizon that she could see in any direction, no further shore; she tried to imagine how hot it must be, how far beneath the ever-moving surface, to keep such a weight of water at the boil. And could not, would not believe it: she'd rather believe her own idea, that something vital and monstrous lurked beneath the steam. She knew the myths of the Dead Waters, as he did not; surely they must have their own counterpart in this mirror-world? Unless the reflection did indeed go the other way, and what was myth in her world had its truth here . . .

Lisan of the Dead Waters, the djinni had called her. Now she really yearned to deny the title; she wanted no part of this.

"Do you think perhaps we ought to go back now?" she asked, and heard the pleading in it and was disgusted by herself. But she'd had enough, truly; the wonder of being here had grown a little stale at last—even the wonder of being alone with Marron, of having his body to hold to every night, when she could do no more than cling like some parasite with secrets—and this last shock was too sinister to refresh it.

"Probably," Marron said. His gaze turned bleak, though, and she thought he was less keen to leave than she was to stay. Which seemed to sum up everything that lay between them, and quite decided her.

"We should find Jemel, and the others," she said, trailing a little temptation in his path, thinking he'd snap at it.

"We'd need to be lucky," he replied. "So many days apart, and so much distance—we must have been faster than them, to reach this place."

"Perhaps. Unless our days are longer." Only three nights they'd had here, when Morakh had promised a week's journey; but she'd lost all track of familiar time. "We won't know, unless we go to see."

"And if we go, and do not find them—what then?"

"We can wait. They will come."

"We don't have enough food. Or water. It would be wiser to go on here, where we don't need it. We could go all the way to Rhabat, and wait for them there . . ."

He was right, of course; but, "Marron, I don't want to walk into Rhabat with you, and without them." Truly, she did not. Hasan had called a council at Rhabat, to urge the tribes of the Sharai into full war with Outremer. If she brought them the Ghost Walker and no temporising voice that they would listen to, for they surely would not listen to hers, she dreaded to think what might result. Marron was the weapon of their prophecy, that they'd waited for so long; and he had small loyalty left to his own people. He might refuse to kill, but that would make little difference. He was still a symbol, who could hold the tribes together more strongly even than Hasan . . .

He looked at her as though he could read all of that in her face and perhaps more too, that she would have preferred to keep private; and he said, "You may be right. I don't want that either. But we could wait here, another day or two. Let's rest a little, at any rate, and think about it."

That was delay, and nothing more; she didn't want to rest, and certainly he had no need to. Nor did she want to spend any longer than she must, beside that writhing water. She nodded her acquiescence, though, thinking that she'd pushed him as far as she could, for now.

"I could bake some bread . . ."

"No. Let's save what we have. Unless you're hungry?"

She was not, and knew he wouldn't be. She only wanted to be busy, not to have to sit and stare at the surging sea.

Instead she turned to look back at how far they'd come across that endless dust that carried no footprints but their own, two tracks that made the faintest of paths between them, perhaps the first this land had ever known. She wondered how long those marks might last: millennia, maybe, in a country without wind or weather. Long after she was dead, at least. She could almost be content with that, she thought, to have left so enduring a memory of her passage through life, of her presence here with Marron these few days.

Almost . . .

Something snagged at her eye, just a moment before she could lose herself entirely in melancholy. Something like an insect in the air, only that there were no insects . . .

She tried to find it again and could not, but there was another suddenly; and no, it was not an insect. It was a hair of darkness, hanging almost at the level of her eyes and twisting like a thread on a spindle: twisting and growing thicker as she watched, a string of smoke, and there was another behind it, and another over there . . .

"Marron," she called softly, urgently. "I do not think we should wait a moment here. Do you see?"

She didn't take her eyes from what she was watching, but she heard his turning, heard his sharp insuck of breath, anticipated his question before he asked it.

"What are they?"

"I think they are 'ifrit. Find your knife, Marron, and let us go."

If the djinn were threads of light and air, all but impossible to see except in darkness—she remembered that flicker of gold that had distorted the sky on their first night here, and thought it must have been a djinni—then it seemed likely to her that 'ifrit would be the opposite of that. She thought she was gazing now at a swarm of them, and far too close.

She heard the hiss of Marron's dagger drawn, heard his gasp of pain as he cut open his arm. Then there was a red blur beside her, the Daughter spreading itself into a welcome gateway.

Her feet itched to make a leap through, but she held back, waiting for Marron; she meant to see him safe first, before she saved herself.

He was slow too, though, seemingly for her sake. Between them, they were both too slow.

The 'ifrit stretched themselves out, longer and longer; like black ropes drawn to an unseen windlass they ran, and that windlass on the further side of the Daughter's portal. Too late to make that leap: she clutched at Marron's arm to hold him back, and only realised when he cried aloud that it was his left arm she was grabbing.

There was a mass of those smoky ropes pouring through the Daughter now, flooding from this world into theirs. She tried to count them, and could not; they writhed as they flowed, but there were certainly dozens.

As one tail flicked through and vanished beyond the blur, another head would follow. By the time she thought of how to stop them, shouting to Marron to call the Daughter back and never mind that they'd be stranded here to face however many remained, it was too late even for that. They were gone, they were all gone through.

She stared at Marron, aghast. "That, that was what they wanted. It wasn't us at all, they only wanted a way into our world, and we gave it to them . . ."

"Not us," he said bleakly. "Me. I did it. Even when I don't mean to, I still betray. This time my whole world . . ."

"Our world," she replied fiercely. "And it was my idea, I called you to it. You can't take this on yourself. But— oh, Marron! Julianne, Jemel . . ."

"They may not be there. We said that, remember? They should not be there yet."

Perhaps not. But still there was a plague of evil passed through, and by their hands. With what intent, she couldn't imagine and didn't want to try. She remembered the one 'ifrit that Julianne had brought through by chance—perhaps by chance: she doubted that, suddenly— and how deadly it had been, how it had taken an arrow specially blessed to kill the thing.

"We have to follow," she said numbly. If only to be there, to fall alone or with their friends; likely the first of many, perhaps very many indeed . . .

"Yes," he said; and drew his sword and stepped through that blurring gateway, and was gone.

She hurried to go after him, fearful that he might find himself in battle immediately and close the gate behind him, leave her stranded rather than let her die.

IT WAS LIKE running into a wall, a fiery wall: she thought for a moment that he had started to close the gate and she'd met the Daughter half-withdrawn and she'd be dead indeed, it would slay her here or suck her through and slay her there or maybe leave her between two worlds, nowhere at all. When flesh met Daughter, flesh ruptured, it blew apart, as though every smallest fragment of it were ripped between irresistible forces . . .

But if she could think so clearly, she couldn't be dying, surely?

Nor was she. She hadn't been splattered, at least, as she had seen men splattered by the Daughter's kiss. That fire-heat had encompassed her entirely—as she had seen the Daughter do, wickedly, to its victims, before it disassembled them—but she knew it now, by its touch inside and out. She'd forgotten its thunderstrike effect, that was all, on stepping from caveshadow or cool pool—or even from golden-warm air beside a boiling sea—into the sudden full heat of the Sands.

She opened her eyes, only realising as she did so that she must have closed them when she made that hectic plunge through in Marron's wake. So much for the clear-eyed heroine, walking boldly to meet her fate at her man's side . . .

But he was not her man in any case; and he stood some paces from her, and seemed to be staring in fascination at his feet while his sword Dard hung slack and disregarded in his hand.

She had her remaining knife in hand, though she couldn't remember drawing it; she hurried to stand at his unprotected back, to watch over him as he would not watch over himself.

There seemed no immediate sign of the 'ifrit, but they could come from any side, or all at once. She said, "Marron, did you see which way they went?"

"Mmm? Oh. Yes. At least, I didn't see, but look . . ."

She risked a quick glance down, where he was pointing; and then a longer stare, as every horizon was still clear of any ink-black shadow that moved. Marron stepped a little way away, and took the Daughter back into his blood. She made no protest.

Here, as in that other country they had so abruptly fled,

the ground fell in a smooth and shallow bank down to the lapping waters of this desert shore. Here the sand was coarse and tawny, seeming tarnished after the glitter and glow of what they'd left; here the water was dark and dirty, and blessedly still . . .

Almost still, she corrected herself, seeing a patch of bubbling disturbance some distance out and moving further. As though a shoal of fish were fighting just under the surface, she thought—except that there were no fish in the Dead Waters, nor anything that lived, except perhaps a monster.

From that point where the Daughter had stood, opening a way between the worlds, the wind-smoothed sand was disrupted, churned into a cattle-track, it seemed; and that track led straight down to the water's edge, and the same line followed underwater would run precisely to that roiling agitation, except that as she watched it settled slowly into nothing more than a shimmer under the sun, and then into nothing at all.

She turned her eyes back to the sand, and crouched to check. No tracks led in any other direction—though 'ifrit might fly in this world as in their own, if they took a shape with wings—and what individual marks she could read were pockmarks rather than prints, little pits that seemed to have been made by spikes or needles . . .

Well, an 'ifrit could take what shape it chose, in this world; by all that she'd heard they favoured monstrous forms. That one that Julianne pulled through and Jemel stepped in to kill, that one had shaped itself into a giant beetle with a demon's head.

She glanced up at Marron and said, "Crabs?"

"Something crab-like," he confirmed. "Something with many legs, sharp little legs that can run on sand and underwater too."

"I wonder why?"

"A good shape to use under the water, I suppose."

"Yes, but why come through here, only to go deep into the Dead Waters?" It must have been planned, so much was obvious. Likely the 'ifrit had shadowed them a great part of their journey waiting for this place, this time to show themselves and so force open a door that the creatures couldn't open on their own account—but why? What lay under the water here, that they could possibly want?

"Safety, perhaps?" Marron was answering her spoken question, but his answer fitted the unspoken as well. "They are not immune to the weapons of men. The Sharai would hunt and kill them gladly, however many lives they lost in that hunt; but not even the Sharai can come at them while they lurk down there. And with the shell and claws of a crab, they can defend themselves against whatever might come at them in the water . . ."

"Nothing will. Hadn't you heard? The waters are dead here, there's nothing living to disturb them." Only ghosts, and she didn't suppose the 'ifrit were susceptible to haunting. But she glowered at the murky surface, blinked away the sun-dazzle that bit back at her eyes, and said, "I don't believe it. Why take so much trouble, only to hide in the end?"

"I didn't say only to hide. They must have some other purpose. But in the meantime, until they are ready, they are very safe."

"Well, perhaps. Perhaps. Are we safe?"

He smiled. "No, of course not. They could come back; if they came slow and quiet, or in another shape, we would not even see the water ruffle."

She eyed the water's edge a little nervously, and skittered to the other side of Marron. Which made him smile, which had been her intent. She tucked her arm through his, and smiled back. "You're not worried, though. Not about them. Are you?"

"No. At the moment, no. If they had meant to kill us, they would have waited for us and done it quickly, before I took the Daughter back. It would be harder for them now, whatever shape they came in. Perhaps they think their way home will be easier, if I am still alive; perhaps I can still surprise them."

"We," she said, "we'll surprise them together. They surprised us, both of us. We owe them, and I always pay my debts."

Not a smile this time, a real grin on his face, and she hadn't seen that for so long. "We, then," he said, "if you can get that dagger blessed. What prayers do the imams put on weapons, do you know?"

"I'll ask, if we ever see an imam. They are rare in the desert, the Sharai have little time for them; that's why blessed weapons are so precious."

"Good enough." He looked about him then, and walked a little way away from her, to the top of the rise, to see better; she followed his every step like a well-trained servant or a well-trained dog, and couldn't even resent herself for doing it.

There was no sign of the rest of their party, no sign of anyone; not even a track to show where people had passed on these dull, dun sands. She remembered that no roads ran close to the Dead Waters. Rhabat was well protected, sheltered both by its towering hills and by age-old custom; either superstition or true caution kept the tribes away from its open waterfront.

"Well, we are here," Marron said, "and so are the 'ifrit; and I'm more worried about us for now. We need food and shelter, and particularly water. Water we can drink," with a scathing glance at the lapping sea behind them. "And for that, I have to depend on you. I don't know the ways of the Sands, where to look or how to find it . . ."

I'm more worried about you, was what he was saying; she understood him perfectly, and her heart thundered in response. He might survive the long trek along the shoreline to the safety of Rhabat, but she could not . . .

"I'll find water," she said confidently. "Food, too. We can hunt; there's always life in the Sands, if you're alert to see it."

The search might lead them far from any hope of meet-

ing their friends, but that she did not need to say; he knew
it already.

"And shelter? This sun will scorch you . . ."

Marron, it will scorch us both. He was bare-chested and
bare-backed; the Daughter would not shield him from the
sun, only stop him feeling how it burned. He was stupid
about his body, he always had been and now he was
worse; he'd neglect it altogether, if she allowed him to.
But she loved his care of her, and the chance to return it.

"No shelter here," she said, stating what was obvious,
"except what we make for ourselves. We can dig a little
into the side of a dune, and find cooler sand to hide in;
there are lizards that bury themselves completely, they
make good examples. We'll move by night, lie up through
the day and hope to meet our friends quickly. That
wound's all but healed now, but you can't walk through
the Sands like that, no one could . . ."

Her fingers trembled just a little where she touched his
deep-scarred shoulder, which was foolish; hadn't they
slept close-wrapped together last night, and several nights
before? But that was in another country, in their solitude,
quite unobserved except by passing spirits who would
give no weight to such an act, as neither perhaps had he.
Here Jemel was close, and Julianne, and others; the clasp
of a hand carried portents that even he might not manage
to misinterpret.

She took her hand away and used it to shield her eyes
as she scanned the far and flat horizons, trying to look
wise in the ways of the desert. In truth it mattered little
which way she led him; or rather it mattered enormously,
but that she saw no signs to say where water might be
found, and so she had to guess. What roads she knew of
were too far to seek, where they might have found wells
in common use.

"We'll go west," she decided. "The others must come
that way, once they reach the Waters; Rhabat lies on the
southern shore, and the other way around is too mountain-
ous. I don't say that we should wait for them, unless we

find water and better shelter than I can see from here, but we can leave signs that they may find and follow . . ."

There were many such signs, that could be carved in• rock or set out in smaller stones, even trampled into sand where no other means afforded. Each tribe had its own, but some at least were understood by all: *you may drink from this well* or *you may not, good hunting here, beware of quicksands ahead . . .*

Here on the rise was good; she gathered pebbles and laid them out in pattern, to say nothing more complex than *we were here, and have gone west.* Even so much was probably not necessary; Jemel or the Dancers would see their tracks, come from nowhere, and know who had made them and where they were headed. The tracks of the 'ifrit might puzzle even Dancers, though; she thought a moment, and added a sigil that meant *beware the water.* It was more usually used to warn travellers of a well that harboured disease, but she could think of nothing better on the spur of the moment. There were those among the party who might make a sound guess as to her meaning, when they had seen those tracks.

Or they might not find this spot at all, of course. She'd done all she could, though; she straightened up and scanned the horizon one more time, against the small chance of seeing a shadow rise. And did not, and so led Marron away on a line a little north of the sun's path west, to give them some distance from the Waters.

AND SO SHE found what she had least expected, tracks that she could read herself, although she did not understand them.

They came from the north, the way her friends must have come; and they were camel-tracks and bare feet to speak of that party, riders and Dancers. The camel-tracks were fresh, made perhaps that morning, there was only a little wind-scuff blurring them; but the feet had come later. Their marks were sharp and clear, a couple of hours old perhaps, no more.

By her count, there were five camels and three men afoot. Which was not enough of either, if this were truly what she hoped against all reason.

"They can't be ahead of us," she said, "how can they?"

Marron shook his head. "Either the Dancers were wrong about how long the journey would take, and I don't believe that—"

"No," she said positively. "I saw it, some of it, before we left them. Easily a week across that ground, and I couldn't see the Waters."

"—Or we were right, that time moves differently in the other world. Why not? The djinn have no need to count the hours. But are you sure that these are our camels?"

"I can't see mine. She had a scar on one pad, and I don't think she's here. But Julianne's white, she's so proud, that one, she throws her feet out as she walks. Look, here . . . I'm not positive, no—but as near as I can be. Though there aren't enough Dancers, either. Only three, and they're hours behind. I don't understand it."

"Perhaps they were delayed, while the riders went ahead; perhaps they met trouble on the way, or they just met news, and have divided. We'll find no answers here. What should we do, follow the tracks? Or go on looking for water?"

"Whoever made these tracks, whether they're our people or not, they've come across the Sands; they'll be looking for water too. Let's follow. We won't catch up with the camels before dark, unless they found a well and chose to rest out the day; but if they found a well and moved on after, their tracks will lead us to it. With luck we'll find the walkers, at least. Come on . . ."

She was more worried than she cared to admit; if the camel-tracks were from their party and the feet did not belong to Dancers, then their friends were being stalked, and probably not by anyone with peaceful intent. She couldn't remember which tribe laid claim to the lands around the

northern end of the Dead Waters, but this was a deadly
time; few of the Sharai would welcome strangers. In isolated areas where no roads ran, at high summer when
water was short and precious, few indeed . . .

She was anxious not to alarm Marron, he was so reluctant to fight, and so adamant in his refusal to kill any
more. She didn't know what he might do if he thought
they were headed for a battle. Wake the Daughter, perhaps, and go back to the land of the djinn? Take her with
him, perhaps, or else leave her to face whatever trouble
she found, quite alone? Every option made her more un-
quiet, and so she held her tongue and could only hope that
his thoughts were following a different, more hopeful
track than hers.

THE LAND WAS rugged here, gravel plain with scattered
dunes rising unpredictably; impossible to see much in any
direction, each dune-top gave a view only as far as the
next. The tracks were easy to follow, though, human toes
breaking camel-pads all the way. Their depth and clarity
renewed her unease; perhaps she was a victim of their legend, but she was surprised to find Dancers leaving so obvious a trail. She'd thought they would walk across dust
and not leave a mark. So perhaps these were not Dancers,
these three men. But if so, where were the Dancers? Left
the group after Marron did, for lack of their Ghost
Walker? That was certainly possible; on the other hand, if
they wanted to find him again, their best choice was to
stay.

To stay, or to follow. That might be it, that they had detached themselves completely but still kept the same
route, holding themselves aloof and apart. That fitted; but
if so, why were they hurrying? No one hurried in the
desert, but these men did. Toes and balls of the feet she
saw, rarely a heel. Their strides were short, so they
weren't running full out, but trotting certainly. Had they
simply let the group get too far ahead for their comfort?

Or was it that they had some insight, perhaps foresight: did they expect Marron to return tonight, and so they closed the distance quickly?

Questions, questions. She struggled to believe the best, and rarely managed it; so that when at last Marron did spot dark figures against the sand, she was hardly surprised to see him gesture her to stillness as he crouched low beside her.

She shaded her eyes against the glare of the lowering sun, and strained to see. There they were, she had them now, three men lying prone in the lee of a dune that ran due west ahead, so that not even their shadows broke the crest.

As she watched, one of them snaked backwards down the slope, not standing until he was sure of avoiding any wary eyes on the further side of the dune. He ran off westward, and she thought she saw a bow in his hand; certainly it was too long and thick to be a riding-stick, and in any case these men had no camels.

Who but the Dancers would venture the Sands without camels? None, that she had ever heard of. She couldn't see whether their robes were blue or black, but she was sure none the less, although she didn't understand it.

"Marron? Can you see more than I can?"

"One of the men is Morakh; the other two were also with us, although I never learned their names."

No, neither had she. Morakh did all the talking, always. "They, uh, they don't look very friendly, do they?"

"No."

"And it must be our friends, beyond that dune . . ."

"It is. I can hear their voices, and the camels. They have found water, I think."

She could hear nothing, but she was growing accustomed by now to how Marron's abilities far overreached her own.

"What did the Dancers say to each other, when that one left? Could you hear that?"

"They didn't speak. I think they used signs, not to be

overheard, but I couldn't see their hands. What should we do?"

"You could call to them, call them off, whatever it is they're doing . . ."

"One has gone, beyond the sound of my voice; the others—well, do you think Morakh would set his plans aside because I bade him? Ordered him, even? They are sworn to serve me; I don't believe that his idea of service includes obedience to any will other than his own."

It was a fault he was familiar with, to judge by his bleak tone and bleaker look; she remembered Marron and his master, Sieur Anton, how hard it had been for the boy to leave the man. And how he had left regardless, she remembered that too. No, oaths bent or broken were nothing new to Marron.

"It would warn Julianne and the others, though. Warn Jemel. If you shouted . . ."

"And perhaps push the Dancers into violence that we might otherwise avoid. A hasty enemy is a dangerous enemy, Elisande; he will kill for convenience."

"A friend alerted is as good as an enemy surprised," she countered, her overheard wisdom for his. Neither one of them knew so much from practice. "And why are they enemies, anyway? They were companions when we left, if not exactly friends . . ."

"A long way from being friends. And we left. They were there for my sake, and I left. With you, without them. What happened after we were gone—well, we can learn that later."

"What do you want to do, then?"

"For the moment, nothing. Watch, and wait. It'll be dark in an hour. If the Dancers move before nightfall, then yes, perhaps I must distract them; but I guess they're waiting for the dark. So can we."

"Marron, that one who slipped away, he was an archer, he had a bow . . ."

"I saw it. So?"

"So what if he shoots Julianne? Jemel? Now, while the

sun's behind him and the light's still good? We can't even
see him from here, we won't have time to interfere . . ."

"If he stands to use his bow," Marron said slowly, deliberately, maddeningly, "then he makes a target of himself; the sun won't hide him, it'll mark him out. His
shadow will cover all the land between, faster than any
arrow he can draw and shoot. Even if that's what they in-
tend, they'll wait till dark."

"And how will he see to shoot then?"

"Jemel will light a fire. That's one reason why they
stopped, perhaps: not only for the water, but to gather fuel
too. There's driftwood along the shore. Jemel will light a
fire, and the bowman will see them outlined against the
flames, and they won't see him at all . . ."

"No. So how do we prevent it, pray for rain?"

"As soon as it's dark, I can take you to the well. I could
do it now, but Morakh would see."

"He'll see after dark, too. He doesn't need firelight, he
has owl's eyes. Like yours."

"No, not like mine. If he sees us at the fire, that's too
late for him. And he won't see us crossing the sand; we'll
go the other way."

"What other way?" she demanded; and felt stupid immediately the words were out of her mouth, didn't need to
see him tap his arm to tell her.

SO THEY WAITED and watched; and as he had predicted,
the Dancers did the same. The sun set in a riot of reds and
purples, that still seemed tawdry to her gold-adapted eyes;
she said, "Now?"

"Wait," he said, "you know Jemel's fires. It'll be a
smoky smudge for the next hour, he won't build it up till
the heat goes from the sand. They won't move yet, so we
don't need to. Not till it's full dark."

True enough, but she was restless with impatience and
anxiety, desperate to carry the warning to their friends.
Darkness swept up from behind them as the sun disap-

peared ahead; she wanted to go immediately, and thought she had her wish when Marron sat up beside her, suddenly alert. She touched his shoulder enquiringly, but he shook his head and gestured her to be still. He seemed to be listening, to something far beyond her hearing; strain though she might, though she did, she could hear nothing but distant sounds of the sea's stirring.

She fidgeted at Marron's side while he listened, turned his head and listened again. At last he reached to take her wrist and tug her gently back into the star-shadow of a dune, safely away from the skyline. She wanted to ask him what he'd been so attentive towards, but he gave her no opportunity; his knife nicked his arm, and the Daughter flowed.

It was only dimly red in the darkness, but when it shaped itself into a doorway, the heart of it glowed brightly; when they stepped through, it was more shocking than the plunge from the steamy heat of the hammam into an ice-cold pool.

They stepped from night into day, from darkness into pearly light that didn't even have that border of gloom on the horizon to say that night was coming. Proof positive that the days of the djinn were longer, or else that time here followed other patterns entirely; she only hoped that none of the Dancers had noticed any flare of light leak from the Daughter as they'd passed through.

Marron might have had the same concern; he closed that doorway behind them, even as his blood ran into the sand, as he staggered from the pain.

"Take it back," she urged him, slipping her shoulder under his arm for support, wrapping her own arm tight around his waist.

"What, for a walk of a hundred paces and then scratch at the door to let it out again?"

"Marron, please . . . For my sake, if not your own? I can't, I can't carry you that far . . ."

She was lying, of course; she could carry him to the moon if she had to. He believed her, though, or let her be-

lieve that he did; either way, the Daughter sucked itself
back under his skin, the bloodflow stopped and his weight
lifted from her body.

A long moment later, she uncoiled her arm and stepped
away.

"At least it should be easier to find the place in the
light," she said determinedly, "even though the land's so
different. Which direction?"

"Over there." They were standing among dunes again,
but dunes of dust that were shaped quite differently from
the sand they'd come from; his pointing finger betrayed
no doubts, though, and she agreed with him. They had no
sun to guide them, nor any sight of the sea, but still that
felt westerly and a little south, it felt absolutely right.

And was right; they were sure when they saw steam rising from a little dip in the dust. As they came closer, they
saw a pool of gently bubbling water at the bottom of the
dip.

"Not too close," he said, leading her away to the south.
"I don't want to risk touching anyone. Not even one of the
camels . . ."

Touching them with the Daughter, he meant; she shuddered at the memory of another night, when he had slain
and slain in the stables of the Roq.

Where he judged it safe, he cut his arm once more.
Elisande thought that even the colour of the Daughter was
stronger here, richer and less smoky, though it still be-
haved like smoke, pouring heavily through the air. Smoke
with a will, she thought, that was in some part its own,
only directed by Marron; here was something at least that
did practise obedience. It would be a day of terror, she
thought, the day that it did not . . .

She stepped forward and through the portal that it
made, back into sudden dark; as she went she heard Marron murmur, "Elisande, beware the south, beware what
comes from the water."

She didn't reply immediately; blind eyes overruled and
she had to stand blinking, lost in utter darkness until her

sight came back to her a little. Then she saw the soft glow that was Jemel's fire, the shadows of her friends and their mounts around.

A voice cried a warning, weapons scraped from their sheaths, and she had no time to question Marron; she stumbled forward, and another voice called her name.

"Shush, Julianne!" she hissed frantically. "All of you, listen to me! You're being watched, Morakh's behind that dune," with a jerk of her head northerly, "and he's been tracking you all day. We tracked him. He's got other Dancers with him. Only three of them altogether, though, I don't know where the others went, they might have circled round to get ahead . . ."

"They're dead," Rudel said shortly. "What more?"

"One of the Dancers has a bow and he went west, along behind that ridge there. I thought he was looking to catch you in the sun but Marron said not, he said he'd take you by the firelight and he was right, so put it out, Jemel . . ."

A sudden barefoot kick, a yelp as the smouldering fire bit even through leathery Sharai soles, a scatter of sand and that little glow was gone.

"Where is Marron?" her father demanded, just a voice in darkness.

"Why, here—"

But she turned as she spoke, sensing at last the absence behind her, where there should have been another human body.

There was nothing: no Marron and no sign of the Daughter, no gateway open or closed . . .

"Didn't he come through?"

"No," Julianne said softly, slipping an arm around her shoulders. "Just you. And barely even you, girl. What have you been doing to yourself? You're so thin . . ."

Was she? She was hungry, she was suddenly, inappropriately aware of that; no, more, she was ravenous, as she had not been for days. Djinn-length days . . .

"Short commons," she said briefly. There would be time later, to eat and talk both; or there would be no chance for either. Even so, even in her urgency, she found just time enough to feel a pang of betrayal. He had gone back—stayed, rather, let her come through alone—to avoid the fight he foresaw, the possibility of his having to kill. He'd abandoned her and all of them to fate or chance, for the sake of his own heavy conscience; and oh, that was bitter to her. He'd said it himself, that he betrayed wherever he touched. She should have trusted his judgement on that, and had not.

"We can move now," Jemel said. "It will be hard to rouse the camels silently, but we can bind their jaws. Where we go may not be seen, if we avoid the sky-line . . ."

But there was doubt in his own voice, and she knew it was the wrong choice. There was no moon, but stars blazed overhead; it was not so dark at all, now that her eyes were accustomed. The Dancers would need no more light than that to see them leave, nor to follow them. Perhaps the archer could even shoot in such a light, though she could not; she might risk a knife, but not with any confidence.

"No," firmly, from Rudel. "Safer to stay where we are; a party on the move is always vulnerable. We can use the camels as shelter against arrows. At close quarters, we have a chance; we have beaten the Dancers before, when there were more of them and we were unprepared. Quickly, come . . ."

"We need the camels," Jemel objected.

"Jemel, we need to live. If the camels die, so may we, granted; but if they die in our stead, their deaths may at least give us the chance of life. We have no other."

No further argument; they huddled close against the sandy bodies of the beasts. Five camels, and four of them: one short, on each count. To save thinking of Marron, Elisande whispered, "Julianne, where's my camel?"

"Oh. Unh, I'll tell you later, I can't think about that now . . ."

Dead, then, somewhere in the Sands; she was sorry. So

would the Sultan be. Julianne was right, though, this was not the time. Elisande lifted her head cautiously, and peered over her warm, protective bulwark.

What had been an open pool in the land of the djinn was a well here, or at least a stone-rimmed pit that ought to signify a well, with a leather rope coiled beside. There was no gleam of light reflecting up from that black hole; the water would lie deep, in such country. If there were water, if it weren't dry and her friends' dipped skins had brought up nothing but dust . . .

The dunes held the well closely; too close, she thought. This was poor ground to defend, as any such isolated well would be. Rudel should have known that. Desert wisdom decreed that camp should always be made a little distance off, on a dune-crest where one could both see and be seen; it was less aggressive, and tactically far safer. With such a well, the wind blew sand against the stones that covered it, and every passing party dug it clear; and so a rampart of dug and discarded sand would build up through the years, all around the well-head. More wind, more nomads, much more time and this was the result, a well at the bottom of a wide, high bowl. Too wide for a small party to protect, and too near a horizon: she could see little further than she could throw a knife. She'd be lucky to have time to make the throw; a man appearing on that short horizon, a running man would be down and among them before she'd done more than yell a warning.

Blade in hand, she scanned her quarter of the skyline grimly, determined to throw before she yelled.

When the man appeared, he was not running; neither was he in her range. He caught just the corner of her eye, a shadow rimmed by starlight, rising to his feet in her father's quarter. She should watch her own horizon, and not his; but that was the archer, his bow was too fine a line but she could read his stance. And her father juggled knives with breathtaking skill until he tried too many, but she'd never seen him throw one. It wasn't he who'd taught her.

Had she doubted that the archer could shoot by night?
At this distance, he could shoot blindfold and not miss.
She crouched lower behind the camel's bulk, and thought
they should have run after all; they had no chance here,
none. Fish in a pond, a child could pick them off . . .

A hiss and a thud, a camel's shriek of pain; the beast
that sheltered her father staggered half to its feet and fell
back grunting. Dead, it would make as good shelter—but
Rudel was standing suddenly, a clear target for the next
arrow.

She opened her mouth to shriek at him, *stupid! get
down!*—and bit the words back unformed, as she saw his
arm cock and hurl. She looked for the glint of a knife in
transit, and didn't see it; he seemed to have thrown a ball
instead, in a high slow lob.

She didn't understand, and wasn't granted the time to
puzzle over it. The archer drew and shot; she saw her father fall.

And did shriek then, wordlessly, and leaped to her feet,
as stupid as he'd been; and so made a target of herself, a
brighter target by far as the well, the camels, her friends,
her father's body and all that lay within that broad bowl
shone suddenly in a flaring light. Harsh sharp shadows
moved and ran into the night beyond the walls of sand.

Startled, she flung herself around—not down, not
clever even now, exposed and helpless—to see that ball of
stuff her father had flung up, now falling fast. Falling and
burning, blazing, trailing a fierce guttering flame of blue
and green, while the core was white as a streaking star.

Down it plummeted, too fast almost for her eyes to follow; too fast surely for a human body to avoid. The archer
seemed not even to try. She saw him standing rooted, gaping as that fireball plunged towards him.

Flame and body met and merged. The ball lost its solidity and seemed to flow, to melt not over the man's body
and robes but into him, into soft flesh and running blood.
He didn't catch fire as a man ought, hair and clothes
aflare and his hands beating, flailing uselessly, his voice a

scream of horror; he burned from the inside and glowed like a lamp, as though his bones were blazing.

When he flung his head back and his mouth gaped, no scream came out of it: no voice at all but only a leap, a vivid flare of light.

Elisande had seen fire-eaters many times; she'd heard boys being burned to death. One was a fairground trick, the other a truth, a memory seared deep. She'd never seen a man eaten by fire, consumed from within; she'd heard such things in stories, and never believed them true. Tricks of the tongue, no more . . .

But that man burned and his tongue was tricked with flame, and shadows danced; and the Sand Dancers added their shadows to the dance, she saw them, two men rising up and running down through that shimmering light.

She was offered horror on the one hand and danger on the other, and she rejected them both. For the moment, while that dread light lasted, she turned her back on her friends in their peril and ran to her father, with never a thought for the strangeness of that choice.

Rudel lay on his back, with the arrow jutting from his chest. She dropped to her knees beside him and reached to lay her hands on his body, one beside that arrow and the other on his head. He was not dead, she could feel his breathing, hard and shallow; her own breath choked her briefly, one quick sob of relief.

His eyes were open, staring up at her; his mouth worked, but only to splutter a thick dark liquid into his beard. He was drowning, she thought, as his lungs and airways filled with blood. She closed her eyes against the desperate sight of him, tried to close ears and mind both to the sounds around, harsh grunts and the clash of steel, the bellows of terrified camels struggling against their hobbles. Never mind that he was her father, with all that meant to her; never mind that her friends were fighting for their own lives and hers also. She distanced herself from all that was happening around her and within her, strug-

gling to focus only on this broken body, seeking as she'd
been taught to with her inner eye.

She felt her fingers tingle as she drew on her own
strength and gave it up to him. After a little, his breathing
seemed to ease; that was a distraction, though, not
enough. Far short of what he needed. Her thoughts
seemed to slide down her arms, down through her hands,
her skin and his; her mind seemed to wander in the path-
ways of his body, till she found what was ripped and torn,
where metal head and wooden shaft had invaded.

Nothing she could do about the arrow now, but she
could stop the blood from flowing out so fast, close up
minor vessels, clot the major. It was patching only, but it
would serve. Time enough later for the slow arts of true
healing. If they were granted time, and the opportunity to
use it . . .

Whether what she saw was real, whether she actually
reached inside his body and touched her thoughts to his
flesh, she couldn't say. It might be only imagination and
knowledge working together, while the undoubted power
that she had found its own way to where it was needed.
But it seemed to her that she did see and touch, as she had
with Marron also, in the land of the djinn; she thought she
saw her father's blood clotting around that brutal arrow, to
stem the leaks that would kill him else.

At last she lifted her hands away, and turned him
quickly onto his side. A little more blood flowed from his
mouth; she watched anxiously in the fading light—fading
as the fire must be dying in the dead Dancer's body, but
she didn't turn her head to see that—until she saw that he
could breathe and not choke now, until she was sure that it
was safe to leave him for a while.

Then she stood and looked around, though it took an
effort to do so. Jemel was fighting blade to blade with
Morakh; he was hard-pressed, but holding. Julianne was
facing the other Dancer, across the struggling body of a
couched and hobbled camel; she had her knives in hand,
but his scimitar slashed and lunged at her above the ani-

mal's back and all she could do was dodge. Elisande pulled a knife from her father's belt and cocked her arm to throw, but in that instant the light was lost to her, as the last lingering flames lost their hold on shrivelled flesh, and darkness fell.

It would take time, too much time for her eyes to find enough light by the stars. Drained though she was she ran instead, a knife in each hand now. She saw one shifting shadow, two, and a third on the ground between them: that was Julianne, that was the camel, this must be the Dancer. She hurled herself at him, blades outstretched, wanting only to wrestle and slash, too close for his sword to find her.

The moment before her body must have plunged into his, he was suddenly not there. She hit only empty air and staggered, fell, fetched up against the surging weight of the camel. Struggled back to her feet, bewildered; and saw him now on the other side of the beast, face to face with Julianne.

Her friend took the same desperate chance that Elisande had, hurling herself across the space between them, a beat ahead of his swinging sword; the blade missed her back by a finger's width. Julianne thudded up against the Dancer, with force enough to send him staggering; but she'd flung her arms wide as she leaped, and now she had no weight behind her knives. She slashed wildly at his face, not even trying for his eyes, as Elisande would have done. He flinched back from the flashing, biting blades, but then rooted his feet and flung her off.

Julianne lost her footing, and fell sprawling. And would have died, as the Dancer at last had room to skewer her; but Elisande threw a blade in that moment, and the next vaulted over the camel with one hand on its back, lashing her feet around to catch the man behind his knees and bring him down.

She landed in a tumble on top of him. Her one knife had taken him in the shoulder; her other she slammed into his side, yanked it out and thrust again. He was still struggling, still strong, writhing beneath her; but then there

was another body falling onto him beside her, and more
blades flashing, sinking deep.

Elisande felt his final shudder, felt him relax into death.
She breathed deeply, once, and lifted her head to find herself eye to eye with Julianne. There was a spray of blood
across her friend's face and a frenzied look to her, her
eyes wide and white behind her tangled hair; absurdly,
Elisande wanted to wipe her clean and tidy her, to bring
back the calm and courtly maiden. Julianne had been
made for another kind of warfare altogether, not this desperate brawling in the dark . . .

But sounds of grating steel and gasping breath pulled
her back to where they were, in deadly danger still. She
jerked upright and saw Jemel blundering backwards,
swinging his scimitar two-handed now and with no art or
skill, battering his opponent's blade aside and barely re-
covering in time to do the same again. It couldn't last;
Morakh stalked him across the sand, merciless and
deadly. Feint and thrust, feint and cut: soon one of those
strokes would tell, it must do. And then he would have the
girls to kill, and that he could do, though he was alone to
do it now; in such a fight victory lay in the head as much
as the hands, and he was their master in both. He knew it,
so did they. So did Jemel.

But Jemel had held him already for longer, far longer
than Elisande would have believed possible; and thanks to
that heroic effort there were still three of them, and so
they might yet have a chance . . .

She scrabbled for her knives, and found one; pushed
herself to her feet and found Julianne at her side, again
with only the one blade in her hand.

"Jump, or throw?" she gasped.

"I throw," Elisande said, *and then I take your knife and
jump, my sweet, you weren't bred for this . . .*

So she poised herself to throw, and almost as if to
oblige her the duelling men shifted, so that Morakh's
broad back was before her. She couldn't miss . . .

Even as her arm began to move, though, a monstrous

shadow blotted out the stars above Jemel's head, as something rose up from behind the crest of the dune. She could see only the creature's silhouette and a glimpse of claws, of a fearsome tossing head; but that was enough to say *ghûl* to her, and just enough to shift her aim. Morakh might kill Jemel with his next lunge, or the one following; the ghûl would do it from behind, immediately and certainly.

She couldn't hope to be accurate, changing her cast so suddenly. Nor was she. Her only chance to kill the ghûl with such a small blade at such a distance was to take it in the throat; she saw the knife sink home into its chest, an arm's length below her mark.

It hissed and roared, louder than Julianne's cry of warning. Jemel perhaps heard both, though he couldn't have understood either. He understood his peril, though, and dived rolling down the dune, beneath Morakh's killing-stroke.

The Dancer wasn't fool enough to turn his back on a wounded ghûl; nor alas was he fool enough to strike at it. Instead he simply flickered out of sight, that legendary ability of his kind. Elisande had heard it told in stories, had seen it once before tonight. She spared time for one quick glance round, but couldn't see him anywhere within the bowl. She ran instead to Jemel's side, with Julianne not slow to follow; the three of them faced the ghûl as it came slowly down towards them.

Behind it, two more appeared above the dune.

Beware the south, Marron had said, *beware what comes from the water.* He had known, somehow—had heard them, perhaps, or understood better what they'd both heard, the sounds of heavy bodies rising from the sea. Certainly he'd been listening to something. And still he'd left . . .

"What should we do?" Julianne whispered.

With a heavy heart, Elisande made swift plans that any swift mind would dismiss as nonsense, as the dreaming of a stupid and frightened girl. "This one's wounded; a second blow will heal it. We must be quick, then. Give me your knife, Julianne. I'll throw. It'll recover; but then you can slay it, Jemel. After that we're in your hands, you must kill the others yourself, or at least delay them till Julianne and I can gather swords from the fallen . . ."

It wouldn't work, it couldn't work; already the first ghûl loomed above them. A foul smell was its herald, salt and filth on damp rank fur. Julianne breathed at her, "Throw, for pity's sake . . . !" But it had to be close, to give Jemel a chance to slay it in the instant of its recovery. She waited, waited—

—and didn't throw at all, she didn't need to. The air thrummed with a bass note, they heard the thud of an arrow striking home. Next moment the ghûl had reared up, its dreadful claws raised high; and in that moment a second arrow shattered its skull, and so it died.

And then they heard men's voices yelling, over the softer sounds of camels ridden hard, ridden at the gallop. Staring, they saw a squadron of Sharai come pouring into the bowl, scimitars drawn.

They could finish the ghûls, however many there might be lurking beyond the dune. Elisande sank down onto one knee, abruptly drained; and then rose up again, as quickly energised, when one boy on foot came running after the riders, skirting round the couched camels by the well, trotting over to join them.

"Marron . . . I thought, I thought you'd left us, for fear of the killing . . ."

"I will not kill again, unless I must," he confirmed softly. "But I heard the ghûls in the water, and I heard riders further off; so I went to fetch the riders, to face the ghûls. I thought you could outface Morakh," he added.

And she thought he was teasing, almost joking, which he never did; and she surprised herself and all of them by bursting into tears, and burying her face in his shoulder as she hugged him.

EASY TO BEGIN, but hard, very hard to stop; harder still to look her friends in the eye, immediately after. Jemel's expression . . .

But there was her father, lying sick and needful. Another surprise, that she'd be so glad to push Marron
away—though by the look of him he was never so glad of
anything, which was no surprise at all—and hurry to
Rudel.

He was no better, though he seemed no worse; that was
as much as she could expect, and perhaps more. She
didn't think she could have treated a death-wound at all, a
week ago. Something she'd gained, from the land of the
djinn: something she'd brought back, perhaps, a little of
the strength she'd felt there, or just a little more understanding.

He was conscious, she saw. He didn't speak, but his
eyes glittered at her.

"Well, what?" she mumbled crossly. "Should I have left
you to die, is that it? Well, perhaps I should. But I thought
Outremer might need you. To speak for it, if Redmond
doesn't get to Rhabat. Though why you'd want to, I don't
know. Save Surayon and let the rest go burn, it isn't worth
the saving . . ."

As she talked she laid a hand against his brow, feeling
for the chill sweat of fever or that simple chilling that can
follow a severe wound, that can kill the patient though the
wound recovers. She found neither; he was cool of skin,
yes, but the night had swallowed the day's heat already
and was turning sharp now, she was starting to shiver herself . . .

"Jemel!" she called. "Get that fire going again—and
build it up, Rudel needs warmth . . ."

"I think we all do," Julianne said, rubbing her arms as
she came running in response. Marron could not, of
course, with the camels there; and so Jemel had not either.
The two boys were standing together on a dune-top,
watching the ghûls being hunted down, she thought. Perhaps that was why she'd called Jemel, because they were
together, and she could not leave her father. She hoped
not, but perhaps . . .

Perhaps Julianne would fail with the fire, and have to

fetch Jemel; burning dung-cakes was an art she might not have.

Perhaps Elisande would grow into a crabbed and bitter soul, jealous to the core of her. Perhaps she had already.

"Talk to me," she said hastily. "Tell me what's been happening to you, why Morakh wants us all dead . . ."

Julianne did that as she built her fire, finding some wood from somewhere to make it blaze, no help needed; and then asked simply, "How is Rudel?"

"He'll live." He was sleeping now, but it was a real sleep, a healing sleep she thought. Thanks to her, he would live. That was something to be considered later, to be made to fit with her conscience, and her ever-burning rage against him. She'd never truly wished him dead, even in her most anger; he was too necessary, too valuable to her beloved land and her people. But still, she'd never thought that she might save his life.

There were more figures on the dune-top at last, the Sharai riders; they paused to speak to Jemel as Marron backed away, and then came slowly down towards the well. A dozen of them, and half had ghûl-heads swinging from their saddles.

The man who led them bore no trophies; he needed none, Elisande thought, seeing the easy confidence in him as he couched his mount and stepped to ground.

He threw his hood back to show himself clearly by the firelight: a man in his early thirties, perhaps, hawk-nosed and trimly bearded. Then he bowed to them Sharai-fashion, a grave inclination of the head and a complex gesture of the hands.

"Lady Elisande d'Albéry, I believe, and Lady Julianne de Rance?" He had them right; Elisande bowed as grace-fully as she could manage, squatting as she was beside her father; Julianne rose only in order to make a full courtly curtsey, meeting manners with formal manners. "I am called Hasan, of the Beni Rus," he went on, his voice soft and mellifluous, his accent an ornament to their tongue. "And this is Rudel?"

It was a moment before either of them could reply, so startled they were; then Elisande stammered, "It, it is . . ." She should perhaps give him a title, but wasn't sure if he wore one. For sure he needed none; Hasan was Hasan, all the tribes would know that name quite unadorned.

"Your father, and he is hurt? How badly?"

He stepped forward to see for himself, and checked suddenly at sight of the arrow still jutting from Rudel's chest. It was the first ungraceful movement that he'd made; Elisande was quite glad to see him human, suscep- tible to shock.

"He should be dead," Hasan said simply. "With such a wound, we would have left him to the vultures."

"He needs to live," Elisande replied, equally simply.

"Perhaps so. I would not have thought God meant him to; but you are from Surayon, of course."

"I am. Though much of what we know, we learned from your people, prince." No harm in flattery, of him or of his people. Besides, she told nothing but truth, in both cases. Without the Sharai, her country would be near as ignorant as its neighbours; and in a land without titles— which this was not—he would still be a prince among men.

"Not this," he said absently. "Not to keep a man alive and without pain, when he should have gone to paradise in minutes."

Well, no—but I am Surayonnaise, and so a witch. Will you burn me for it?

No, of course he would not. It was her own people who kept fires for the likes of her.

"The arrow must still be removed," she said quietly.

"My men can do that, if you are not able . . . ?"

"Thank you, prince. I'd be glad if they would." She was able, but not particularly willing, now that the need was gone. If ever a man deserved to carry a blade in his heart, that man was Rudel; far be it from her to remove it. Though this was not a blade and not in his heart, the symbolism still mattered to her. "The sooner the better, if you please. I can hold him asleep, to make it easier for all."

He nodded, beckoning some of his men forward and speaking to them in rapid Catari: the man lived by the lady's skill, but the arrow must be drawn, and swiftly . . .

It took little effort on her part to keep Rudel unconscious through their knifework; she cradled his head in her lap and stroked his temples gently, whispering under her breath. This was only a subtle variation on the *sodar,* a tendril of her mind whispering to a tendril of his. Just as well: she'd all but drained herself with that first hurried healing, and then she'd had to fight after. She was exhausted now, almost slipping into sleep herself despite her rabid hunger as she lulled her father's mind and numbed his body to any pain.

Almost—but not quite. Exhaustion never touched her curiosity. Hasan was speaking with Julianne behind her, and she could listen while she lulled, while she lolled.

"Lady, it was a great surprise to me when your companion gave me your name. I think I was only ever once more startled in my life."

"Oh? And when was that, ah, prince?"

"You need not call me so," with a chuckle. "It is a politeness of the Lady Elisande, but I am not a prince. My name is Hasan, that only. When was it? A short time ago, when the Ghost Walker came running half-naked out of tales and terrified my camel."

"Ah. Yes, he would do that. I hope the surprise of finding me was not so terrifying? To you or to your camel?"

"Not at all. She is a placid beast ordinarily, she takes what comes, as a servant of God should do. Alas, I cannot be so stolid, faced with such beauty. The surprise is as pleasant as it is remarkable. That your father came to my council was unforeseen, but not in truth unaccountable; he has done such things before. That you should choose to do the same is a grace quite unlooked-for."

"My father, Hasan?"

"Yes. Did you not know?"

"I, ah, had been told. How is he, is he well?"

"Quite well, I believe. He seemed so this morning, at least. If he was expecting you, he did not mention it."

"No. I think I will surprise him also, if we come safely to Rhabat."

"Lady, trust me; I will bring you there."

"My name is Julianne. Prince. But there are dangers you may not be aware of . . ."

"Not in these lands, Julianne. You are on my territory here; I know every rock, and every insect that inhabits them."

"Oh? How many ghûls have you killed tonight—and how many before tonight?"

"A few, before—but never in a pack, as they were tonight. That I confess."

"Cut into their tongues, Hasan, and see what you find there."

He gave the order, and waited in silence until the thing was done, and the results shown him; then, "What are these? And how did you know . . . ?"

"They are a device the 'ifrit use, that give them power over ghûls. I am told that they are stones from the land of the djinn; I have not seen that country for myself, but I believe it."

"As do I; their warmth confirms the story. You continue to surprise me, Julianne—though the greater surprise is that there is something you do not know for yourself."

"Oh, many things. I'm only a girl yet . . ."

"Then I would like to see you grow into a woman. Would you marry me, Julianne? If your father consented to the match?"

A pause, and then a laugh, more breathless than amused: "Alas, Hasan, I am married already."

"What of that? So am I, several times. But of course, your customs are different; and you are not a man. Tell me his name, then, that I may kill him."

"Oh, no. Would you make me a widow before I have been made a woman?"

His turn to pause, and the lightness was gone from his voice when he spoke again. "No, Julianne, I would not do that. Perhaps I will not need to. I will speak to your father on the subject. But for now, it is time to rest. You have the well; we will make camp beyond the ridge there."

"Keep a good watch overnight, Hasan. There is a Sand Dancer unaccounted for, with brethren to avenge; he sought our blood, he may seek yours also, whether you have a quarrel with him or no. I think he is mad, myself."

"All Sand Dancers are mad; but your Ghost Walker may have given them reason. That one makes me anxious myself. My thanks for the warning; we will guard your camp as well as our own. Sleep easy, lady."

"I will, prince . . ."

SHE DIDN'T, THOUGH. Elisande set herself to wake several times during the night, to check on her father and keep him deep asleep. Each time she was aware of Julianne's restlessness, each time she expected her friend to sit up when she did, and share whatever was disturbing her; each time she was disappointed.

IN THE MORNING, as they broke camp, Elisande surprised Hasan on her own account, telling him of the 'ifrit in the Dead Waters. She took him to see the tracks, at his insistence. They found hoofprints also, where the ghûls had come up out of the sea; and they found one thing more, the prints of a barefoot man that overlay the ghûls'. Elisande couldn't identify them with certainty, but Jemel could. He said they were Morakh's.